REMEMBERING THE JUICE MANGO

REMEMBERING THE JUICE MANGO

Neena Kahlon

Rupa & Co

Copyright © Neena Kahlon 2009

Published 2009 by

Rupa . Co

7/16, Ansari Road, Daryaganj,
New Delhi 110 002

Sales Centres:

Allahabad Bangalooru Chandigarh Chennai
Hyderabad Jaipur Kathmandu
Kolkata Mumbai

All rights reserved.
No part of this publication may be reproduced, stored in a
retrieval system, or transmitted, in any form or by any means,
electronic, mechanical, photocopying, recording or otherwise,
without the prior permission of the publishers.

The author asserts the moral right to be identified
as the author of this work.

Typeset by
Mindways Design
1410 Chiranjiv Tower
43 Nehru Place
New Delhi 110 019

Printed in India by
Rekha Printers Pvt Ltd.
A-102/1, Okhla Industrial Area, Phase-II,
New Delhi-110 020

For my mother, Pritam K. Sarkaria, whose thinking inspired me to write what should never be forgotten

Contents

Note from the Author	ix
Genealogy chart	x
Acknowledgements	xi
Prologue	xiii

Part One: India, 1947 — 1
1. The Nightmare — 3
2. A Long Journey — 12

Part Two: Pre-Partition Years, 1940-47 — 19
3. A Privileged Child — 21
4. The Bride's Dowry — 30
5. The Girl Child — 39
6. Calm Before the Storm — 48
7. Troubled Times — 58
8. Independence and Partition — 71

Part Three: Independent India, 1947 — 81
9. The Promised Land — 83
10. The Welcome — 94
11. First Rays of Light — 104
12. Wonder Years — 114
13. Glimpses of a Rainbow — 121
14. Where the Sun Shines — 132
15. One of Us — 140

16	Happy Days	148
17	The Betrayal	159
18	Remember the Juice Mango	172
19	The Child is the Parent	186

Part Four: 1958-78 — 193

20	The Engagement	195
21	Marriages Made in Heaven	205
22	Making Do with Life's Lemons	215
23	The Cool Breath of Security	230
24	Bride and Mother	243
25	And Life Goes On . . .	251
26	Another Baby, Another War	260

Part Five: 1978 — 271

27	Cycles of Life	273
28	Spring Branches on Old Trees	284
29	Choices Pave the Way to Destiny	291
30	Broken	299
31	A Heart that is Tender	303
32	Physician Heal Thyself	305
33	Search for a Meaning	310
34	A Daughter's Struggle	317
35	Ratna Stands Tall, Again	325
36	Dawn	331

Appendix: Cultural Titbits	337
Terms of Address Used in the Story	338
Glossary	340

Note from the Author

Of all the memories I still cherish from my childhood in Punjab of 1950s and 1960s, the mango parties we had in summer seem the sweetest.

We usually spent our summer vacation on a farm—an aunt's, a cousin's or ours. All those farmhouses had one thing in common—a tubewell to irrigate the parched land. The water pulled up with a generator-operated pump, and collected in a deep cement tank, was released when needed for irrigating the fields. These tanks, open on the top, usually had some shade from surrounding trees and at least one adjoining side with a raised brick patio large enough for the family to sit, socialise or have a mango party.

During these much anticipated parties, we girls sat with our salwaars (like harem pants) rolled up to our knees, feet dangling in cool water, drinking deeply from the native, tiny juice mangoes, chilled on ice blocks in metal tubs. Any wormy fruit went straight into the rubbish pile. The rest we squished between our two palms, one puny juice mango at a time. When soft, we pulled out the stem. Then throwing our heads back caught the two or three swallows of mango juice, before discarding the shell and reaching for another juice mango.

At one such family gathering, long before the table-variety of hybrid mangoes became popular, my mother's analogy between a diseased juice mango and a toxic human being planted a seed that birthed this book.

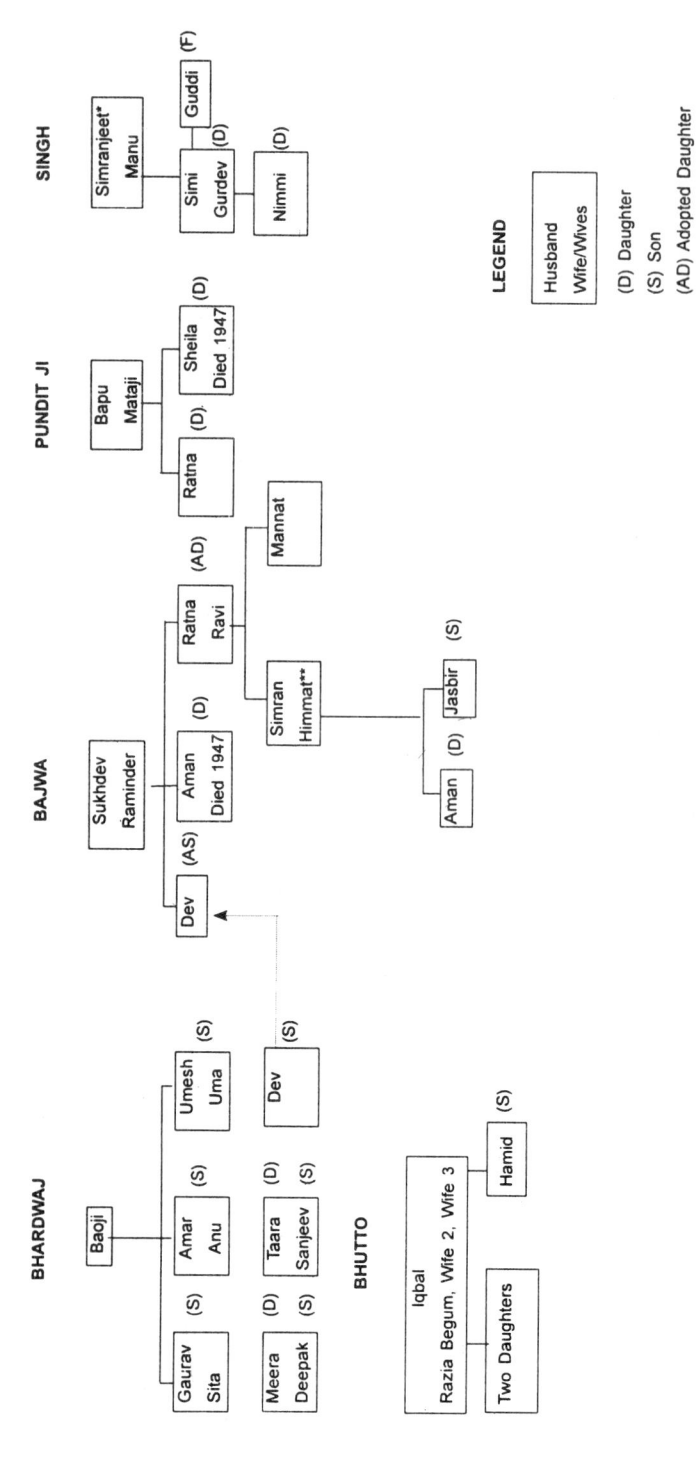

GENEALOGY

BHARDWAJ

- Baoji
  - Amar (S) — Anu
    - Gaurav (S) — Sita
    - Meera (D) — Deepak
    - Taara (D) — Sanjeev (S)
  - Umesh (S) — Uma
  - Dev (S)

BAJWA

- Sukhdev — Raminder
  - Aman (D) — Died 1947
  - Ratna (AD) — Ravi
    - Mannat
    - Simran — Himmat**
      - Aman (D)
      - Jasbir (S)
  - Dev (AS)

PUNDIT JI

- Bapu — Mataji
  - Ratna (D)
  - Sheila (D) — Died 1947

SINGH

- Simranjeet* — Manu
  - Guddi (F)
  - Simi (D) — Gurdev
  - Nimmi (D)

BHUTTO

- Iqbal — Razia Begum, Wife 2, Wife 3
  - Two Daughters
  - Hamid (S)

LEGEND

- Husband
- Wife/Wives
- (D) Daughter
- (S) Son
- (AD) Adopted Daughter
- (AS) Adopted son
- (F) Friend
- *Raminder's brother
- **Guddi's son

Acknowledgements

I'm deeply indebted to all who have experienced violent acts of aggression in their micro or macro world, but still carry the torch of hope instead of the sword of revenge.

Thanks to my sister and brother-in-law, Surinder K. and Dr R.S. Sandhu, and my friend Jaswinder Kumar, for picking up stories of Partition where mother left off. Thanks to the readers of my unpolished first draft, Swarna Mohan, Surjit Kalha and my niece Manjot K. Pannu, for providing me encouragement in spite of the dubious merits of the rough version of the manuscript. Thanks to my niece's husband, Hardip S. Pannu, for drawing the chart of genealogy. Generous thanks to my writing buddies from the Freelance Writers Network of Fort Worth, Texas—Dr Mike Bumagin, Linda Austin, Lucile Davis, Olyve Abbott, Marilyn Komechak, and to the rest of that remarkable group.

Thanks to Jim Lee, Ruth Orren and Judy Reveal for their support. A special thanks to my soul sister Emily Seate, who has been especially generous with her time, astute observations and kind suggestions.

Prologue
Partitioning of India

On 15 August 1947, Great Britain freed its 'crown jewel', ending two centuries of colonial rule in India. Before withdrawing, the imperial pen modified the map of the country by carving from it a nation for the Muslims, a country called Pakistan. To mark the boundaries of the two countries, Britain sketched a 'Radcliffe Awards Line' across the states of Punjab and Bengal on the western and eastern borders of colonial India. This partitioning of land along religious demographics created a panic of such magnitude that it triggered the worst known riots in Indian history, killing over a million people and displacing ten million more.

Ignoring the mayhem thus created, Britain walked away from the bleeding land.

PART ONE
India-1947

'Long years ago we made a tryst with destiny and now the time comes when we shall redeem our pledge . . . At the stroke of midnight hour, when the world sleeps, India shall awaken to life and freedom. . . .'

—JAWAHARLAL NEHRU
In his Speech on 14 August 1947

1
The Nightmare

Punjab, 15 August 1947

Three bodies lie side by side near the temple altar—her father, mother and little Sheila. White sheets cover them. The moon creates eerie shadows in the dark as it peeps through ancient banyan trees that surround the temple. Alone and scared, she can neither move nor scream. They will come, and then she too will lie covered in a white sheet. . . .

Her heart thumping, nine-year-old Ratna bolted upright from the nightmare. The morning, heavy with smells of charred wood and a sour stench, churned her stomach, reinforcing the dream's terror in her. She wrapped her arms around herself and took a guttural breath.

The previous night, her mistress Uma had led her and Dev to the back of a raised platform in a partially burned house. 'Stay here, children,' Uma said. 'Keep hidden behind this wall. You'll be safe.' With Uma's assurance, they had both slumped to the ground and fallen asleep.

Now, drenched in perspiration and still not fully awake, Ratna blinked at her surroundings through the shrouded morning light. Her clothes, her hands and her tangled braids reeked of smoke and ashes. Reaching for her crumpled veil lying next to her, she shook the dust from it, wiped the sweat from her face and covered her head. As she straightened her long tunic over her loose-cuffed pants, the relentless drone of flies nearby attracted her attention. A man's severed head lay open-eyed in thickened blood a few yards away. Shuddering, she hugged herself again, tighter, while the actual memory—not just the frightening nightmare—of the massacre at the temple flooded her mind. More vivid than the severed head, images of her father, mother and little sister slaughtered near the Bhardwaj temple flashed by, choking her into silence.

Panting, she looked around for her mistress, Uma, and found little Dev curled up at her feet. She shook his shoulder. 'Wake up, Dev babu. Your ma is gone.' She addressed Dev with respect. He was the master now, she still the servant girl.

Dev scrambled to his feet, half-asleep, and collected his belongings. In short-pants and sandals, he appeared younger than his age—seven years. 'Ma,' he whimpered, looking around.

'Your ma is gone. Come on, Dev babu, we have to look for her,' she said, offering him her hand. Dev's lower lip trembled as he reached for Ratna. Coming around the wall that had protected them, they saw Uma lying on the ground.

Running to her side, the boy screamed, 'Ma! Ma!' He dropped his sack and sliding down, lifted his mother's head onto his lap. Caressing her face, he moved away stray hair from her eyes as his tears spilled unchecked. 'Ma, open your eyes. It's me—your little prince.'

Ratna, the impoverished priest's daughter, held back, her breath erratic. Oblivious to her surroundings, she stumbled down the steps from the platform and circled around a sobbing Dev and his unconscious mother. Still in a zombie-like state, she climbed back. Clutching her small sack of belongings to her chest, she stared at Uma who lay naked and bleeding, amidst blood-soaked clothing. Just like my mother, she thought.

Dark blood clotted Uma's wounds, and flies buzzed around her. Ratna's heart missed a beat when she saw the woman's chest rise—her mistress still breathed! She bounded down the steps and kneeling by her side cried out, 'Oh, my dear, dear Uma bibiji.'

Ratna leaned closer to hear her. Uma's lips moved, her eyelids fluttered as she whispered, 'Cover me with . . . a dhoti.'

Ratna found the two cloth-sacks the dying woman had carried the previous night, and opened the master's bag. Pulling out a cotton loincloth, she covered her mistress with its ample yardage. Squatting on her haunches, she used a corner of her veil to shoo flies away from Uma's face and wiped her own nose with the back of her other hand.

'Bottom of my bag . . . a small pouch. Get it for Dev,' mumbled her mistress.

Ratna rummaged through the bag, and, finding the heavy pouch, handed it to the boy. Uma's eyes opened a sliver to look at her son. 'Guard it well,' she whispered. 'Give . . . to your aunt Anu chachi, in Jullunder.'

He gulped and swiped his sleeve across his eyes. 'Ma, we won't leave without you.'

Bright blood dribbled from Uma's mouth as she strained to speak. 'Dev, listen. Carry the bags . . . take Ratna . . . find your father at our store. Go to Jullunder to your Anu chachi. Now go . . . without me.' She stopped, gasping for breath.

Ratna bent forward and with a corner of her veil, again wiped the mouth of the woman who meant much more to her than a mere mistress.

Uma peered at Ratna, and then focussed on Dev. 'Join a kafila. Leave me here . . . take care of Ratna. And, and remember the juice mang . . .' Her voice rattled with a peculiar gurgling sound, as her eyes closed.

'Hush, Ma,' whispered the boy, and he bent to kiss his mother's cheek. 'You rest now. I'll keep awake and take care of you.' With his dead mother's head resting in his lap, Dev's lips moved in prayer and his sobs subsided. He imitated his mother, who often repeated the invocation—Ram, Ram, Ram—during stressful times, praying to Lord Ram for guidance and protection.

Ratna arose and sat on the steps, a few paces away from the mother and son. With her chin on her knees, she rocked herself back and forth, trying to lose the images of her own family's lifeless, blood-soaked bodies. Now her mistress lay dead too. 'I knew Uma bibiji would die. She prayed too much. Just like my mataji,' she mumbled to herself.

Ratna's parents had worked in Uma and Dev's household—her bapu, her father, as the priest in the Bhardwaj temple, and mataji, her mother, as a maid. As far back as she could remember, they had always addressed

Uma respectfully, as bibiji. Ratna too called her Uma bibiji, but she resented being coerced by her destitute parents to show respect to little Dev, heir to the Bhardwaj estate, by addressing him as Dev babu.

The white loincloth covering Uma's body turned a spotty crimson. Dev changed his leg position, causing dark-red, thick fluid to ooze from his mother's stiff mouth. The coppery smell gagged Ratna, just as a sudden commotion made her look up. A caravan of Sikh and Hindu refugees moved slowly down the road. 'Dev Babu, Uma bibiji said to travel with a kafila,' she called, reminding Dev of the urgency and seriousness of their situation.

Dev turned his head with a slow, almost regal move, to face her. 'We'll leave when ma wakes up.'

'But . . . but the kafila is passing us by,' she said, pointing to the caravan of refugees.

Dev glared at her. 'We can't leave ma behind!' Touching his mother's face once more, he shuddered. 'Her face feels like, like Baoji's feet did when I touched them last night.' His voice quivered, as if the reality of his mother's demise had finally dawned upon him.

Ratna took a deep breath and whispered, 'They killed her, like they killed your grandfather, Baoji. They also killed my bapu, my little Sheila . . . They killed them all!' Her voice shook as tears threatened to spill. 'Dev babu, cover Uma bibiji's face with the dhoti, the way we covered your Baoji's face.'

'Why?'

'Because, like Baoji, she's not going to wake up. They killed her.'

'Don't say that! She's sleeping, but she'll open her eyes after she has rested. I know she will. She loves me and . . . and. . . .' His voice trailed off into a flurry of sobs.

The miles-long caravan passed them. Ratna watched the travellers throw pitiful glances at them, but no one stepped forward to help. She sat staring at the road long after the caravan disappeared.

Soon, another caravan moved towards them slowly. The refugees carried their belongings on bullock carts, rickshaws, ponies, donkeys and on whatever else that could move. Army trucks and turbaned Sikh soldiers circled the caravan, guiding the Hindus and Sikhs to safety.

She noticed a young Sikh couple walking with the caravan. The bearded man shod in scuffed oxfords, wore a magenta turban, a cream-coloured short-sleeved shirt and well-tailored pants on his tall frame. Ratna recognised his expensive English shoes, as she had often polished similar shoes for the men in Dev's household. A slim, pretty woman walked beside the turbaned man. She wore a crumpled, printed blue tunic and loose-cuffed harem pants, the salwaar kameez, with a matching blue dupatta veil. Ratna thought they made a fine couple—he attired in a white man's clothing and she in traditional Indian garb, her dupatta draped gracefully over her head. They reminded Ratna of Dev's rich parents. 'They look so sad,' she mumbled to no one in particular. 'The woman in blue looks like she is struggling with *jinn bhoot*.' Ratna stared at the woman whose face looked contorted as if struggling with unseen ghosts.

Suddenly, Dev shook his mother. 'Wake up Ma . . . all the people are leaving. Ma, please . . . they'll leave us behind if you don't wake up.'

Dev's piercing cry jolted the demon-grappling woman. She stopped, looked at Dev and walking over, bent to hug the boy as she asked her turbaned husband, 'Can we take him with us?'

The man nodded and moved to help Dev with his belongings.

Dev pointed to Ratna. 'Can she come too?'

'Of course,' replied the woman. 'Is she your sister?' she asked, wiping Dev's tear-stained face with her dupatta veil.

'No. She's Punditji's daughter. Ma told me to take care of her.'

The turbaned Sikh man offered Ratna his hand. With his help she rose. 'Dev Babu is going to die,' she whispered. 'They are going to kill him. I know it. He was praying.'

'We'll protect you both,' said the man. He turned and bent to cover the dead woman's face with the bloodstained loincloth.

Unbidden, Ratna paid homage to Uma by touching her feet and placing her hands over her heart. Dev imitated her. Picking up their cloth sacks, they both stared at the two bags Uma had carried. The turbaned man noticed and bent to take Uma's bags, putting them atop a pathetic looking mule that carried his and his wife's sparse belongings. Ratna and Dev carried their cloth sacks over their shoulders and walked with the unknown adults. They held hands, crying, wiping the tears with their knuckles and cleaning their noses on shirtsleeves.

'Ratna, when ma wakes up, how will she find us?' whimpered Dev.

'She . . . she won't wake up,' answered Ratna with a stifled sob.

Dev wiped his tears. Letting go of Ratna's hand, he put his arm around her shoulder. 'Don't cry,' he said. 'I'll take care of you. From now on, I'll be your Dev bhaiya.'

Ratna smiled through her tears. Dev wanted to be her brother, her bhaiya, even though she had never even tied a rakhi around his wrist. The sacred ritual of tying a rakhi—a coloured string—on a brother's wrist would be a declaration of a sister's love and a brother's promise of protection. The thought gave her strength.

'Ratna, what should we call them?' he whispered pointing to the Sikh couple.

'How should I know?' she blurted. 'Why don't you ask them?'

Dev nodded, but did not ask.

They walked in silence with the unknown couple for about an hour when the caravan came to an abrupt halt. It was past noon and the army escorts gave them time to eat and rest, warning the travellers over megaphones, to stay alert when passing through the city of Lahore which now belonged to Pakistan. They also announced that after passing Lahore, the caravan would stop only once more in the evening to rest. They would start the next morning towards the land designated for the Sikhs and Hindus.

Ratna noticed a Hindu well, guarded by the army. 'Look! A Hindu well.'

'So?' asked Dev.

'Silly, it means we can refill our water containers. Hindus and Sikhs do not draw water from Muslim wells. Didn't your fancy folks teach you anything?' Turning back to the two adults, she offered to refill their water receptacles also.

Before she left, Dev whispered, 'I'm hungry. I know the paranthas and pickle are for the journey to Jullunder, but I want to eat now.' Pointing to the couple, he said, 'Should I offer the food to them also?'

Ratna nodded and picked up the empty containers. The tall man moved to accompany her with two more brass containers. When they returned, all four of them sat huddled a short distance away from the caravan, under the shade of an old pipal tree. To avoid the hungry eyes of the less fortunate, they lowered their heads, hunched over in a tight circle and ate their unleavened fried bread and pickle.

Soon, the army started them on their way. As they walked, Ratna held Dev's hand, leading him on the bridge over the river Ravi. Midway, she looked down from the bridge and gasped. All along the shallow banks of the river, hundreds of mutilated, dead women and girls floated in the river, creating little dams with their bodies and billowy clothes.

Dev pulled at her tunic. 'Will they throw ma in the river too?' he asked, his voice laced with horror.

Ratna did not answer. The previous night Uma bibiji had cautioned them. 'You must be extra careful. The rioting mobs are very cruel to unprotected women and children.' Thinking of her dead mistress, a cold shiver slithered up her spine, her body jerking in response. The two adults gently pulled them away from the haunting sight.

As they walked, Dev seemed to know where they were. 'We'll stop at the fabric store down the road,' he whispered. Ratna nodded.

Turning to the unknown woman, Dev muttered in a voice quivering with emotion, 'Ratna and I will leave you soon. Our fabric store is on the way and my father is waiting for us there.'

The woman did not respond.

After another mile, they neared the Bhardwaj Fabric Store. The doors lay broken and ajar and the store entrance stood devoid of decorations of fancy clothing and materials for sale. Letting go of Ratna's hand, Dev ran towards the shop, screaming for his father. Ratna followed. The turbaned man rushed after them, leaving his wife standing with the mule.

The deserted store held nothing but trash and dried blood. Ratna turned to look at the Bhardwaj Jewellery Store across the road, but found that empty too.

Dev saw the dismal scene and shrieked. 'This can't be. My father was supposed to wait for me. Ma said so!'

Akbar, the Muslim manager of the store, peeked from behind a broken door at the back of the shop, and seeing the children, emerged. Dev ran and clung to his legs, begging for his father.

The Muslim slipped to the floor and addressing Dev as a son, said, 'Beta, I'm sorry. I'm so sorry. Your father is dead.'

'He can't die. Ma said he'd take me to Jullunder.'

'Your father is dead,' repeated Akbar softly. 'A mob looted the store and killed him. I'm a Muslim, so they spared my life.' Pointing to the Sikh man, he urged, 'Little one, go with the Sardarji'.

Ratna helped Dev rise. Akbar stood up and said, 'Sardarji, take good care of our Dev Beta'. He used a respectful term of address for the Sikh—a Sardarji, a benevolent landlord. Asking them to wait, Akbar ran to the back of the store, soon returning with his young son. He handed over a sack filled with an old tarp, two cotton blankets and cooking utensils. His son brought them an old army tote, filled with a bunch of bananas, dry food and spices.

The Muslim's generosity surprised Ratna. He seemed almost as compassionate as the turbaned Sikh. The man couldn't possibly be one of 'them'—the ones who killed her family. She took a deep breath and picked up the bulky sack. The turbaned man thanked the Muslim and picking up the other bag, also gathered Dev in his arms. Together, he and Ratna went to rejoin the woman-in-blue, and the caravan. The man set Dev down beside his wife, took Ratna's burden and along with his own sack, put them on their mule.

Before they resumed the journey, Ratna hugged Dev, who clung to her. 'Ratna, they killed him. They killed my father.' Between sobs, he asked, 'Why?'

'I don't know . . . but, I'll never leave you,' she whispered.

He nodded and reached for her hand. The children stayed close to the Sikh couple, shedding silent tears. After a short while, at Ratna's prompting, Dev took a few deep breaths, wiped his eyes and asked the woman, 'What should we call you?'

'My name is Raminder.' Pointing to her husband she said, 'He's Sukhdev Singh Bajwa.'

The children nodded, even though the answer did not resolve their dilemma. Ratna's mataji had taught her never to address her elders by their names. 'Maybe we can call them auntie and uncle,' she whispered.

Ahead, vultures flew in a tight circle and all too soon, decomposing bodies covered with flies lay in their path. Stepping over or around them, they walked in silence, breathing the fierce odour of rotting body parts through open mouths, parched lips and dry tongues.

'I've heard no Hindu can cross Lahore alive. They kill everyone there.'

'Don't worry. I'll take care of you,' said Dev, squeezing her hand.

They encountered no mobs in Lahore, but the bloodcurdling fear persisted well after they crossed the city. Even babies in the caravan whimpered but faintly to complain. Ratna heard only intermittent coughing, shuffling feet, clip clopping of animal hooves, creaking bullock carts and the stone crunching under heavy army trucks. Beneath these sounds, she sensed something deeper; an uneasy silence—a silence pulsating with grief and horror.

2
A Long Journey

15-16 August 1947

Raminder put one foot in front of the other, lulled by the caravan's slow, steady pace. Tall and graceful, she seemed to be fighting invisible demons as she slipped in and out of a trance-like state. In the suffocating heat, her tired limbs barely supported her body, a body fatigued by troubling thoughts and a broken heart.

Two children walked with her, crying like adults—quietly, too quietly. She wondered what deep trauma taught them not to howl like the little children they still were. Who were they? She had no remembrance. Suddenly, the startling scene of the bewildered child with his dead mother's head in his lap seared her consciousness, bringing her back to reality. The girl, she realised with a shock, was not her daughter Aman, but then who was she? She was the punditji's daughter, the boy had explained.

She shuddered. What happened to her orderly world?

Raminder recalled being led out of their home by her kind Muslim maid, Nasibaan, who had packed their belongings, and put two water-filled brass pots on a wobbly cart. She remembered sitting in the cart, crying. For how long? Was it for two days or maybe three? She looked back at the sad-looking mule. Where was the cart? And . . . and . . . what happened to her Aman?

Again, she looked around with frenzied intensity until Sukhdev, her husband, moved over and put his arm around her shoulder. 'Everything will be all right. *Vaheguru Raakha!*' God is our guardian.

She took a deep breath. Clinging to her husband's reassurance, she forced her tired legs and blistered feet to keep their pace. Their belongings, she realised, rode on the back of a mule. They had traded the relative comfort of their bullock cart for a mule, as one pregnant woman, accompanied by her husband and a feeble mother-in-law needed it more.

By late afternoon, the caravan ground to a halt. She wondered at the sudden stop. It looked like the refugee men were moving out to join the guards. Why? Could it be to provide greater security to the caravan? The women had started huddling in the centre. Just then, using megaphones, the army escorts requested able women to assist a young woman in labour. To aid this miracle in the midst of madness, some of the men had moved outwards voluntarily to provide a stronger shield around the stationary caravan.

Raminder guessed it to be the same pregnant woman they had helped climb onto their bullock cart. Since the birth would take time, everyone prepared to camp overnight. A few women stayed with the birthing mother, the others turned to help their families' camp overnight.

'Hey Vaheguru!'—Dear God—'I hope they have clothes for the newborn,' Raminder exclaimed.

Dev turned to fumble in one of his bags. 'I have my father's dhoti in this bag. Do you think the new mother could use it for her baby?' His concern melted her heart and reaching for the white cotton loincloth, Raminder also gathered Dev in her arms. She knew the clean, soft dhoti material could easily be used to make a few cozy receiving blankets or even napkins for the baby.

'You hug like my ma,' Dev muttered.

'Beta, what's your name?' she asked.

'Dev,' he replied and pointing to the priest's daughter added, 'She's Ratna.'

Raminder nodded, smiling a gentle smile, sensing a new reality through the tenuous anchor the children seemed to provide.

She turned to watch the soon-to-be-born baby's father go out with a borrowed bucket, to get water for the delivery. Just then her husband Sukhdev asked, 'Raminder, can you cook something for the new mother?'

'Maybe. Let's see.'

They unloaded the mule and she examined the staples Akbar had given them. 'Yes. We have lentils and some seasoning. I can cook daal, if we still have enough water.'

'I think we should have plenty to cook the soup. Don't forget that Ratna and I filled our containers at the last stop. One of them should still be full.'

Raminder turned to Ratna and Dev. 'Take a drink of water and go to the nearby fields to collect any wood or kindling you can find. But stay close to each other and the kafila, within the range of the protective army guards.'

After the two children left, Sukhdev helped her set up a temporary fireplace by placing rocks and broken bricks in a triangle, to support the cooking vessel. Then checking the water receptacles, he picked up the almost empty one. 'Use up the water from this. I'll go and refill. . . .'

Sudden rifle shots and screams left his words hanging.

The refugees who had wandered away, stampeded back to the caravan. Raminder watched anxiously as Sukhdev ran towards those who returned, looking for Ratna and Dev. When he found them, the frightened children leapt into his arms. Sukhdev hugged them tight and shepherded them back to safety.

Someone screamed, 'He tried drawing water from à Muslim well.'

'Why?'

'For his baby's delivery. There is no drinking water in the Hindu well, only floating corpses of women and girls.'

'It . . . it smells horrible.'

'It's lucky our soldiers had rifles, otherwise those bastards would have killed him.'

'Bad omen.'

By now the Sikh soldiers had become alert again, their rifles cocked and ready. In the face of well-armed soldiers and a few refugee men carrying bamboo clubs, the Muslim mob retreated, and soon order prevailed.

Raminder asked, 'Ratna, what are you carrying?'

Ratna, still clutching the two open corners of her long tunic, relaxed and gingerly opened the temporary receptacle she had made with her kameez, revealing its contents. 'We found these scalded potatoes in a burned down vegetable stall.'

'Great!'

'I found this kindling and a stump of wood,' said Dev, showing off his contribution.

'You two have been very helpful. Come, let's cook.' She smiled.

While cooking, she heard subdued cheers of gratitude from the refugees announcing the birth of a healthy baby boy.

Raminder served a supper of lentil soup and paranthas. When done eating, she directed the two children to rest on homespun cotton blankets that Sukhdev had spread on a small open spot. She poured some precious water into Dev's small water can, and picking up a parantha and hot daal, walked over to feed the new mother. The woman broke off two bites from the fried bread to eat with her lentil soup, and gave the rest to her husband and mother-in-law. She then took a long refreshing swig of water before passing the water can to her family. Turning to Raminder, she said, 'Behenji, bless you for your kindness. We've had nothing to eat for two days. *Vaheguru meher kare.*' God Bless.

Amid chaos, the premature baby, naked under his mother's veil, slept in peace. The parents, helpless in the barrenness of the caravan, accepted Raminder's offering of a clean white dhoti with deep gratitude.

As soon as the family of the new baby finished eating, Raminder proposed to do ardaas, a Sikh prayer, for the newborn. So she, the newborn's turbaned father and grandmother stood around the mother and child, and prayed. More and more people joined them. Very soon, every waking person stood up, head covered and bowed, to give silent thanks for the baby's safe birth, thanks for a ray of light in the time of darkness. Not everyone could hear the words of the ardaas but they joined in the thanksgiving anyway. Sikhs and Hindus stood praying together, gathering strength from that moment of grace.

The next morning, the day after Independence and Partition, Raminder stared at the charred and wasted landscape all around her. The innocence of a new day seemed deceiving, its silence unsettling. Hoping that the pristine morning would bring clouds and relief from the scorching afternoon heat, she started the day by coaxing Dev's damp stump of wood into a smoky fire and stuck Ratna's scalded potatoes into it.

After boiling tealeaves in hot water, she took a few warmed roasted potatoes and bananas and fed her husband and the two children. Then, while Sukhdev gathered their belongings and tied them on the mule, she watched Ratna douse the stump of wood with handfuls of loose dirt, to save it for future use. Raminder smiled at the ingenuity of the little girl. 'I'm glad you didn't waste any precious water. Smart girl!'

Ratna beamed. Raminder turned to rummage through Akbar's giftsack, and pulling out a bronze tumbler, she poured dark tea into it. After adding turmeric to the tea water, for faster healing, she picked up the leftover potatoes and a parantha, and walked over to feed the newborn's mother. She also carried for them the tarp Akbar had gifted, for the newborn's protection from impending monsoon rains.

The new mother accepted the gifts with kind blessings and again shared the food with her husband and mother-in-law. When Raminder made a move to leave after picking up the empty tumbler, the young mother reached for her hand, 'May Vaheguru reward your kindness and may He bless your family with long lives.'

Raminder forced a tearful smile and turned away. She could not yet talk about her nine-year old daughter, Aman. A couple of days earlier, their only child had gone to school, never to return. As Raminder walked back, she kept seeing her Aman, decapitated and floating in the school well. Trembling convulsively, she hoped her child's end was quick. When she gagged, she took a couple of deep breaths. If throwing-up could ease heartache, she thought, then everyone in the caravan would be retching. Struggling with her emotions, she stumbled and fell into a heap near her husband. Sukhdev put a gentle hand on her shoulder.

Feeling like an abandoned puppy, Ratna walked with the caravan. She no longer talked, but held Dev's hand, and watched helplessly as the world she had known drifted farther and farther away. By now the horror of seeing and smelling putrid dead bodies had softened, but the pain of losing her family still held her in a strong grip threatening to crush her with its intensity.

At a distance, she saw hundreds of covered heads, gently bobbing up and down. Before she knew it, the Sikh army escorts herded them, like goats, off the main road to allow passing room to the incoming refugees. She realised that the approaching wave of humanity was not a mirage but a caravan of Muslims fleeing the new India. Ratna's mataji, her mother, had often explained how the Hindus, Sikhs and Muslims were like three separate streams merging into the same river called Bharat Ma—Mother India. But now, the streams flowed within assigned boundaries, not daring to merge, unable to flow as one.

While the Sikhs and Hindus waited beside the road to allow the Muslim caravan to pass, everyone had prayers on their terrified lips. The Hindus mumbled, 'Ram, Ram, Ram,' invoking Lord Ram for protection. The Sikhs repeated, 'Vaheguru, Vaheguru.' God is great and merciful.

Once the road cleared, they were back on the trail, shuffling, dragging their bodies forward. Around noon, scattered clouds moved in with a light rain. Even with a benign drizzle, Ratna's teeth chattered and her body shivered. Not understanding the excruciating pain, she let go of Dev's hand and held her stomach. She remembered her bapu, her beloved father, butchered beside the Bhardwaj temple altar and her mataji and little sister Sheila, bludgeoned to death inside their room. Even the mighty Baoji, Dev's grandfather, lay slaughtered near one of the pillars of the private Hindu temple. She shook her head to rid herself of the horrible images, all the while struggling to keep up with the caravan.

'Ratna, what are we going to do?' whined Dev.

She avoided his eyes and shrugged.

'Child, are you all right?' asked Sukhdev.

'I'm dizzy,' she mumbled.

Sukhdev stepped forward and bent down on his knees. 'Hop onto my back.'

Out of desperation, she did. The kind touch of another human made her feel strangely secure in her terrifying new world. She put her head on Sukhdev's shoulder and from that vantage point, noticed scattered houses along the sides of the road. Muslim women and children stood on their rooftops and in front of open windows, gaping. Every now and then, a little Muslim child waved to the caravan made up of Sikhs and Hindus, but no one returned the wave. Ratna wondered if those children sensed her pain.

In her short life, she had never experienced such agony and terror. Her Mataji had often explained how being a poor man's daughter and a mere girl-child, made her a 'lesser' being. Now, with her head still on Sukhdev's shoulder, Ratna tried to understand the logic. If she was already 'less', then why did it get worse? She recalled nothing wayward she had done to deserve losing her secure world. Maybe, she decided, this was a part of a bigger sin of not being able to figure out what made her less, and why she was a 'mere girl-child'.

She also needed to understand what happened to Dev babu, who now wanted to be her brother and not her master. Why? What did he do to fall into the same dismal hole of 'less' with her? Shifting her troubled head to Sukhdev's other shoulder she hoped the kind couple, Sukhdev and Raminder, would care enough to take both her and Dev to safety.

Ratna shuddered as her body burned with fever. The harder she willed the lump in her throat to soften, the more it solidified. Too exhausted to sleep, her mind wandered to simpler times, to her childhood world, which held promises without any fear.

Part Two

Pre-Partition Years 1940-47

'The entire Universe is born of One Light, [Then how can anyone say] one [being] is good and the other bad? . . . There is but one clay from which the Creator has created innumerable different forms. There is no imperfection in the clay vessel nor in the Potter.'

—Bhagat Kabir
Guru Granth Sahib
(Translated by Dr R.S. Sandhu)

3
A Privileged Child

Simpler Times, 1940

Uma, the matriarch of the large Bhardwaj family, waddled towards the birthing room supported by a maid on one side and her sister-in-law, Anu, on the other. After twelve years of marriage to the oldest Bhardwaj son, Umesh, Uma finally hoped to give an heir to her wealthy joint family. Six adults lived under one roof to form this joint family, better known as the mighty Bhardwaj clan. The family waited anxiously to welcome a newborn into their midst.

Uma's father-in-law, Baoji, a widower and father of three grown sons, was the patriarch of this clan. Addressing his younger daughter-in-law, Baoji announced, 'Anu, I plan to spend the day at the temple. Do not . . . and I repeat . . . do not disturb me if it's a girl. Of course, if it's a boy, whosoever brings me the news of a grandson will receive *mooh manga inaam*—a reward of whatever the heart desires.'

'Yes, Baoji,' replied Anu, as she kept moving Uma towards the birthing room on the other side of the courtyard. Uma had already ensured that the room had been aired and dusted—the same birthing room where Baoji, her husband Umesh, and her two younger brothers-in-law had been born.

Anu, the midwife and the maids helped settle her inside the room. Once comfortable, Uma suggested Anu to leave and supervise the daily chores, promising to call her at the time of birth.

However, the baby arrived with such unusual speed that it allowed no time to summon Anu. As soon as the midwife snipped the umbilical cord, Uma relaxed, and shifted her perspiring head and matted hair on the pillow. The midwife's scream, 'It's a boy! It's a boy!' rang in a pitch high enough, it seemed, not only to summon Anu, but also to raise the entire village. Uma smiled. The jubilant cry announcing the birth of an heir to the most powerful Hindu Brahmin family in the village of Shahadra seemed to vibrate throughout the huge mansion. Like temple bells, it echoed joyously from one corner to the other, through happy chattering of the servants and cleaning women.

Since Baoji had promised "mooh manga inaam", to whoever brought him the happy news, Uma was not surprised to see two beaming maids scramble from the birthing room, hustling to convey happy tidings to the family. The younger maid, announcing her intentions, ran with lissome strides through the iron gate at the back of the mansion, to the temple. The other, older maid, shuffled towards the kitchen on legs too aged to carry a body weight so heavy. She met Anu just outside the screen door of the birthing room. 'Anu Bibiji! Anu Bibiji! We have a boy! A loud, lusty boy,' she panted.

'A loud, lusty boy, eh?' Anu laughed, as she walked into the room.

'Believe me, Bibiji, this little one is going to put his uncle Gaurav's outbursts to shame. The baby has powerful lungs,' said the maid laughing.

Uma watched as Anu smiled at the faithful family servant, excusing her on this happy occasion for the brazen reference to Gaurav's temper. He was the youngest and only bachelor Bhardwaj son.

After bending to hug and congratulate Uma, Anu walked to where the midwife cleaned the newborn. 'Oh, he's so precious!' she cried. A beaming Uma pulled herself up in bed in preparation to receive her baby. As soon as the midwife handed the bundle to her, Anu left, whispering, 'I'll send a messenger to inform the lucky father.'

From the huge backyard outside, Uma overheard Anu's summons ordering the coach keeper, Saleem, to fetch Umesh, the newborn's father, from the family owned place of business in the nearby city of Lahore. A surge of warmth enveloped Uma as she held her baby, marvelling at the little toes, tiny hands and the soft skin, while tears of joy spilled down her cheeks. Smiling and using her dupatta veil to wipe her face, she looked out through the open window beside her bed, at the backyard of the family mansion that bubbled with happy commotion. She heard the servants whisper about the expected showering of gifts.

The haveli, as the three-storied Bhardwaj mansion was called, had an enormous brick courtyard and a verandah in its enclosed backyard. On the far side of the brick patio, close to an imposing dark iron gate, stood a cluster of medicinal neem trees, guava and pomegranate fruit trees, and multihued vines. Outside Uma's open window, Anu instructed the servants to cover all trees, bushes, even the bougainvillea vines growing around the lofty pillars of the verandah, with lights, to celebrate the birth of an heir. Summoning a servant, Anu dispatched him to obtain sweets, dried fruit and nuts from the nearby city of Lahore.

Reassured that her sister-in-law prepared well for the anticipated flood of well-wishers, Uma nestled the sleeping baby next to her body and prepared to rest. But before she could settle into restful sleep, the village hermaphrodites, the *hijraas*, arrived outside the estate, surprising her with their loud drums. Raising herself on the pillows, Uma looked through the open window. She shook her head, amazed at the speed with which the news of the baby boy's birth had spread through their village. As usual, the hermaphrodites showed up en masse to celebrate a male child's birth. The wild cavalcade tumbled into the mansion's backyard, clapping, singing, and dancing with exaggerated vulgar movements. Anu, her eyes on the dancers, her hands coming together to the beat of drums, performed her own rhythmic dance backward, towards the shade of the verandah.

In order to see better, Uma picked up her baby and giving a gentle squeeze to the precious bundle, raised herself further on the bed. The maids rushed to place more pillows to support her back. Hearing the sound of a horse-drawn carriage outside the haveli walls, she knew it would be her husband. She waited with abated breath for Umesh's arrival. When he finally walked through the back iron gate, her heart skipped, her eyes danced and, she smiled.

An avalanche of merry-makers greeted him. Blocking his path, they looked for an appropriate reward at such a happy occasion. She could see Umesh's pride in the way he held himself erect, and walked into the midst of merry dancers. As per custom, he had to dance a round, before being released to visit his newborn. The hijraas, decked in showy women's clothing, pranced in a circle around him. The dancing continued until Umesh produced a few bundles of ten-rupee notes and started sprinkling them ceremoniously over the dancers like one would rose petals, bringing the merry-making to a sudden halt. The hermaphrodites looked stunned by the lavish gift and prepared to leave. Scrambling to gather the money, they showered loving blessings on the happy Bhardwaj clan and left.

With quiet restored to the backyard, Uma, holding the baby in her arms, turned to face the door. As soon as Umesh entered the room, the midwife and the maids giggled and, paying obeisance, withdrew, shutting the door behind them. Umesh bent down to kiss Uma's forehead while his eyes sought the sleeping baby. Sitting beside her on the bed, he took out two ruby and diamond studded thick gold bangles from his inner pocket and slipped them onto his wife's arms. 'These don't even begin to show how thankful I am for the child you've given me.' He turned to gaze at his newborn. 'He's very good looking.'

'He looks like you,' said Uma, smiling.

'Maybe he took my colouring but he has your chiselled features. I hope he also inherits your wisdom and loving heart.' Umesh beamed and kissed her cheek. 'You've made me the happiest man alive.'

Uma whispered, 'Here . . . take my *jigger-da-tukra*, Dev,' and she offered the tiny slice-of-her-heart to her husband.

'Dev, eh?' said Umesh, taking the little miracle in his arms.

'Yes. I'd like to name him Dev Anand,' murmured Uma.

'I like that. Dev Anand Bhardwaj,' he said, nodding with satisfaction.

Minutes later, Baoji walked into the room to greet his grandson. He blessed Uma. His hand still lingering over her head, he turned to the newborn. 'I overheard the name you've picked for him and I like it. Dev Anand Bhardwaj. It's a great name for my grandson. Heh! Heh!'

As Umesh accepted his father's congratulations, Baoji ordered, 'Get ten acres of land cleared and tilled.'

'What for?'

'To plant hybrid Langra mango saplings, as a gift for the newborn and his mother. Tell the workers to clear and till the land beyond our native juice mango orchard. Leave space for a marble water fountain in the centre. On the newly tilled side, plant new hybrid mango saplings. I shall order a pure white marble sculpture of a mother and child from Italy, which shall be placed on a white streaked marble pedestal in the centre of the fountain.' He smiled. 'The bubbling water fountain will create a tranquil haven for my bahu and her little prince, Dev.'

'Baoji, we have no running water. So, how is the fountain going to work?' asked Umesh laughing. Uma smiled.

'We shall build the fountain now and worry about running water later. The trees must be planted right away.' Reaching to pick up the baby, he added, 'After all, the mother and the heir to the Bhardwaj estate deserve nothing but the best.'

To announce baby Dev's birth, Uma requested Anu to distribute laddoos—sugared gram-flour balls—to the poor, and colourful baskets filled with nuts, dried fruits and expensive burfi sweets—white milk toffee—to their affluent neighbours and relatives. Anu even sent messengers carrying similar colourful baskets to relatives living in Lahore and beyond.

Two days after the baby's birth, Uma asked to sit beneath large trees nestled against the back wall, beyond the spacious courtyard. A maid carried the sleeping baby and put him next to his mother. Uma, caught in the music of life, listened to the birds chirp and inhaled deeply the sweet-smelling spring fragrances. Her newborn's soft breathing brought a surge of peace. Serene and content, she looked at the magnificent Bhardwaj mansion with indulgent eyes.

The paved Grand Trunk Road from Lahore split at their gate, becoming two dirt roads that circled around the haveli before entering the village of Shahadra. The one on the right turned into a narrow pathway between the tall mansion walls and the village pond; the other ran as a wider, bumpy dirt road along lush green fields and orchards to the left. Their haveli stood like a sentry, guarding the entrance to Shahadra.

Hearing a commotion at the front entrance, Uma called a maid to sit with the baby and walked to the front of the mansion. There she saw Baoji strutting around like a peacock, near the open front gate. He stopped every villager walking to or from the village, and distributed sweets and cotton dhotis—loincloths—to them. Apprising the villagers of the baby's health, Baoji bowed to the lowest of villagers with folded hands, and looking skywards said, 'Lord Ram is great.' The poor villagers, flustered by the kindness shown by the regal old man, stammered blessings in return.

Uma smiled, turned back, and reaching her newborn, started rocking him. She sang a gentle lullaby, celebrating the good fortune that Lord Ram had bestowed upon her.

Umesh walked over from the verandah, where he and the other Bhardwaj men ate their breakfast. 'I'm going to the temple,' he said, and bent to kiss the baby.

'Do request the Punditji to ring the temple bells daily, at the exact hour of the baby's birth, until Dev turns forty days old,' said Uma.

Thus, the temple bells rang daily at the appointed hour, the family distributed gifts and Uma sang lullabies, as baby Dev grew. On the fortieth day, Uma and the entire Bhardwaj clan brought the baby to their private temple for God's blessings, showering the priest's small family with gifts.

Uma noticed the priest's only child, a toddler, lying listlessly on a worn out comforter, in the shade of a temple pillar. Flies hovered over and around her, but the little girl seemed oblivious to their maddening buzz. When Uma talked to her, the child did not respond.

'Punditji, what does the doctor say is wrong with Ratna?' Uma asked the priest.

'Bibiji, we cannot afford to consult the medicine man,' mumbled the priest. With folded hands and downcast eyes, he continued in a higher pitch, 'My wife and I have prayed and made offerings to Lord Ram to heal our Ratna. Bibiji, our baby is slipping away. . . .' He broke down sobbing, as did his wife who stood next to him.

The anguish of the helpless parents seared Uma's heart. Her troubled eyes moved to peek at the contented baby sleeping in her own arms. Giving him a tender squeeze, she silently thanked Lord Ram, and turned to look at the wilted girl with huge lustreless eyes. The poor, simple folks had named their only child Ratna—a jewel. How could she allow their jewel to be lost forever, before it even had a chance to be polished to its promised radiance?

As soon as she returned to the haveli, she summoned the coach-keeper, Saleem, and sent him to Lahore to fetch Dr Simranjeet, the family doctor, to examine the punditji's ailing toddler. After three long weeks, the girl recovered and upon Uma's generous invitation, became a regular visitor to the Bhardwaj haveli.

Uma spent most of her mornings sitting on the shaded side of the patio, next to the trees, while baby Dev cooed and gurgled in his embossed sterling silver jhula bassinet, next to her. The swing bassinet had been retrieved from the birthing room. According to family folklore, Baoji's great grandfather got the jhula made to his own specifications, for his descendents. Since then, every generation of Bhardwaj babies were rocked in the same jhula.

On most mornings, after the men left for work, Anu, the wife of Baoji's middle son Amar, joined Uma under the trees. The two sisters-in-law breakfasted together and discussed their plans for the day. The matriarch, Uma, knitted sweaters and shawls for the family, and attended to the overall management of the household. Anu, on the other hand, made all cooking decisions and supervised the cleaning of the mansion.

One morning, during their breakfast, the poor priest's wife arrived to launder the family's clothes. Her little girl Ratna ran to the ayah—the nanny—clamouring to sit on a stool near the baby. 'I want to lo . . . lock him,' she lisped.

Noticing the ayah's hesitance, Uma laughed. 'Salma, let her rock him. Do watch her though, so that she doesn't fall off her perch.'

With the determination of a confident child, Ratna climbed the stool, refusing Salma ayah's help. Within minutes, the jhula's back and forth rhythm made her drowsy, and the ayah had to lay her on a clean cotton carpet to rest.

Uma's knitting stopped in mid-stitch. She sat shaking her head.

'What?' asked Anu.

'Nothing . . . just thinking about her.' She nodded in the sleeping girl's direction. 'Look at her dimples and her long eyelashes. The beautiful child is oblivious to the harsh destiny that awaits her. She's carefree and unaware that she was born only to serve.'

Anu looked at the girl. 'She sure is cute.' Both the women indulged the girl with sweets, fruit and pretty clothes to wear. And that kept Ratna returning to the mansion for more.

Soon, Uma started hearing whispers amongst the servants. Some said, 'The Bhardwajs are spoiling Punditji's little girl, Ratna.' Others complained, 'Uma bibiji treats her as if the poor girl is worthy of attention. She indulges in Ratna as though she were the son of a rich man.'

One day, Uma asked Ratna's mother what the fuss was about. 'Bibiji, I think it's jealousy. They complain because you are so kind to us. You allow our Ratna to play with Dev babu.'

'How does it affect them?'

'It doesn't, but the servants are hypocrites. They tell me, "Sister, you must have good kismet. Your Ratna was born to be a princess. Look at her. She goes to the haveli to play and she doesn't even have to lift a finger".'

'But she is not even three! What kind of work can she do?' asked Uma. She dropped the subject and dismissed Ratna's mother by getting back to her knitting.

After Ratna's mother left, Uma's mind drifted to her beloved sister-in-law. She enjoyed having the forever smiling, short and plump Anu near her. Anu's carefree, easygoing personality balanced Uma's organised and compulsive nature. Anu's constant humming of happy tunes seemed to attract joy like some flowers attract butterflies. After Dev's birth, Uma realised that she, an only child, had found not just a friend in Anu but also a sister and a masi—mother's sister, an aunt—for little Dev. Anu adored the baby and oftentimes took care of him at night so Uma could rest. Even though Uma knew she could easily afford one or more nighttime ayah, she found it easier to trust her baby to Anu.

Besides Anu, the only other close friend in the village Uma had was Razia Begum, a Muslim. Baoji treated her friend's husband, Iqbal Bhutto, as his fourth son. Iqbal had three wives and Razia Begum was the oldest and his favourite. Affluent in their own right, the Bhuttos became such dear family friends that the Bhardwaj men and Iqbal did nothing without consulting each other first. Uma taught Dev to address Iqbal as chacha and Razia Begum as khalajaan—uncle and aunt. This unusual family friendship between two dissimilar religious icons of the village gave Uma a feeling of pride, like successfully fitting two swords in one sheath.

However, as the country awoke to dreams of Independence, rumblings amongst orthodox Hindus and Muslims generated scepticism among ordinary citizens. The Muslim League and the Indian National Congress started displaying glaring signs of distrust of each other. For the common man, tolerance of each other's religious practices and constraints, cultivated over centuries, started crumbling slowly but surely. Conscious of the changing times, Uma still hoped and prayed the two swords would never be unsheathed.

4
The Bride's Dowry

Spring, 1942

Early one morning, Uma walked out of their detached kitchen and saw her youngest brother-in-law standing, his feet firmly planted at the foot of the stairs. 'Gaurav, come here,' she called out.

Gaurav, dressed in jodhpurs to go horseback riding, stood gulping a glass of fresh-churned buttermilk. Taller and better looking than his two older brothers, he handed the empty glass to a maid and twirled his moustache.

'What is it, Bhabi?' he asked his sister-in-law Uma.

'I have good news to give.' Uma smiled at him. 'Did anyone tell you we have arranged a suitable match for you? I believe the girl is exceptionally good looking, and she's been educated in English medium institutions in Delhi.'

'I heard.'

'Who told you?'

'I met Iqbal bhaiya yesterday. He mentioned it.'

'Iqbal bhaiya is the trading partner of the girl's father, a wealthy Hindu Brahmin businessman in Delhi. Razia Begum is a friend of the girl's mother.'

Gaurav knew his family trusted Iqbal and Razia Begum's judgement enough to agree to the match without any questions or demands. 'Uma Bhabi, have you met her?'

'No, but Razia Begum has a very high opinion of the girl's looks and her temperament.'

'What's her name?'

'Oh, you are so shameless Gaurav,' Uma teased. 'Why do you need to know your bride's name? You will find out soon enough after marriage. Look at you. You don't even look embarrassed.'

'I am. I'm sooo embarrassed.' Gaurav smiled.

'No, you are not. You are sooo silly. Her name is Sita. Wait till I tell your brother how shameless and curious you are.'

'Does . . . um . . . Sita come from a rich family?'

'I just told you they are very wealthy. Anyway, does it matter?' Uma asked.

'Of course it matters. If Sita's family is rich then we can demand a bigger dowry,' Gaurav explained, his tone condescending.

Dumbfounded by Gaurav's boldness, her smile vanished. She wondered why he thought the family would not do the right thing for him. His questions dishonoured the family wisdom, its shared love and traditions. Didn't he know joint families survived and thrived only as a part of a whole? Could mango blossoms mature into luscious fruit without being nurtured by the mango tree?

She shook her head and snapped, 'I'll pretend I didn't hear that. We Bhardwajs are proud people. By God's grace, we have more than enough for our needs. At my wedding and at Anu's wedding, no demands of dowry were made and we are not about to start with you, Gaurav.'

'Why not? We could use all the dowry her family can afford.'

'You amaze me,' said Uma, shaking her head again. 'What is it you don't understand? Did you hear what I just said? We have . . . and I repeat . . . we have more than enough and do not intend to ask for any dowry from Sita's family.'

She wondered where she went wrong in raising her brother-in-law. Gaurav was only nine, and motherless, when she married Umesh. It was she who had helped nurture Gaurav to maturity.

'You and Umesh bhaiya have enough, but what about me? I am the youngest son of the family, and nobody cares about the youngest.'

'You know, we . . . your family cares—'

'Those are empty words, Bhabi. What do I have that I can call my own? Huh? I have no house, no property. In fact,' he whined, 'getting a decent dowry is my only option if I want to lead a respectable life.'

Blood creeping up her face, Uma started to walk away, but stopped upon hearing her father-in-law's heavy footsteps.

Baoji bellowed, 'What's the matter, Gaurav? Did you quarrel with your bhabi again?'

Gaurav twirled his mustache as he turned to face his father. 'Baoji, I'm not sure what's troubling her. All I asked was if my intended came from a rich family, so we could demand a decent dowry.'

'Was that all? Foolish boy! Are you questioning your family's decision? Have you no shame? You think we don't know what to look for?' He stared at his son. 'I often wonder if you were born an imbecile or simply become one when it suits you. Go, apologise to your bhabi.'

Uma watched Gaurav cringe as Baoji continued thundering in his I-am-the-master-of-this-house voice. 'Gaurav, it's not in mortal hands to dictate whether the spouse brings dowry or not. It is all one's karma. You'll get what you deserve, but for heaven's sake, have enough sense not to ask stupid questions, especially not from a bhabi who brought you up like a mother would.' Breathing heavy, Baoji scoffed under his breath, '*Budhu na hove te!*' Bloody Idiot!

Gaurav offered Uma a lukewarm apology. The subject of dowry never came up again.

That morning, Baoji informed Uma that Gaurav would be getting married by the end of the following month. Without batting an eyelid, Uma immersed herself in wedding preparations in earnest. Not once did she question her father-in-law's decision or complain about the short notice.

Since wedding celebrations usually lasted for days—both before and after the marriage ceremony—Uma ensured that the Bhardwaj mansion was scoured, sanitised and whitewashed. Under her directions, the haveli stood like a well-scrubbed child on the first day of school. Tall arches flanked the front entrance, covered with fragrant white jasmine, golden marigolds and crimson roses. Hired chefs cooked outside in open-fire pits, adding delicious aromas to the fragrant flowers. Colourful cloth canopies not only shaded the cooking areas but also provided shade to arriving guests. The canopies, the house and the big pipal tree in the front yard, all draped with lights, spoke of an extravagance unheard of in Shahadra. The villagers gaped at the lights twinkling on the manor house night after night, for almost three weeks. Mothers from neighbouring villages, needing an excuse to step out of their closed quarters, brought their children in the evenings to see the spectacular sight.

Every evening, while the women sang and danced, the men settled down to drink and discuss politics. Uma did not appreciate that, preferring the men to relax and enjoy the festivities instead of talking about the worsening political situation in the country.

'That's not possible,' her husband explained. 'You know as well as I do, that deeper and deeper cracks of distrust are appearing between the Muslims and us.'

'So? All I'm saying is let this be a happy time for the family.'

'I understand,' he replied. 'But, the rift between Muslims and non-Muslims is affecting our friendships.'

'I can't seem to reach you! Tell me, did we Hindus start the rift?'

Umesh stared at her.

'Why should we have to pay the price? Huh?' she insisted.

'Uma, please calm down. No one community started anything. This is just an ugly byproduct of the freedom movement, which has now branched into two demands—one for Independence and the other for Muslim autonomy in a separate land for "the pure".'

Uma walked away shaking her head. She did understand the reality of social unrest but life still had to be lived. She had a wedding to manage. So, ignoring the men, she bustled around taking care of the guests, managing the chefs, the servants, the decorations and the festivities.

Every day, during the evening's merrymaking, Uma watched her younger sister-in-law, Anu, singing and dancing with happy abandon, with friends and relatives. Uma's toddler, Dev, followed Anu around clapping and squealing. She and Anu often tried but could not coax the punditji's daughter Ratna, now a bashful four-year-old, to join in the evening entertainments. Ratna took to hiding behind doors and furniture, peeping and laughing. The more they cajoled, the faster Ratna chuckled and ran. Catching her in hiding, little Dev oftentimes tried to drag her into the middle of dancing women, but Ratna, giggling and hissing, demanded that he leave her alone.

Uma shook her head at their antics, and smiled.

Outside the haveli walls, the political climate changed at a fast pace. She did not like what she saw and heard.

'Uma,' Umesh said one night, a week before the wedding, 'the rioting is escalating. These days it's neither easy nor safe to travel.'

'I heard. Punditji stopped by today and said two Muslim boys threw stones at him when he went to buy vegetables at the village market,' said Uma.

'Did he say who they were?'

'No. He said their faces were covered and they slung racial slurs at him.'

'This really worries me. I think to be on the safe side maybe only the men should travel to Delhi for the wedding.'

She agreed, suggesting Umesh arrange for extra servants to travel with them, there being safety in numbers. 'It seems these days you can't be too careful.'

Thus, the men travelled with extra servants attending to their needs.

The Bhardwaj men returned from the wedding in Delhi after five days. Uma arranged a warm reception for the newlyweds, not only at the haveli but also at the Lahore station. She sent both the Bhardwaj carriages decorated with red roses and fragrant tuberoses, one to receive the groom and Baoji, the other for Umesh and his brother Amar. She also arranged a palki—a bridal carriage—and four palki bearers to bring Sita, the bride, to her new home. A group of village musicians dressed in crisp red and white uniforms waited to play the wedding music and to lead the slow procession to Shahadra.

At the expected time of arrival of the doli—the groom's party returning with the bride—the Bhardwaj haveli sparkled as brilliantly as the new bride. Fresh tuberoses adorned the arches while the walls and the haveli pillars could hardly be seen for the marigold garlands. Punjabi wedding songs blared through loudspeakers, and the women, dressed in fine silks, talked and laughed, enjoying the fragrant air.

Soon the village urchins, with stray dogs trailing them, raced to the haveli gates, pointing backwards, shouting, 'The doli. The doli.'

As soon as the doli arrived at the entrance to the Bhardwaj mansion, the majestic iron gates opened to welcome the newlyweds. The blaring music in the haveli hushed. Gaurav's female relatives and guests gathered to receive the bride, their long skirted silk ghagaras flowing in the breeze. Some danced and twirled in joyous merriment while others carried lighted diyas—earthen lamps with oil and wicks—on sparkling bronze platters, to welcome the new bride. The bearers lowered the palki, and with the help of Gaurav's female cousins, Bimla and Vimla, the bride emerged, her luxurious silks trailing behind her.

Baoji commanded Gaurav to stand next to Sita, whose gold and tomato-red ghagara shimmered in the morning light. Gaurav, twirling his mustache, moved closer to his bride. His cousins, Bimla and Vimla did the arti—the welcome prayer—with lighted earthen lamps, to receive blessings of a bright future for the newlyweds.

Then Uma and Anu came forward to welcome the bride. Uma lifted the bride's veil, hugged her and put a heavy gold wedding necklace around her neck. She also pushed twelve ruby-studded gold bangles onto her arms—a welcoming gift from the matriarch of the Bhardwaj family. Sita bent to touch Uma's feet as a sign of respect, and Uma directed her to touch Anu's feet too.

Anu giggled when Sita bent towards her feet, and as soon as the bride straightened up, Anu led her to one of two ornate chairs placed side by side on a dais decorated with fragrant roses. Sita sat on the first chair. A beaming Gaurav walked up to sit beside her.

Anu brought a toddler. 'This is Dev, Uma bhabi's son,' she said, and placed Dev in the blushing bride's lap. Sita's blush revealed she understood the significance of this little ritual—the family's hope that she too would produce a male offspring.

'Me, me, me,' clamoured a bright-eyed, dimpled girl, jumping on her tippy-toes.

'Oh, this is Ratna, our punditji's daughter,' said Anu.

Sita bent over to caress Ratna's face.

All of sudden the village hijraas erupted from the open iron gate, in a colourful, loud procession like hot lava from a volcano. The guests parted to allow the brazen group some dancing room and the hermaphrodites, dressed in gaudy saris, danced, clapped and made a racket. Gradually the family and guests joined in the merry making.

Uma saw Sita steal a glance at her handsome groom only to find him smiling at her. Blushing and lowering her eyes, Sita smiled shyly and turned her attention to the restless toddler in her lap.

In the months following the wedding, Uma did her best to ease the bride's transition into married life. Sita was the first woman in the village of Shahadra to have completed a Bachelor's Degree from an English medium institution. Talking it over with Anu, Uma realised they both were in awe of their new sister-in-law. However, Dev seemed neither intimidated by her education, nor her stunning looks, and followed her around like a shadow.

One day, as Uma watched, Anu pointed to Sita and explained, 'Dev, she too is your chachi.'

'Anu chachi?' little Dev asked.

'No, she is Sita chachi. I'm Anu chachi.'

Dev nodded, and reaching for Sita, lisped, 'You no Shita. You my Shweet chachi' Smiling, Dev's sweet aunt, Sita, bent down to kiss him.

Uma included Sita in the household's predictable routines. After Gaurav left in the mornings to supervise the large farm, she invited Sita to spend her mornings either helping Anu in the kitchen or to sit with her under the trees to relax. After lunch, Sita retired to her room to rest or read the English newspaper. Since Gaurav usually did not return until five or six in the evening, Uma suggested Ratna spend a couple of hours every afternoon with her, to give Sita some company. For Ratna and her parents, this was a welcome opportunity for their little girl to rest on hot afternoons in the cool of an electric fan in Sita's room.

One day, Ratna's mother mentioned that the girl had a cold and would not be visiting in the afternoon. So, Uma and Anu decided to wait until Dev woke up from his afternoon nap and pay Sita a visit in her quarters on the uppermost floor of the haveli. At four o'clock in the afternoon, Uma ordered tea and cookies, along with hot milk for Dev, to be brought upstairs to Sita's suite. When the two sisters-in-law reached the top floor, they found the door to the sitting room ajar and heard voices from the open bedroom.

Gaurav sat flirting with his wife, who held Tagore's *Gitanjali* in her hands. Smiling, Uma raised her finger to her lips to warn Anu. Neither had expected to find Gaurav back from work so early.

They heard Sita laugh and screech, 'What?'

'Nothing.' Gaurav winked. 'Sita, when you look at me with that beauty mark and those dimples, it unravels my heart. God! What a figure. I wonder which bard's fantasy moulded your body to such perfection—'

'Flatterer!' They saw a blush spreading on Sita's face, as Gaurav pulled her to their bed.

Both Uma and Anu turned red at witnessing the innocent play turn into an intimate moment between the newlyweds. They retreated as unobtrusively as possible, taking Dev with them, directing the maid to take the evening tea to the table on the back verandah.

Uma realised that of the three brothers, Gaurav's life, after almost a year of marriage, still seemed to revolve only around his wife. He no longer joined the family in the evenings, spending most of the time in their suite on the third floor of the mansion. Whenever Uma and Anu sat on their back verandah cleaning and preparing lentils and vegetables for supper, they often heard Sita and Gaurav laughing, giggling, and sometimes talking in English. One day, Anu asked Uma, 'What do you think has turned Gaurav into a drooling idiot—Sita's looks or her education? He sure acts foolish—'

Uma, breaking into a smile, interrupted, 'You call that being foolish? He's more like a gushing, blabbering Ranjha.' He acts like a lovesick Romeo.

'Bhabi, do you think we should hire a tutor to teach both of us some English?' asked Anu.

'Whatever for?'

'Well, Sita knows English.'

'So?' asked Uma.

'If both of us learn it too, then we three Bhardwaj mistresses could converse in *git-mit* amongst ourselves, and impress all our maids and servants with our speech.'

They both burst out laughing at the notion of talking in English to impress the simple village folk. But the unspoken thoughts made Uma realise that like her, even Anu feared the unthinkable—what if their own husbands started comparing them to Sita?

5
The Girl Child

Spring, 1943

In the spring following the wedding, Uma watched Gaurav strut around whistling a cheerful tune. The haveli buzzed with excitement awaiting the arrival of Sita's new baby. She was not surprised when Baoji decreed, 'Uma, make sure no effort is spared to ensure a male offspring. Take Sita to all places of worship and promise the gods a full hundred-rupee donation for a boy baby.'

So, Uma encouraged Gaurav to offer money, gold, silver and sweets to the family gods, the family priest and even the midwife, in exchange for a male child. Every morning Uma accompanied Sita and her maids to visit the family temple built by Baoji's grandfather. Some mornings, contrary to accepted norms, Gaurav accompanied them, following the path lined by fragrant juice mango trees, alive with blossoms and the promise of fruit. Ancient banyan trees with thick beard-like growth surrounded and bathed the temple in ethereal silence.

Punditji, the family priest, rang the temple bells, offered flowers, laddoos and dried coconuts, soliciting the gods to bless the couple with a male child. The days sped by pleasantly while preparations for the new arrival gathered momentum.

As per custom, Uma suggested to Gaurav that Sita be taken to her parents in Delhi for her first delivery.

'No, I'm fine here,' Sita replied to Gaurav's query. 'Uma bhabi and Anu bhabi are very good to me. I want to stay in Shahadra, as I want you to be by my side for our baby's birth.'

During her eighth month, Sita became ill, running a low fever. A frantic Gaurav asked his Uma bhabi to take his expectant wife, not to a hakim—a native herbal doctor—but to a medical doctor in the city of Lahore.

'Oh! *Maere Mai*. You know very well that the doctor of female troubles in Lahore is a male. How can she go to him in her condition?' asked Uma. 'Gaurav, this is your wife for God's sake. Do you have no shame in exposing her to another man?'

'In Delhi, there are women doctors for female problems. Maybe we can look for a similar lady doctor in Lahore?' suggested Sita.

The midwife, who had been summoned earlier by Uma, suggested her hakim give the patient his puriyas—the powdered medicine—to chase the fever away. It would cost them only two rupees for the hakim, another rupee for the tonga fare from and to Lahore, and maybe a rupee or two for her services. 'Remember, when Uma bibiji started running a fever during her pregnancy, it was our hakim Tarachand who took care of her? He felt her pulse and gave her the appropriate medicine without compromising her modesty, and she got better, didn't she?' she argued.

Gaurav looked like he had no answer, so he parted with six rupees for the hakim, the fare, the medicine and the midwife's services. Helpless, he stood attempting to twirl his mustache. But Sita's condition did not improve. Her retching started early one morning and within a couple of hours, she went into early labour. The midwife, summoned in great haste, could not even start the fire or fetch water for boiling before Sita delivered a stillborn girl.

Gaurav sat on an armchair in their back verandah, dumbfounded with the news of a daughter born dead. 'How could the gods do this to me after all I offered?' he kept asking over and over. 'A dead girl baby? How did that happen?'

To Uma it seemed he grieved not for the child being stillborn, but for it being a girl.

Five-year-old Ratna walked up the side stairs to Sita's room and knocked on the door. No one answered. It was early afternoon—time for her afternoon visit with Sita bibiji—but the door stood locked. She skipped down the inner courtyard stairs and asked a maid, 'Where's Sita bibiji?'

'She's not well. Didn't you know?'

'No. What's wrong with her?'

'Hai Ram! You are such a pest. Go home.'

Coming down the verandah stairs, Ratna saw Gaurav sitting in an armchair, his head in his hands. Sensing something peculiar going on, she hid behind a door and watched him from a safe distance. Gaurav babu scared her. Even under normal circumstances, Gaurav babu was nasty and this, whatever ailed him, did not seem normal, she decided.

She peeped from behind a partially open door and choked as Gaurav stared back at her, his face contorted with misery or anger. Before she could figure out which it was, he yelled, 'What? Have you never seen me before?' Ratna tried to breathe before he barked again. 'Go home and ask your rotten father if he still remembers all we offered for a male child. Ungrateful bastard! He probably did not even pray on our behalf.'

Ratna stood rooted, unable to move, her mouth agape.

Gaurav stomped his foot and bellowed, 'Scoot!'

Her heart thumping, Ratna took off as fast as her five-year-old legs could carry her, through the courtyard, the iron gate, the mango grove and beyond. On the way, her tiny dupatta got caught in the low tree branches. Yanking it hard, she tore it, but did not slow down until she reached the grove of ancient banyan trees, close to the temple. Once safe amongst those trees, Ratna stopped and looked back, tears welling up in her eyes. Brushing off her tears impatiently, she resolved not to discuss the nasty Gaurav babu with her parents, as that would trigger another of her mataji's meaningless lectures about her being a mere girl-child and 'him' being her master.

'Gaurav babu. Indeed!' she muttered, shaking her head in anger.

Looking up at the banyan trees, she demanded out loud, 'How come everyone at the haveli is my master? Huh?'

The ancient trees swayed in the cool breeze, but offered no answer.

Uma sat on a chair near Sita's bed in the birthing room. Anu, the midwife and the maids worked silently to make Sita comfortable after the delivery. Uma thought of the time when she too had lost her firstborn girl. Her mother helped her through the grief and pain. Placing a comforting hand on Sita's shoulder, she said, 'When I lost my first born, my mataji told me in God's kingdom, *der hai, andher nahin.*' There is delay but not the darkness of injustice and denial. 'Sita, believe me, you'll get a healthy baby one day.'

'Look at me,' cried Anu, 'I've been married for seven years and am still hoping and praying for a child.'

Sita choked back her tears.

Anu sat on the bed and took Sita's hands in hers. 'Little sister, have faith in God. Trust me, one day you'll get a healthy baby. Did you know, for the last six years I've been keeping a fast on Tuesdays, praying for a child? Our punditji assures me our family gods will hear my prayers.'

'I don't have your strength and faith . . . wish I did,' Sita mumbled.

'From now on maybe both of us can pray and keep the fasts together. What do you say?' cajoled Anu.

Sita nodded feebly through her tears.

Uma watched her two younger sisters-in-law sharing each other's pain and felt excluded, almost guilty and acutely aware of her own good fortune. Her Dev was a beautiful child with features like hers, his father's fair complexion and light hair cascading in curls over his head. Throwing a quick prayer to Lord Ram, reminding him (in case he forgot) about the loss she had suffered with her firstborn, Uma made a deal. She too would fast on Tuesdays and pray with her sisters-in-law, as long as he would keep her precious Dev under his protection.

Prayers aside, Uma knew she also had to be careful about other people's *buri nazar*—their evil eye. So, she walked briskly over to the kitchen, picked up some ashes from the wood stove, mixed them with red-hot chili peppers and threw them over her son's right shoulder, to ward off evil. For added measure, she applied a black kohl mark behind Dev's ear.

The Girl Child | 43

A couple of months after Sita's loss, Baoji returned from a visit to the family temple, breaking the tranquility of the morning by his roar. 'Bahu!'

When agitated, he addressed Uma as Bahu in an exceptionally loud voice. Uma, in her confusion at being summoned in such a venomous tone, dropped the shawl she was knitting and ran to see her distraught father-in-law dragging a weeping Dev.

'Here, take care of your son,' growled Baoji, in his I-am-the-master-of-this-house voice.

'What happened, Baoji?' she asked, running to her sobbing son's aid.

'What happened? Huh? What happened? I'll tell you what happened. Woman, do you have to have everything spelled out for you? Do you not see that Ratna is five years old and is still running around with my grandson? I can't even take him to the temple because that good for nothing girl lures him out to play.' Uma waited while he took time to shake his head before continuing, 'Did you know I caught them playing near the unprotected water well? What if Dev had fallen into it?'

Baoji stomped away giving one last warning, 'Tell Punditji his girl need not come to the haveli uninvited. She can help you in the kitchen if you like. As for my grandson, he needs no girls. Get him boys of his own status to play with. Women!' He trailed off, shaking his head again.

Uma realised that by encouraging the children's friendship, she had put the priest's little daughter in the midst of this controversy. Since it was her fault, she had to find a way to make the child's banishment as painless as possible, for both Ratna and her impoverished parents. She also puzzled over the best way to explain Ratna's sudden disappearance to Dev.

Late in the afternoon, she left Dev sleeping in Salma's care, and walked down to the temple to talk to Ratna's parents, hoping for an easy way out of this embarrassing situation. The punditji's wife sat in shade on the raised platform on one side of the temple, shelling peas for supper. She saw Ratna walking about collecting wood for the evening cooking, as her mother was now too big with a child to be doing much bending and lifting. Uma greeted the woman with a kind *namaste*—I bow to God and his divinity within you.

The priest's wife, with folded hands and a humble smile, struggled to her feet. She had stopped washing clothes at the haveli a month earlier. Uma helped the poor woman sit down again, asking, 'When is the little one due?'

'Any time now, Bibiji.'

'You will soon have your hands full. We know Ratna is old enough to help you with the baby. Keep her at home from now on. She doesn't need to come to the haveli anymore. If I ever need her help, I'll send for her.'

'*Jo hukam*, Bibiji.' Your request will be honoured, Ma'am.

Uma started to walk back to the haveli. 'Oh! I almost forgot to mention,' she turned around, 'make sure Ratna and the baby do not play near the open water well. There is a beautiful clearing in those banyan trees between our mango orchard and this temple. Ratna knows about it, as I've seen her there sometimes. Ask Punditji to put up a swing in those trees for Ratna. The cosy glade will be safer for your children. Even the baby will have room to crawl and play in a safe environment.'

After giving permission and money for a new swing, to soften the blow of banishment, Uma left. Sighing with relief, she realised the task had turned out to be simpler than she had anticipated.

During the brief conversation between her mother and Uma, Ratna had sat close by, building a smoky fire in their clay stove. Perplexed by adult behaviour, she wondered why Uma bibiji did not even bother to talk to her or acknowledge her smile. Grown-ups, she mumbled shaking her head, one minute they are fine and the next they ignore you.

Ratna's father walked out of the temple and, nodding towards Uma's receding figure said, 'Bibiji didn't come into the temple. What did she want?'

Ratna's mataji exploded. 'She doesn't want our girl at the haveli anymore. It seems all of a sudden Ratna is too old to play with Dev babu.'

'They say, *samahjdaar ko ishara kafi.*' A simple hint to the wise is enough. 'You remember how angry Baoji was when he saw Dev babu playing near the well with our Ratna? That is one precious little boy they have in that family,' said Ratna's bapu.

'Our child is precious too. Just because we are poor doesn't mean our child can be summoned or banished at the will of the rich and mighty,' screeched Mataji.

'Come, Come. You know Uma bibiji well. Don't you remember what she did for our Ratna when we almost lost her? Uma bibiji would never shun our child just because she is a poor man's daughter. They are right though. We should impress on Ratna that playing near the well is neither safe nor acceptable.'

'But what is our poor girl going to do? Where can she play safely if she can't play at the haveli? Bibiji gave this money to put up a swing for Ratna on those banyan trees . . . as if a swing can compensate for the pride of the rich!' Still grumbling, she handed the money to her husband.

'I'm sure she'll like the swing. I'll put it up in the evening. We can also encourage her to play with the other little girls in the village,' he replied.

'*Tauba, Tauba, Tauba!*' God forbid. 'You want a Hindu Brahmin child to play with Muslim girls of the village?'

'Come on. There are plenty of Hindu and Sikh girls in the village. What about Vinod's daughters?'

'Hai Ram! We are Brahmins and those girls are from a much lower Hindu caste. They are practically untouchables. And did you ever see the filthy slum they live in? That is one disease-ridden hellhole. There the village elders eat opium and smoke hookah pipes the whole day long, while their children run around naked with big bellies and running noses.'

'Well,' said Punditji, scratching the stubble on his chin, 'we can always admit her to the village school.'

'No, we can't. There they teach only Urdu. What purpose will that serve? All our sacred writings are in Sanskrit.'

'How about I teach her Hindi and Sanskrit during the day? That should keep her occupied until our new baby arrives. And maybe, once in a while, we can allow her to play with Sikh and Hindu girls who are not untouchables.'

They talked as if Ratna was invisible, but she heard the argument. The fire in the stove had started, so she got up and walked towards her parents. 'Bapu,' she said, 'it's okay. Don't worry. You teach me Hindi. I hate the haveli anyway. Mataji tells me to obey everyone at the haveli, especially that little monster Dev, like . . . like he's the boss of me!'

'Hush, wicked girl. You can't talk like that. What if somebody hears you? You don't even have sense enough to know you are a poor man's child and a mere girl-child at that,' hissed her mother.

'Mataji, what did I do to be a mere girl-child?'

'It was your karma, you ignorant girl.'

'Does it make me different from Dev?'

'Hai Ram! You are so dense. Ratna, you will get us in trouble. Always remember you are not his equal. Do you understand? You will call him Dev babu. You hear me, girl?'

'Mataji, you said children must never take the name of anyone older than them. But Dev does. Shouldn't he call me Ratna didi because I'm older than him? It's only fair I call him Dev instead of Dev babu because he's younger?'

Before the mother answered, Ratna fussed. 'Dev is an idiot anyway, calling me "Atna! Atna!" when I remind him constantly my name is Ratna.'

'Hush you stupid child. Try to remember who you are. A poor man's—'

'I don't care. I know I'm special and Dev is not,' Ratna muttered.

'You are a foolish girl . . . and he is not Dev but Dev babu to you. Do you hear me?'

Ratna shrugged her shoulders and ran off to the tranquil haven amongst the centuries-old grove of banyan trees.

Within a week of Ratna's banishment from the haveli, her mataji delivered a baby girl they named Sheila. Ratna, thrilled with her new big-sister status, adored her baby sister, feeling important to be taking care of her. She felt special for another reason—her bapu took the time to teach her, when none of the other girls she knew in the village could read or write. It pleased her not to have to go to the haveli anymore and not to have to deal with Dev.

A day before Dev's third birthday, Uma came to the temple to discuss the timing of the prayers for the birthday celebrations and for his mundan ceremony—the Hindu ritual of initiation by shaving the head. The celebrations were to take place not at the temple but in their haveli, and Uma wanted Punditji to prepare for a havan, to be performed with the usual chanting and feeding the fire deity with ghee—clarified butter—and with the sprinkling of holy water from the river Ganges. The rich, the poor and even the infirm from the village slums were invited for the feast.

Uma gave Ratna a personal invitation for Dev's special day. 'Ratna, do come with Punditji. Dev misses you a lot and would love to see you.' Uma smiled at her but Ratna pursed her tiny lips.

After Uma left, Punditji said, 'Ratna, isn't that nice? Bibiji invited you personally.'

'I'm not going!' she shouted.

'Bibiji said Dev babu will like it,' coaxed her bapu.

'I said I'm not going,' and she ran off towards the banyan trees.

The next day she still stubbornly declined to attend the ceremonies. While her father went to the haveli to perform his priestly duties, Ratna, angry and hurt, sat on her new swing in the banyan grove, convincing herself that she hated everyone, including that stupid Dev who could not even pronounce her name and called her Atna. She dragged her unshod feet in the dirt, and sat on the swing wondering how she could have ever cared for that three-year-old baby. The pain and rage she felt for being banished from the haveli made her decide that not only was Dev a spoiled, pampered, rich boy but an idiot as well, so she tried to reject all warm feelings for him. She had to. After all, did not Baoji scream at her for playing with Dev near the well? How did playing suddenly become a crime? She would show them she did not care.

She was Ratna, a jewel, after all.

6
Calm Before the Storm

1945-46

Uma watched her father-in-law spoil her son without shame or remorse and worried that such pampering would damage her child emotionally. Baoji provided Dev with the best of everything, fulfilling the child's every whim, often times vetoing Uma's and her husband's wishes. Whenever she protested, he thundered, 'You may be the mother but Dev is *my* grandson. He is the sole heir to my estate—the one and only Bhardwaj estate. You know it as well as I do, even if there are more grandsons, it is he who will inherit almost everything and become the lord of these lands—the haveli, the farm, the three orchards and the stores in Lahore.'

Finding no other recourse, she requested her husband to talk to his father.

'Baoji,' started Umesh, 'if Dev is to become a wise head of the future Bhardwaj clan, we think he needs to be taught to derive his values in life from the Vedas, the source book of all knowledge. Uma and I both think we should hire the best pundits available to coach Dev in Sanskrit.'

Baoji smirked. 'You fool, which world do you live in? Wake up. What will learning to read Sanskrit do for him? Dev needs to learn English, so that he can be educated at Oxford in future. Your wise pundits can teach him nothing about survival in the ever-changing world that exists beyond our haveli walls.'

Baoji admitted five-year-old Dev to Aitchison, an English school in Lahore, in spite of his parents' misgivings. He then directed Sita, Dev's English-educated aunt to help him with his schoolwork. Both Umesh and Uma thanked Lord Ram that Baoji did not think of hiring an English nanny for Dev's education. At least, with Sita as his tutor, they could still influence the child's thinking and give him sound Hindu values.

Under Sita's coaching, Dev moved to the head of his class long before the school year ended. Proud of his grandson's achievement, Baoji bought a sparkling Austin, hired a Muslim chauffeur named Omar, so Dev could go to school in a chauffeur driven car, as befitted the little prince.

The sparkling black car, still smelling of fresh leather and paint, arrived outside the open haveli gates. The car's side windows screened with dark drapes for purdah, sort of beckoned the women of the family to travel in privacy.

As the first car in Shahadra village, it received more fanfare than any English man's visit to the village. The news of its arrival spread through the village like a flash flood, disrupting the daily activities of the curious villagers. Leaving their tasks, the village men hustled to see the marvel. With determined expressions, wearing grimy loincloths, they armed themselves with rough-hewn bamboo sticks to ward off stray village dogs in their path. The women, heads covered with dupatta veils or wearing burqas, gathered on each other's flat rooftops and waited, laughing and giggling. Little children materialised in scanty clothes. Young boys flying kites or trying their skill at breath control in kabaddi, suspended their games and ran on unshod feet to see the new wonder. They arrived with eyes opened wide, staring at the amazing motor car.

Even stray village dogs, attracted by the commotion, joined the proceedings, standing patiently, breathing with their mouths open, tongues hanging, their tails wagging in anticipation.

Baoji, dressed in a starched white loincloth and kurta, holding a regal looking sterling silver walking stick, surveyed the admirers around the car and the flat-topped roofs, and beamed the smug smile of a rich man. The villagers begged the chauffeur to let them touch and feel the car's silky smooth surface. Omar, the chauffeur, looked at Baoji and, pursing his lips, shook his head.

Baoji and his three sons strutted about grinning. Amidst much yelling, the crowd of men and boys waited like restless children at the circus, to see the car perform. Baoji instructed the handsome young chauffeur to ensure no one scratched the brand new vehicle. The villagers heard and moved back reluctantly. Omar stood guard, proud, smiling, and vigilant.

Over the years, Uma had resigned herself to Baoji's extravagances, but this shining black car was a bigger deal than anything she had ever imagined. Pulling down the dupatta veil draped over her head, in order to cover her face, she called Anu and Sita to join her, and walked towards the car. She guessed the villagers had probably seen cars in Lahore and other big cities, but this was different. Hearing a touch of pride in their voices warmed her heart. Owning a car had probably put the Bhardwaj family on an equal footing with the rich British rulers.

Dev's two aunts, with heads and faces covered in dupatta veils, followed Uma and sat with her in the backseat of the car. Dev joined them, sitting in the front seat with the driver. Baoji ordered Omar to take the precious cargo to Iqbal and Razia Begum's haveli on the other side of their orange orchard.

At the sound of the engine roaring to life, the villagers applauded, whistled and screamed with collective excitement. The village boys ran after the car, competing with the machine. The stray dogs barked and followed in hot pursuit of the car that left clouds of dust in its trail. Uma leaned back into the luxurious comfort of soft leather and closed her eyes, relishing the vehicles effortless motion. When she opened her eyes to look back, the village men and boys had started shuffling and turning towards the village. The women too moved to desert the rooftops.

Uma and her sisters-in-law returned within twenty minutes, laughing and talking. They found the Bhardwaj men sitting on their back verandah.

'How was it?' asked Anu's husband Amar.

The three women answered in a chorus. 'Great.'

Baoji, shaking his head, laughed out loud. 'I'm glad you enjoyed the ride. Even the villagers had an amazing reaction to the car.'

The sisters-in-law pulled chairs to join their men.

Umesh smiled. 'I heard one of them say, "Wait till I tell my woman about this machine that can move faster than the fastest horse, without the need to eat hay or oats"!'

'Another asked his grown son, "What can top this marvel? Huh? Maybe next, man will try to go to the moon"!' said Gaurav.

The men laughed. The women looked at each other with pride in their eyes. Uma felt overwhelmed by her good fortune and threw a silent prayer of thanksgiving.

Baoji shook his head, and smiled.

One morning, in the early spring of 1946, Uma overheard Baoji talking to Gaurav. 'You are the best horseman in the family. I want you to give Dev his first riding lessons.'

'Baoji,' Uma blurted, 'Dev is still too young to learn riding.'

'Nonsense. He's six years old. You can't keep him tied to your apron strings all his life!'

Neither she nor Umesh could convince Baoji otherwise. So, the parents gave in to his wishes once more, as they usually did in the end.

But Uma was relieved to find that Gaurav was a good teacher and Dev a quick learner. By the end of the first month, she noticed Dev riding Diadil—an Arabian filly that his Baoji gifted him on his sixth birthday—at every opportunity he could get. The young horse had a sweet temperament, suitable for little children. Dev seemed to love the horse and under Gaurav's direction, he arose early each morning to feed Diadil black peas that Ladda Ram, the horse's caretaker, prepared and soaked the night before. Ladda Ram cleaned, combed and rubbed Diadil's coat and mane to a perfect shine. Uma kept an eye on Ladda Ram to ensure he not only cleaned the mare's stall but also kept her watered, fed and exercised.

One cloudy Sunday morning, shortly after his lessons began, Uma overheard Gaurav offer to take Dev and Diadil to visit the Bhuttos. The offer carried one condition. In order to ensure his safety, Dev had to agree to allow Ladda Ram to run by the side of the horse. When Dev nodded in agreement, Gaurav urged, 'Go, put on a sweater. It's a chilly day.'

Sitting under the shade trees, as usual, Uma watched as Dev ran to Salma, his ayah, to help him dress appropriately, while Gaurav, dressed in his native garb of a kurta pyjama, a tunic and leg-hugging pyjama, went to his suite to throw a warm shawl over his cream-coloured silk outfit. Uma looked up when she heard her son's footsteps. Dressed in a crisp riding outfit, Dev took her breath away. She could see his father in the child. He seemed so confident for a six-year-old.

Gaurav clattered down and without breaking stride said, 'Let's go!' What a sight to behold! Uma's heart swelled with pride as she walked over to the back gate to watch Gaurav on his stallion, Dev on Diadil and Ladda Ram standing beside Dev and Diadil. After the riders left, Uma returned to her chair under the trees and motioned for Ratna, who had just arrived to help with the kitchen chores. She directed the girl to carry a shawl she had knitted as a gift for Razia Begum.

Eight-year-old Ratna washed her hands and left the haveli with eager steps. About fifteen minutes after Ratna left, Uma saw her running back, huffing, still holding the gift shawl. 'Accident . . .' she screeched, taking big gulps of breath. Pointing towards the Bhutto haveli, she screamed, 'Dev babu . . . the horse . . . blood everywhere—'

Uma leapt and reaching the girl, shook her. 'What . . . what happened?'

Still struggling to catch her breath, Ratna replied, 'Diadil flipped . . . crushed Dev babu.'

Stunned, Uma asked no more, and taking off on wings of fear, she reached the scene of the accident within minutes. Dishevelled, shocked and still panting from her sprint, she dropped to her knees next to Dev, muttering, 'Hold on, Baby. You are going to be fine. Open your eyes my little prince. I am here.' Dev lay comatose and bleeding, outside Razia Begum's haveli.

'Ram, Ram, Ram,' Uma prayed.

Emerging from her haveli, Razia Begum, dressed in a black burqa, hastened to the scene. The fabric peepholes in her burqa cloak revealed only her worried eyes. A maid followed her, and two servants carried a makeshift stretcher made of bamboo poles, to carry the bleeding child. Uma felt Razia Begum's arms around her, helping her rise.

As the servants carefully placed Dev on the stretcher, Uma clambered onto the Bhutto coach. Gaurav, with a swollen ankle hobbled up next. Many hands helped to place the stretcher with an unconscious Dev over the laps of the two adults.

'Take them to the hospital,' Razia Begum ordered her coach-keeper. 'Hurry!'

As the coach-keeper whipped the horse into a gallop, Uma wiped the blood from her son's face with her dupatta, and clutching Dev's tiny hand, whispered, 'Ram, Ram, Ram'.

Watching his sister-in-law shiver, Gaurav took off his symbol of opulence, the white pashmina dushala shawl, and offered it to her. She accepted the shawl but used it to cover her unconscious, bleeding child.

'Bhabi, I'll hold the stretcher while you put pressure with your hand on the wound in his groin,' Gaurav advised. Using her left hand to clamp Dev's bleeding wound, Uma used her right hand to wipe the blood and perspiration from Dev's face. The white shawl turned crimson.

'Diadil is a gentle horse. I don't understand,' said Uma, in between taking deep breaths.

'A black cobra slithering in his path startled Diadil. As the horse reared, he lost his balance. I tried to catch his reins but he pulled me from the saddle. I fell and hurt my ankle.'

'Where was Ladda Ram?'

'Right where he should have been, Bhabi. No one could control such a frightened horse.'

Uma momentarily closed her eyes in acknowledgment. 'We need to make a quick stop at our haveli to send a messenger to the men.'

Gaurav nodded. Since the chauffeur had his day off, and no one else knew how to drive the car, Gaurav sent Saleem, their coach-keeper, to deliver the message to the Bhardwaj men.

Baoji, Umesh and Amar arrived in record time and waited with Uma, on the lawn of the hospital, for news of the extent of Dev's injuries. Nobody paid much attention to Gaurav's swollen ankle. The doctors released him after wrapping his ankle and giving him crutches and a mild painkiller. They admitted Dev to the hospital with a broken nose, a bleeding groin and still unknown internal injuries. Dev lay unconscious, while his parents and the extended family waited and prayed.

Late that night, Dev regained consciousness and the doctor allowed Uma and Umesh to visit him for a few minutes.

'How bad is it?' Uma asked the doctor.

'It's bad . . . very critical. But if he makes it through the night, he would probably recover.'

Uma and Umesh stayed with their child that night.

The news of the seriousness of the accident spread through the village faster than the juiciest rumour. By the next morning, villagers gathered outside the haveli gates for news of the doctor's prognosis.

Even Ratna and Punditji arrived early to inquire about Dev babu's condition. Baoji, shaken and nervous, barely acknowledged them before requesting Punditji to return to the temple and pray for the speedy recovery of the family's 'little sunshine'. Ratna stayed back to help with chores around the haveli. Even though she knew about Gaurav babu's ankle, she did not bother to ask Sita bibiji how her husband was doing. She had never liked Gaurav babu, and was positive he had not done enough to keep Dev babu safe. He deserved to have his ankle hurt. After all, Dev babu was a little child and the nasty Gaurav babu made him ride a big horse. How could Uma bibiji trust that man?

Umesh returned from the hospital, in time to join the family for breakfast. As Ratna walked in with a tray to serve them, he greeted his family. 'Thank you for your prayers. Our Dev is out of danger.'

'By when will he come home?' asked Amar.

'We are not sure. The doctors think maybe a week or two. Uma will stay with him.'

Baoji said, 'Good. Now hurry and finish your breakfast. We're all going to the temple.'

When Baoji spoke, the family listened. Ratna knew that Gaurav babu did not usually participate in family activities, so was surprised to see him reach for his crutches. Her Sita bibiji motioned to her to help support the nasty, hobbling babu. Ratna could not refuse to help the bad-tempered man, but consoled herself that she was doing it for the sake of her Sita bibiji.

They were barely out of the haveli gate when the nasty Babu turned to his wife, and said in a loud voice, 'I feel helpless. If anything happens to Dev, I'll never be able to forgive myself.'

'It wasn't your fault,' she whispered.

He is such a hypocrite, thought Ratna. She wondered how her kind Sita bibiji could be so blind, especially after all the education she had had. Everybody could see it was Gaurav babu's fault. He should have been more careful. Was he not the adult in charge of the safety of a little boy? Ratna was surprised when none of the other adults commented on his outburst. She had hoped, at least Baoji would have the courage to tell off his mean son.

That night, upon Anu's request, Ratna moved to the haveli for the duration of Dev's stay in the hospital. Anu unlocked the vacant birthing room for Ratna to sleep in.

Even though the room smelled musty, Ratna was amazed at the opulence she was ushered into. Anu gave her a cotton-filled mattress, a pillow and bedsheets to sleep on, and explained how to lock the door from inside, showing her how to switch on the electric light and the fan.

Ratna made her makeshift bed on the rich wool carpet on the floor. The first night, with the electric light on, she bolted the door and window of the room, but before settling on her pallet, tiptoed to sit on the magnificent four-poster bed, draped in a silky soft mosquito net. Lifting the mosquito net, she moved her hands admiringly over the crimson, velvet bedspread. She put her head down on the luxurious fabric, and smiling, arose to sit on each of the three brocade-covered chairs in the room. Even as she felt guilty for tasting the forbidden luxury, she enjoyed feeling like a pampered princess.

In the morning, she joined the family to pray for Dev's speedy recovery. Nobody guessed she was not the same Ratna—the one born only to serve. The night before, she had tasted abundance. Life had opened doors, revealing gentle dreams. When the family went to the temple, she eagerly rang the temple bells and thanked Lord Ram for saving the life of the little heir to the Bhardwaj estate.

During the days, she washed and ironed Uma and Dev's clothes, cooked food for them, but at night she turned into a pampered princess and the birthing room became her castle.

Within days of Dev's hospitalisation, the family started working on a schedule. Baoji accompanied Umesh to the hospital in the mornings and Amar and Anu went with him in the evenings. Sometimes, Anu took Ratna along to help Uma with Dev's caretaking. Gaurav never went, claiming his swollen ankle made it difficult for him to walk. Sita usually stayed to take care of him.

Even though the doctors believed he was mending, Dev still complained of acute pain in his groin. During his ten-day stay at the hospital, Ratna surprised herself with the realisation that she cared a whole lot for the boy. When Dev returned from the hospital, she worried about his bruised eyes that had turned pale shades of purple, red and blue; she worried about his nose taped in bandages, and she worried because he needed support to walk.

Ratna wished she could hug or comfort him in some way but it was not in her position as a maid to show concern for the rich boy. So, she prayed in loud whispers in the hope that little Dev and his mother would understand her concern. She even talked to her bapu, the priest, asking if keeping a fast on every Tuesday would help Dev babu heal faster.

'Just pray. That'll be enough,' replied her bapu indulgently.

Ratna noticed that even Uma bibiji had lost a lot of weight while at the hospital. But what surprised her more was Gaurav babu's concern. 'Bhabi, what happened to you?' he asked.

Ratna inhaled deeply. Maybe the man did have a heart after all.

'I'm very worried,' Uma replied. 'Even though the doctor insists Dev is fine, he still complains of excruciating pain. Dev seems to experience severe discomfort when passing urine. I wish the doctors could fathom the extent of his internal injuries.' Uma walked away, leading her son towards his bedroom.

It was another week before Dev's bandages were removed. Ratna was shocked when she noticed the change; where once a regal-looking, chiseled nose graced the child's face, now stood an irregular, bulbous one, looking comic enough to be cute.

Long after Ratna returned to her temple home, she worried about Dev babu's health. Even though he complained less and less about internal pain, Ratna still prayed for him, but now she prayed silently. She realised that somehow she had started regarding him like a little brother she never had. She did not want to remember the times when she thought he was an idiot or the times when she told herself he was too full of himself. Dev's accident bewildered her to know that she could harbour conflicting emotions of love and hatred at the same time. It did not seem normal to love the person you hate. Maybe, prayers could relieve her from the bad emotions, she decided.

For the next several months, every time she noticed the boy's bulbous nose, it reminded her to pray for his health. Then, as she gradually realised that Dev's nose was not swollen and would from now on be permanently enormous, her newfound spirituality faded. Even then, every time she experienced feelings of hatred, jealousy or even sisterly love for Dev, it threw her in a frenzy of prayers, lest her unfamiliar emotions somehow thrust Dev babu into another accident.

7
Troubled Times

1946-47

One hazy, hot August morning in 1946, Uma and Sita sat talking under the shade of trees in their backyard, when a loud banging on the iron gate made them both look for the gatekeeper. Not finding him at his post, Sita got up to open the gate. As she struggled with the iron slide on the lock, Uma joined her. Together they opened the heavy gate to find a distraught Ratna standing outside with Anu's protective arm around her shoulders.

Staring at the dishevelled girl, Uma exclaimed, 'What on earth happened to you?' She took Ratna's hand and shepherded her towards the shaded trees, as Anu explained. 'On my way back from the temple, I heard screams and found Ratna stumbling through the orchard, with her shirt ripped and her dupatta veil missing. I brought her home with me to calm her down.'

Sita moved over to hug Ratna. 'What happened?' she asked.

'Bibiji I . . . I went to the village to buy lentils, and Mahmood's son pulled off my dupatta. He said I was a kafir. He tore my shirt. All his friends hooted and told him to remove my salwaar too—'

'Where were the villagers? How come no one helped?'

'I don't know. I saw Razia Begum's carriage and ran screaming towards it, but it didn't stop. When I turned and cut across the mango orchard, the boys ran away.'

Uma turned to Anu and said, 'Do you have a spare salwaar kameez and a dupatta? My clothes will be too big on her.'

'Come,' said Anu, smiling. 'Ratna, you are getting real tall.' Barely five feet herself, Anu comfortably put her arms around Ratna's shoulders. 'At this rate you'll probably be taller than me before you are ten years old. Come, let's see what we can find for you.'

As soon as Anu and Ratna were out of earshot, Sita said, 'I wonder why Razia Begum didn't stop to help her.'

'She travels in purdah and probably didn't see Ratna. As for their carriage driver—he is Mahmood's brother. With the way things are these days, it isn't worth the trouble for a Muslim to save a poor Hindu girl.'

'It's very scary . . . Jinnah with his demand for a separate land for Muslims is putting wrong ideas in the minds of ordinary people.' Sita shuddered.

'I hope this partition thing is just a rumour,' said Uma, shaking her head.

'It's not a rumour, Bhabi. Partition will happen. The boundaries of the two new countries will slice through Punjab and Bengal.'

'Why only Punjab and Bengal? What about the rest of India?' Uma asked her well-read and opinionated sister-in-law.

'The states on the extreme east or extreme west of India that are mostly Muslim, will be partitioned off to form a separate country for the Muslims. Since Muslim states in the heart of India cannot be sliced off, Bengal on the east coast and Punjab on the west—both on the periphery, with mixed population—will suffer the consequences of this partitioning of land.'

'That doesn't make sense. What happens to people like us? Our village has almost an equal number of Muslims and Sikhs plus a few Hindus,' said Uma.

Sita had read enough in the English newspapers to understand the tensions and fears scuttling through the communities. 'What does Umesh bhaiya think?' she asked without addressing Uma's concerns.

'He's extremely troubled.'

'Why?'

'He thinks Jinnah is making an unfair demand for a separate land for the Muslims. Jinnah is proposing that this so-called "land for the pure" be named Pakistan. The sad part is, most Muslims follow Jinnah blindly.'

'Just like the Hindus and Sikhs follow Mahatma Gandhi and Nehru?' asked Sita with a smirk.

Ignoring Sita's tart comment, Uma said, 'Yesterday I overheard Baoji say that Mahatma Gandhi will ensure a peaceful Independence. I agree. This partition thing is just pure nonsense.'

'And how is Gandhiji going to do that?' asked Sita.

'He has charisma and the white men pay attention to him. Anyway, this is our village. We've lived here for generations. Baoji's great grandfather settled in Shahadra in 1842. How can the English or anyone else oust us from our lands?' Uma demanded.

'Bhabi,' reasoned Sita, 'ever since religion became a part of the equation, our country's Independence and Partition mean nothing but trouble. I think the country will be divided and if we have to move, there's nothing anyone can do about it. Personally, I don't think we'll be safe in Shahadra.'

'So, what in your opinion is the worst that can happen to us?' inquired Uma.

'You tell me. What happened to the Sikhs and Hindus under Muslim emperors like Aurangzeb?' Sita asked and without waiting for a reply added, 'Anyone who believed in a faith other than Islam was a marked man. The staunch Muslim emperors set out to cleanse the country of all non-believers and committed unmitigated carnage.'

'I get the point, but Sita, that was a long time ago.'

'Obviously not that long ago. Humans make the same mistakes over and over, never learning from history. Look at what happened to Jews in Europe in this day and age!' Sita referred to the horror stories brought back by her uncle when he returned from the war in Europe. She had often discussed those stories with her sisters-in-law, so Uma understood that particular shameful episode in world history.

When Anu returned with a calmer Ratna, she called Salma, the Muslim ayah, to escort the girl to her temple home. She also instructed the ayah to take Ratna to the kitchen and let her take some lentils home. After Salma and Ratna left, Anu turned to her two sisters-in-law and asked, 'What are you two talking about?'

'About the curious fact that when religious animosities surface within diverse communities, life's not sacred anymore,' Sita replied.

'Have you ever wondered how we women can sense the coming upheaval but our men are both deaf and blind? Why don't they see that our family's very existence is at stake?' asked Anu.

Just then, they heard banging on the back-gate again. By now the gatekeeper had returned to his post and he opened the gate to usher in Vimla and Bimla, their husbands' cousins. The visit surprised the sisters-in-law, as this was neither the festival of rakhi nor any family gathering when they usually came. The guests rushed over to hug their cousin sisters-in-law and without any preliminaries, Bimla faced Sita and asked, 'Bhabi, have you heard the news?'

'What news?'

'Jinnah's "Direct Action Day", on fourteenth of August, in Calcutta?'

'Hey Ram! That was yesterday. I'd heard about his threat but . . .'

The two women married to men in Shahadra looked alarmed. Vimla and Bimla's parental home was in Calcutta. 'Some teenagers painted "kafirs" on our front gates and shouted threats of a massacre of Sikhs and Hindus, similar to what happened in Calcutta yesterday. If a massacre took place in Bengal yesterday, would they not talk about it in the English newspapers of Punjab today?'

'Yes, they would. But I haven't read the paper as yet. I usually read it in the afternoons.' Sita directed a maid to bring the newspaper from her bedroom. The front page carried appalling pictures and news of the bloodshed on the 'Direct Action Day' in Calcutta the previous day.

Throwing her arms around the slim sisters, Uma said, 'I'll talk to your Umesh bhaiya to find out how your family is doing. Don't worry, Lord Ram will take care of them.'

The two sisters nodded and thanking their wealthy relatives, left as abruptly as they had appeared, too distressed to accept an offer of tea.

The disturbing events of the day convinced the three sisters-in-law to discuss and make tentative plans for the family's safety. Uma, an only child had lost both her parents. Sita's parents lived in faraway New Delhi, the capital of India. Only Anu's family lived close by. Her parental village Garha, near Jullunder, was easily accessible. The sisters-in-law held Anu's only sibling, a brother named Sanjay, in high esteem. Jullunder, they decided, would definitely fall within the Indian boundaries as it was heavily populated with Sikhs and Hindus. 'If the worst happens, we'll temporarily live in Garha with Anu's family,' they agreed.

For their future security and peace of mind, Sita suggested they send some of their jewellery and money to Garha with Anu, to help the joint-family start life all over again, if necessary. Even though their men were not paying attention to changing times, they, the women of the family, planned to be prepared.

This act of faith drew the sisters-in-law closer to each other.

As the troubling winter of 1946 turned into a harrowing spring of 1947, Uma realised the need to be more involved. She needed to make a conscious effort to listen to and understand the news on the radio. A major political upheaval like the partitioning of land would affect everyone. No women, even the ones as secure as she was within her haveli walls, could ignore politics any longer. She listened to the daily news on the radio and discussed her fears and worries with Sita and Anu. The Bhardwaj men did not think women needed to worry about politics but the sisters-in-law, like good friends, decided otherwise.

In April of 1947, Sita confided in Uma, 'Bhabi, I am about three months late. Since I had major problems during my last pregnancy, may I go to Delhi for my delivery this time?'

'Absolutely!' replied Uma. She still had not recovered from the guilt she felt for suggesting they not take Sita to a white male doctor the previous time. 'Sita,' she continued, 'why don't you and Gaurav go to Delhi now, while it's still comfortable for you to travel? We all know the trip to Delhi is long, and with all this talk of dividing the country, now might be a better time to travel—just in case the political situation gets more chaotic later on. We know that Delhi will be safer than Shahadra or Lahore during these difficult times.'

When Sita concurred, Uma had another suggestion. 'I think both of you might want to travel with Iqbal bhaiya. Yesterday Razia Begum mentioned that Iqbal bhaiya was planning one of his extended trips to Delhi. He'll be travelling alone.'

'No problem. But I'm curious why we need—'

'Sita, the way things are, it'll be safer for him to travel with Hindu friends because Delhi is heavily populated by Hindus and Sikhs. On the other hand, it'll be safer for Gaurav and you to return to Shahadra accompanied by a Muslim. After all, our village, as you've pointed out often, is in the land of Muslim majority.'

Sita nodded. This time around, there were no happy celebrations in anticipation of the baby, only more precautions. Sita and Gaurav left for New Delhi, the capital of India, in May. Iqbal Bhutto accompanied them.

During the ensuing anxious days, Uma heard radios blaring in Shahadra and watched the villagers squatting under pipal trees, smoking their hookah pipes, listening and discussing politics. While the village men exchanged horror stories of rioting in big cities, she heard the women whisper and worry.

During this tense period, Uma learned that Ratna's mother could no longer work because of severe arthritis, so Ratna, who turned nine that year, had to take over the mother's chores at the haveli.

'Uma Bibiji,' said Ratna, one day, 'my mataji worries about rioting and killings but bapu says, "Baoji's family will let nothing happen to us".'

When Uma did not respond, Ratna asked, 'Is bapu right, Bibiji? Can something bad happen to us?'

'I'm not sure what can happen, Ratna. There's talk of separating the Muslims from non-Muslims. If that happens, we might have to move. So, yes, if anything bad happens, we'll take care of your family,' replied Uma.

Ratna smiled and went about doing her chores.

Uma decided to remind Umesh again about the worsening political conditions and about the massacre of Vimla and Bimla's family in Calcutta the previous August. She hoped her constant reminders about atrocities the three communities were committing against each other not only in Punjab but also in places like Calcutta, Jasor, Khulna and Comilla in Bengal, would make the men pay heed to their warnings.

As her uneasiness over the current political situation grew, Uma wondered how to convince Baoji about the peril they were in. Baoji refused to recognise the problem brewing outside their haveli walls. He had screamed at her when she had mustered enough courage to question the wisdom of not planning any escape route for the family, in case of Partition. 'Bahu, stay out of my business,' he said. 'Go worry about nappies and cooking!'

Uma's husband Umesh was a quiet man. She knew that he carried a heavy sense of duty, so she coaxed him to talk some caution into his father. Umesh promised to approach the old man at the appropriate time. One such moment presented itself very soon. One day, because of intense rioting in Lahore, their businesses had to be closed. He, Baoji and Amar returned home for lunch. This was a godsend, Uma reminded him—an opportunity for him and Amar to discuss the ramifications of Partition with Baoji.

Their non-Muslim servants had stopped coming to the haveli because of widespread disturbances, so Anu and Uma had to do the cooking. When the three men returned for lunch that day, Uma served them a simple fare of lentil soup, spiced vegetables and yoghurt on traditional Indian round bronze trays, while the nine-year-old Ratna made fresh chapatti bread. Anu poured home-churned buttermilk into glasses.

As soon as the men sat down to eat, Umesh asked, 'Baoji, what are the plans? What can we do to ensure the safety of our family?'

'What do you mean? Our family is safe in the haveli,' replied Baoji.

'Should we not discuss our strategy for relocating from here to some safer place in the future India? I worry about this constant tension and the riots around us.'

'Worry, worry, worry! What is it this time? Is it the British or is it Jinnah and the Muslim League's threatening demands that scare you?' asked Baoji, putting his glass of buttermilk down and wiping his wet moustache with the back of his left hand.

'Both of those and more. I'm even worried about Gandhiji and Nehru. Even though Mahatma Gandhi does not want the land partitioned, Nehru and the Indian National Congress are amenable. Baoji, do you realise they plan to slice up our beloved Punjab?'

'Son, aren't you being presumptuous? Just because Nehru and the Congress have agreed to partition the country doesn't mean it'll be done.'

'Yes, it does,' said Umesh. 'Besides, Gandhiji cannot stop it, not after the British have agreed to split the country into two. Now Nehru and the Congress are taking the position that if the country can be divided, so can the states of Punjab and Bengal.'

Baoji banged his fist on the table. The glasses rattled and Uma and Anu looked at each other in alarm. 'Without Gandhiji's permission, nothing of the sort will happen. Now eat your food.' Baoji twirled his mustache and glared at him.

Neither Uma nor Anu participated in the discussion. As per custom, good women stayed mute when their men argued. Uma felt helpless in the face of Baoji's belligerence. She could not side with her husband, but at the same time, could not stifle the pride she felt when he did not give up.

'Baoji, by refusing to accept reality you can't stop the change. Trust me, there will be a major upheaval. Have you forgotten Jinnah's "Direct Action Day" and the carnage in Calcutta, and the massacre of more than three thousand Sikhs in Rawalpindi this past month? The Muslims have made it clear that they want Punjab and Bengal cleansed of kafirs like us.'

'We are not kafirs. We do believe in God—it's just not their god,' shouted the old man.

'I agree,' replied Umesh. 'None of us feels like a kafir. But the fact remains that no one is listening—Muslim or non-Muslim. After this March's massacre in Rawalpindi, the Sikhs have made repeated appeals to Nehru for a planned movement of people caught in this maelstrom to safer areas. But who is listening?'

'We are not Sikhs, so how does their appeal affect us?' demanded Baoji.

Umesh's voice rose. 'See what I mean? Even you are not listening. I know we are not Sikhs, but they are our friends and allies. If they are concerned, then we need to pay attention.'

'Umesh, you forget your *aukaat*,'—your status and manners—'I am your father and I say Punjab will not be partitioned. And that's that.'

Umesh stared at his father. Then shaking his head, he turned to look at Amar.

'Believe me Baoji, Punjab will be partitioned,' said Amar.

Amar's soft-spoken assertion seemed to sink in and the old man turned towards Umesh, asking, 'Well then, how do we know if our village will be part of India or the future Pakistan?'

'That's exactly the problem,' repeated Umesh. 'We don't know. But the probability is that Lahore and our ancestral land will fall into Pakistan. As I've mentioned many times, the British have made no plans to mark the boundaries between the two countries and no provisions have been made to divide the country fairly.'

'So?' demanded Baoji.

'I fear there'll be political and social turmoil when the time comes to partition the land.'

'Umesh, you sound like a broken record. You mean there is going to be chaos just because you are not aware of any plans. Don't you believe Gandhiji is thinking about all these problems? He will ensure that the common man's concerns are resolved satisfactorily—just like he got us the promise of our freedom through a non-violent struggle.'

'Baoji,' said Amar, 'how can you talk of non-violence while Punjab and Bengal are burning? I think Umesh bhaiya does have a point. We should consider it seriously.'

'I have complete faith in Gandhiji. It's amazing how he single-handedly got the British to agree to give us our Independence,' answered the old man, looking smug.

'Mahatma Gandhi is only one of the forces that secured our freedom. Thousands of Indians like Subhash Chandra Bose, Bhagat Singh, Uddam Singh, Lala Lajpat Rai—and the list goes on and on—sacrificed their lives, struggling for a free India,' said Umesh. 'Then there is another hidden reason—the war in Europe between the allied forces of Britain and USA against the Axis powers of Germany, Italy and Japan. In terms of human lives lost, this "big" war caused havoc for the British. They can't afford loss of more life. Considering everything, I think now is the perfect time for our Independence.'

'What do you mean?' asked Baoji, his tone mellower.

'I mean exactly what I say.' Umesh's voice picked up strength. 'Agreeing to give the country its freedom is not a choice for the British anymore. It's a pressing reality. Millions of Indian soldiers who have returned from the war in Europe, have been trained hard and well for the war effort. I think the British understand that if the Indians revolt now, they—the English people—do not have enough manpower to quell this well-trained Indian army.'

'And what Indian army can stand up to the mighty English?' questioned the old man who, as Uma was well aware, still carried the centuries-old burden of fear of the white man's wrath. 'Have you forgotten the massacre at Jallianwalla Baagh at the hands of General Dyer? Where was the brave Indian army then? Who are the Indian soldiers who have suddenly become brave enough to provoke the wrath of this ruthless race?'

'The Indian army trained by the British to fight the war in Europe. The brave regiments of Sikhs, Gurkhas and Rajputs are now equipped with weapons which they did not have access to earlier,' replied Umesh, looking his father in the eye.

Her husband's brilliant argument made Uma proud.

'And why would the British not subdue these so-called tough Indian soldiers?' asked Baoji.

'Because they no longer have the means. After the death and destruction the British suffered in the war in Europe, they can't afford to lose any more English men.'

'I'm not sure what you're arguing about. You just wait and see the most peaceful changing of the guard the world has ever witnessed!' replied Baoji, rubbing the back of his neck.

'And watch Punjab and Bengal burn?' asked Umesh.

The old man did not respond.

Frustrated, Umesh stared at his plate, trying to concentrate on his food. Uma's heart went out to him. Their beloved family's very existence was in jeopardy and Baoji refused to plan. In the ensuing days and weeks, Umesh, Amar and their wives, often discussed their worries with each other. On 3 June 1947, they sat listening to Lord Mountbatten's broadcast over the radio. Britain, he announced, would free India and create Pakistan by 15 August 1947, much sooner than the original date of India's Independence by June 1948, as promised by 'His Majesty'.

'Good Lord! Amar, did you hear what Mountbatten just announced?' When the younger brother nodded gravely, Umesh continued, 'I wish Baoji had agreed to take some precautions.'

'I know. We tried but he doesn't listen, does he? At that time, we thought we still had a whole year to plan. One whole year! Now Mountbatten has the audacity to announce that the British will be quitting India almost a year sooner than anticipated—in two or three months' time.' Umesh shuddered.

'They are leaving India now, in 1947 itself, and all this without training or planning for a safe transfer of power. What can they be thinking?' said Amar.

'The war in Europe has scrambled their brains!'

'But the country's day-to-day working depends upon them!' said Amar. 'They never trained Indians to be administrators. Do they think a handful of educated Nehrus and Jinnahs can run a country? Can politicians make good administrators?'

'Once the British leave, the country's working structure is bound to collapse. That'll mean total mayhem.'

Amar, his elbow on the armrest, chin cradled by his palm, lips pursed, nodded.

'There's no chance now for a peaceful Partition.' Umesh worried about the future. 'To separate the three communities without any plans is bound to cause confusion, pain and suffering. The uprooting of thousands of innocent people is bound to take place, because of division of land around religious demographics. But there is no designated land marked for displaced people.'

To everyone's dismay, Baoji still insisted, 'I heard what Mountbatten announced, but I know the communities and properties will be exchanged fair and square across borders. You just wait and see.'

'How does one separate the veins and arteries on the same limb, without causing excruciating pain and unbelievable suffering?' asked Umesh.

The old man ignored the question.

In mid-July, Anu received a telegram that her widowed mother had passed away. She and Amar made immediate plans to leave for Garha. Since the trains were not safe, Baoji suggested they take the car. 'Take Omar with you. A Muslim chauffeur would provide extra security in these troubled times.'

'But Baoji, will Omar be safe in Jullunder?' asked Uma.

'Of course he'll be safe. Amar and Anu will be with him, won't they?'

Baoji never apologised for his earlier blind folly but now, somehow, talked about Partition as a given. 'I think Jullunder and Amritsar are definitely falling within the Indian territory and they'll be safer for Hindus.' Turning to face Amar, he added, 'Keep the car in Garha and send the chauffeur back by train. You never know.'

Amar and Anu packed in a hurry. Uma advised them to take enough clothes for at least two months and to carry some jewels from their jewellery store, for safety. In a strange way, the timing of the tragedy was right, she thought. It would put two more family members out of harm's way.

Uma saw her world in turmoil, but Baoji, reassured by his family name and wealth, acted as though wealth brought a benevolent destiny.

By the end of July, a couple of weeks before the 15 August deadline, demarcation lines between India and future Pakistan still remained vague. Uma mulled over what Umesh had told her about the innumerable disputed areas like Gurdaspur and Ferozpur on the Punjab border, and Khulna district, Jessore and Murshidabad on the East Coast, in Bengal. She watched the rioting and the massacres continue to escalate—all in the name of religion. Still, Baoji like the common man, denied reality, retaining the belief that the choice to leave or stay was still his to make.

'Staying in Shahadra is in the best interests of our family,' Baoji insisted. 'The land, the haveli and the businesses have been accumulated over generations of the Bhardwaj family. Where can we go, leaving all this behind?' he maintained.

Uma, saddened that even Umesh could not help Baoji change his mind, watched the political situation spiral out of control as 15 August moved closer. In Shahadra, just outside the Bhardwaj haveli walls, shouts of *'Pakistan leke rahenge'* and *'Pakistan zindabad'* could be heard throughout the day. These shouts of 'We will get (our) Pakistan' and 'Long live Pakistan' finally seemed to shake Baoji out of complacency and slumber. Uma sensed he finally heard the anger, the jeopardy and the harsh reality threatening the safety of their haveli. But what could they do now?

The tension kept brewing, thickening like a witch's potion. Glued to the radio, Uma learned about the meaningless curfew that engulfed the city of Lahore that did nothing to keep the looting, rioting and the killing from escalating. 'This burdensome state of anarchy is not our problem,' the English reporters quoted in newspapers. 'These bloody natives deserve to be taught a lesson!'

The rioting continued to mount. The Muslims shouted 'Pakistan leke rahenge'. The Sikhs and Hindus dreaded the future in Muslim-land, while the British, the keepers-of-the-law, scrambled to flee the land.

And Uma watched their Baoji, who, looking scared out of his wits, shut his eyes like a pigeon faced by a cat, hoping that the danger would pass.

8
Independence and Partition

August 1947

Uma felt lonely and apprehensive. With Amar, Gaurav and their wives gone, silence draped across the Bhardwaj mansion like a thick blanket. Summer vacation in schools was extended indefinitely and that worried her more. The family businesses remained shuttered because of looting and rioting in Lahore. It seemed to Uma that Baoji aged ten years in a few days. He laboured as he walked to the temple in the mornings and spent the rest of the day in silence. Umesh still went back and forth to Lahore, for a couple of hours a day, to check on family businesses.

Seven-year-old Dev walked around the enclosed backyard, shooing the crows and birds from trees, plucking flowers just to crush them under his heels. His few Hindu playmates had already left for India, while Iqbal Bhutto's children were now an unspoken taboo. Muslim and Hindu children could no longer play together safely. Seeing Dev's restlessness, Uma invited Ratna and her sister to come play with him.

'Dev, look who's here,' she called.

He came over to look but walked away mumbling, 'Girls are no fun.'

Left with nothing to do, Ratna sat little Sheila on the swing in the courtyard and softly sang sad songs of loss.

'Ratna, I didn't know you could sing so well. Who taught you?' asked Uma.

'No one,' mumbled Ratna. She stood staring at her unshod feet, her right toes moving over her left foot.

'Did your mataji teach you?'

'No. She doesn't like me to sing. She says it makes me . . . like . . . like a bad girl. But I can't help it.' She shrugged her shoulders.

'Help what?'

'To go to the mud houses at night and listen to Bulashah sing.'

'Why?'

'Because . . . he's very good, Bibiji. I learn the words he sings.'

Uma had heard good things about Bulashah, the village minstrel. But it was no longer safe for little girls to run around the village after dark. 'Ratna, if your mataji doesn't like you to sneak around at night, then you mustn't.'

Ratna nodded, still looking at her feet.

As the days moved closer to the time of Independence and Partition, Dev's ayah Salma, and her husband, the coach-keeper Saleem were the only two servants who still came to help Uma with her daily chores. Their Islamic faith made it safe for them, so they came, while the Hindu and Sikh servants either started on their journey towards the Indian land or stayed within the safety of their own homes.

With no non-Muslim maids and servants to help her, Uma spent her days cooking, cleaning and packing small bags of clothes and necessities for everyone in the family. Each bag she packed had two changes of clothes, some money and a small bottle of pure drinking water. Uma made the preparations just in case they were forced to leave temporarily, when, as planned, they would leave for Garha, Jullunder, to live with Anu's family.

Early on the morning of 14 August, Umesh woke up with a high fever. 'Uma,' he said, 'I'm not feeling well. I need to go to Lahore to Dr Simranjeet's dispensary. After I get medication, I'll check on the two stores before returning home.'

'Could Baoji check on the stores while you return to rest in bed?' she asked.

'With so much unrest in the city, I would rather have him stay home and be safe. Baoji is too old to have to deal with all this.'

'You sound worried. Is the usual rioting and unrest accelerating?'

'Uma, how do you define "usual"? Do you forget what the Muslims did two days ago?'

Uma shook her head, not comprehending.

'On 12 August, they sent a train from Lahore station to Amritsar, loaded with bloodied, mutilated bodies of Sikhs and Hindus. The body parts of the dead hung out of its windows and doors. Is that normal? Is it usual?'

'Hai Ram!' Uma gasped. 'Please be careful. What if you get caught in these hateful disturbances?'

'Uma, I need to do what's necessary. Hopefully, today, the Muslims will be too busy celebrating their Independence to waste energy on rioting.'

'I thought the Independence is tomorrow—the fifteenth of August,' she blurted.

'Mountbatten has promised to hand over the reins of Pakistan to Jinnah, and those of new India to Nehru, at midnight tonight,' he replied. 'But rumours have it that the new nation of Pakistan is celebrating it today. The Indians will celebrate it tomorrow.'

After Umesh left, Uma felt claustrophobic. The haveli had become a prison she shared with Dev and Baoji, a prison created by self-imposed constraints of staying within the safety of its walls. She prayed to ease her worry about Umesh being in Lahore, without the protection of the family name or the tall walls of their mansion.

Since Saleem, the coach-keeper, took Umesh to the doctor in the morning, Uma called his wife Salma, the only servant left, and said, 'Go over to the temple and ask Punditji to send Ratna. I need her to do small chores around the haveli.'

A very subdued Salma returned with Ratna. After Uma told Ratna to sweep the huge patio, Salma walked over to Uma and said, 'Bibiji, you need to visit Razia Begum today. She's very distraught.'

'Why?'

'On my way to the temple I met my older sister, Noor, who works for them. Noor was hysterical. She said Razia Begum's parents, her newly married younger brother and his bride were on their way from Amritsar in the morning's train to Lahore. . . .' Salma broke down sobbing.

'And they didn't show up?' prompted Uma.

'They did show up . . . but . . . but arrived in more pieces than one,' blurted Salma. 'The train arrived from Amritsar loaded with corpses of Muslims. Every single person on the train lay butchered, with the mutilated bodies of women, along with their babies and children sprawled all over. At the station, there is just blood and the stench of death. Some men from Razia Begum's family have gone to identify and claim the bodies.' Salma sobbed, trying to still her shaking hands.

Uma, paralysed with fear, knew she needed to be with her Muslim friend, but the terror clutching at her very marrow kept her locked in the safety of her home. She decided to go see Razia Begum as soon as Umesh returned from the doctor, and spent the rest of the day in shock, questioning how one community could do that to another.

Around three o'clock in the afternoon, Uma heard a commotion. Looking up, she saw a dishevelled Saleem without a turban, opening the haveli gate and letting out a strangled cry.

Umesh was not with him.

'Bibiji, bibiji, you have to leave right now!' he screamed, his voice laced with terror.

'Leave for where? What happened? Where is your babuji?' Uma tried desperately to remain calm in front of the servant.

'He's still in Lahore . . . trying to reason with the rioters looting our stores. He wanted me to get you, Baoji and Dev babu to the train station. Plan to leave for Jullunder immediately. I'll run to the temple to get Baoji. We must leave before five o'clock at the latest, to catch the night train to Jullunder.'

Rattled by this sudden turn of events, Uma forgot to ask if Umesh felt any better after the doctor's visit. She found herself scrambling around the haveli, gathering the bundles she had prepared for everyone, while Saleem flew through the back gate to get Baoji from the temple.

She called Dev and Ratna, and fed them in haste. 'Salma,' she told the ayah, 'come and cook some paranthas for our journey.'

Salma gave Uma a quizzical look. She, a Muslim, had never been asked to enter their kitchen before. The Bhardwajs were Brahmins, the highest Hindu caste, and living within the confines of their caste-system, they did not allow any Muslims into their Hindu kitchen. Over the past centuries, each community honoured the other's constraints, often with resentment, but abided by nonetheless.

'Yes, Bibiji,' replied Salma quietly. 'Can you please show me where things are in your kitchen?'

Uma grasped the message—in spite of her willingness to help, Salma wanted to ensure Uma understood the implications of allowing a Muslim into her Hindu kitchen. Uma hurried Salma through the kitchen, showing her around. 'We'll need about twenty or thirty paranthas. Fry the parantha bread in pure ghee from that canister. Pack them in this metal container with mango pickle on the side. Use a clean cloth duster to wrap the fried bread.'

She then hustled to gather her belongings and her child, giving Dev a small bag and a metal container filled with water, to hold. She tied a small pouch around Dev's loins and told him not to mention that pouch to anyone, as it contained a stack of money as insurance for his future. Collecting the bags she had prepared for such a journey, she told Ratna to hold Baoji's bag along with the bundle of paranthas Salma had made.

Even though fear reflected in their eyes, still, the children asked no questions.

Five o'clock came and went, but Saleem did not return with Baoji.

'Bibiji, may I go home?' asked Ratna.

Uma shook her head, fearing for the girl's life. 'I can't let you go. It's not safe.'

Salma offered to go and look for her husband Saleem and Baoji, at the temple. 'Ratna, I can also give a message to your parents if you like,' Salma offered, but Ratna shrugged her shoulders and looked at Uma.

Salma's religion would keep her safe outside the haveli walls, whereas Ratna's would not. 'Salma,' said Uma, 'tell the Punditji's family to prepare to leave immediately. They should reach the station as soon as they can. If they have no means of reaching the station then tell them to come with Baoji. They should bring a change or two for themselves and for the girls.'

After Salma left, screams from beyond pierced the eerie silence that enveloped the haveli. 'Bibiji, can you smell smoke?' asked Ratna.

Uma nodded.

By 7.30 pm, with no signs of Baoji, the Punditji's family or the Muslim servants, Uma finally decided to vacate the haveli, and go looking for them at the temple. She locked her dark mansion and taking both the children by hand, started through the mango grove.

The stables outside the formidable iron gate had no lights. All animals were gone and so was Dev's old carriage. 'Ma, look! Diadil is not in her stall. Where's Ladda Ram? You think he took my horse to exercise it?' asked Dev.

Uma did not reply.

Dev tugged at her long tunic kameez for an answer but Uma put her finger to her lips, 'Shhh!' she said, while struggling to digest the chilling reality, wondering why none of the rioters came inside her home to loot and kill.

When she turned around to take one last look at her haveli, she saw and understood. All along their outer walls, as far as her eyes could see, someone had painted white, crescent moons—an indication that the haveli was under Muslim occupation. It must have been Saleem, she mused, their kind Muslim coach-keeper, who probably masterminded the graffiti to save them from immediate harm.

Uma hurried down the narrow path, dragging the children towards the temple. Feeling her legs slipping away but her heart racing ahead, she kept hoping and willing the temple bells to ring and the temple lights to blink. But all she saw were the ancient banyan trees, standing silent and still, with their thick, gnarled branches, like stalactites and stalagmites, casting haunting shadows. Not a bird or an animal stirred. She sensed the piercing silence in her bones. It seemed as if even the mosquitoes, fireflies, frogs and beetles, had all suspended their rich and noisy evening rituals.

The temple sat dark and deserted. With horror, they discovered Baoji's body lying face down in a pool of blood. Dev, with his mouth open, eyes unblinking, clung to her kameez while Uma leaned against a pillar, shaking, sobbing and praying, 'Ram, Ram, Ram'.

Ratna's screams jolted Uma from her own horror. The girl had discovered the mutilated and lifeless bodies of her family. Ratna's bapu's body lay near the altar, but her mataji's and four-year-old Sheila's bodies were in a room inside.

Uma scrambled to reach the shrieking girl and collected the hysterical child in her arms. 'Hush, dear child! And pray.'

'Why?' asked Ratna, sobbing. 'My bapu and mataji prayed all the time and look what happened to them. I never prayed and I'm still alive.'

Uma's hands shook as she tried to calm the girl. 'Ram, Ram, Ram,' she prayed.

Ratna's mother's naked body, her stomach and breasts slashed into a bloody mess, seemed like a macabre warning of death and extinction to non-believers—the kafirs. Uma remembered with horror the morning train from Amritsar, carrying mutilated bodies of Muslim women and girls—a calculated message from the Hindus and Sikhs across the border to their Muslim counterparts. Now this. A reply: With each girl and woman's demise, a slice of the enemy's future dies.

Uma understood the game of chess the three communities played—a woman was a mere mohra, a pawn. To rape, kill or mutilate each other's women was to send a message to the opponent: We win, you lose.

Dizzy with apprehension, Uma helped Ratna cover the bodies of her massacred mother and sister with bedsheets. With trembling hands, she took out one white dhoti from Baoji's bag and gave it to Ratna, to cover her bapu's body. She then asked Dev to help her cover Baoji's body with another white loincloth. If these had been normal times, her husband, Umesh, would have lit Baoji's pyre. But these were neither normal times nor normal circumstances. So, Uma made Dev, the only heir to the mighty family, touch his grandfather's cold, dead feet to pay his final respect.

The evening darkness spread its cold fingers in every direction, choking all life around them. In the distance, she heard screams.

Uma realised that the responsibility of getting out alive from this nightmare lay upon her, but she did not know how to get to the Lahore railway station. No one had prepared her for self-reliance in a world beyond her haveli walls. She had always travelled in purdah, so never learnt the route to the city of Lahore.

'I know how to get to the main road to Lahore,' said Dev. Both the Bhardwaj stores were on it and he passed the stores every morning, on his way to school. But he did not know how to reach the station. Uma steadied her nerves by praying to Lord Ram and telling herself to reach the stores.

She picked up two changes of clothing for Ratna, packing them in Baoji's almost empty bag, and gave it to her to hold. As Ratna still wailed, Uma put her hand on the girl's mouth. 'Hush,' she said. 'Get hold of yourself.' Her voice and hands both shook. 'Ratna, you must stay quiet, but strong, if you want to survive.'

Within fifteen minutes, weary, shaken and traumatised, they took to the village pathways, through the fields, and under Ratna's able directions reached the dirt road.

The unpaved road carried many other quietly stupefied travellers, slithering stealthily towards Lahore. They were barely out of sight of the village when Uma saw a mob carrying fire torches and sturdy bamboo clubs, coming towards the village. *'Pakistan hamara hai.'* Pakistan is ours. 'Pakistan zindabad', they shouted.

Pulling the two children with her, Uma jumped into a ditch filled with muddy slush.

The mob passed, dragging a body. Uma's lips moved. 'Ram, Ram, Ram.'

Once the immediate danger passed, Uma and the children climbed out of the ditch covered with filth. She made them change into clean, dry clothes. Since it was too risky to walk close to the dirt road, they moved fifty yards away from it, staying close to the tall sugarcane fields. Any movement, including the sounds of other fleeing Sikh and Hindu refugees, scared her enough to hold her breath and hide in the fields with the children.

They arrived at the Grand Trunk road to Lahore at midnight. She led the exhausted children to the back of a newly burned house. The ruins sat on a platform alongside the road. She knew they had missed the night train but thought they could make it on time for the morning train, after the children had rested. 'You two sleep here,' she told them, settling them to rest behind a partially standing cement wall. 'Do not come out of hiding until daybreak.'

Uma walked towards the front of the ruins and facing the road, sat down on the steps to rest, but sleep would not come. Baoji's bloodied body and the bodies of the priest and his family intruded into her thoughts. Why them? She besought her god for answers, but none came.

What should she do now—go to the Bhardwaj Fabric Store to meet Umesh or find the way to the railway station? She remembered Dev did not know the way to Lahore station, so it made sense to go to their fabric store or their jewellery store, which Dev knew how to reach. If Umesh had already left, she believed, any employee would take them to the railway station. The plan calmed her. She closed her eyes, catching brief moments of troubled sleep.

Early the next morning, Uma woke up with a start and like an animal stunned by bright light, she stared paralysed at a mob of Muslims surrounding her. She knew instantly the horror she had brought upon herself. Her indiscretion at sleeping in the open, un-chaperoned and un-clad in a burqa, had aroused carnal demons and inflamed the lecherous mob to encircle her. Noticing the centre of the circle open for the sacrifice and slaughter, she pulled her dupatta veil tighter around her body. The mob's lascivious smiles broke into guffaws. They raped her, one after another after another, and Uma, in her defenceless state, could not scream for fear of luring Dev and Ratna out of hiding. When done with her, the mob slashed her breasts and genitals to a pulp and left her to die.

Bleeding profusely and unable to move, Uma willed herself not to lose consciousness until she could help her beloved son, her little prince Dev, to safety.

Part Three
Independent India 1947

'Borders are scratched across the hearts of men
By strangers with a calm, judicial pen
And when the borders bleed, we watch with dread
The lines of ink along the map turn red'
—Marya Mannes
'Gaza Strip'

9
The Promised Land

16 August 1947

A day after Partition, in the suffocating heat of an August afternoon, Dev dragged his tired body, walking beside the unknown couple, while the bearded man, Sukhdev, carried the sick Ratna on his back. Dev tried but could not shake off the intense images of the previous day. His mother's last words played in his head over and over. 'Carry the bags . . . take Ratna. Find your father at the store. Go to Jullunder to your Anu chachi. Now, Go! Without me.' And then she had mumbled, 'You must join a kafila, leave me here . . . to rest. Dev, take care of Ratna and remember the juice mang. . . .' He could still hear the last, peculiar gurgling sounds his mother had made before closing her eyes.

A sudden fierce need for comfort made him reach for Ratna's limp hand hanging from Sukhdev's shoulder. The mere touch of her hot sweaty hand jolted him to look, really look, at Ratna's face. Noticing her fever-shot eyes, her wild delirious stare, he panicked, and tugged at the tall man's arm. Pointing to Ratna, he asked if they had any water for her. The man nodded, and putting Ratna down, wiped the perspiration from his face with a grimy handkerchief. He gave Ratna a tumbler of water and taking a drink himself, asked, 'Child, can you walk now? I'm too exhausted to carry you further.'

Taking a sip or two, Ratna staggered onwards. Dev reached for her burning hand.

Late that evening, Sukhdev, exhausted, helpless and angry, wondered how the British, the keepers-of-the-law, could walk away so casually from the haemorrhaging land. He, his wife and the two orphans dragged their feet, striving to keep up with the caravan that kept pushing at a slow, steady pace.

'Auntie, please hold my hand. I feel light-headed,' mumbled Ratna, wobbling as if her legs would soon crumble into mush.

'Sure.'

Before Raminder reached her, Sukhdev shuffled to give Ratna his hand for support. He knew his wife was too exhausted to support Ratna, just as he himself was too tired to carry the feverish girl on his back as he had done earlier in the day.

Raminder sighed. 'Ratna, Dev . . . I think we're going to be together in this wretched situation for a long time. Both of you may call me biji or ma if you like.'

'And you may call me papaji,' added Sukhdev.

Ratna and Dev nodded, seeming to gather strength from the warm caress of compassion, even while their eyes mirrored the terrifying new reality.

Sukhdev sensed the beginnings of a new family.

Later that evening, the air felt less fraught with fear. Somehow, Sukhdev suspected that they had arrived in safer territory, even though he found no tangible signs of the border dividing the two countries. Turbaned Sikh men cluttered the road ahead with free stalls, providing cool drinking water and ice-cold sweetened milk. Somehow, as the liquid cooled his deep body thirst, the emotional thirst left unquenched, engulfed him with remorseless intensity. Sukhdev wondered if anything would ever be able to soothe it.

The place seemed like the end of their journey. They had arrived in the "promised land", but neither he nor his fellow refugees displayed any signs of relief. As far as the eye could see, the road, the fields, the raised banks of water canals, all were littered either with refugees or dead bodies, and the stench of putrid flesh filled the air. Every direction he turned, flies hummed their relentless drone over the dead. Vultures hovered in the fading skies.

In this cauldron of wretchedness, he noticed one distinct difference. Here, the lifeless bodies littering the countryside were of Muslims. The bloated bodies floating in the wells and streams belonged to burqa-clad Muslim women and girls. He knew blood had paid for blood. Even so, the loquacious silence of the slaughtered was deep, their accusations haunting.

Sukhdev watched Ratna and Dev plodding along, showing no recognition of the change in scenery around them. He shook his head thinking, dead bodies are dead bodies—they are neither Muslim nor Sikh nor Hindu. His mind wandered to his beloved Aman, wondering if their child had not died, would he and Raminder have still helped the orphans. Ratna seemed to be about his Aman's age, and so helpless. Thinking of Aman and the massacre at her school, he shuddered.

As the kafila disbanded, he realised he had suspected correctly—they had crossed the border. Now it was up to each family to fend for itself. 'Sir, how far are the government sponsored refugee camps?' he asked an army guard.

'Fifteen miles or more up the road, closer to Amritsar.'

Sukhdev, exhausted and anxious, struggled to lead his family another mile or two. They needed shelter, so Ratna, the sick child, could rest under a roof in case of threatening monsoon rains. Dragging their weary bodies down the road, they came to a village and knocked on several doors but no one stirred in unlit houses.

Disheartened, they were about to retrace their steps when Dev pointed to a dim light some distance away. 'Look!' he cried.

They followed the light to the outskirts of this nameless village and reached a bungalow with tall brick boundary walls. The huge gate stood wide open. Inside the gate, they saw a sea of refugees. When they walked through the gates, the owner looked at the feverish Ratna, and offered them the use of a verandah at the back of the house.

Two other families with sick children squatted on the verandah. They rose to make room for the newcomers. With Dev's help, Sukhdev unloaded their belongings along with a little hay he had picked up on the way. After feeding and watering the mule, he tied it to a tree. In the meantime, Raminder spread the two cotton blankets for sleeping, one for Ratna and the second for the rest of the family.

With dark monsoon clouds moving in, the temperature started to plummet. The little wood they carried was damp and Raminder could not start a fire to warm the ailing child. She helped Ratna change into clean clothes, to make her more comfortable. After retrieving a pair of hand knitted woollen socks and a sweater from her own small metal box, she gave them to the child. Ratna slipped them on, and drew the oversized woollens close to her body as Raminder fed her the last mushy banana.

'My mouth is dry . . . may I have some water?' asked Ratna.

As soon as Raminder arose to get her water, the lady of the house walked over with hot milk for the sick. The other refugees called the kind woman, "Sardarniji". She was the wife of a large-hearted Sikh landlord who had opened his house to the refugees. Raminder touched the angel's feet with gratitude, and proceeded to put turmeric and sugar into the hot milk.

'What's the raw turmeric for?' asked Sukhdev.

'It cures the fever.' Holding the delirious girl in her arms, Raminder fed her the milky brew. After taking care of Ratna, she, Sukhdev and Dev sat down to share the last two paranthas and snuggled up in the only other bedding.

Sukhdev lay in restless slumber, his feet swollen, body hurting and his spirit shattered. He lay awake listening to a radio blaring inside the house, realising that the euphoria of Independence had not dissipated. Nehru talked incessantly about the country's promising future, but Sukhdev understood the unspoken. Neither he, nor the millions of fellow refugees, seemed to be a part of the present or the future India. They were already the past—a sad statistic. Nothing more than a troubling open sore that made all non-refugees avert their eyes in mild uneasiness.

At the dawn of Independence, their heartache had already been forgotten.

His mind wandered from Nehru's speech and he lay thinking about the cost of freedom. He thought of his retired English friend, Colonel Wright, who lived next door to his 'S.S.B. Flour Mill' in Sialkot. Even though his friend was often condescending, Sukhdev had still enjoyed the Colonel's company. A couple of years earlier, they had a heated discussion about the possibility of a partition of the country, and the retired Colonel had stated that if ever it did take place, the British would plan a smooth transition. 'The main reason the sun never sets on the British Empire is because we are master planners and executioners. We never do anything haphazardly,' the Colonel had announced. Sukhdev had watched the Colonel display smug conviction and arrogance, apparently born from the knowledge of ruling many lands.

Sukhdev wondered what the Colonel would have to say now. The British scurried from the land they had ruled for over two centuries, betraying millions with their sheer indifference. Their sudden departure created this widespread chaos. They had casually cracked India, creating a new boundary along these ragged cracks, and called it the 'Radcliffe Awards' line. They sliced off the western and eastern borders of British India, creating a new country on either side of India, naming the two disjointed pieces of land collectively as Pakistan.

West and East Pakistan flanked India on its two borders. It made Sukhdev angry that with a single stroke of a pen, the British had created countless refugees, without making any arrangements for them. The 'master planners' had offered no workable solution for an organised demarcation of new borders between the two countries. He wondered if Colonel Wright witnessed this injustice or if he too left the country of his birth in haste, for the safer shores of Great Britain.

That first night in the 'promised land', Sukhdev slept and dreamt terrifying dreams. Between nightmares, he lay grieving for his dead child, Aman, named for 'peace'. His soul in torment and body in pain, he listened to Ratna, who, delirious in her sleep, sang snatches of lullabies to her baby sister Sheila, while Dev whimpered again and again, 'Ma, wake up. People are all leaving.'

By the next morning, Raminder knew that something drastic had to be done as they were losing the little girl. Even though Ratna had stopped shivering, she still burned with a high fever. Raminder dragged her tired body into action, tearing one of her cotton dupattas to make a couple of big bandages. She filled one bronze bowl with cool water from the hand pump and woke Dev up to wet the cloth in water, squeeze it as best as he could, and put the cool bandage on Ratna's forehead.

Dev dipped, squeezed and applied the bandage over and over for almost an hour. At last, Ratna's delirium subsided and she drifted into peaceful slumber. While Dev worked to cool Ratna's forehead, Raminder took everyone's dirty clothes, scrubbed them with the only soap bar in her metal box and spread them to dry on a rope tied between two columns in the verandah.

After Ratna dozed off, Dev still sat with her, mumbling, 'Ram, Ram, Ram.'

Raminder knew the two children were not related by blood but watching them together, she sensed invisible threads of love binding them.

She needed a strong cup of tea to relieve her headache, but try as she might to start the fire, the damp wood smoked and died out. Just then, Sardarniji came with a glass full of steaming hot milk. Raminder hated to wake Ratna who had fallen into restful sleep, but the milk would get cold, so she added sugar and turmeric to half the milk—saving the rest for Dev—and woke up the sick girl. Sitting on the ground, she supported Ratna's limp body, while the child sipped the milky concoction.

After finishing the hot drink, Ratna looked at Dev sitting with wet rags and a tumbler of cool water. Turning to Raminder, she asked if the festival of rakhi had passed. It had, but Raminder understood the sentiments and pulling a simple red coloured thread from the thick cotton blanket, asked Dev to bend over so Ratna could tie the rakhi on his wrist, to sanctify this new relationship of a brother and a sister.

Little Dev seemed to understand the meaning of the ritual and smiled a weak smile, kissing his new older sister on her forehead. Raminder watched Ratna melt at the sight of Dev's lopsided smile, even as the girl had a spasm of coughing.

In an attempt to warm some water to soothe Ratna's cough, Raminder tried lighting the fire one more time. To make it work, she finally rose to get old newspapers from the Sardarniji. The newspapers caught fire and soon the flames licked the smoking wood. Raminder first warmed water for Ratna, and then made hot tea and a pot of porridge. She next coaxed and fed the sick girl, before feeding the rest. The breakfast refreshed them as no meal had since their nightmare began. Then to save the charred piece of wood for another time, Raminder smothered it with water.

When done with breakfast, she fished out a five-rupee bill from the knot tied at the end of her dupatta. Handing the only cash she had over to Sukhdev, she said, 'Please go to the village and buy a little black pepper, fresh ginger and some dry wood.' She burst into sobs. 'Ratna's cough is getting worse and we don't have the resources to help her.'

Dev heard this exchange and said, 'Each of the bags Ratna and I carry contain a little money. Use it to help Ratna.'

Raminder rushed over, fishing a stack of about a hundred rupees from Dev's father's bag. Delighted with her find, she hugged Dev and giving another twenty rupees to Sukhdev, said, 'Bring some ground turmeric and a bottle of honey. Also, see if you can find a hakim to look at Ratna.' A native herbal doctor would be cheaper than a medical doctor she reasoned.

Everyone in this newly formed family lacked clean, dry clothes, as Raminder had washed the only other set of clothes each had and they were still damp. However, dry clothes were needed to rest at night, so she asked Sukhdev and Dev to change into the damp clothes she had washed earlier in the day, before stepping out under overcast, threatening skies.

As Sukhdev and Dev left, she sat watching them drag their feet towards the village, thinking how she had never been so weary. From behind her, the sound of a deep cough resonating with phlegm jolted her to reality. She saw Ratna turn red with the spasm and rushed over with a tumbler of water. After the cough subsided, she tucked Ratna back in bed and dropped into a heap next to the child, beaten and crying. She tried to remind herself that the worst was behind them, but she could not stop the tears that tumbled over her face.

Raminder wept for Aman, her only child who never returned from school.

She cried for little Dev who had sat beseeching his dead mother to wake up, for fear of being left behind.

She cried for the sick little Ratna, groping in the dark for her baby sister, Sheila.

She cried for the thousands of dead bodies littering the countryside or floating in wells and rivers.

She cried and cried. And then she cried some more.

She woke up with a start when a gentle hand touched her shoulder. Raising her head, Raminder looked into the sad eyes of her husband. Sukhdev helped her rise, pointed to a pile of dry wood, and handed her the ginger, honey, black pepper and turmeric.

'Can you spare a pot and the few bronze bowls we've been using as tumblers?' he asked.

'Yes. Why?'

'We will need them at the village gurdwara,' he replied. She understood Sukhdev must have gone to the gurdwara, their place of worship, for help.

'Is the gurdwara open?'

'Yes. The gurdwara kitchen seems to open around four o'clock for an early langar—a free community kitchen run at all Sikh places of worship—to feed the refugees. Dev and I could go and bring back some daal and chapattis.'

'Langar food will be so welcome. Did you find a hakim for Ratna?'

'No. The only hakim in the village was a Muslim who left for Pakistan,' he replied without looking at her. Raminder looked long and hard at her husband, and seeing him avoid her eyes, understood the tragedy that must have befallen the Muslim herbal doctor. She looked down, and picking up a little dry wood, started a fire to cook lunch.

Since they both wore damp clothes, made worse by the steady drizzle, Raminder motioned without looking up, 'You two go and change into dry clothes. Sit under the blanket to get warm while I cook.'

Sukhdev tied the thin rope directly over the fire for their wet clothes. Since they all were tired and cold, Raminder put a few broken bricks near the fire to heat them for their aching feet and tired bodies.

She made tea with honey and ginger accompanied by a lentil and rice concoction, and served it to Sukhdev and Dev before sitting down to feed Ratna. When done, she wrapped the hot bricks in cut up cotton bandages, handed a brick each to her husband and Dev, before placing one beside Ratna. The girl curled herself around the warmth, as did Sukhdev and little Dev. Only after she had taken care of the family did Raminder eat. Then she made a mixture of finely chopped ginger, pepper and honey, and retrieved her own warm brick from the dying embers. Lying down beside Ratna, she medicated the child with the ginger potion every time she started to cough.

Later in the afternoon, Ratna opened her eyes. 'Ma, my throat feels better but my head still hurts, and I still feel feverish,' she whispered.

Raminder's heart melted. Ratna had called her ma. Soothed by this gentle balm, her insides hurt less. She sat up, and taking Ratna's head in her lap started massaging it.

Outside, the rain fell steadily on the hundreds of refugees in the yard, huddled under the trees for shelter. Raminder prayed for all. *'Vaheguru, meher kar.'* Dear God, bless us all.

In late afternoon, Sukhdev and Dev changed into their damp clothes again, which by now also smelled of smoke, and left for the gurdwara to bring supper for the family.

By the third morning, Ratna's fever subsided and her cough seemed under control. So, as soon as they finished breakfast, Raminder sat down with Sukhdev and said, 'Ratna is better and will soon be well enough to travel. Where do we go from here?'

'First, let us go to Amritsar and if I have luck finding work, we'll stay, else go to Jullunder,' replied her husband.

'We are not staying with your brother in Jullunder, are we?'

Sukhdev had no quick answer for her. He and his brother Harpal, almost fifteen years his senior, were not close. His dadima—paternal grandmother—had often talked about how his parents died in a train crash. Harpal, being the older son, inherited a rich collection of properties and the position of a father figure to his five-year-old brother Sukhdev.

Dadima said that neither Harpal nor his seventeen-year-old wife, Gursharan, were ready for the responsibility the sudden death of his parents thrust upon them. 'Why did your mother have to die and leave this *balaah* for me to raise?' the belligerent sister-in-law would ask while pointing to Sukhdev, who remembered being timid but he did not think he looked like a balaah—a she-devil.

When he turned six, his brother Harpal told him that for the sake of peace in the house, he had got Sukhdev admitted to an English boarding school on the hill-station of Dehradun. Whenever Sukhdev returned home for his vacation, his sister-in-law ordered him to stay with his dadima. The feeble, old grandmother lived in a dingy room in the servants' quarters, away from the huge house. She was the only relative who gave Sukhdev love, emotional support and moral guidance. Dadima died before his sixteenth birthday.

As soon as Sukhdev finished schooling, Harpal packed him off to the village of Ugoke to manage a small piece of land belonging to their father's younger brother, a poor uncle who had died without an heir and whose property reverted to their family. Ugoke, a village close to Sialkot, was about a hundred and fifty miles beyond Jullunder, to its northwest. Harpal showed no interest in managing the small piece of land. So, Sukhdev inherited that property and moved there, thus bringing peace to Harpal's household.

Through hard work, Sukhdev continued adding more land to his property. He took care of his uncle's widow and put himself through college in Sialkot, while his farm grew. By the time Partition took place, he had caught up with Harpal financially. The farm in Ugoke was close to three hundred acres. The "S.S.B. Flour Mill", that he had built in Sialkot, flourished and brought in more than enough money to live comfortably. His marriage to Raminder brought him greater prosperity. Her affluent parents gifted them a car and many other material goods at the wedding. He had balked at accepting the dowry, but Raminder's parents insisted the gifts were for their daughter.

Thoughts of Raminder eased him back to the present. 'Raminder, I don't have an answer that would please you. Since we don't have many options, we might have to stay with my brother Harpal—but only till I find some work.'

Raminder did not bat an eyelid at Sukhdev's belated answer and picked up the conversation where she had left off. 'We have two impressionable children with us. Should we not exhaust all other options before deciding to stay with your brother's family?'

'Jaan, my precious, we have no other options.'

'I think we do. I could write to my sister-in-law's parents in Ambala. My brother and his family are probably with them. I'm sure we could stay with them until you find some work.'

'We don't have enough money to travel that far. It may be possible later.'

10
The Welcome

24 August 1947

One bright sunny day, after Ratna gained enough strength to travel, the Bajwas took leave of their kind hosts. Before parting, Sardarniji filled Dev's metal can with refreshing home-churned buttermilk and gave them a few potatoes and a small bag of basmati rice. Armed with food and dry wood, they set out for Amritsar, half a day's journey away.

Upon arrival, they found the city swarming with refugees, but the place seemed rich with compassion. Hospitable city folks fed them whatever they could spare, sometimes even half a slice of chapatti bread. Housewives came out to share their meagre resources. Through narrow streets, the family trudged towards the sacred Sikh gurdwara, Harmandir Sahib—the Golden Temple—where they ate wholesome food donated by the kind people of Amritsar.

Ratna, surprised to see less rigid observance of purdah in this new land, found it very liberating. Women and young girls without burqas served the refugees. They helped shoulder to shoulder with men. She decided to test what she thought she saw. In one slick move, she pulled her cumbersome dupatta veil off her head, and when no one tapped on her shoulder to remind her of her immodesty, she pursed her lips and smiled. She liked the new freedom.

At Harmandir Sahib, they were given a place to stay, as well as two square meals a day. In the safety of the gurdwara and its routine, Ratna began to relax.

She and Raminder helped in the gurdwara langar, the community kitchen, while Sukhdev and Dev searched for a job. The second afternoon of their arrival, Ratna complained of a headache and Raminder suggested she rest, giving her a rolled up towel to use as a pillow. Ratna slept fitfully, and waking, pressed the towel to her ears, crying.

Raminder gathered her in her arms. 'What . . . what is it child?'

Ratna wailed, 'I can hear 'em screaming—'

'Hear whom screaming?'

'My mataji and Sheila. Please, please help them. Make them stop hurting.'

Raminder held her until the screams subsided and Ratna dozed off.

The next morning, while braiding Ratna's long hair, Raminder asked, 'Was Dev always this quiet?'

'Oh no, that child talks too much. I think he likes his own voice,' Ratna declared nodding her head, as if she had just uttered a weighty truth.

'What about you?' Raminder laughed.

'What about me?'

'Don't you love to hear your voice?'

'Oh Ma!'

'Did Dev have any other brothers and sisters?'

'No. My mataji always said, "Dev babu came with good kismet—a lucky boy in a big household".'

'So, he had a large family?'

'Yes, and very rich too. He had two married uncles, living in the haveli with Dev's parents, but he was the only child there. Everyone spoiled him, especially his grandfather, Baoji, who acted as if Dev was the centre of the universe.'

'Do you honestly believe Dev is spoiled?'

Ratna nodded.

'Even after the way he took care of you during your recent illness?'

Ratna pressed her lips and shrugged. 'Maybe he changed.'

'What was his mother like?' asked Raminder.

'You remind me of her. Uma bibiji was tall, pretty and very nice, just like you. She often let me and my sister Sheila play with Dev. Sometimes she gave us toys and cookies, and at times she even plucked sweet juice mangoes from their orchard for my little sister and me.'

Thinking about Dev's past with awe, she added, 'Did you know they sent Dev to an English school in Lahore, in his own coach? Then last year his grandfather bought him a new car to go to school in. Can you believe it—his own car and a chauffeur to take him to school!'

'Ratna,' asked Raminder, 'did your family live with Dev's parents?'

'No. We lived in the small temple behind their haveli. My mataji reminded me constantly that Dev was the boss' son and I could never get cross with him. I had to agree with every stupid idea he proposed. And he had plenty of those. My bapu . . .'

She broke down. Ratna sobbed and talked about their last day in Shahadra, remembering how her slain family lay amid splattered blood. 'My bapu . : . my bapu was . . . they killed them all. My mataji lay without clothes, butchered, and my little sister Sheila lay in blood next to her,' she said, and snuggled close to Raminder. 'I miss them.'

Raminder, with tears sparkling in her eyes whispered, 'The Muslims murdered our young daughter Aman too. She was as old as you, and I miss her so very much.'

'Why are Muslims so bad?' Ratna mumbled her question through sobs and spasms.

'I . . . I don't . . .' stammered Raminder. 'Ratna, it's not religion that makes people bad. Some Muslims are good and some bad—like us.'

'They are not like us! My mataji scolded me often and if I answered her back, she beat me and was bad to me . . . but she was not nasty enough to kill me. I'm mean to people sometimes but I never ever killed anybody. No, Muslims are not like us. Definitely not.'

'Ratna, all Muslims are not bad, only some are, just like some Sikhs and Hindus are good and some not. The rotten ones amongst us killed a lot of good Muslims,' said Raminder. 'Remember the thousands of slain Muslims littering the road leading to Amritsar, and, the burqa-clad lifeless women floating in rivers and wells? The bad Sikhs and Hindus killed them.'

'Then how do you know the good from the bad?' Ratna asked.

Raminder had no answer. 'I don't know child.'

After days of trying, Sukhdev and Dev found nothing to do other than an occasional odd job. Raminder suggested they work as porters at the railway station. The suggestion seemed good at the time, but Raminder found them returning within a couple of hours on their first day, with Sukhdev carrying a hysterical Dev, who kept whimpering, 'He was my chacha!'—The man was his uncle.

Sukhdev put Dev down near Raminder. 'He was my chacha!' Dev cried. He repeated the lament over and over like the heartrending pleas of someone drowning in quicksand.

Raminder, not knowing what had happened, took Dev in her fold, repeating, 'It is okay. You are safe now.' She chanted softly, 'Sat Naam, Sat Naam, Sat Naamji, Vaheguru, Vaheguru, Vaheguruji'—the Sikh chant of 'God is the truth', and 'God is great and merciful'.

Late that night, with the children tucked in their makeshift bed, she asked Sukhdev what happened. He said he was not sure how Dev landed where he did or saw what he saw.

Raminder shook her head. 'I don't understand.'

'After my first errand as a porter, I returned to the spot where I'd left Dev. He wasn't there. I heard him screaming and saw him running towards an angry mob. I ran and grabbed him before he pushed his way to the centre of the crowd where they had just bludgeoned a Muslim to death.' Sukhdev sobbed. Raminder watched her tall, proud husband shrink right before her eyes, in angst over man's cruelty to man.

Gathering himself, Sukhdev continued, 'Dev kicked, screamed and pleaded, "don't hurt him please! He is my chacha". After they removed the body, I asked Dev what his uncle's name was and, still sobbing, he replied, "Iqbal Chacha". The slain Muslim must have been a very close family friend for our Dev to call him chacha. He was still hysterical and since I could not calm him, I brought him back to you.'

Raminder sat shaking her head, marvelling at the strength that it must have taken her husband to carry a hysterical seven-year-old for almost five miles—all the way from the railway station.

She laid the boy beside Sukhdev that night. Dev pleaded intermittently, 'Please don't hurt him. He's my chacha!' or 'Ma, wake up. People are all leaving.' Sukhdev took Dev in his arms, crying with him, holding him until the wave of each such nightmare passed.

The next morning, Dev woke up as if nothing had happened. 'How far is Jullunder from here?' he asked.

Raminder found his calm uncanny. 'I'm not sure. By train, it could take three or four hours I suppose. But on foot, it might take us three or four days,' she replied, wondering what he was getting at.

'Let's go there. Ma told me Anu chachi will take care of us there,' he said, offering her money from one of his bags, so they could travel by train.

'Do you or Ratna know where your Anu chachi lives?' Raminder inquired, taking the money.

'No, but Anu chachi will find us. Ma said so,' he answered with the unwavering innocence of a child.

Raminder and Sukhdev looked at each other and decided it was best they leave the place that had caused such trauma. She agreed to stay with Sukhdev's brother Harpal for a short while, and packed to go to the railway station.

On the way, they gave away their mule to another struggling refugee family.

Travelling in the train for the first time in her life distracted Ratna enough to look around her with mild interest. They reached Jullunder in the early hours of the morning and renting a tonga, rode to Harpal's house.

Harpal and his wife, Gursharan, stared in stunned silence at relatives dressed like beggars, at their door. Gursharan took them inside her spacious bungalow, and gave them old clean clothes to change into after washing up. While they bathed, Gursharan's servants made chai, spicy scrambled eggs and paranthas to feed them.

A scrumptious breakfast rekindled their spirits, and Ratna and Dev got up to peep into the room next door. Gursharan, with her back to the door, cleared her throat and in a cantankerous voice asked her husband, 'Who is that riffraff your brother has brought with him? The girl is too dark skinned to be their daughter. Didn't their daughter have a Sikh name, Amar, Aman or something like that? I know it was not Ratna,' and warming up, added, 'We never heard of their ever getting a son . . . and . . . and he wears no turban. He must be some Muslim's worthless bastard.'

Ratna felt her face turn red. 'He's not a Muslim and he's not a bastard!' she growled. And before the woman could turn or get over her shock of being challenged, Ratna dragged Dev back to shelter with her new parents.

Gursharan ushered Raminder and Sukhdev into a room in the servants' quarters, at the back of the bungalow. 'You may eat with us in the afternoon but from tonight, cook your own food,' she admonished, handing Raminder the key to the room. 'I'm tired of helping useless refugees, especially ones with big mouths!'

Not having said anything to aggravate her sister-in-law, Raminder wondered what Gursharan meant, but let it go. 'Beggars can't be choosers,' her father had always quoted.

Late that afternoon, while Sukhdev and the two children went to shop for groceries, Raminder swept and cleaned the room to make it more livable. She started a fire in the small earthen fireplace in one corner of their room, and cooked the potatoes and rice that the generous Sardarniji had given them before they left for Amritsar.

Their room had no bathroom, which meant they had to use the open field at the back of the servants' quarters for any calls of nature. One wall of the room had a small opening leading outside to an open sewer. Raminder decided they would use that spot, not only for washing the utensils and clothes, but also for their daily baths.

The next morning, she borrowed a bucket from one of the servants and while one bathed, the others sat outside on the grass. With small change in his pocket, and a paltry breakfast cooked on a temporary stove made of loose bricks, Sukhdev left to look for a job, while Ratna and Dev stepped out to explore their surroundings.

Their room was one among five separate rooms for the servants. The rooms stood side by side, and they found two rooms beside theirs, occupied. The two rooms beyond their own had sturdy padlocks bolting them.

Pointing to the last room, Ratna said, 'I swear I heard someone sobbing in that locked room.' Dev went to check but said he heard nothing.

Raminder overheard their little exchange and in the afternoon noticed a servant take food into that room. He returned with empty dishes after re-locking the room and pocketing the key. Late in the evening, as Raminder stood looking out the window from her room, she watched her brother-in-law enter the locked room. Fifteen minutes later, she heard some whimpering from within, and saw Harpal leave the room whistling happy tunes. One by one, three other men went in, did their business, and emerged looking smug.

The sobbing continued for long hours.

The servants whispered that a thirteen-year-old Muslim girl was locked in the room and told Raminder how the child was raped night after night by multiple men. Fear of the master's wrath sealed their lips. In an effort to alleviate the guilt over this terrible injustice, they claimed they could do nothing for the helpless child. Nobody knew the whereabouts of the Muslim girl's family, or knew how she came to be in such a tragic situation.

'Alas!' asked the servants, 'where could the girl go now with her shame?' They whispered how no one would accept her, even if someone helped her cross the border into Pakistan. Her own family, if still alive, would disown her for having brought shame to herself. If freed, she would definitely kill herself. 'The poor child must have some terrible karma to be in such an unforgiving situation, at such a tender age.'

As Raminder placed wood in the stove and prepared to cook, she heard Dev and Ratna talk in whispers outside their open window.

Dev asked Ratna, 'Why is the girl kept a prisoner?'

'Pure meanness,' explained Ratna. 'But, at least, they give her food to eat and give her company in the evening. That is a little comforting.' Ratna sighed like grown-ups.

'But why does everyone keep talking about "her shame"? What do they mean?' insisted little Dev.

'You silly! Don't you realise the girl is probably not wearing a burqa when all these unrelated men go in to keep her company in the evenings?

Muslim women must live in purdah. They have to wear burqas in front of all men other than their own immediate family. To show one's bare face in front of unrelated men is considered very shameful in their community,' she replied.

Raminder heard them talk but how was she to explain the truth? Too disturbed to think, she left her cooking and rose to talk to her sister-in-law Gursharan, the mistress of the house with dark whispers.

'Is it true that a young Muslim girl is imprisoned in those quarters for men's pleasure?' Raminder confronted Gursharan.

'Who told you?' asked Gursharan, her voice quivering.

'No one. I heard a girl sobbing when each of the men left the room,' replied Raminder, sensing she had come knocking on a door that was not even shut—the dark secrets inside were begging an audience.

'I have a young daughter myself and . . . and . . . I'm so ashamed of what is going on. There is nothing I can do about it. Your brother-in-law does not listen. He refuses to discuss it,' sobbed Gursharan.

Raminder, overwhelmed by this fleeting glimpse of warm human emotions in her surly sister-in-law, put an arm around her shoulder. Once Gursharan calmed down, Raminder moved towards her own quarters.

Gursharan called out after her. 'Listen. I have some old clothes my children have outgrown. Do you think you could use them for your children?'

Raminder turned and nodded while her insides hurt at what she, a proud woman, had been reduced to. If she could afford the clothes herself, she would not mind being asked to wear "used clothing". It was her situation that made her hurt, even though she realised Gursharan was only trying to help. The awful truth seeped into her body and wiggled around until she painfully acknowledged that her situation was not Gursharan's fault. It was her life and she had to deal with it.

'I can spare two old comforters. Can you use them?' Gursharan asked. When Raminder nodded again, her sister-in-law added, 'Wait . . . wait a minute. I can also give you some wheat-flour and a griddle to make chapattis.' She left to bring the griddle, a rolling pin, wheat-flour, old clothes and the comforters.

'Thank you, Behenji.' Thank you, sister, mumbled an overwhelmed Raminder. Conflicting emotions swamped her—gratitude for compassion shown, anger at her own fate, fear of an uncertain future and the constant hammering of the relentless question. Why? Why did this happen to her? Why did she lose her precious Aman? What did she or Sukhdev do to deserve this? A subdued Raminder, laden with clothes, comforters and groceries, returned to her quarters.

'Ma, did you ask her why they locked up the Muslim girl? Did you? Ma . . . did you?' pestered Ratna. 'Ma, say something. Can't you make it better for the poor Muslim girl?'

'I don't know how.'

'Can she live with us?'

Raminder did not reply.

When Sukhdev returned that night, beaten and tired, Raminder showed him the gifts Gursharan had given and shared the secret of the Muslim girl.

'I'm so ashamed of my blood,' he said. 'He's my brother, but I don't have the courage or the means to stop him.'

Early the next morning, one of the servants came banging on their door. 'Did you hear the news?' Before Raminder could find her voice, the maidservant shrieked, 'The Muslim girl bled to death last night.'

'W . . . hat?'

'The servant who went in with her meals last night told us how pale and sickly she looked. The room, he said, reeked of putrid blood. We pressured him to tell the mistress, which he said he had already done a few times, without any results. So, all of us went to beg for a doctor for the girl. The doctor showed up just now. The poor girl's been dead for hours.'

Raminder sank to her knees. Sukhdev stepped out and raised her to her feet. Leading her to the makeshift bed on the floor,' he helped her sit, and brought her a tumbler of water. 'Jaan, I'm sorry. You didn't deserve to witness this. I wish we could get away from here. If only we had some money . . .'

Dev opened his eyes and sat up. 'Biji, I have some money that might help.'

Dev called Raminder 'biji', not 'ma', as Ratna did, but it's a start, thought Raminder. 'What money?' she asked.

'Before we left the haveli, my ma tied a bag of money around my loins and said it was for my future. Do you think we could use it now to get out of this place?' he asked, handing her a bundle of hundred rupee notes. The bundle had more money than Raminder had ever seen at one time. Hugging Dev, she silently thanked the wise woman who bore him.

Raminder and Sukhdev talked it over.

'There are no jobs out there. Maybe I should look for a small business,' said Sukhdev.

Raminder made lunch for him, as he would probably be out the whole day looking for a business. She had no butter or oil to make paranthas, so she made chapattis and spiced potatoes, and packed them for lunch.

Sukhdev left early, taking Dev with him for consultation. 'A new business is a decision to be made by the men of the house,' he told Dev. Raminder smiled. Sukhdev was a good man.

Sukhdev and Dev were gone the whole day and when they returned, they brought a few bananas, mustard oil, lentils and onions, along with encouraging news. 'We've bought a small bicycle repair shop and rented the room and kitchen above the store. We can move right away.'

The next morning, the family quickly and unceremoniously relocated to their own house.

11
First Rays of Light

Winter 1947-Spring 1948

'Ratna, when will we go back to my haveli?' Dev asked. Like a newly weaned puppy, he still looked disoriented in his new surroundings.

'Probably never. Dev, listen to me. We have no other family left except Ma, Papaji and each other.'

Dev nodded with tears in his eyes.

Ratna understood his ache as she hurt too. They often talked of dreams. They talked of a fairytale path, which would lead them back to their warm past, a past sprinkled with laughter, love and security. She talked about the past as a pleasant dream, whereas Dev seemed to view it as only a matter of time before the dream would turn to reality.

Ratna knew that this new standard of living was unthinkable for Dev when compared to his previous life, but for her, life opened up. Her new parents, she sensed, would not only help her survive but help her rise above this. Ratna marvelled at how during the day, under Sukhdev's guidance, even Dev learned to do odd jobs in their repair shop. She came downstairs in the mornings to help with the cleaning of the store, while Raminder stayed upstairs, cooking, cleaning, sewing and knitting.

The family's bicycle business picked up, and within the first month, the shop started making a tiny profit. Ratna overheard her new parents talking. 'If we live frugally, I think we might be able to buy this tiny apartment soon,' said her mother.

'If anyone can make it happen, I know you can,' replied her father, smiling.

Their new home had one large room, a small kitchen, an attached bathroom to be used only for bathing and washing clothes. The so-called bathroom had no running water and no toilet, but was private enough to bathe. There they kept a few buckets that Sukhdev filled with water for bathing purposes.

The bright and spacious main room had light streaking not only through a broken window but also from the two ventilators, close to the high ceiling of the room. With Ratna's help, Sukhdev boarded the broken side of the window with plywood, leaving the half that still functioned untouched, so they could have fresh air.

The tiny kitchen had two earthen fireplaces—one for burning coal and the other for wood. The kitchen had one broken ventilator, which stayed open permanently. When Ratna suggested they board it, Raminder didn't want that. 'I don't mind the open ventilator as it keeps the smoke away from the living quarters.'

The privy stood on the ground floor of the old structure, behind their bicycle shop. With constant monsoon rains, the poorly constructed septic tank overflowed, making it virtually impossible for them to use it. This small structure turned into a visual revolting mess, reeking of undesirable smells, which even Ratna, accustomed to poor living conditions, found repulsive. But choices were few and Raminder helped them learn to live with it, knowing that once the monsoons passed, the weather and their surroundings would take a turn for the better.

The stairs, with wooden banisters, leading to the apartment, stood on the outside of the shop and since there was no running water, every morning Sukhdev carried up four large buckets of water for their baths, from the hand-pump that stood next to the stairs on the ground floor. For their other daily needs, throughout the day, Ratna lugged more water upstairs.

Ratna loved the new freedom of going up and down the stairs at will. Her new mother never insisted she cover her head with the dupatta the way her mataji had insisted. Raminder bought her two small buckets to carry the water, and Ratna turned this chore into an enjoyable game.

Every time she carried the full pails upstairs without spilling, she knew it would be a great day. If she spilled it on the first five steps, she promised herself an extra chore to please her new mother; if she spilled any time later, she had to be extra diligent that day to please both her new parents. Most of the days, this little ritual set a happy pace for Ratna's days, especially since on her way down the stairs, nobody reprimanded her for acting like a child, skipping to a happy tune in her head.

She and Dev loved the flat rooftop above their one-roomed apartment. It was accessible from the same wooden stairs leading to their home and up to the roof. The rooftop had a raised three-foot high brick wall in a basket-weave pattern around its outer parametres. On the side opposite the wooden stairway sat a tiny unfinished room with a tin roof. The room had three walls with no door or windows. An old wood-framed woven jute cot, left by the previous occupants, took up most of the space in that partially completed room.

Sukhdev needed Dev's help during the busy mornings and evenings, but the afternoons belonged to Ratna and Dev. The rooftop became their playground where Ratna allowed herself the luxury to dream. Sometimes she turned the cot into a raised platform and the room into a temple. She was punditji, the priest. At other times, she encouraged Dev to turn the half-done room into his castle where he was the king and Ratna his subject. With an active imagination, Ratna invented new games while Dev usually followed like a motherless puppy, desiring to please. He agreed to do whatever Ratna suggested—play, dream or just talk.

On one side of the unfinished room, a clothesline stretched between bamboo poles. Next to it, sat a huge rusty metal tub filled with dirt, overgrown with mint. On days when she had no lentils or vegetables to cook, Raminder made chutney—a paste with onions, a few dried pomegranate seeds, salt, chilies and mint—and served it with fresh chapatti bread.

She often sat with Ratna and Dev on the rooftop in the afternoons. While the children played, Raminder prepared for the approaching winter, knitting and basking in the warmth of the sun. Often times she heard Ratna singing softly in an unusually melodious voice. A good sign, she thought. Ratna was connecting to her new life and Raminder prayed for Dev to reach a similar state of grace.

She spent her mornings and evenings cooking, washing, cleaning and teaching Ratna the art of living a woman's life. She loved the little girl who had become not only her friend but also her confidante in this new, vast, unfamiliar world.

Raminder often talked about her daughter Aman, an only child, born after six years of marriage. Ratna, on the other hand, talked constantly about her Bapu, her wise old father who taught her to read and write Hindi. She was his special child, his jewel. Ratna also spoke of her adorable baby sister, though she confessed Sheila was never as special as she was to her Bapu. 'But I think my mataji loved Sheila more.'

'What makes you say that?' asked Raminder.

'I just know it. It's just that Sheila was little and had more needs . . . and . . . she was so cute, with light skin, big doe-eyes and wavy hair. However, I could never understand one thing.'

'And that is—?'

'Why my mataji resented Uma bibiji.'

'Wasn't Uma Dev's mother?' asked Raminder.

'Yes, and she was very kind.'

'Then why do you think your mataji didn't like her?'

'Just because I know. My bapu often told me I was special, so I guess I just understand such things.'

'How?' Raminder persisted.

'Well, whenever my mataji was in a sour mood she'd scream, "why did you have to be born a girl? Why could you not be a boy like that woman's child?" she asked, pointing towards the haveli. So I just know she hated Uma bibiji.'

'Does Dev know about this?'

'Of course not! You think I'm stupid. Why would I tell him that?'

'Did your father ever hear your mataji fuss like that?'

'Yes. But he was too nice. All he said was, *"Rehan-de"*.' Let it go.

Such interactions helped Raminder understand the girl. On rare occasions when she and Sukhdev had some privacy, they talked about the children. 'I think Ratna has started trusting me but Dev is still unreachable. I never know what's going on with him.'

'Don't worry, girls just open up faster. Remember how our Aman talked to you about everything—well, boys and men are different. We find it harder to share feelings. I know I do. I hate myself for not telling Aman how much I loved her. Now I wish I had—maybe the pain would be less, if only I had told her.'

Raminder reached over to press his hand.

'I do think Dev is coming around though. He has started looking up to me . . . I can tell from the way he relates to me in the shop.'

Raminder nodded. 'Let's hope so.'

Once they secured a roof over their heads, Raminder started worrying about other problems. With winter approaching, she taught Ratna to knit warm sweaters and socks. Both of them worked furiously to prepare for the winter. Struggling for the barest necessities, Raminder and Ratna spent long hours in unending lines at the 'Bhargava Refugee Camp', first to get their refugee ration cards made, and later for cheaper or free rations. Raminder often let Ratna stand in queue, while she went around the camp searching for her missing relatives.

The loved ones Raminder left behind in Pakistan, haunted her during her waking hours. She had no idea how to track down her parents or her younger sister Preet. They lived a long way off, in Rawalpindi. Her own village, Ugoke, near Sialkot, was farther south and closer to Lahore. She had not heard from her parents for almost a year now. If they made it across the border, she knew her family would probably look for her in Amritsar or Jullunder.

While at Amritsar, she had added the Bajwa name to the 'refugee list' available to them at the Golden Temple, to notify her loved ones that she and Sukhdev had gone to Jullunder. Her only brother, a doctor, had lived and practiced in Lahore, and Raminder hoped to find him. She sometimes went to the gurdwara or the post office to check the lists of handwritten notes from relatives and friends looking for lost loved ones. But there was no note from her family. Amongst millions of refugees, no one looked for her. Raminder felt as if her stomach carried a boa constrictor tied up in knots, waiting to uncoil and strangle the life out of her. If only she could find a loved one, any one of them, perhaps then it would be easier to carry on. The only way to track her married brother's family was through her sister-in-law's family in Ambala. Even though she did not remember her bhabi's parental address, she took a chance and wrote to her brother in care of her sister-in-law's parents' family name on an envelope, mentioning the landmarks she could remember. Raminder enclosed her new Jullunder address in the letter.

Seven months after they set up house in the tiny apartment, she still had no news of her brother or the rest of her family. Nurturing two traumatised children, Raminder often longed for a strong dose of good old-fashioned 'mothering' for herself. She too needed the security of a mother's love, like the kind only her bebeji could give. Her bebeji stated her thinking with guileless innocence as if it were an obvious truth. Her mother talked sparingly, but when she did, it was to announce weighty declarations, which she assumed were as evident to everyone as they were to her. Raminder smiled at the thought of her mother, a loving simpleton, who in an artless, naive manner could deliver a 'sense of control' back to her.

Raminder often talked of her happy childhood in their haveli in Rawalpindi. 'While growing up,' she told Ratna, 'we had no running water or electricity in the house, but I grew up in a secure world, surrounded by a loving family. One night, when I was about eight years old, my bebeji asked me to get water from the well. "Bebeji, I'm scared," I mumbled.

' "How's that possible?" she asked. "Sikh girls are brave. They don't get scared." And then gently, very gently, she put her arms around me and kissed me on the head and my world suddenly seemed safe. With the trust of a secure child, I had no further need to question my mother's philosophy. After that, every time I admitted to being scared, I got the same answer, delivered in the same loving manner.'

In lonely times during the day, when Ratna and Dev were occupied, Raminder longed for her bebeji, wanting to lay her head in her mother's lap, to forget her heartache. She was tired of her life. She was tired beyond her skin, muscles and bones, way beyond, in the depths of her very soul, and she was scared. She wanted desperately for her bebeji to tell her the lie that metamorphosed into a powerful truth on the wings of faith. It was the lie that questioned her fears, the lie that somehow transformed itself into a truth, the lie that stated it was not possible for Sikh girls to be scared. All Raminder wanted was just one strong shoulder to cry on but her bebeji was not there with her comforting lap or her admonition that 'Sikh girls don't get scared,' to lighten her heavy heart.

One day, during that first spring in their new one-room dwelling, Raminder came face to face with her recent past. While shopping, she and Ratna met the mother of the newborn child, the child born during their march out of Pakistan. It was the mother who had given birth to a baby boy on the bullock cart belonging to them.

Overwhelmed by this chance meeting under gentler circumstances, they hugged each other like old friends. For Raminder, meeting a familiar face in a world of uncertainty was akin to finding a well-trodden path while lost in a jungle.

'It feels like I've met a long lost sister and I don't even know your name!' Raminder gushed, hugging the woman one more time.

'I'm Baljeet and this is my son Baldev, the one you all helped deliver. This is Jagjit bhabi,' she said motioning towards her brother's wife who accompanied her.

After appropriate inquiries about each other's health and family, Baljeet invited them to her house in the nearby village of Garha. 'Why don't all of you come over for Vaisakhi celebrations this weekend? We are having paath'—prayers—'in the morning and a party in the afternoon. The men will join the village bhangra dancers, and we women will do giddha dancing in our backyard,' said Baljeet.

Before Raminder recovered from her happiness at meeting a familiar face, Baljeet added, 'The children will have a good time.'

'Please Ma, let's go,' pleaded Ratna.

'Okay, but we have to check with your papaji first.'

They parted with warm feelings, making tentative plans for the following Sunday.

As soon as they returned home, Ratna flew into the store yelling, 'Dev, Dev, guess who we met in the market today?' Before Dev could guess, she told him about the new baby's mother. 'Remember the war baby? He's turned out so adorable! The mother's name is Baljeet and Ma said we could call her Baljeet auntie . . . and she was dressed up nice like your Uma ma used to. She invited us for Vaisakhi celebrations.'

Turning to Raminder, she asked excitedly, 'Ma, ask papaji if he'll close the store that day and take us.'

'Okay, what is all this about?' asked a smiling Sukhdev, who had overheard part of the conversation.

Out came the whole story, invitation and all.

'You children have been very good. I think a little fun and play can be arranged,' he said.

Ratna and Dev grinned in anticipation.

On Sunday morning, the children bathed and dressed in their best clothes. Sukhdev, wearing his cleanest pair of pants, a good shirt and polished shoes, picked up his favourite bicycle with a rear seat and presented it to the family with a flourish. Ratna positioned herself on the bar in front of Sukhdev's bike as gracefully as an English lady riding sidesaddle. Raminder sat on the back seat with Dev in her lap. Impossible as it seemed, all four of them made the six miles to the village with Sukhdev pedalling the bicycle. Raminder noticed no one gave them a second glance, this being a common sight in those post-Partition days—whole families piled up on the only means of transportation the poor could afford.

Once in Garha, Raminder learned how Baljeet's parents had helped set them up with a small three-room house and about thirty acres of land. Baljeet's parents and her younger brother lived close by, in the same village.

The visit to Baljeet and Harjinder's place turned out to be a great success. After months in close quarters, Raminder watched Ratna and Dev enjoy the wide, open spaces, hitting the seven-stacked tiles with a ball, running, screaming and laughing just for the joy of it. Seeing Baljeet's family surrounded by friends and family was gratifying, reminding the Bajwas of happier times. They talked of nothing else for days.

But, soon after this much discussed visit, Dev started having terrifying nightmares again. Sometimes he woke up screaming, 'No! Don't hurt him. He's my chacha.' At other times, he woke up crying for his aunt, Anu chachi, or for his mother, wailing, 'Ma, wake up! People will leave us behind.' Sometimes he repeated an unfathomable mantra: 'Remember the juice mango. Remember the juice mango.'

One night, Dev seemed especially restless. Raminder woke up Ratna and guided her to Dev's cot, while Sukhdev picked up the sleeping Dev from his cot and carried him to Raminder's pallet. Dev snuggled up to Raminder and together they helped chase away each other's night-time demons.

The next morning, Raminder suggested Sukhdev go downstairs to work, promising to send Dev later. She wanted to talk to Dev, to see if she could find a way to help him with the horrors of his past. However, when Dev woke up, he made it easy for her with an abrupt question, 'Biji, why did Anu chachi not find me?'

'Beta, where was she to look for you?' Raminder asked.

'She could've asked you,' he replied with effortless innocence.

'Your Anu chachi doesn't know me, beta.'

'Ma said Anu chachi will take care of me in Jullunder,' he sobbed. 'I've waited and waited for her to come and . . . and . . . I've been so good. But I guess she doesn't like me any more. Biji, you saw it. I didn't leave my ma behind on purpose. I didn't want to leave her. I didn't!' Dev's wet face twitched with a nervous tic.

'Oh, my poor baby. You didn't do anything wrong.' Raminder hugged him.

'Ma told me to go without her. She did! Ma told me to take care of Ratna. And I try to. I'm not a bad boy. Am I Biji? Why is Anu chachi angry with me?'

"Beta, nobody is angry with you. I'm sure your uncles and aunts love you very much, but they don't know where to look for you. Your papaji and I are proud of you for the way you are handling all this. You must miss them a lot. I am so sorry,' she said, hugging him tight, hoping to cement a bond that seemed to have already taken root.

'I miss my ma. I do. I know she died that day and I will never see her again but I wish she would somehow tell me she is not angry with me.' A brave whimper escaped him.

'Dev, I can tell you this much. Your ma is not angry with you. She still loves you very much and is now your farishta—your guardian angel. You can talk to her whenever you miss her. She will hear you, even though she will not be able to answer you.'

Sudden light shinning in his eyes, Dev whispered, 'My ma made up the mantra to "remember the juice mango". She made it only for me. Yeah . . . that's how I can still be with her.'

Raminder decided not to ask him about the mantra. He would tell her when ready. 'Beta, what did your ma say before she died?'

'She told me to take care of Ratna and go to the Bhardwaj Fabric Store where my father would meet us and take us to Anu chachi's place in Jullunder. She said, "go without me. I want to rest now".'

Suddenly, Dev seemed to remember something and getting up searched his belongings. Raminder and Ratna watched him as he picked up the heavy but tattered, dirty pouch that he often clung to as his security blanket, and brought it to show her.

'Uma bibiji made me promise to help Dev guard that ugly thing,' whispered Ratna.

'Before ma died, she gave me this.' Dev showed Raminder the pouch. 'She told me to give it to Anu chachi. But how am I supposed to give it to her if Anu chachi doesn't even try to find me?' he sobbed. His lips trembling, he extended his hands and said, 'I want you to have this. You are my mother now. You take care of me.' He thrust the tattered cloth sack into Raminder's hands.

Raminder, touched by this simple, sweet child, asked what was inside the pouch and Dev, not knowing, shrugged. The heavy pouch was stitched over with several layers of cloth. Upon removing the stitching, the three of them sat dumbfounded to find pearls, rubies and other priceless jewels inside the pouch.

12
Wonder Years

Summer, 1948

Eight months after they moved into their tiny apartment, Raminder found her world turning mellower. Dev's pouch of jewels had provided them the means to buy twenty-two acres of land in the village of Garha, next to Baljeet and Harjinder's land. Since Sukhdev had the bicycle repair shop to take care of, they had no option but to accept Harjinder's offer to work their land and share the profits fifty-fifty.

This small parcel of land brought Raminder a sense of security. One day she told Dev, 'Beta, with your jewels we've been able to set roots in this foreign land. I think we'll make it here after all, and you made it possible. Thank you.'

Dev beamed.

At the beginning of summer, because of poor ventilation and no fan, their apartment heated up like the inside of a furnace. During the days, Raminder kept the window and the door open to allow air to circulate but at night, the door had to be shut. So, in order to get away from the suffocating heat of their apartment, they started sleeping on cots on their rooftop.

One night Ratna whispered, 'Ma, I feel so safe here. It's like . . . like sleeping on top of the world.'

'It is,' assured Raminder, hugging her.

Every night the children sat cross-legged on Sukhdev's cot, under starlit skies, and he told them bedtime stories of famous maharajas; of Muslim emperors and their Mughal courts; tales from the Arabian Nights; and stories of the Sikh gurus. Raminder shared stories from her own childhood, stories of the people of Punjab, stories about their heritage. The family relaxed and the parents showered unconditional attention on Ratna and Dev. Raminder often noticed that the evenings ignited a peculiar fire in the children's eyes. This ritual seemed to transport them to happy lands of make-believe and, imperceptibly but surely, anchored them to their new lives.

During the day, either one or both the children helped their father in the store. One day, as Ratna and Dev worked in the store, Raminder came downstairs and said, 'I have a surprise for both of you. Come.' She extended her arms to shepherd them upstairs.

Ratna and Dev looked inquiringly at their father who nodded his okay and both followed her up the stairs. A smiling Raminder stopped them at the door and blindfolded them. Taking each child by the hand, she led them indoors and sat them on two chairs, next to a small table. With the blindfolds removed, the children opened eyes that danced with joyful anticipation.

Somehow, Ratna's smile vanished when all she saw on the table were two notebooks, two pencils, two primers—one each in English and Hindi—and a book of numbers.

'Is this the surprise?' Ratna pouted.

'Aren't you happy?' asked Raminder. 'We want both of you to prepare for school.'

'Wow!' breathed Dev. 'Will we go to an English school? Can we go to school in a carriage? Will you or Papaji drop us?'

'Slow down, slow down.' Raminder laughed. 'Yes, you'll go to an English school but not in a carriage. Your Papaji will take you.'

'You know, in my old English school, they prayed in a place called a church. It was not a temple. They had no idols and no bells in the church and everyone sat on wooden benches to pray. No one sat on the ground like we did at our Shahadra temple. In front of the church, where we used to have idols in our temple, they just had one big picture of a mother goddess and her baby, and a sort of a wooden pole. And on the pole was their God, with his arms stretched . . . like . . . like this,' and Dev spread his arms like an eagle. 'They called their god Jesus Christ. He wore a loincloth, just like Mahatma Gandhi does and—'

'What was the name of your school?' interrupted Raminder, hoping to give direction to his babble.

'Aitchison,' he replied, his voice still excited. 'My Baoji got me admitted to that English school in Lahore, and he bought me a big car to take me to school. And . . . and . . . my Sita chachi helped me with my homework. She knew English and she sat with me in our library everyday to help me study. I called her, "shweet chachi" because as a child I lisped. By the time I was old enough to know better, she insisted she loved it. So, she'll always be my "shweet chachi".' Dev rambled on and on without taking a breath.

Raminder laughed and, ruffling his pretty head of hair she glanced at Ratna who still pouted.

Unaware of Ratna's disgruntlement, Dev chuckled. 'You know after my first day in that English school, when my ma greeted me at the haveli, I imitated my Baoji. I stood tall like him and announced in a loud voice, "Ma, I've learnt to speak English!"'

'Did you tell her how much you knew?' asked Raminder in English.

Taken aback, Dev, his lips parted, stared at Raminder, and mumbled, 'I didn't know you knew English.'

Raminder smiled and switched back to their native Punjabi. 'How did you tell your ma how much English you'd learned?'

'I told her I'd learned to say my prayers in English.'

'And did you?'

He chuckled again. 'No. All I remembered was a part of a sentence. "Our father who . . . in heaven—"'

'Was she impressed?' Raminder laughed at his joyful exuberance.

His eyes full of mischief, Dev replied, 'Yes. Since I couldn't remember the rest of the prayer I said, "and then you speak some more English".'

Raminder realised, Dev's Uma Ma would have probably been more upset by the thought that her child was not learning her religion, but a foreign one. She used his enthusiasm to win Ratna over.

Both Raminder and Sukhdev coached the children daily, to prepare them for the entrance exams. Since Ratna had never attended school and Dev had missed school for a whole year, they had to work extra hard. Ratna struggled. Even though her Bapu had taught her Hindi, she needed extensive coaching in English and Math. Since neither Raminder nor Sukhdev knew Hindi—having learned only English and Urdu—Ratna had to tutor Dev in that.

During those hectic days of learning, the children sat on a cot on their rooftop, studying inside the battered, unfinished tin-roofed room. Raminder watched them study hard for hours on end, helping each other read, helping each other be a teacher and a student at the same time.

The pressure of studies made Ratna edgy. She could not understand the knots in her stomach or the anger in her heart. Why could she not hum and sing any more? Even at night, unknown demons haunted her. She woke up, lost and scared, from a recurring nightmare, witnessing fields upon fields littered with dead bodies, the corpses covered in white sheets. When she jolted into wakefulness on such nights, awash in perspiration, she remembered none of the faceless dead. The nightmare made no sense and she slipped back into sleep. By morning, it felt like any other recurring dream, and she put it behind her without discussing it with anyone, focussing only on her studies.

One day, about two months into this feverish preparation for school entrance exams, Raminder walked up to the rooftop, sat on a cot facing the children and asked, 'By what name do you want to be called in school?'

'Huh?' stammered Ratna.

Raminder laughed. 'I mean, when you are asked at the entrance exam in school, "What is your name?" how will you reply?'

'I'll say, "My name is Ratna Bajwa",' replied Ratna.

'I am Dev Anand Bhardwaj,' said Dev, stopping to think out his thoughts. 'Maybe I'll say, "My name is Dev Anand Bajwa".' He offered a compromise.

Raminder looked at them deep and hard. 'You know, your papaji and I are Sikhs and those are not Sikh names.' Stopping to ensure they were following, she continued, 'How about we call you "Ratnagar Kaur Bajwa" and "Devinder Singh Bajwa"?'

Ratna and Dev stared at her, their eyes opened wide, jaws hanging.

'You do know Sikh girls have to have "Kaur", and the boys have to have "Singh" as the middle or last name?' explained Raminder.

'What does Singh mean?' asked Dev.

'It means brave like a lion.'

'What about Kaur?'

'It means a princess.'

'Ma,. I'm not sure about this,' said Ratna. 'My Bapu said Ratna means a jewel. I like that. It means I'm as special as a jewel. My name reminds me of my Bapu. I hate Ratnagar.'

'Do you know what Ratnagar means?'

'No! And I don't care! I still like Ratna.'

'Ratnagar means an "ocean of jewels". In other words, it means, someone who is very special and precious. Anyway, those will be your official names. We will still call you Ratna and Dev for short.'

Ratna thought for a moment. 'Well . . . does that mean we won't be allowed to go to the Hindu temple anymore?'

'No. All it means is that from now on strangers do not need to know you are adopted and not our birth children. We will always love you. Nothing else will change and you can go to the temple whenever you want to.'

'Okay,' said the trusting Dev.

Still not sure, Ratna nodded reluctantly.

'Now we need to figure out your ages and birthdays,' said Raminder. 'Dev, do you know how old you are and the date of your birth?'

'Yes. I turned eight years old this year, before the festival of Vaisakhi. My birthday is on 3 April.'

'Oh! Your birthday passed and you didn't tell us?'

Dev looked at Ratna, who shrugged her shoulders and turned to face Raminder. 'Ma, he did tell me but I assured him his birthdays didn't mean a thing any more. We weren't going to plan a fancy feast or prayers to celebrate his birthday. Anyway, we don't know anyone here, so who could we invite?' Ratna asked. 'And another thing. Now that I'm his sister, either we celebrate both our birthdays or we celebrate neither! Ma, don't you agree?'

'Absolutely. Both of you are equally special and your birthdays are important, but Ratna, even if we can't invite others, we can still celebrate birthdays amongst our own family. Right? And that brings me back to the original question. When is your birthday?'

'I don't know. My Mataji often told me I was about two years older than Dev, so I must be ten years old,' answered Ratna.

Since they had no birth date for Ratna, Raminder picked 24 February 1938, because that date had a special meaning. Raminder hugged Ratna with misty eyes and said, 'I see Aman in you. Hope you don't mind sharing your birthday with a sister?'

'No, Ma. It makes me feel I belong. Thank you.'

Raminder cooked a special meal that evening, and bought them sweets to celebrate their belated birthdays.

Raminder did everything in her power to ensure that the children knew they were very important in the lives and hearts of their adoptive parents. She wanted Ratna and Dev to feel their reality changing for the better, even though the pain of the lost past would still haunt them for a long, long time.

On the much-anticipated day of the entrance examination, Raminder said the ardaas—a Sikh prayer—and Sukhdev took his neatly dressed children to the new school on a bicycle. She and Sukhdev had discussed their options and decided upon this school. St. Jude's High School was an English medium school, run by south Indian missionaries. The school taught both English and Hindi, making the students proficient in both the languages from an early age. Dev did extremely well in the entrance exam but Ratna floundered. The principal admitted Dev to the third grade and reluctantly offered to do the same for Ratna. The place had separate sections for same sex students. So, Dev would join the boys section and Ratna the girls section of the same class.

Raminder, especially pleased about Ratna's admission to the third grade, prepared the children's favourite meal of poori-chole—puffed fried bread with spiced chickpeas—to celebrate the occasion. After supper, she decided to go to the gurdwara to offer thanks, and Sukhdev offered to take Dev and Ratna to the Hindu temple.

The children talked softly to each other, and after what seemed like a quick consultation, Ratna said, 'Ma, both of us would like to go to the gurdwara with you.'

So they all went to the Sikh place of worship together.

On the first day of school, there was no carriage and no horse to take them. Dev sat on the bicycle bar, sidesaddle style in front of Sukhdev, and Ratna sat on the seat behind. But Raminder knew one could not have found a prouder father, taking his well-scrubbed, well-dressed children to an English school.

13
Glimpses of a Rainbow

Summer, 1949

One evening, as Dev helped his father in the workshop, Raminder brought an empty canister and asked Sukhdev to get it refilled with mustard oil for cooking the evening meal. After Sukhdev left, Dev sat on a short stool licking his lower lip, his hands testing a bicycle tire tube in a bucket of water. Finding the exact location of a puncture, he primed the area, applied glue and put on a rubber patch to fix it.

A car screeched to a halt in front of their store. Dev looked up to see a tall, well-dressed, turbaned Sikh man get out of the car and limp towards him. 'How can I help you?'

'Is this Sukhdev's store?'

'Yes. I'm his son.'

The man stared at him for a second. 'Is your mother's name Raminder?'

'Yes. But who are you?'

Ignoring the child's question, he asked, 'Can I speak to either of your parents?'

'I'll go and get my Biji,' replied Dev, and getting up, ran upstairs.

'Biji, there is a sahib who wants to see you.'

'Did the gentleman give his name?' asked Raminder.

'No, but he looks vaguely familiar. He limps when he walks.'

*

Raminder got up from the jute-woven seat of a peerhi stool where she sat chopping onions for the okra she planned to cook. She did not know anyone with a limp. Looking around for a towel to wipe her hands and finding none, she wiped her hands with the corner of her dupatta before walking downstairs.

Dev ran ahead and Ratna followed.

When Raminder saw the gentleman at the foot of the stairs, she gasped and fell against the stair railing. 'Vaheguru. Vaheguru. Simranjeet!'—Oh my God. Oh my God. Simranjeet!—she screamed and flew down the stairs into the arms of her brother. They clung to each other, sobbing, laughing and talking.

When the shock of finding each other passed, Raminder noticed Ratna standing on the last step, her mouth open. 'This is our daughter Ratna,' she said, introducing the girl to Simranjeet. 'You've already met our son Dev.'

Simranjeet limped over to hug the children but his gaze wandered. 'Where is Aman?'

Dev and Ratna held their breath and stared at their mother. Simranjeet looked at the stricken faces and understood. He turned to take his sobbing sister in his arms. The brother and sister stood locked in that loving embrace when Sukhdev walked in.

'Simranjeet!' he cried, and hugged them both.

'Dev Beta, let's close the shop and take him home. He is your mother's brother and both of you may call him mamaji.' He led everyone up the stairs.

After Raminder served dinner and cleaned up, Sukhdev marched her and her brother upstairs to the rooftop to sleep, while he and the children slept in their apartment. This allowed the siblings some privacy. Once on the rooftop, Raminder sat cross-legged on a cot, while Simranjeet sat on the edge of another cot, facing his sister, his back erect, his feet on the brick floor.

They talked long into the warm summer night. Neither of them had any idea about the whereabouts of their parents or Preet, their younger sister.

'You think they survived?' Simranjeet asked.

'I pray and hope so. I worry about Preet. She is so young and pretty. After what happened to my Aman, I fear for her. Vaheguru raakha.' God is our guardian.

'I've searched for them everywhere, in the refugee camps and gurdwaras of Ferozpur, Amritsar and Jullunder, but have found no leads anywhere.'

Raminder shuddered, reliving the sights she had witnessed during their flight to safety. One recurring image haunted her. She remembered seeing a young girl, bleeding and holding her bloodstained shirt where her breasts should have been. She was doubled over with pain while her elderly grandmother stood wailing, imploring those who passed by for help. Having lost much blood, the girl did not have enough strength left to join their caravan. Raminder recalled how all she could do was share one parantha and a little water with them—providing food for the body when she knew sustenance was needed for the spirit. In an effort to shake that horrible image away, she looked Simranjeet in the eye. 'How are Simi and Manu bhabi?'

'With *Vaheguru di meher*,'—with God's grace—'my family's safe.'

'How did you find me?' she asked next.

'It took me a couple of months to be united with my family and then as soon as I could, I started visiting the refugee camps in Amritsar and Jullunder in hopes of finding you or our parents. Last· week, at Manu's suggestion, I spent the whole day at the Ambala post office, going through every list of refugees they had, but found nothing. While I was there, a postman suggested I go through the tons of undeliverable mail scheduled for destruction. Hundreds of people were doing that, in a huge warehouse at the back of the post office. Seeing no harm, I too started going through it and miraculously found your undeliverable letter that had the wrong address of my in-laws.'

Raminder remembered that other lonely day on their rooftop, when she had longed for her mother's comfort. Now she had her brother's. Through poignant grief, bearable only because he was there,·Raminder told him how Aman died and how they came to find the two orphan children.

'How come Dev does not wear a turban?' he asked.

'Because he had Hindu parents. When the children grow up, they will decide what religion they want to follow.'

'Do you know who their parents were? Are they related by birth?'

'No, they are not. He is the only heir to some very rich and powerful family from a village near Lahore. His father's name was Umesh Bhardwaj I believe, and his mother was called Uma. Ratna on the other hand, is the daughter of their punditji who took care of the family temple.'

'Did you say Umesh? Was it *the* Umesh Bhardwaj from the village Shahadra?'

'Uh huh. Did you know him?'

'Yes. I was their family doctor. Come to think of it, Umesh came to see me a day or two before Partition. He was running a high fever and I gave him medication and advised complete rest. Oh, my God! So that's why Dev looks so familiar,' he said. 'And, I believe I even treated the punditji's daughter at Uma behenji's request, when the child was just a toddler. I can't believe this.' Raising his hands and looking up, he added, '*Rabb de rung!*'—God's magnificence!

Raminder noticed that Simranjeet called Dev's mother 'Uma behenji', giving Uma the same respect that he gave her, by addressing her as an elder sister.

Simranjeet shook his head. 'It's so hard to see you and Dev in such an impoverished state.' Then, as if remembering something, he looked at her and said, 'Dev comes from a very large family who will sooner or later claim him. Behenji, please don't get too attached to him or you'll be hurt again.'

Raminder dismissed her brother's misgivings. She felt she had earned the right of a mother to love and be loved by the child. 'Dev lost his parents and grandfather during Partition. When we found him, he sat caressing his dead mother's face, her head in his lap. We are not sure about the whereabouts of the rest of his relatives. Anyway, we love him very much and he's our son now.'

Changing the subject, she bombarded him with questions. 'I gathered from your last letter before Partition, that Manu bhabi and Simi were already on this side of the border with bhabi's parents. But how did you survive? When did you leave Lahore and how did you cross the border?'

'It's a long story. Even though Manu and Simi had left for Ambala, I was still on Muslim soil. I decided to rough it till things calmed down and the family could return.'

'Then why did you leave?'

'Because Rashid, my Muslim servant, did not think it a good idea to keep my medical practice open in those troubled times. Gangs of rioters from different parts of the city prowled the streets, killing, robbing and looting Sikh and Hindu businesses. No one could stop them. A day after Partition, the killings and looting got so bad that Rashid insisted I leave temporarily, for safety's sake. He somehow managed to get me to the station and helped me board a train to Amritsar.'

Raminder started rocking her body back and forth, in agitation. 'Vaheguru! Vaheguru! I believe the Muslims butchered everyone on board the trains that arrived in India carrying only corpses. How did you manage to escape?'

'I didn't know any better. I just concentrated on surviving.' Simranjeet reached over to put a calming hand on her shoulder. Once Raminder recovered, he continued, 'When Rashid and I reached the station, the locomotive bulged with hundreds of people on the roof of the carriage and many hung out the open doors. I somehow managed to squeeze in but before we left the station, an angry mob of Muslims, carrying hatchets, swords and lathis, attacked us. I heard blood-curdling screams and before I grasped the situation, someone pierced my shoulder with a sword. I tripped and fell, hitting my head on the metal door.

'I must have passed out because I have no remembrance of the butchering. When I came around, I was too paralysed with fear to move. And the train moved slowly, very slowly. I lay under a heap of dismembered, lifeless bodies, but did not move because I realised the only way I'd live to see another day was to act dead.'

'Bebeji always said you were a survivor.' Her voice quivered with the shock of visualising Simranjeet lying with the dead.

He stood up to hug his sister. Once she calmed down, he returned to his cot and continued, 'Not only did the train move slowly, but every so often it stopped. When it did, angry mobs peered in and shouted, "Allah-u-Akbar!" Then after what seemed like an eternity, it careened forward, jolting from side to side as it gathered speed. Loaded with dead bodies, it suddenly raced, as if on an unending slide downhill, with no one at its controls. It took a long time before I summoned courage to rise from under the shroud of dead bodies. When I looked out, I saw turbaned Sikh men in fields along the side of railroad tracks. They stood open mouthed, staring at the carnage. Thinking we had either passed Amritsar or were close, I jumped out of the fast moving train but have no remembrance of where I landed. I woke up the next morning to find myself lying on a cot with clean sheets, in a refugee shelter.'

'Is that how you hurt your leg?'

'Yes. I broke it during the jump. My shoulder had been securely wrapped but my leg needed a cast. A doctor was summoned from Amritsar. He arrived on a bicycle, carrying rudimentary supplies. Without the necessary equipment, he did the best he could. I'm glad I can still walk without crutches. The shelter turned out to be a temporary camp for ailing refugees.'

'Was it a government sponsored refugee camp?'

'No. The caretaker, the bhaiji, at a nearby gurdwara had organised this shelter and he fed everyone from the free gurdwara langar. We were near the village of Attari, where the landlords had pooled their resources to help the sick and the wounded. Their help ensured a supply of rudimentary medicines procured from Amritsar. As the only doctor in that makeshift facility, my word carried weight. Upon my insistence, the volunteers started boiling all drinking water, and that along with a few basic medicines, controlled the cholera and typhoid which ran rampant among the refugees.'

'How long did you stay in the camp?'

'About a month in the shelter and another month in the gurdwara. When I had enough strength to travel, I borrowed a little money from the bhaiji and reached Ambala.'

Raminder wiped her face with her dupatta and asked, 'Will your leg get better?'

'My leg is better. I think what you want to know is, will I walk with a limp all my life? Yes, I'm afraid so.'

'Have you started practicing medicine again?'
'Not yet, but now I will.' He smiled.

Simranjeet left the next morning, returning within a couple of hours, his car loaded with a pedestal fan, a sewing machine, groceries, fruits and clothes for the family, toys and storybooks for the children.

Ratna struggled during the first difficult months of schooling while Dev took to his schoolwork like willow roots to water. Were it not for her mother's loving encouragement and her brother's unconditional support, Ratna might have given up.

Dev, on the other hand, excelled in his studies and by the end of his first year in the new school, he received a double-promotion, skipping the fourth class and graduating to the fifth. Ratna, surprised and troubled at being left behind, wondered how Dev could embarrass her so. She vowed on her bapu's soul that she would catch up with the rich man's son and prove she was as good as him. She would not let her bapu down; after all, she was his jewel.

So, she studied day and night.

Raminder sometimes found her sitting in their tiny bathroom after dark, reading her schoolbooks in the dim light. 'Beti, you will ruin your eyes if you do not slow down. What is this new passion with books?' she asked one day.

Ratna shifted her chair, turning her back towards her.

Raminder ignored Ratna's unspoken rudeness. 'We do not think any less of you because Dev is ahead in school. You are both very bright. He is ahead, not because he is brighter but because he has had more schooling than you.'

'Leave me alone!'

Before the end of the second school year, Ratna caught up with her brother and fulfilled her promise to her bapu. Once she received the double-promotion, she somehow felt grateful to Dev for setting a higher standard. Proud of herself for having risen to the challenge, she realised that Dev had a big part in her success. All through the prior year, whenever she needed it, he helped her in English, Math and Sciences. But because of her own insecurities, she had cut him off.

Once in the same class as Dev, Ratna relaxed and chose to become a better sister. To make up for her insensitivity, she tried writing a note of apology but, after several unsuccessful attempts, she decided to write a note of thanks instead. She wrote her first unseasoned thoughts—a poem in English—on a crumpled piece of paper. Dev read and giggled over the silly mush:

> I have a brother
> And I want no other
> He loves me and protects me
> He comforts me and helps me
> I sometimes ignore him but
> He forgives me
> He knows the secret to my heart
> Is to love me
> Thank you God for giving me a brother
> A brother who really really loves me.

Thus, Ratna made peace with her brother, but more than that, she made peace with herself.

One day, about a month into the new school year, Dev asked her to join him at their rooftop hideout. He said he needed to discuss a problem with her, in private. 'Ratna, do you know Raghu, my closest friend?'

Ratna nodded.

'Well, today at school he said, "Dev, how come your father wears a turban and you don't?" I didn't know what to say, so I just shrugged and walked away.'

They had never discussed this issue, as the question of their religion had never come up. Ratna explained, 'You don't wear it because you are a Hindu. You are a Brahmin by birth.'

'But our papaji and biji are Sikhs.'

Ratna stared at Dev, the truth hitting her—of course, papaji and ma were their only reality now. 'Maybe we should talk to them.'

They both went down the stairs to the apartment and asked to talk to their parents. Raminder walked in from the kitchen with a tray, carrying hot tea for herself and her husband, and cookies and milk for both the children. Setting the tray on the table she passed them milk and cookies and poured tea into the two cups. Picking up her cup she asked, 'Dev, what do you want to talk about?'

'When can I start wearing a turban like papaji?' said Dev, coming straight to the point.

Raminder's hands trembled, spilling the chai. Taken aback, even Sukhdev put his teacup back on the saucer. 'Beta, we didn't know you wanted to become a Sikh. Have you thought it through and discussed it with your sister?' asked Raminder.

'Yes, I have.'

'Even so,' said Raminder, 'honouring the tenets of Sikhism is a difficult commitment to keep and you are still too young to decide. Why don't you wait a few more years before—'

'You know your parents were Brahmin Hindus,' Sukhdev interrupted, 'and you might want to follow their beliefs. Give yourself a chance to grow up before making an irrevocable commitment.'

'But now, our parents are Sikhs,' said Ratna, smiling, 'and we have decided we want to grow up Sikhs, just like you.'

'But—' started Raminder.

'Ma, my mataji's only brother was a Sikh,' said Ratna.

'But I thought your father was a Hindu Brahmin? Was he not the punditji at the temple?' asked Sukhdev, surprised.

'Yes, my father was a Hindu and my mother was the oldest child in a Hindu Brahmin family. However, my mataji's mother, my nanima, gave birth to four sons, who either died at birth or in their infancy. She prayed to her gods and promised if she ever got blessed with a healthy male child, she would bring him up as a Sikh—strong, brave and god-fearing. So, when my uncle was born healthy, she kept her promise and brought him up as a Sikh.'

'Wow! I didn't know that,' said Dev.

Ratna smiled and turning towards her parents said, 'My mataji said Sikhs do not pray in front of idols nor do they believe in various deities like Hindus do. They believe in only one God. Is that true?'

When Raminder and Sukhdev nodded, she continued, 'I believe my nanima also prayed regularly from *Guru Granth Sahib*—isn't that the spiritual guide of Sikhs?'

Raminder and Sukhdev nodded again.

'Do you know where your uncle lived?' asked Raminder.

'I'm not sure. All I remember is after he got married, they moved to some place called Lyallpur. The last time we met his family, I was about six. His name was Mannat Singh.'

'Biji, you look so surprised,' said Dev. 'Don't be. Ratna and I have talked and decided that we want to share not just your love but also your faith.'

'Beta, let's wait until your summer vacation. You may grow your hair at that time, unless you change your mind by then. In the meantime, I will try to educate both of you about your new religion.'

Towards the end of their summer vacation, Ratna, pleased that Dev's curly hair had grown enough to be tied into a small knot on his head, explained the ceremony to Dev. Her mataji had taught her how, in traditional Sikh families, it was customary for a maternal uncle to tie the first turban on a nephew. So, when Simranjeet came for the turban tying ceremony and brought his wife Manu and daughter Simi, Dev felt important and loved.

They celebrated the *dastaar bandi*, the turban tying ceremony, a couple of weeks before the schools reopened. Besides Simranjeet's family, Baljeet and Harjinder's extended family, and Dev's friend Raghu and his father came from the village of Garha.

When Raghu arrived accompanied only by his father, Ratna asked like a little hostess, 'Where is your mataji? You should have brought her with you.'

'I don't have a mother. She died in an accident when I was eight,' he mumbled.

'So, who takes care of you?' asked Dev with deep concern.

'My buaji does. She's my father's younger sister.'

'You should have brought her with you,' insisted Dev.

'It's a little hard to fit a father, son, an aunt and her twins, all on one motorbike.' Raghu laughed. He sounded very proud of his father's old Harley Davidson, a status symbol in their village.

The prayers and the ceremony went well.

'Ratna,' Dev said after the ceremony, 'I think we two are now officially part of our new family. We are real Bajwas now!'

Over the next few years, Ratna realised Dev seemed to have come to terms with his past. He spoke lovingly about his early childhood in that fairyland village of Shahadra, Pakistan. He talked with great love for his Uma ma, his grandfather, his aunts—Anu chachi, Sita chachi—and all the other angels who were once an integral part of his everyday life. 'I'm finally at peace. Even my nightmares occur less and less often,' he told her, but Ratna noticed he never called Raminder 'ma', and she knew, Raminder would always be his 'biji' and Uma, his 'ma'.

Ratna smiled remembering she too was no longer the lost little girl with a smart mouth, whom Raminder and Sukhdev adopted when nine years old. Over the years, without even trying, the sauciness and sarcasm had slipped from her personality like used clothing. Both Raminder and Sukhdev provided strong shoulders to lean on and Ratna marvelled how with their support, this unconventional family dared to weave an invisible shield of love and hope and dreams around each other.

14
Where the Sun Shines

July 1954

Raminder's scrimping and saving, and Sukhdev's sharp business acumen paid off. Within seven short years after Partition, their tiny bicycle shop blossomed into a small but lucrative bicycle factory, employing twenty workers. By the time Ratna and Dev graduated to the ninth class, the hard work put in by their parents made them more secure financially. The children now rode individual bikes to school, and no longer needed to depend on their father for transport.

And, Raminder started dreaming of a house on their land in Garha.

As soon as the schools closed for summer vacation, Raminder and Sukhdev took Dev and Ratna to the village, to decide upon the location of their future home. They planned to start small, with a three-room house, a bathroom with a toilet and running water, a water-well and a kitchen, with the intention of adding to the house, when they could.

Ratna whispered to Raminder behind her brother's back, 'I think Dev would like it if our new house and backyard are enclosed within a tall brick wall—like a haveli.'

'Beti, times have changed. Partition and the separation from Muslim culture has taken away the necessity of home privacy for women,' replied Raminder.

'Ma, I'm not suggesting we build a haveli for him. I'm saying it might help anchor Dev, by reminding him of his old village of Shahadra.'

Raminder stared at Ratna, shaking her head.

'What?' Ratna asked.

'Nothing . . . it's serious talk coming from a sixteen-year-old.' Raminder laughed and moved to hug Ratna. 'Anything to ease old wounds is acceptable,' she said.

So, she and Sukhdev decided to enclose an acre of rectangular land within a brick wall. Raminder proposed they start the house on the smaller side of the enclosed rectangle and when more funds became available, add more rooms. She and Sukhdev discussed their options and decided it would be a two-storied house, with a water tank on raised pillars, to ensure running water. By pulling water from a well with a generator-operated pump, the tank would be filled.

Raminder asked to leave more than half the brick-fenced property for a lawn, fruit trees, flowers and a small herb garden. Sukhdev agreed but suggested they build a wide brick courtyard next to an existing old neem tree, between the yard and the main house.

Raminder loved having a full-grown neem tree on her property, not only because she could hang a swing on its sturdy branches but also because of the medicinal properties the tree leaves and its branches provided. Until now they had to buy neem twigs, as she had always insisted her family use them as toothbrushes, by masticating them and releasing the medicinal goodness for tooth and gum health. Before leaving that first day, the family cut small branches from the tree for brushing their teeth.

With the site for their new home selected, Sukhdev and Raminder hired a contractor to do the work. They asked that the brick enclosure be built first. Under Sukhdev and Dev's watchful eyes the haveli started taking shape. Foundations for the living quarters were laid on the smaller side of the rectangle. In the corner adjoining the three rooms, they dug a well, close to a tall juice mango tree. Raminder proposed they replace it with a good quality hybrid mango, but both Dev and Ratna objected. Juice mangoes carried too many fond memories for them. So the old tree stayed.

The monsoons slowed the work to some extent. As soon as the schools reopened, Raminder took Dev's place and started alternating with Sukhdev for supervisory duties. Foundations for a spacious kitchen, an eating area and a kitchen pantry were laid, and the building of rooms was started before the end of the year. Between the newly dug well and the future kitchen stood the only opening to the house. Their new neighbours, Baljeet and Harjinder, helped them find a shop for made-to-order carved wooden doors, that they wanted to use at the entrance to the house.

The idea of building the kitchen adjoining the house did not even occur to them. After all, in every proper house they knew, the kitchens were always detached from the main building. Eventually, they hoped to add a verandah, a dining room, a drawing room and a library on the ground floor, with more bedrooms and attached bathrooms on the upper floor.

Before the children entered their senior year of school called 'matriculation'—the tenth class—the initial phase of the house was complete, with three livable rooms, a verandah and a paved patio leading to the garden. The Bajwas sold their one-roomed apartment and moved to their new place.

A little over seven years after Partition, they finally arrived home.

The weekend after they moved in, they had house-warming celebrations, with prayers followed by langar, the community sharing of a meal together. The few families they knew in the new village were all invited. Simranjeet and his family drove from Amritsar to join the celebrations in Garha.

It turned out to be a cool sunny day. Even the sky seemed laundered extra clean in the purest of blue for the occasion. The prayers started in the morning, and women dressed in colourful salwaar kameezes came with their heads covered in dupattas. Most of the boys and men wore turbans except Dev's Hindu friend Raghu and his father. Those two were provided with large handkerchiefs to cover their heads, to show respect in the presence of *Guru Granth Sahib*.

The prayers were held on the patio, under the shade of the huge neem tree. Ratna and Raminder prepared the langar food for the congregation. With their heads covered, the mother and daughter worked in the kitchen listening to the prayers in silence. Baljeet came in early to help them make the bread dough and to roll fresh chapattis. They had just finished their first batch of chapattis when a woman walked into the kitchen humming.

'I'm Raghu's aunt,' she said. 'I'd like to help.'

After greetings, Raminder made room for her to sit and help. Ratna looked up and her jaw dropped. Getting up abruptly, she ran out screaming, 'Dev! Dev!'

Raminder ran after her. 'Ratna hush,' she whispered crossly. 'The ardaas has not been performed as yet. You better sit down and pay attention, young lady,' she hissed, pulling Ratna down with her, to sit for the prayers.

'But—' started Ratna.

'No buts. You are smart enough to know that until the ardaas is performed, you must not create any disruption. Sit quietly for the prayers to end,' whispered Raminder sternly.

Ratna sat down, her eyes seeking Dev, her mind not on the prayers but on the turmoil in her heart. After the ardaas, Dev came over to see what had caused the commotion and the altercation between mother and daughter. Raminder looked at them and saw a peculiar look in Ratna's eyes. She instantly understood that her child had something weighty to share. Ratna, speechless in her confusion, grabbed Dev and dragged him to the kitchen. Raminder followed. When they reached the kitchen, Ratna pointed to Raghu's aunt and said, 'Look!'

Dev stood with his mouth open, gaping at the woman. Upon seeing the two teenagers pointing to her, the unsuspecting woman stopped her humming and looked at them.

'Anu chachi,' stammered Dev, 'Is that you?'

'Yes . . . I am Anu, but I don't understand—'

'Dev,' he interrupted, and ran to cling to her.

'Oh! My God! Is that you Dev beta? Is it my Dev?' said Anu, her eyes wide. Raminder watched Dev cling to Anu as if to a life support, while Ratna, her upper teeth on her curled lower lip, played with the corner of her dupatta.

Raminder led Anu and the two children to her bedroom to cry, to talk and maybe to heal. But she shivered involuntarily, fearful of losing her beloved child to his aunt. Her brother Simranjeet had warned her about this a long time ago. Taking a couple of deep breaths, she prayed to Vaheguru for strength, reminding herself that it was she who had nurtured the lost child into a wholesome being. No law could prove Dev was not her son. They were refugees and only Dev could decide which family he wanted. In a flash of inner composure, Raminder knew. She somehow understood in the warmest part of her being that Dev would choose her. She was his mother.

Raminder sat quietly while the children and Anu talked. Dev described their last day in the haveli and the loss of all their loved ones, asking Anu, 'How come you didn't look for me? Why didn't you even try to find me?'

'Oh, my dear child, we did,' she cried, hugging him. 'Every morning for more than a month after Partition, your Amar chacha went to the refugee-camps looking for all of you. Sometimes I went with him and we'd spend hours and hours walking, searching and looking. We spent most of the time at the Bhargava Camp on the Jullunder/Nakodar road. But every now and then, we also went to the smaller refugee camps in the area. We knew if you all made it safely across the border, you would come to Garha or at least Jullunder, as per our plan.'

She stopped to take a sip from the glass of water Raminder offered and continued, 'It was the second month after Partition when your Amar chacha got sick with typhoid. The doctor said it was because he spent too much time in those disease-ridden refugee camps, drinking polluted water from the hand pumps, which drew water from the sub-soil overloaded with the monsoon rains and the filth of camps—'

Baljeet interrupted by knocking on the door, bringing them langar food. 'I'm sorry,' said Raminder, 'for leaving you by yourself to serve langar.'

'Don't worry. I asked my sister-in-law and mother to help,' replied Baljeet.

Ratna went out, returning with glasses filled with water for everyone. Anu picked at her food while continuing with her story. 'In a strange way we found ourselves happy and sad at the same time. Partition and the ensuing loss tortured us on the one hand and on the other, we learned our prayers had been answered and we were finally about to become parents. Sorry, I digress. Anyway, taking care of my sick husband and my sister-in-law, who also was very ill, took all my strength. Going through a difficult pregnancy and taking care of two sick patients, I had no energy left to go looking for you by myself. My brother, Sanjay bhaiya, knew your parents well, so he started searching for all of you but without any luck,' she stopped, choking with emotion. 'Your Amar chacha passed away in November of that year. He never even saw his own twins.'

Raminder instinctively got up to hug her. 'Behenji, I'm so sorry. I wish we had met you at the refugee camps. Ratna and I visited the camps often, first to get our ration cards and later to procure the necessities, but Dev never accompanied us. He often asked for you but we didn't know how or where to look for you.'

Noticing her distraught son, Raminder moved to comfort Dev while Anu's tears flowed unchecked. Raminder's suggestion to take a deep breath, helped calm the boy. Something still bothered her though. Turning to Anu she questioned, 'I wonder why your Sanjay bhaiya never recognised Dev. Raghu and Dev have been friends for years.'

Anu pressed her lips, and raising her eyebrows, shrugged, not understanding it either.

'Probably because he never met me until the day I had my turban tying ceremony. He couldn't recognise me with a turban,' said Dev.

'How about you? Didn't you recognise him?' Raminder asked.

'No. I never paid much attention. Sanjay uncle did look a little familiar the few times I met him, but he lived in Garha, and ma had drilled into me that Anu chachi lived in Jullunder. It didn't occur to me Garha was in Jullunder,' Dev answered.

A soft sigh escaped her and turning to Anu, Raminder asked, 'How old are your twins now?'

'They turned seven this spring. Sanjeev is the spitting image of his father. It seems Taara favours me. She is short and plump.'

Smiling indulgently, Anu called the twins to introduce them to their new relatives. While the children made friends with each other, Raminder ventured to ask her about Iqbal.

'He is a family friend,' replied Anu. 'Even though he's a Muslim, our Baoji treated him like his fourth son. In fact, towards the end of August 1947, my brother-in-law Gaurav came to see us. He had Iqbal bhaiya with him to help him cross the border to Pakistan. Gaurav also picked up some jewellery his wife Sita had left in my safe-keeping.' She stopped and after a few moments added, 'I have some things Uma bhabi left for Dev. Please come over tomorrow and take what belongs to him.'

Raminder nodded, relieved that Anu had no intentions of claiming her precious Dev. Seeing the children walk out of the room, she whispered, 'I believe, your family friend, Iqbal, was butchered at the Amritsar railway station. Dev witnessed the gruesome act.'

'Hai Ram!' Anu shuddered with a sudden sigh. Her voice breaking, she said, 'I hope Gaurav is okay. We never heard from him or Sita again. I often wonder what happened to them. They do not even know my husband passed away. And they don't know about my twins either. I hope they are safe. Sita was pregnant when they left Shahadra for Delhi prior to Partition.'

Raminder wrapped her arms around herself and shivered, feeling her own poorly-put-together-dam of healing burst. She sensed even Anu, with her shattered life, begged for a friend. They talked, attempting to comfort, instinctively addressing each other as Behenji, as per an expected Punjabi mode of address. Since neither had the right words to soothe, each provided a shoulder to the other to cry on.

That night, Dev thanked Raminder and Sukhdev for bringing him to Garha. 'If we had built a house near our bicycle shop in Jullunder, we would never have found my Anu chachi.'

'Beta, your jewels made all this possible,' said Sukhdev, bending down to kiss his son goodnight.

'Your Uma ma's farishta guided us to your beloved Anu chachi,' Raminder added. Dev, a serene smile on his lips, closed his eyes and rolled over.

The next morning, Raminder and the children visited Anu, who lived with her brother, Sanjay, in a house very close to their new home. Sanjay's house was a sprawling one-storey structure with about fourteen or fifteen rooms, built single file around the three sides of a brick patio. Beyond the patio, a well-tended garden, alive with flowers and fruit trees, bustled with butterflies, fragrant jasmine and multihued roses in bloom. At the entrance to the house stood the servants' quarters and a huge garage, which housed the Harley Davidson and Anu's black Austin.

Raminder looked around. On one side of the garden grew a pomegranate tree and on the other side thrived two mango trees laden with unripe fruit, their boughs bending with the weight. A verandah circled two sides of the house where bougainvillea vines wound around the verandah's majestic pillars. Dev whispered, 'Those vibrant bougainvilleas remind me of my haveli in Shahadra.' Raminder saw Ratna squeeze his hand.

With the greetings over, Anu brought out a tray of sweets and steaming tea. Dev, Anu's nephew Raghu, and the twins went out to play while Ratna and the two women sat sipping chai, talking of days gone by.

Once their cups ran cold, the hot tea long finished, Anu went to her room and returned with a bag Uma had given her long years ago, for safekeeping. She offered it to Raminder saying, 'This is Uma bhabi's *amaanat*,'—a gift left in safekeeping—'for Dev.'

The bag contained five thousand rupees, two ruby bracelets, twelve gold bangles and a heavy gold chain with a ruby pendent.

15
One of Us

Summer, 1955

That first year in their new haveli, Ratna luxuriated in her surroundings, enjoying the peace and security of their new home. One Sunday morning, Anu and her eight-year-old daughter, Taara, paid a surprise visit. Raminder sat cross-legged on a cot covered with a bedspread, knitting a sweater for Sukhdev, while Ratna dragged her feet sitting on a swing hanging from the neem tree next to the patio. Taara looked around for Ratna, and seeing her exclaimed, 'Didi, didi, look at my new doll and her beautiful sari!'

Ratna liked to be called didi by Taara, as it reminded her of her Hindu roots. 'What's her name?' Ratna asked, and getting off the swing, she bent over to reach the child's eye level.

'Geetu.'

'You think Geetu would like to sit on the swing?'

'Yes. But she wants to sit in my lap and, I want to sit in yours.'

Ratna smiled and sitting back on the swing, she lifted Taara and her doll onto her lap.

'Ratna Didi, mummy says Dev bhaiya is our cousin. You are his sister, so you must be our cousin too,' said Taara, nodding, as if pleased with herself for grasping such a weighty truth.

Ratna laughed, giving Taara a warm squeeze.

'I love you, Didi,' giggled Taara, snuggling up to Ratna.

'I love you too, Pisti.'

'Didi, when you know my name is Taara, why do you call me Pisti?'

'Because you are one!' Ratna laughed. 'You are tiny and precious like a pistachio. A long time ago, I knew someone just like you. I called her my Pisti.'

'Who was she?'

'She was my chhoti behen, my little sister.'

'But you don't have a chhoti behen,' Taara replied, with sparkling eyes and a puzzled expression.

'I did, but I lost her.'

'How come your ma and papaji didn't look for her?'

'They didn't know my little sister. I lost my other parents, so nobody could look—'

'You could have. . .' started Taara, before her train of thought switched tracks. 'How come you have other parents? Where are they?' she asked.

Ratna shuddered. 'They died during Partition.'

'Oh. I lost my father during Partition too. I never met him.' Taara stated the fact with no emotions involved.

Ratna sighed. Was it a blessing Taara had no emotions invested in her father? Would losing her own bapu have been easier if she had never known or loved him? Who was the luckier—the one who never experienced a father's love or someone like her who experienced it twice, once with her bapu and now with her papaji?

Pointing to Raminder, Taara asked, 'If you had other parents, how come you call her ma?'

'Because she and papaji adopted Dev and me.'

'What does "adopted" mean?'

'Adopted means to include someone in your family because of love born from here.' Ratna placed her hand on Taara's heart.

'Oh, I understand. You mean, like Sanjay and I grew in mummy's tummy, you and Dev bhaiya grew in your ma's heart?'

'Something like that,' said Ratna, smiling at Taara's uncomplicated logic.

'And can you choose your little sisters too?'

'Yes. That's why I chose you.' Ratna smiled, tickling the giggling child in her lap.

'I choose you too.' Taara chuckled and, making a quick turn, kissed Ratna on her cheek. 'Didi, did your other father wear a turban like your papaji?' she asked.

'No.'

'How come?'

'Because he was a Hindu and papaji is a Sikh.'

'So I can adopt Geetu even though me and my mummy both wear salwaar kameez and Geetu wears a sari?'

'Yes, if you love her enough,' said Ratna laughing.

Anu, humming a happy tune, walked over to the swing and asked Ratna, 'Is she bothering you with her incessant questions? Really, she is such an inquisitive child!' Ratna smiled. Bending to face Taara, Anu said, 'Taara, run over to Baljeet auntie's house and see if you can play with Baldev and your brother. Ratna didi needs to spend some time with us.'

Baldev, the 'war baby'—as Ratna and Dev called him—was six months older than the twins. All three studied in the same class and went to the same school in a shared rickshaw.

After Taara jumped off Ratna's lap to go play with her brother Sanjeev and his friend Baldev, Ratna walked over to join the two women.

'Ratna, your ma wants me to take you to Jullunder tomorrow, to my cousin's music store to buy you a sitar,' said Anu.

'Really, Ma?' shrieked an excited Ratna, and fell into her mother's arms.

'Beti, you've never asked us for anything but we know how crazy you are about music. Your papaji and I often see you drumming your fingers on the bench under that mango tree. We hear no music but by watching you drum, we sense a tune in your head.'

'Thank you. Thank you, Ma. I'll try my best to make you proud.'

'We know you will.' Raminder hugged her tight. 'Since we don't know the first thing about musical instruments, your Anu chachi's cousin will help you pick up a good piece. Your papaji has already arranged for a sitar teacher. You'll be starting your music lessons this coming Wednesday . . . in the evening from five to six.'

Dev appeared for his final university matriculation exams at fifteen, his friend—Anu's nephew—Raghu, at sixteen. One lazy summer day after their examinations, they both stood near the village pond skipping stones on water, out of sheer boredom. Black water buffaloes lay in peace, chewing their cud in the shallow and murky water of the pond. Flies buzzed around scattered dunghills. A few ducks swam among the reeds on the far side of the pond, and the boys had nothing better to do than aim their stones at the frolicking ducks.

Pointing to blackened rubble in the distance, Dev said, 'Look, Raghu, there's Pintoo and Pappu near the ruins. Let's join them for a game of kabaddi.'

'I can't,' answered Raghu, holding another stone flat before sending it skimming across the pond.

'Why not?'

'Because I hate that place. It . . . it belonged to my uncle before it burned down. My mataji died from the burns she received when that haveli caught fire,' blurted Raghu, sliding to the ground, looking tired and defeated.

'Really?' stammered Dev, aware he had touched a sizzling, live wire of painful memories, and now had no idea how to deal with it. 'I thought your mataji died in an accident,' he murmured, squatting on his haunches next to Raghu.

'My Baoji said it was an accident. Nobody meant to kill her.'

'What happened?' Dev ventured, rubbing one side of his face with his hand, where it had started twitching.

'My Baoji had a joint business with my Khan uncle.' Raghu broke down. 'When riots broke out in the summer of 1947, we hid our Muslim friends in our house. Khan uncle, his wife and their two daughters, Naaz and Nadia, stayed in hiding with us for over two months. By the time we realised things were not going to get better, it was already too late. The arrangement had worked fine until Partition, but it soon became perilous, as violence against Muslims became intense.'

'Why did the Khans not leave India?' asked Dev.

'How could they? If caught, they would have been killed on the spot. We could have helped take them to the Jullunder railway station, but no one would guarantee their safety at the Amritsar station, where all Muslims were massacred, their bodies dumped in the train for Lahore.'

Raghu's narrative had an unsettling effect on Dev, who slipped to the ground, looking pale and spent. He remembered the Amritsar station the day his Muslim uncle, Iqbal chacha was slaughtered. A shudder shot through his body.

He remembered another scene he and Ratna had witnessed on their first train journey when the train made an unscheduled stop near a small village. A mob of Sikh and Hindu teenagers, armed with spears and swords, chased a nine or ten-year-old Muslim boy dressed in white salwaar kurta and a crocheted topee—the traditional Muslim skullcap. The teenagers caught up with the child, severed his head, and spearing it, danced with the bloodied, dripping head!

Dev threw up his guts while Ratna screamed herself hoarse. They cried, screamed and retched long after their train started moving. Their new mother Raminder held both of them close to her, mumbling, 'Sat Naam, Sat Naam, Sat Namji. Vaheguru, Vaheguru, Vaheguruji.' God is the truth. God is merciful.

Remembering that spurt of blood from the Muslim child's neck made Dev sick to his stomach, again. He was glad when Raghu continued. 'By middle of September, Baoji arranged a passage for the Khans to reach Pakistan. He took them in a truck to a pre-arranged spot. From there, they were to be smuggled into Pakistan. It was a risky scheme. We knew my Baoji and the Khans could be ambushed by a mob.

'While Baoji was away, someone leaked a rumour that the Khans were still alive and in the village. One night, a mob from a neighbouring village, sprinkled kerosene on the Khan haveli and lit it. A handful of neighbours and servants ran with buckets of water to put the fire out. My mataji was among the helpers.'

'How come they didn't call the fire brigade?' asked an incredulous Dev.

'It was still too soon after Partition. There were no fire-brigades, no telephones, no running water and no real police one could depend upon,' exclaimed Raghu, tears streaming down his face. 'Mataji helped by pulling water from the well, one bucket at a time, but the helpers were too few and resources not enough to stop the blaze. The fire raged out of control and my mataji got caught in it. Friends and neighbours brought her back on a cot, charred and unconscious, while the Khan haveli burned to ashes that night.'

'Why didn't Anu chachi and Amar chacha help? I know they were living with you at that time,' whispered Dev.

'Uncle Amar was very sick and Anu buaji had to stay home to take care of him. I was not allowed to help either, as mataji said I was too young and could get injured in the fire. So I sat on the roof of our house and watched Khan uncle's haveli burn right before my eyes.'

Dev hesitated before asking, 'Did your mataji die that night?'

'No. She started getting better, especially after Baoji returned. In fact, she did not pass away until a month or so after uncle Amar died. The night of the fire, she received very severe burns but no doctors were available to help her. Only Anu buaji helped. She took care of Mataji—grinding and applying poultices and creams made of herbs, on mataji's wounds.'

Softly, so as not to disturb the fragile air, Dev whispered, 'What happened?'

'The wounds healed but complications with her lungs developed, causing breathing difficulties.' Raghu shut his eyes, cupped his nose between his curled fist and thumb, and wailed, 'The smells, the smells. I can't get those smells of burnt flesh and poultices out of my head.' Through his sobs, he gasped for air. 'Mataji's lungs stopped working and she choked to death.'

Dev put an arm around Raghu, wishing the study of medicine would also teach how to mend broken hearts. He hoped to be a doctor, a healer. There were so many like his friend, with deep invisible wounds. Perhaps, then he could heal the scars in his own heart too.

When he returned home that evening, he could hear Ratna practicing her music, as usual. Walking past the drawing room, he saw her sitting on the carpet, her long fingers playing the sitar, picking up the notes where her music teacher left off. Dev stood listening, mesmerised by the dance of music—the teacher's notes melding into fluid notes of the student—sa, re, ga, ma, pa, dha, ne . . . and on and on the liquid sounds played. Dev stood still, enthralled with the melodies his sister played on the sitar, sensing his sister had found her passion.

He stood leaning against a pillar, his eyes closed, head moving to the rhythm, waiting for the lesson to be over. As soon as the music teacher left, Ratna came looking for him.

'What is it, Dev? Were you looking for me?' she asked.

'Yes . . . but your music is so good, I forget the reason.'

Ratna burst out laughing. 'Very funny. Anyway, thanks for the compliment.'

'I had a long chat with Raghu and guess what? He is also one of us.'

'Meaning?'

'Come on Ratna, you know what I mean,' he blurted.

'No, I don't!' Ratna rolled her eyes and arched her right eyebrow in an insolent question.

'Raghu suffered during Partition just like we did. Well, almost like us.' Dev repeated the tale of Raghu's mataji's death and the story of Raghu's Muslim uncle and his family. He walked away remembering his own lost ones, sensing the dichotomy in his life—the unrelenting pain of losing his birth parents and the gratitude of receiving loving adoptive parents.

A couple of days later, while Ratna and Dev sat on a bench reading at their favourite spot under the juice mango tree, Raghu ran through their haveli gates and blurted breathlessly, 'Dev! Dev! We just heard from some friends in Ferozpur and learnt that the Khans reached Pakistan safely. They settled close to Shahadra, the same village where your family used to live. Anu buaji is so happy she hasn't stopped talking about that wonderful place ever since.'

The two friends, quasi-brothers, hugged each other.

'How come you got the news now after so many years?' asked Ratna.

'There was no way to communicate. Our mutual friends heard the news from Pakistan only recently.' Turning to Dev, Raghu said, 'And guess what? Nadia, who is a year older than me, is getting married to Hamid. I believe he is the son of some friends of your Shahadra family. Anu buaji said he is your Iqbal uncle's only son.'

As soon as Raghu mentioned his Iqbal uncle, Ratna noticed colour draining from Dev's face. She moved to kiss her brother on his forehead. Dev took a deep breath, stood up and putting his arm around Raghu's shoulder, walked away.

Ratna remembered Hamid, his two half sisters and stepmother, Razia Begum. Hamid, she remembered, was a spoiled brat. 'I hope Hamid grew up to be a better person than he used to be,' she muttered, looking up to the mango tree laden with dense clusters of small juice mangoes.

16
Happy Days

1955-56

While scanning the matriculation exam results in the morning's *Tribune*, Ratna's eyes widened. 'Papaji, Ma, look . . . Dev topped the university! Oh my God! I've always known he is good but . . . but this. Wow! Dev, Dev, Ma—'

'Hush, Beti,' said an ecstatic Raminder, hurrying towards her daughter.

Dev sauntered in smiling.

'Did you know? Dev, did you ever imagine?' inquired Ratna jumping, her eyes dancing, her hands fluttering as if trying to dry them.

'I thought it possible.'

'Thought it possible? Huh?' Ratna yelled some more, and hugged him.

Sukhdev and Raminder moved in to embrace and congratulate him.

'And how did you do?' asked Dev.

'Not as well as you did for sure. Actually, I haven't checked,' replied Ratna. Going over the list in the newspaper of other successful matriculates, she beamed, saying, 'Oh! There I am. One, two, three . . . I think I'm tenth or eleventh in the university.'

'Not bad. Not bad,' exclaimed Sukhdev. 'Who would have guessed that in a little over seven short years, you two would be among the best students in the state of Punjab? I'm so proud.' He extended his arms and hugged them, kissing both on their foreheads.

After Ratna and Dev's tremendous success, they sat down to discuss college plans with their parents. Ratna intended to study instrumental music and specialise in sitar, an instrument that enticed her to create music of peace and joy. Dev wanted to be a healer, aspiring to pursue a career in medicine, following the footsteps of his Simranjeet mamaji.

However, Ratna did not want to go to college at Jullunder but in Amritsar, which was about sixty miles to the northwest of Jullunder. Amritsar not only had a good government sponsored college for girls but also boasted of an excellent medical college. This way she knew she could stay close to her brother.

Since Simranjeet lived and practiced medicine in Amritsar, he invited both Ratna and Dev to stay in his home and complete their studies. Ratna took up the offer but Dev joined the D.A.V. College for Men, where his friend Raghu and he had planned to live in the same hostel. After finishing his pre-medical studies, Dev hoped to join the medical college.

Ratna loved her Simranjeet uncle and his small family. As a little girl, she had often wondered why her Manu mamiji, who could afford a life of luxury, rarely left the kitchen. With her head covered in a coloured silk dupatta veil, matching the colour of her salwaar kameez, her aunt sat on a peerhi stool, supervising the maids. Never idle, her mamiji chopped vegetables, churned the yogurt in big vats to make butter or stirred the pot of daal soup. However, when she did leave the kitchen, her aunt's tall stature and pleasant face radiated power, peace and compassion. Ratna's uncle, her mamaji, equally charismatic, spent a major part of his days dispensing free consultation, food and medicine to the poor. The couple made a loving team of compassion and hope. Food prepared in their kitchen fed not only the family, but also a daily procession of poor patients.

In Ratna's younger days, after every visit to Amritsar, her mother always fussed how her brother and his wife spent too much time in charitable endeavours, allowing their daughter Simi to be brought up by her illiterate ayahs, with little or no supervision. 'Why don't you talk to Simranjeet mamaji about your worries?' Ratna remembered asking.

'I have. But he is not worried. He says Vaheguru has blessed him in so many ways that He will take care of their daughter too.'

Ratna had to admit, Vaheguru had taken good care of her cousin. Simi emerged from her privileged childhood, unspoiled and loving. Safe in India when Partition took place, Simi did not have to pick up the pieces of her broken heart, one tiny fragment at a time. As a result, Simi showed no fear of the past but only talked of the pleasant world she left behind in Pakistan, a world that carried dreams but no nightmares.

A week before the colleges were to open, Ratna and Raminder travelled by train and hired a tonga at the Amritsar station to go to Simranjeet's house. On the way, Raminder tried to prepare Ratna for a new phase in her life. 'Beti, my brother and bhabi are good people, but there may be things you might not approve of—'

'Ma, what are you saying? I love them. Why wouldn't I approve of the way they live their lives?'

'I just wanted to say that Manu bhabi is kind-hearted but she pays no attention to keeping a clean house. I thought that might bother you considering how picky you are about cleanliness.'

'You are worse than me.'

'I know. Ratna, just remember that their hearts are in the right place, and that's what matters.'

When their pony trap entered the rusted gate of her uncle's house, Ratna noticed its ugly architecture for the first time. Simranjeet's gardener came running to help them with the luggage. As soon as Ratna alighted, the pony relieved itself and she had to jump to safety to avoid being sprayed by the offensive hot mist.

She looked about her at the garage on her left and noticed two dreary rooms beyond the garage, built in a straight line. Why had she never noticed those rooms or their clutter of temporary cots earlier? Poor patients and their families sat on the cots or squatted around them. The dispensary stood on the right side of the gate, with three rooms in an 'L' shape, smelling of chemicals. Through the open doors and windows of one room, Ratna saw a long, marble-topped table, littered with mortar and pestles. Two young men dressed in men's Indian tunic set—the kurta pyjama—sat grinding medical concoctions. They worked for her mamaji, as his compounding pharmacists.

A nondescript sign, hanging by one rusted nail, announced the office and dispensary of 'Dr Simranjeet Singh'. Amid all these medicinal smells and sickness, Ratna's well-groomed mamaji, his beard rolled up around a cord tied on his head, wearing a blue turban, limped about dispensing medicine and cheer to his sick patients.

When Simranjeet saw his sister and niece, he walked over flashing a smile, and greeted them, '*Sat Sri Akaal.*' God is truth. Hugging them both, he said, '*Ji ayanh nooh.*' Welcome.

Raminder and Ratna turned to follow the gardener and their luggage over a cobblestone path that meandered beyond the cluttered dispensary and the clinic, leading through a garden to the steps of the raised patio of the house. Ratna stopped on the cobblestone path struck by the charming flower garden in the midst of messy surroundings. Her eyes followed a gold and black butterfly, fluttering over a lush green lawn to settle on the jasmines. On her right grew fruit trees, medicinal plants and the kitchen garden. One tall lone mango tree bustling with blue jays and nightingales stood at the edge of the garden. Ratna savoured the welcoming garden and trees.

Manu walked out of the kitchen as they climbed the steps of the patio. Smiling, she folded her hands together in salutation. 'Sat Sri Akaal.' Manu moved to hug Raminder and Ratna. 'Simi, they are here!'

Manu ordered chairs to be brought out and tea served to the adults and cool lemonade to the girls. Ratna thought of her earlier conversation with her mother, noting the patio littered with dry leaves, chicken droppings and old newspapers. During her childhood she had visited her uncle's family often but nothing beyond the warmth and compassion of her relatives had ever made any impression on her. Now, for the first time, she saw through her mother's eyes. Other than an immaculate garden, an efficient and well-run kitchen, the rest of her mamiji's household seemed to thrive on benign neglect.

Ratna looked around, wondering which room she would be given to live in for the next four college years. The house had four spacious bedrooms, a large living room and two tiny windowless cells—in constant use for overnight guests. She hoped she would not have to stay in one of those windowless rooms. While Ratna sipped the refreshing lemonade, her aunt said, 'You can move your luggage into the spare bedroom next to Simi's room.' Ratna nodded, smiling. Even though she loved her cousin, it was lucky they did not have to share a room, as Simi, like her mother, seemed to thrive on messy surroundings.

Her uncle and aunt shared the biggest room in the centre of the house. Manu's widowed aunt occupied the bedroom furthest from the master bedroom. The house had no dining room. They ate in the huge, detached kitchen, sitting on low peerhi stools, eating food served in sparkling bronze platters, on individual brass-topped tables.

After tea, both the girls stood up to move Ratna's luggage into her new room. As they carried her stuff indoors, Ratna asked, 'Simi, what should I call your Waddeh Buaji?' She needed to know how to address Manu mamiji's elderly, wise and respected aunt, since no one had formally introduced them. Technically, the old woman was the aunt of an aunt, so Ratna had no idea how to address her.

'Waddeh Buaji is a sweet soul and you may call her Waddeh Buaji too. I'm sure she'll like that,' Simi replied.

'I've seen her here many, many times. Does she live with you?' asked Ratna.

'Actually, we live with her. Waddeh Buaji became a widow at a very young age and lost her only son and her son's family during Partition. Left without a family of her own, she needed the comfort and we needed a home,' answered Simi, sitting on Ratna's bed.

Ratna opened the wooden closet and started putting her things away. 'Is she your grandfather's sister?'

'Yes. After she lost her husband, her father—my mother's grandfather—built this house for her. My mother is her only niece and since she is very fond of mummy, she offered to share the house with us after we lost our house to Partition. "My house," she is fond of saying, "belongs to Manu—from one daughter of the family to the next".'

'Considering all she's lost in life, she doesn't seem bitter.'

'Uh-huh.' Simi agreed. 'Waddeh Buaji is fun to have around. I love her. Anyway, to finish my story, once we moved to Amritsar, papaji borrowed money from my grandparents and built the dispensary and clinic. So, here we are.' Simi smiled and patted the bed, inviting Ratna to sit with her.

'Guessing from the number of patients, it seems mamaji's practice is flourishing,' said Ratna, sitting next to Simi.

'Yes. He is doing extremely well. He returned all the money he borrowed within the first two years. Now he insists he does not need so much, so he provides free care to the poor.'

'Simi, it looks like he not only provides medical care, but even houses and feeds his patients for free,' Ratna said laughing.

'Don't laugh. It's true,' Simi replied. 'We do not need four milking buffaloes and all those chickens for our small family. The livestock is kept simply to have a constant supply of milk, butter and eggs for the poor patients who cannot afford them.'

Ratna felt a sudden surge of love for her relatives. The feeling wrapped her like a warm shawl in freezing Amritsar winters. 'I'm so happy to be here,' she said, giving Simi a hug.

Once she settled in her new surroundings, Ratna had a standard answer for anyone who asked her if she missed home. 'The one thing that keeps me from missing home is the rooster that sits on the neem tree outside my window, and trills its early morning wake-up call. Waking up to the sounds of my village every morning, keeps me grounded,' she laughed.

Her room sat close to the backyard where the stables stood. Since her uncle did not own any horses, he used the place as a cowshed for his milking buffaloes. On one side of the stables lived families of three servants and a gardener. A huge dirt yard separated the building from the main house. Milking buffaloes, chickens, roosters and servant children played about without constraint in this yard.

Repugnant smells of animal waste wafted into her room. The smells turned especially overpowering in summers, as Ratna had to open the windows whenever electric fans did not work because of repeated power failures. She, however, did not complain.

The animals in the backyard stayed within their confines but the chicken often strayed onto the paved front patio, littering the place with tiny piles of faecal matter. Throughout the day, Ratna could hear startled cackling, as the chicken, ousted by the gardener from his grounds, flew up the walls or onto the roof in alarm, sprinkling little squiggles of droppings in their path. Since she was raised in a clean, well-tended village home, she had to learn to tolerate the mess and confusion of her mamaji's city home.

Ratna and Simi went together for admissions to the Government College for Women. When Simi guided her to a collection of scattered, crumbling structures, Ratna exclaimed, 'Surely, this is not our institute of higher learning!'

Simi smiled. 'Don't go by the looks. It's still the best women's college in Amritsar.'

'Even our tiny school in Jullunder had a better building,' Ratna commented.

'Ratna, you seem to be forgetting something,' said Simi. 'Amritsar sits on the border of India, where damage from arson was the heaviest during Partition. Luckily for us, the Punjab government, with its limited resources, has decided that good education has a higher priority than well-built structures. This college has the best-trained teachers in Punjab. Putting together land and resources for a proper building will take a little longer.'

Five dilapidated Victorian bungalows spread out among sprawling lawns, made up the college premises. One of the mansions was reserved for pre-medical students. Tall green hedges effectively separated it from the main college. Ratna and Simi's days revolved around the two central buildings, reserved for Liberal Arts students. The two houses beyond were again separated from the rest of the college with tall evergreen hedges. One housed the administrative offices and the Principal's living quarters, while the other served as a hostel for girls.

A huge brick wall surrounded the five battered mansions, lawns and all. An iron gate at the entrance topped by a curved, half-crescent metal sign, declaring it to be the Government College for Women, gave the ancient structures some credibility.

The lecturers, Ratna discovered, usually obliged if the students clamoured to study on the lawns on cool, pleasant days. The teachers sat on chairs, brought out by eager students, while the girls sat on the grass, picnic style. But as time passed, Ratna learned that these idyllic surroundings were mired in problems.

During the monsoons, only a few rooms other than the library stayed dry. With the arrival of monsoon rains, the classrooms were equipped with empty pails to collect the rainwater, which came not in droplets but in steady streams from the leaky roofs. On certain days, the rooms had more pails than dry desks and on such days, the room assignments held no meaning. The teachers had to send their representatives scouting around for the driest rooms. The students who found dry rooms could be educated, while the rest simply donned their raincoats or their umbrellas and headed for home.

She and Simi preferred to go to college on their bicycles, which allowed them the freedom to come and go as they pleased. Although both had a common interest in music, one took vocal music and the other, sitar. They built new friendships, with a few friends common to both. They especially liked one girl named Guddi, the captain of the college athletics team.

Over the course of the first year, the three girls became inseparable, known as "the big three". One or the other of these three girls served in all the coveted positions of the student body, from being the president of the literary society, the music society and the captain of the college athletics team. They supported each other in almost every college activity. If one faltered, the others encouraged. All of them excelled in studies and sports.

For Ratna, college seemed to be a release into the fresh air of freedom. She had graduated from a very regimented and puritanical school that insisted on turning out proper ladies, willing or not. College made her dizzy with expectations of the future. Life seemed sweet.

One day Simi said, 'Ratna, yesterday Indu suggested we both participate in the inter-collegiate music competitions in November. What do you say?'

Ratna felt fortunate that Indu, the "head girl", the college president of the student body, had befriended them and acted as their unofficial student mentor.

'I won't be able to do that. I'm not good enough!' she exclaimed. 'Besides, I don't think I could play in front of hundreds of people.'

'Of course, you can. You have a natural gift. As long as you concentrate on your music, you'll do beautifully. Anyway, you'll never know what you are capable of unless you try.'

Ratna laughed. Simi sounded like her mother. During the first hard years of her schooling in Jullunder, she would often get disheartened and her mother would say those exact words to her, over and over again.

She agreed to participate, surprising not just herself, but her family too with her mastery of the instrument. It seemed that with the sitar in her hands, an invisible presence guided her to an alternate dimension, a place so warm, so secure, it soothed her still shattered soul. Her fingers flowed effortlessly over sitar strings, the rhythms resonating in joy, not just with her living loved-ones but also with the ones she lost in her childhood.

Every morning, when the rooster crowed, Ratna got up to practice sitar. Invariably, she sat with her eyes closed, her fingers gliding over the instrument, her head moving in a trance-like state. Surrounded by the peace of early dawn and sitar music, Simi sometimes added a vocal melody of her own. The sweet melodies carried Ratna to the most sacred and purest part of her being—the part that had been nurtured by the wise old banyan trees of her childhood, in Shahadra, Pakistan. To be transported to that secret sanctuary every morning soothed her. It rejuvenated her and heightened her awareness of the beauty around her.

When she started giving music recitals, Dev always attended, glowing with pride at his sister's accomplishment. 'Ratna,' he confessed one day, 'in my Shahadra family no one ever played any musical instrument, so it is hard for me to describe my feelings. Somehow, every time I hear you play the sitar, I feel strangely secure and think of Uma ma, Anu chachi and Sita chachi. It is as if your sitar awakens a memory of all the nurturers in my prior life.'

'Dev, that is the sweetest compliment anyone has ever paid me.' Ratna squeezed her brother's hand. It made her feel good to have Dev in the same city with her. The bond between them seemed to grow stronger.

The close proximity and the common passion of music moved her closer to Simi too. One day, while the two cousins sat relaxing with the radio, Waddeh Buaji joined them and fussed with Simi. 'I wish your mother would spend less time in the kitchen and more time with you. Simi, this constant wasting of time listening to the radio is terrible. If it's not the radio, it's your friends! I only wish you could learn a lesson or two from Ratna in womanly arts.'

'Waddeh Buaji, you are embarrassing me,' said Ratna, flustered. 'Look, I'm listening to the music too.'

'Yes, you are. But you are also knitting a sweater while Simi is just wasting her time.'

'Stop it, Waddeh Buaji,' Simi responded. 'You just worry too much.'

'I'm telling you, Simi, we are going to lose you to your silly friends and the radio.'

'Ha! Look who is talking! Did anyone lose you to your friends? Remember what you used to do in your youth?'

'Why do you have to bring up my past?'

'Because it's funny! You spent more time with your friends than I do. Remember, you yourself told me?'

'Okay, don't listen. See if I care.' Waddeh Buaji laughed indulgently.

Ratna watched the usual lighthearted bickering between the two and smiled. She felt she had become a part of her mamaji's household.

Even though Dev lived and studied in the D.A.V. College for Men, he visited them often, asserting that he missed not only his sister but his aunt's home cooking as well. Ratna thought she knew otherwise. What he seemed to love the most was to spend time in their mamaji's dispensary, doling out love and hope to his uncle's patients. Surrounded by women at home, her uncle too seemed to welcome his nephew's company at the clinic.

When the frequency of Dev's visits increased, but his visits to their uncle's dispensary dwindled, Ratna started suspecting a new attraction—her friend Guddi. It seemed, in Guddi's presence, Dev paid special attention to his attire, his manners, even his jokes, and spent longer hours at the house.

Even though Ratna believed she had stumbled on Dev's secret, no one else in the household suspected anything. But then, no one knew Dev as well as she did. She worried about him, knowing boys and girls were not supposed to fall in love before marriage. Her upbringing and her culture had conditioned her to believe that falling in love was a privilege only married people could afford. She knew that elders arranged the marriage and the children accepted it. That is how it had been done for centuries and that was how Dev would be expected to do it.

When the colleges broke for winter vacation, she travelled with Dev by bus to Garha. On the way, she broached the subject. Using her term of endearment for him, she said, 'Bhaiya—'

'Uh-oh! What did I do now?' He made a comic face.

'Nothing major,' she answered. 'I think you like someone I know.'

'Do I sense jealousy?' He laughed his spontaneous laugh.

'No, I'm serious. If you like her as much as I think you do, maybe we should talk to ma about it. She could arrange it in the proper way. I think it would work, especially since you are studying to be a doctor. You are kind and loving. What better match could Guddi's mother want for her daughter?'

'I d-didn't think a-anyone knew,' stammered Dev, his face twitching with a nervous tic.

'I don't think Guddi is aware of your interest in her. It's for the better. This way her mother won't panic and do something we'll regret later.'

'I don't know how to approach it with biji. I'm not even sixteen years old. Maybe once I get admitted to medical school and am a little older, I'll be able to talk to biji about it,' he mumbled.

It hurt Ratna to see her brother struggle with his emotions. She squeezed his hand to let him know she understood.

17

The Betrayal

1956

One January, eight-and-a-half years after Partition, Raminder heard rumours that Wagah border near Amritsar would open up for tourists between India and Pakistan. A friendly cricket match between the two countries had been arranged and Indians were invited. Raminder understood it to mean that visitors to Pakistan would require no passports or visas to cross the border. This suggested an opportunity for her and her family to visit Pakistan without fear of being harmed.

By February, the rumours became a reality. She learned that visitors had only to supply a photograph, complete and sign a form in front of a Pakistani official, at a makeshift immigration office in Amritsar, and permission was granted. From all the excitement this news generated, it seemed to Raminder, everyone she knew wanted to visit Pakistan—not to watch the cricket match but to get closure on personal issues.

For her, even after all these years, the beckoning call of those she had left behind was unrelenting. She and her brother Simranjeet needed to return to Rawalpindi, their parental city, in an effort to trace their missing family. But most of all, she and Sukhdev needed to mourn their daughter Aman in the village of Ugoke. They had always found it painful to talk to each other about Aman. Each had tried to deal with the pain in private ways, but both knew it didn't work. For them this opportunity to make the pilgrimage together meant a chance to help each other heal.

After various conferences, Raminder and her extended family decided to visit Pakistan in two separate cars. Anu, Ratna, Dev, Anu's brother Sanjay and nephew Raghu planned to travel in one car, since all of them meant to go only over the border to Lahore and Shahadra. They decided to leave on the fifth day of March and return by the eighth.

Raminder, Sukhdev, Simranjeet and Manu would take another car. Their destination, Rawalpindi, was much further than Shahadra. They too were to commence their journey on fifth of March, but planned to return later on the twelfth.

Waddeh Buaji offered to stay with Simi and would have gladly taken care of Anu's twins too, but they had their school finals and Anu left them with Baljeet, the 'war baby's' mother.

Under normal circumstances, Raminder would not have allowed Ratna and Dev to go on such an emotionally charged visit, so close to university finals in April. The stakes were much higher for Dev and Raghu. They both needed to do especially well in their pre-medical exams for a chance at admission to the Amritsar Medical College.

But these were neither normal circumstances nor normal times.

Ratna hoped the ambience of her temple-home amongst the sage banyan trees would help calm her mind, letting the ghosts of the carnage at the temple rest in peace. She prayed for the angels of her childhood to help soothe and release the smouldering ache in her heart.

She and Dev discussed the visit and his need to revisit the past in order to understand what really happened to his father, his Sita chachi and Gaurav chacha. He hoped for peace.

On the appointed date, Anu, Sanjay and Raghu picked up Ratna and Dev from Amritsar in the black Austin. Long before they reached the Wagah border, about eighteen miles from Simranjeet's house, Ratna's silent tears flowed like gentle rain calming a rough and dusty terrain.

Dev became visibly disturbed when they reached the outskirts of Lahore. His face twitched and his eyes mirrored tumultuous emotions while he surveyed the surroundings. But Anu, who sat with Ratna and Dev in the back seat, uttered not one soothing word to calm him.

Ratna stared at Anu with moist eyes, posing an unasked question. Anu shrugged. 'This is my first trip to Lahore without purdah. Nothing seems familiar. I'm not sure how to help.'

Ratna understood why Anu chachi looked so bewildered. She remembered those days, when, even though non-Muslim women did not wear burqas, they still moved around in purdah—by covering their faces with dupatta veils, and thus had no knowledge of places and buildings.

A few familiar landmarks made Dev nostalgic for his Baoji and his trips back and forth to school in the horse driven carriage. He still remembered the lovable coach-keeper named Saleem, the gentle mountain-of-a-man, who took him back and forth to school, without complaining of the freezing cold of the winters, the heat of the summers or the rain of the monsoons. Basking in the glow of those warm memories, Dev relaxed, breaking into a smile, but before the smile had time to settle, his mood changed again—sudden painful memories, like gathering clouds, choked the light and warmth from his cherished past.

Frantic, he looked around mumbling, 'Where are they?'

'Where's what?' asked Raghu.

'Our stores. They were supposed to be right there,' he said, pointing to a cluster of dhabas—roadside eating-places.

'Beta, maybe they are further down the road,' ventured Anu.

'No. The Bhardwaj Fabric Store was close to that tall four-legged electricity pole and the Jewellery Shop was close to those two kachnar trees over there,' he said. As the car moved closer, he exclaimed, 'Wow! The trees are loaded with buds! Saleem and I used to pluck those buds, and take them home to cook for supper. Baoji loved kachnar buds.'

'I know,' whispered Anu. 'I can almost smell the aroma of those buds. It was a delicacy Baoji relished when he could, as within a week of their first appearance, the buds opened into stunning but inedible blooms.'

'You want us to stop and inquire?' asked Sanjay, slowing the car.

'No, not—'

Before Dev could finish, Anu interrupted. 'Dev, did you know Baoji bought this motor car for you?'

'Yes.'

'Do you remember the commotion it created in the village the day Baoji brought it home?' she asked. Dev nodded.

Slipping as if into another time and place, Anu whispered, 'Sita, Uma bhabi, and I often marvelled at our kismet. We felt so blessed. There was no fear of the future, only hopes and dreams.' She threw her head back, and shut her eyes tight to squash unwelcome tears. 'And then, Partition happened!' Ratna reached over to hold her hand.

After a few more miles of travel, much sooner than Dev remembered, they reached the crossroads where one road turned towards the village of Shahadra. The ruins where Dev's mother had died were gone and in their place stood a new housing development. Sanjay stopped the car and Anu, Ratna and Dev got out without saying a word. Dev walked over to the gate of a nearby walled house. Ratna and Anu followed. A shabbily dressed teenager worked in the yard. 'Come in! Come in!' he called and ran towards the house yelling, 'Visitors have come to see you'.

Outside the house wall, Anu asked Dev, 'Beta, do you want to talk to these people?' Leaning against the wall for support, he nodded, allowing tears to course down his face in haphazard little streams, like sudden rains during monsoons. Ratna walked over, kissed him on his forehead and put an arm around his shoulder.

A tall, handsome man wearing a white starched salwaar kurta came out and looked inquiringly at the group. Anu's brother, Sanjay, got out of the car apologising, 'We are sorry for barging in like this. I am Sanjay and I have my sister and other relatives with me, from India. We are on our way to visit their old home.' Pointing to Dev, he added, 'Our nephew lost his mother in the ruins that were here around the time of Partition. He wanted to stop and pay homage to her memory.'

'Of course! Of course!' said the man. 'We moved here only two years ago. When we bought the place, there were no ruins in the area. I'm sorry, but please do come in.'

Dev shook his head and stood staring into nothingness. His tears had dried but he had a peculiar expression.

Ratna asked, 'Bhaiya, are you well?'

He nodded. 'I can sense my Uma ma's presence. I think she's at peace,' he whispered.

The kind host waved his hand in the direction of the village of Shahadra and asked, 'Are you originally from these parts?'

'My sister and the two children are,' Sanjay answered. 'They are from the Bhardwaj family that used to live in the village.'

'Ma'sh Allah!'—Praise be to God who willed this—'You mean *the* Bhardwajs from the haveli?' Sanjay nodded. 'Then you must allow me to take you there personally,' said the man. Without waiting for a reply, he announced, 'I'll be back in a minute. I've to tell my parents I'm going with you to Shahadra.'

As they waited, Ratna whispered, 'He seems so kind. Who is he?'

No one knew him. The man returned, stared at the car briefly and folding his hands in humility said, 'I am Omar. My uncle Saleem was the coach-keeper for the Bhardwajs,' he said.

Dev turned to look at Omar, who continued, 'It was my uncle who helped me buy this house. Uncle lives in the Bhardwaj haveli. For a long time, he insisted that the haveli in Shahadra still belonged to the Bhardwajs and waited for their return . . .' Omar stopped in mid-sentence and asked, 'Is there enough room in the car for me? Maybe, I should guide you on my bicycle.'

'We can all squeeze in,' said Sanjay. 'It shouldn't be more than a couple of miles. Please join us.' Raghu moved to the back of the car, accommodating Omar in the front.

As soon as Omar sat down, he addressed Anu respectfully as a sister—Apa. Without turning around to face her—custom dictated it would be rude, as the woman was not wearing a veil to cover her face—he asked, 'Apa, please forgive my impertinence, but are you married to one of the younger Bhardwaj brothers?'

'Yes. I was married to Amar.'

'You said was. He too? But I don't understand. I left both of you safely in Garha. Remember? I was your chauffeur and this was the very car I drove you in before Partition.' Dev was surprised. Some memories seemed so blurred he had not recognised Omar. 'Amar babuji couldn't have been killed in his own country? Could he? I don't understand.'

'He died of typhoid that same year,' replied Anu.

'I'm so sorry.'

When even Anu chachi and Omar did not recognise each other, Dev knew it was because in pre-Partition days she always travelled in purdah. Throwing a quick glance at Dev, Anu ventured to ask, 'What happened to Umesh bhaiya?'

'Allah kasam,'—I swear by God—'it's hard to relive that day,' whispered Omar. His voice quivered. 'The mob killed him in the Bhardwaj Fabric Store in Lahore and dragged his butchered body all the way home. Once in Shahadra, they lit fire to the kerosene-drenched haveli and . . . and threw Umesh babuji's body on that pyre!'

Dev gasped—his father's body! He relived their flight from the village on that fateful night, and shuddered thinking of the screaming mob. He remembered how as soon as they spotted the mob dragging a dead body, his mother jumped into a ditch of cold, muddy water, taking him and Ratna with her. She had mumbled, 'Ram, Ram, Ram'—invoking her God to have mercy on humans. Did his Uma ma even suspect whose body the mob dragged?

His eyes shot to Ratna. Did she know? Watching her jaw drop and eyes widen, Dev knew Ratna too had just discovered what they did not know then. Anu looked at him and put her arm around him. He tucked his trembling hands between his legs.

'Apa, please forgive me one more time,' said Omar. 'Did Uma bibiji and Dev babu make it safely to the border?'

'Uma bhabi did not make it,' replied Anu. 'She got massacred at the ruins near your home. Dev here survived. A Sikh family adopted him. We live close to each other.'

Omar's body jerked as soon as Anu mentioned Dev being in the same car. Turning around, he took Dev's hands in his, kissing them tenderly. Dev kissed Omar's hands in return, whispering, 'I'm not a babu. Please call me Dev.'

When they reached the village, Dev barely recognised the ruined haveli. Some of the living quarters had been rebuilt but it was nowhere close to its old grandeur. Omar ran in and returned with a startled Saleem, followed by two women, both bustling to get into their burqas.

Saleem, still a huge man, beamed with disbelief and stared at them. Before his eyes registered recognition, Dev embraced the old man. One of the women in burqa advanced towards Anu, hesitated, then hugged her. 'It's me, Salma. Do you remember me? I was Dev babu's ayah,' she gushed.

'Please address me as Dev. I'm nobody's master,' mumbled a red-faced Dev.

Saleem led the procession indoors, where the two women relinquished their burqas and Salma introduced the young woman as their daughter and Omar's wife, Hassina. While they all took seats, Hassina went in to bring hot chai and snacks.

As Salma served refreshments, she came to Ratna and took a double take. 'Is that you, Ratna?' she exclaimed, and took Ratna into an embrace. 'Beti, I'm so sorry. I knew about the massacre at the temple. Uma bibiji had sent me to get Baoji and your family in order to leave for the railway station. But I never made it to the temple. A crazed mob blocked my way. Hai Allah. They didn't even allow me to retrace my steps to the haveli to warn my gentle Uma bibiji to flee. I survived only because of my religion. I'm so sorry.' Pointing to Dev and Anu, she asked, 'Do you all live together?'

'No,' said Anu before Ratna replied. 'Uma bhabi was massacred on the road to Lahore and a Sikh refugee couple adopted both Ratna and Dev. I and my twins live with my brother,' and pointed to Sanjay. 'But we do live close to each other in the same village.'

Salma looked at Dev exclaiming, 'Ma'sh Allah! I'm so relieved you found a loving family.' Then turning to Anu, she continued, 'Bibiji—'

'Please call me "Apa",' interrupted Anu, who wanted to be addressed as a sister rather than as a mistress. Dev, well versed in the three cultures, smiled. He knew where a Muslim would address a sister as 'Apa', a Hindu would call her 'Didi', and a Sikh as 'Behen' or 'Behenji'.

'Apa, you must stay with us for as long as you stay in Pakistan,' said Salma, exuding warmth and welcome.

Anu looked at her brother and Sanjay nodded his consent.

'Do you know any Khans who live close to Shahadra?' asked Sanjay.

'We know a couple of Khan families who live close by,' answered Saleem.

'The ones I'm looking for used to live in Garha, close to our haveli. If we can locate them then Raghu and I would like to spend one night with them.'

Saleem nodded, and Anu said, 'Does Razia Begum's family still live in the village?'

'Yes,' replied Salma. 'But they are not as affluent as they were when you knew them. They lost their business and most of their wealth during Partition. Did you know Hamid's abbajaan,'—his father—'never returned from India?'

Dev wondered why Salma called him 'Hamid's abbajaan' instead of 'Iqbal', but realised that as per custom, she could not take Iqbal chacha's name. The man belonged not only to a higher social status than the ayah, but was older in age too. Dev stared stoically at Salma, without any trace of emotion at the mention of his murdered Muslim uncle.

Anu gave a quick glance to Dev before asking Salma, 'Do Hamid and his wife live with Razia Begum?'

'Yes. The girl he married is the sweetest little thing, but Hamid is good for nothing, just a drunk and a womanizer. He does not treat any woman with respect.'

'Can we go over to see Razia Begum?'

'We can do better than that. How about we request her to visit us?' said Salma.

'Would it be possible to invite Hamid's wife too? She is the daughter of the Khans we are looking for.'

Salma sent a messenger to invite Razia Begum and her daughter-in-law for a visit.

Within the hour, a carriage stopped outside the haveli and out emerged two women in burqas, one carrying herself like royalty, the other following her timorously with her head bowed. After introducing her daughter-in-law, and some small talk, Razia Begum veered the conversation towards her husband, Iqbal Bhutto. 'The last time I saw him was when he left for New Delhi, shortly before Partition. Do you know if he returned to Pakistan, or is he still in India? Does Gaurav know of his whereabouts?'

Even though Dev had witnessed the massacre at the Amritsar station, he struggled to stay calm. The only way to get answers to unanswered questions that had troubled him all these years, was not to mention the murder of Iqbal chacha. 'Khalajaan, I'm sorry,' he said. 'We have no news of Iqbal chacha or Gaurav chacha. We do not even know Gaurav chacha's address in Delhi.' He answered Razia Begum with the slightest of a facial twitch and such amazing steadiness that both Ratna and his aunt stared at him. Ratna opened her mouth to say something, but Dev's pleading look and Anu's restraining hand stopped her. Grateful to his aunt for trusting him, he gave her a weak smile.

Anu in turn gave a meaningful look to her brother Sanjay, who piped in, 'Nadia Beti, how are you? Where have your parents settled? We've come all this way to see them.' It seemed to please Nadia to be addressed as beti, as a daughter, but in her bashfulness, she did not acknowledge her old friend, Raghu. It took a while before she started asking questions, hesitantly at first and then more animatedly, about their haveli and neighbours in Garha. She gave Sanjay the address of her parents, informing him they lived not too far from the village, close to uncle Omar's house.

Razia Begum turned to Dev and said, 'I can't believe how different you look, and how grownup! Uma must be so proud of you.'

Anu had to set the record straight, again. 'Uma bhabi died during Partition and a Sikh family adopted both Dev and the punditji's daughter, Ratna.'

Her eyes watering, Razia Begum turned to Anu and without acknowledging Ratna or commenting upon Uma or Dev's fate, asked, 'Anu, do you remember how a year before Partition, we appointed my cousin Ahmed as a manager at our business in Delhi?' When Anu nodded, Razia Begum continued, 'Well, shortly before Partition, he returned and said, "Your husband has temporarily turned the business over to Gaurav, who has renamed it 'Bhardwaj Import/Export Ltd'." As you know, the times were such that Muslim businesses in Delhi were being burned and looted, so taking a Hindu name seemed prudent, until calmer times prevailed.'

'Gaurav, I'm told,' continued Razia Begum, 'was to take my husband to Amritsar and help him cross over to Pakistan through the Wagah border. But we have had no news from anyone about his whereabouts all these years. I have written to him a couple of times at our Delhi business address—c/o Gaurav Bhardwaj. Perhaps the letters never made it across the border. Maybe he left Delhi after handing over the reins of the business to Gaurav. Hai Allah! There are so many unanswered questions,' she exclaimed, throwing up her hands.

Dev, face twitching, got up to hug Razia Begum. 'Khalajaan, I'm sure Iqbal chacha is safe and under Allah's protection. Give us his address and I will write to you if I get any information.' He passed a piece of paper to Ratna. Razia Begum dictated the address, which Ratna took down with trembling hands. Trusting his own instincts, Dev put a calming hand on Ratna's shoulder.

Over numerous cups of chai, the conversation soon turned to old times. They relaxed as they talked, and Dev looked around, marvelling how people from different countries and different religions could still celebrate the common 'humanness' in each other. As the day slipped into darkness, Razia Begum got up and taking leave, she and her stepdaughter-in-law called for their carriage.

After dinner, Sanjay and Raghu left with Omar and his wife to see their friends, the Khans, while Saleem and Dev helped with the cots, fixing guest beds for Anu, Ratna and Dev in the spare bedroom. Anu and Ratna went to help the hostess with supper. Salma first served dinner to the men on the back verandah, as in the old days. She then served the women in the detached kitchen. After supper, when Anu and Ratna walked into the guest room, Dev had already changed for the night.

Anu seemed ready for some answers. Looking Dev straight in the eye, she demanded, 'Why did you deliberately tell a lie? Why didn't you tell Razia Begum that her husband was massacred?'

Dev, face twitching, sat down on his cot and and patting his bed, motioned for his aunt and Ratna to sit with him. 'Remember the story of me witnessing Iqbal chacha's murder at the Amritsar station?' he began.

'Well, there is more to the story. I never divulged the whole truth to anyone. I couldn't. It just didn't make any sense. I needed answers to many troubling questions.'

Dev's eyes misted, as he broke his painful silence. 'One day, a couple of weeks after Partition, papaji started working as a porter at the Amritsar station. He left me sitting on a bench with instructions not to wander off. Soon, a train pulled in and I heard shouts all around me, "Kill those Musalmaan haramzadas"—kill the Muslim bastards. Carrying swords and clubs, the mob methodically peeped into all coaches of the slowing train, looking for Muslims. I suddenly saw Gaurav chacha standing near the open door to one coach. He stood in his usual stance, his feet apart but firmly planted. He held the handrail with one hand and twirled his mustache with the other—just as he used to every morning, before his morning horseback riding in Shahadra. Excited, I ran screaming for him along the side of the train, but the mob reached him from the other direction before I did.

'Gaurav chacha shouted, "There is one Musalmaan haramzada in here," and pointed to Iqbal chacha, who with eyes opened wide in shock and fear, pleaded with the angry mob, denying the allegation.

' "Believe me, the haramzada is a Muslim. Take off his pyjamas and see for yourself," said Gaurav chacha.'

'Dev, you were so young. Did you know what he meant?' asked Anu, her mouth open.

'No, not then, but the mob did. After checking whether he had been circumcised, they dragged Iqbal chacha down from the train, while Gaurav chacha walked away as if nothing had happened. I screamed and ran to save my Muslim uncle from the mob. A tall, muscular man wielded a shinning sword . . . and Iqbal chacha's bloodied head rolled to the ground, his eyes opened wide in horror. Paralysed with shock, I stared at his accusing eyes and watched his blood run in tiny streams. No one bent down to shut those terrified eyes. Those eyes . . . they . . . they still haunt me.' Dev's voice trembled. Taking a deep breath, he continued, 'When papaji came looking, he grabbed and took me away from that horrific scene. I looked back but found no trace of Gaurav chacha.'

Dev took another guttural breath before continuing with the story. 'I could not understand all these years how Gaurav chacha could do something so terrible.'

Anu's breath came in spurts. Dev continued, 'It was the ultimate betrayal of one human towards another. Why? I kept asking myself all these years. Today, I think, I got the answer I've been looking for,' he said. 'Khalajaan told us that Iqbal chacha's business was legally transferred to my uncle, until calmer times prevailed. Getting the Muslim uncle killed was a sure way for Gaurav chacha to ensure calmer times did not prevail—ever. I've often wondered if Gaurav chacha too has nightmares over what he did. I wonder if Iqbal chacha's accusing eyes haunt him too?' wailed Dev, ending his tale abruptly.

Anu sat in stunned silence, listening to this tale of betrayal. Ratna placed a hand on Anu's shoulder and asked, 'Are you okay?'

'I'm not sure. This brings back terrible memories of a time where a neighbour killed a neighbour, a friend betrayed a friend, and a brother mistrusted a brother,' Anu mumbled.

The room suddenly became quiet, so quiet they could hear each other's erratic breathing. As they sat on the bed, Ratna remembered Gaurav as the haughtiest Bhardwaj in Dev's family. As a poor man's child, she had never liked him, but now she hated him even more. She remembered how he often passed their temple home, riding his horse. As soon as he approached, her poverty-stricken parents would abruptly stop doing whatever they did and stand with their heads bowed, hands folded in humility. The nasty man rode away without acknowledging their presence. Poverty had made her parents invisible.

Once, as a six-year-old, she sat on a swing in the banyan trees, keeping an eye on her baby sister Sheila. Upon hearing a horse's hoofs, she noticed her sister crawling towards the dirt path. Ratna barely lifted her sister out of harm's way, before Gaurav's horse sped by.

Soon, her father came looking for her and scolded, 'Ratna, don't ever let your sister get in Gaurav babu's way again. He said he had no time to be stopping for riffraff.'

'But Bapu, he could have been more careful. He knows where we play.'

Her bapu moved his hand in a wide circle, and said, 'Beti, this whole place belongs to his family. If he says you are wrong then you are wrong.'

Ratna still sulked. 'No one else in his family is as mean as him. Why Bapu?'

'All five fingers of a hand are not of the same length.' And shaking his head philosophically, added, 'It seems every good family has at least one *khota paisa*.'

'What's a khota paisa?' she asked.

'It's a bad coin'—a bad penny—'thoroughly useless . . . like a wormy mango,' replied her father.

18

Remember the Juice Mango

1956

Early the next morning, Ratna, though awake, lay in bed absorbed in suffocating thoughts and fears, thinking about the temple and the old well snuggled close to the grove of gigantic banyan trees. How would she deal with her empty childhood home and her memories? If she met any of the acquaintances from the village, she wondered if they would accept her, not as the poor priest's daughter but as Dev's sister.

Salma knocked on their door and walked in carrying morning tea for them. All three sat up on their cots and reached for chai. Upon being invited, Salma too picked one cup and sat with Anu. As the four of them sipped hot tea, they made plans for the day.

'Ratna, would you like to see the temple today?' asked Salma.

Ratna nodded.

'I must warn you though. The temple is in ruins. The banyan grove, however, is still there with the same peaceful ambience.'

With a catch in her voice, Ratna asked, 'Does the water well still function?'

'Beti, I don't know how to say it . . .' Salma's face turned a deeper shade. 'Some terrible things were done to people during the time of Partition. The bodies of the butchered were disposed by dumping them in the temple well. When the surroundings started smelling, we had to get the well filled up.'

Thinking of the general massacre of non-Muslims, Ratna gagged. Dev got up to hug her and taking her hands in his, sat with her. She took a few deep breaths.

Ratna realised that the well had served as a collective grave for the butchered non-Muslims—for the rich and the poor, men and women, for Brahmins and the untouchables. Her parents and her little sister, Sheila, lay buried in the same well with Baoji, the mighty Bhardwaj. In the end, did social status and caste matter? Did the Brahmins get a more privileged burial than the untouchables? She shook her head in deep thought. Dust had turned to dust, playing no favourites.

A long time ago, on her way to safety, Ratna remembered seeing floating bodies of women and girls in wells that stood testimony to the price of freedom. But the wells were now filled. History had forgotten the sacrifices. It carried no remembrance of her pain or Dev's speechless bewilderment as he sat with his dead mother's head in his lap.

Without remembrance, Ratna feared, history would repeat itself.

She sat, eyes half closed, shaking her head with visions of stinking, bloated bodies of faceless humanity in water wells, willing gentle tears to wash away the pain inside her soul.

'Is the mango grove still around?' Anu asked.

'Yes, it is,' said Salma. 'And so is the orange orchard.'

'Could we pack some food, and after a visit to the temple, return for a picnic under the mango trees?' asked Anu. 'That is, if it's okay with Ratna.'

Ratna saw everyone look at her for approval. Numb with angst, she nodded, and getting out of bed, went to the bathroom. She felt calmer when she emerged after a good cry.

Soon the house bustled with morning activities. While the guests dressed, Salma cooked chickpeas, spiced potatoes and fried poori bread for the picnic. Delectable aromas of these comfort foods wafted from the kitchen.

After breakfast, they left, starting out through the back iron gate of the haveli, over the dirt path towards the temple. Wearing a black burqa, Salma took the lead. Ratna and Anu, with dupattas draped over their heads, followed her. Dev accompanied them.

'Ratna, after Partition, most of the private Hindu temples and small Sikh gurdwaras fell apart because of lack of maintenance,' said Salma. 'I'm telling you this to prepare you for what you'll find. The temple doesn't look like it used to. I haven't been to see it for years, but I understand it no longer houses any bells or idols. Even though the bells and idols are gone, a couple of dilapidated rooms still stand.'

Ratna wondered about a temple without bells and idols. 'I understand,' she said to make Salma feel at ease, but Ratna did not understand. She wished she had the homespun wisdom and effortless faith of her bapu, the punditji. Maybe someday she would understand God's ways; she surely did not understand man's.

They walked past the mango orchard to the grove of ancient banyan trees. Ratna stopped and leaned against one of the old tree trunks. Tears welled up, arriving unbidden at this reunion with her roots.

Over the years, whenever she thought of this place—her childhood playground—she had never experienced her bapu's presence the way she did now. The wisdom of the centuries enveloped her. She closed her eyes and in one breathtaking, serene moment, she heard the temple bells and smelled the incense floating from the altar. She heard her baby sister, Sheila, squealing with delight and her mataji humming and pulling up water from the well under sunny, blue skies. And, she sensed in the very essence of her being that her loved ones were watching over her.

Suddenly at peace, Ratna relaxed. She looked about her at the branches and beards of the banyan trees, watched the birds chirp, the squirrels frolic, and the emerald leaves shimmer in the sun. The trees danced with an elegance so pure that for a moment, life stood still for her. The mellow trees soothed her wounded heart as tenderly as a mother's lullaby. As she savoured those precious moments, the weight of a terrible emptiness became lighter.

Everyone seemed immersed in the healing breath of nature, until Ratna announced, 'I can't go to the temple today. I feel too overwhelmed. Maybe by tomorrow I'll be more prepared. Then Dev and I could visit both the temple and the well.'

'Yes, we could,' said Dev. 'But, I also need to visit the temple today—by myself,' and he turned to walk in the opposite direction.

Salma's forewarning did not prepare Dev for what he found. Once he recognised the temple ruins, he had to reconstruct the place in his mind, and walked to the spot where he thought his beloved Baoji had lain in a pool of blood. Kneeling down, he bowed and said, 'Ram, Ram, Ram' just the way his Uma ma used to pray. Then, standing up and not knowing how else to pay his respects to the departed, he folded his hands, closed his eyes and said the Sikh ardaas prayer biji had taught him.

Instinct had driven Dev to visit the ruins alone, but what happened to him there, surprised him. By that simple act of prayer, he unburdened himself of old pain and sorrow, the release helping him to experience Baoji's embrace one more time. He inhaled deeply of his grandfather's scent, relishing the love he still felt for his first family and basked in the richness of happy memories. The little ritual made him feel lighter as he turned and walked back to join the others.

When he caught up with them, they had already reached the chosen picnic spot, in the mango grove. The maids had set up bed-sheets in an 'L' shaped temporary screen, on the sides facing the village. In the seclusion of temporary purdah, Salma had shed her burqa and she and Anu chachi had spread the cotton blanket next to the screen, in a little clearing under the mango trees.

It had rained the previous night, cajoling the orchard to life with the sweetness of freshly laundered earth, the spring leaves and the fragrance of mango trees just beginning to erupt into panicles of tiny mango buds. The birds chirped while the milking buffaloes grazed, lazed and masticated noisily. In spite of the whisperings of birds and animals, or maybe because of them, Dev sensed a deep and profound silence in the mango grove. He found Ratna standing close by, enjoying the balmy peace under the shade of a mango tree.

He walked over and placed a hand on her shoulder. 'Behen, we have come home.'

Ratna nodded and reached for his hand, just as a maid called to tell them that food had been laid out for the picnic. They walked over to join the aunts, who sat cross-legged on the cotton blanket, immersed in disjointed chatter.

'In the beginning, we somehow believed you all would return,' said Salma. 'But as the years passed, we concluded it would never happen, so we started rebuilding.'

As Salma passed around dishes, Ratna asked, 'Dev, do you remember how Uma bibiji loved this mango orchard?'

'Yes. She brought me down here often. Some of my fondest memories from those days are amongst these trees.'

Anu asked, 'Dev, did you know how we got all these orchards?'

'No. How?'

'You are partially to be blamed for this one.' Anu winked at him. 'When your ma was expecting you, she would request your father to get her mangoes from Lahore. She craved them constantly. When you were born, Baoji was so overjoyed with your birth, he instructed your father to extend our existing orchard with a bigger, better-looking hybrid variety of mangoes. It was to be a gift for the mother and the newborn child.'

'Really? I didn't know that.'

'Yes. That's why the fountain in the centre of the garden has a marble sculpture of a mother and child. Baoji imported the sculpture from Italy. Your father planted the hybrid, table variety of mangoes on the other side of the fountain and left the old juice mango trees on this side. Though Uma bhabi was appreciative of this gesture of love, I think she still enjoyed the native juice mangoes more.'

'You are right,' said Dev. 'She always did like the tiny, juice mangoes more. She often commented how this side of the orchard brought her great peace and joy.'

Ratna piped in. 'One day my little Sheila and I were going by, when Uma bibiji called us and asked, "Would you like to have some mangoes?" We nodded and she told me to make a receptacle by holding the corners of my kameez and filled it with mangoes! She was so sweet.'

'Once she plucked a juice mango for me but it had a wriggling worm inside,' Dev said. 'I was about to throw the diseased mango away, when ma took it from me. "Beta," she said, "come here and sit with me". We sat on a rock and she said, "Dev, sometimes anger, prejudice and other bad emotions muddle grown-ups, like the worm in this juice mango. If you were to squeeze this wormy mango, you would receive undesirable, rotten juice. In the same way, a messed up, angry or an egotistical human being is undesirable company that does not bring love and joy to anyone".'

'You were only around six or seven then,' said Salma. 'Did you understand what she meant?'

'Not really,' he replied. 'But I nodded anyway. Ma continued, "Always make sure you grow up as good as a wholesome juice mango. Deal with your troubling emotions when they happen, before they rot your heart away. Learn to forgive and live your life with love. That way in stressful times, you will still be able to give love and joy. Always remember the juice mango", and so saying she plucked and gave me some delicious, wholesome mangoes to eat.'

Dev paused for a moment. 'After that day, whenever I was angry or threw a tantrum, my ma would hug and tickle me, all the while whispering in my ear, "Remember the juice mango. Be nice. Live with love." We would both laugh. It became our secret code—our private mantra.

'After losing ma, I was naïve enough to believe that by just repeating, "remember the juice mango", things would get better. Oddly, it often worked for me, not because I understood what the mantra meant but because it was my mother's secret gift for me and me alone. It calmed me.' No sooner did he articulate his mother's mantra, a surge of peace and warmth enveloped him again.

As he sat quiet like the rest of them, Salma passed around a plate of cut up oranges. With juice dripping from her mouth, Ratna exclaimed, 'These are so succulent. Are these from the orchard beyond the temple?'

'Yes' replied Salma, and looking at Anu with merry eyes, asked, 'And who is responsible for that orchard?'

'I am,' answered Anu, choking with laughter. 'Actually my husband was,' she corrected herself. 'I used to come to the temple every Tuesday, praying for a child. One day, my husband walked with me, and while passing through this mango orchard, I commented how blessed Uma bhabi was to have a child plus an orchard to call her own. My husband stopped, looked me in the eye and laughed. "I can't seem to give you one gift, but I can definitely arrange for you to have an orchard in your name!" And, he started the orange grove.'

'And is Sita bibiji responsible for the pear orchard?' Salma asked.

'No. That came with the land.'

After their picnic, Dev returned to the haveli with mixed emotions, even as Ratna looked more relaxed.

The next morning at breakfast, Saleem said, 'Dev Beta, how about you and I spend the day together, while the ladies do what they need to. Actually, your uncle Sanjay and Raghu should be returning soon. Then we could go to Lahore. What do you think?'

'Sounds good, but—'

'I would like to take you around the farm first. Later we could go to Lahore and visit all the places you knew there.'

'I would have loved to, but I promised to accompany Ratna to the temple.'

'You go ahead, Dev,' said Ratna. 'I can go with Anu chachi.'

'Are you sure?'

'Don't worry Beta,' said Anu. 'I too want to visit the temple and the orange grove.'

Saleem turned to ask Dev, 'Do you know how to ride a bicycle?' After Dev nodded, they took off for the farm, postponing the visit to Lahore until later.

Soon after Dev and Saleem left, Ratna, Anu and Salma started planning their day. They were still at the breakfast table when a messenger brought a note from Razia Begum. She asked Anu to meet her around three in the afternoon, in the orange orchard under the lone pipal tree.

'Razia Begum's request has perfect timing,' said Salma. 'I have some other commitments to take care of, so, could you two visit the temple and meet Razia Begum in the orange orchard by yourselves?'

'Yes,' said Ratna. 'That pipal tree is only a short distance from the temple. We'll be able to find it.' Ratna remembered how she sometimes walked her baby sister to the pipal tree to show her nests and bird eggs. She could almost hear little Sheila's squeals at the thought.

Salma asked Anu, 'Apa, you mentioned you'd be leaving for India tomorrow. I need to know the time.'

'We should probably leave soon after breakfast.'

'Then, I've to share something with you right away,' and so saying, Salma led Ratna and Anu to her room. There, on one side sat an old metal box. She motioned for them to sit on the bed next to it. 'I got this box out of the store room. It holds some of your things. We salvaged the things from the ruins, saving them in the hope that one day someone from the family might return,' she said.

Ratna and Anu sat in quiet suspense. Salma opened the box and pulled out a sterling silver rattle, wrapped in a child's faded frock. This she handed to Ratna saying, 'This and one *garhvi*'—a small metal pitcher—'which I think belonged to your father, was all we could salvage from the temple ruins.' It was Ratna's baby sister's frock and the sterling silver rattle, a gift given by Anu and Uma. With misty eyes, Ratna pressed the priceless gifts to her heart.

Salma pushed the trunk towards Anu, who bent to pull out a box full of old family photographs from the box. She hummed, smiled and sorted the pictures, making one pile for herself and another for Dev. Ratna noticed Anu did not select any picture of Gaurav and Sita for herself, but put one in Dev's pile. She left the rest of the pictures in the box. 'If Gaurav and Sita ever visit Shahadra, they would enjoy collecting their own mementos.'

Next, Anu reached for some clothing in the box, selecting her wedding outfit and a jacket belonging to her late husband. The salwaar from that set was charred, but the kameez and the dupatta were still in excellent condition. Going through the rest, she pulled out a vibrant phulkari—a hand-woven and embroidered, ocher-colored cotton shawl—that belonged to Uma. This she saved for Dev, along with his father's gold pocket-watch and his sterling silver baby spoon, glass and a small bowl. She still rummaged through the things, looking, searching.

'Are you looking for something specific?' inquired Salma.

'I wish we had something belonging to Baoji. Dev loved him so much.'

'Doesn't that sterling silver walking stick at the bottom of the box belong to him?'

'Yes! That's it. Baoji never left home without it.' Anu reached for it. 'Salma, your warm hospitality and these priceless gifts have helped soothe some very painful memories. Thank you.' Her eyes brimming, she rose to hug Salma.

Both Ratna and Anu walked back to their room, silent, nostalgic, engrossed in sorting their emotions.

When Sanjay and Raghu returned from their overnight visit with the Khans, Ratna noticed a peculiar fire in Raghu's eyes. Could those be signs of love? Ratna refused to believe her intuition. She knew a union between Raghu and Khan's daughter, Naaz, could never take place. No one could alter the fact that Naaz was a Muslim and Raghu, not just any Hindu but a Brahmin, the highest of all castes. To her young mind, marriage between a Hindu and a Muslim seemed unthinkable.

Saleem and Dev, flushed by the exercise, returned shortly after Sanjay and Raghu did. During lunch they discussed their plans. 'Dev, would you like to see where your family's stores used to be?' asked Saleem.

Ratna stared at Dev. Her heart went out to him. How would he handle seeing the place where his father was massacred? As Dev walked out the door, she whispered, 'Bhaiya.'

Dev stopped. 'What's up, Behen?' He instinctively switched to a matching term of endearment for her.

'Nothing much,' Ratna mumbled. With a catch in her voice, she said, 'Just take care and, remember the juice mango.'

His eyes glistening, he replied, 'Behen, you do that too, at the temple.'

Soon after the men left, Ratna and Anu got up for their rendezvous with Razia Begum. They left earlier than necessary, to have extra time for a visit to the temple before the meeting. Walking through the mango grove and enjoying the pervasive fragrance of trees laden with tiny mangoes, Ratna only stopped when they reached the banyan trees. Leaning against one tree, she closed her eyes and breathed deeply. Anu waited. When Ratna opened her eyes, they walked in silence towards the ruined temple well. A brick dome covered the original opening of the well. Here Ratna bent down, kissed the bricks and then, standing up, paused in silent prayer over the grave of her loved ones.

When she walked towards the temple ruins, Anu cautioned, 'Ratna, do be careful. Old ruins sometimes have snakes and other vile creatures.' Anu sat down on a rock, a short distance away from the ruins.

Ratna seemed not to hear Anu's warning. She moved from one crumbling room to the next, as if in a daze, stepping over weeds and vines, brushing aside years of cobwebs. Light filtered inside through gaping holes in walls and the roof. Field mice scurried around, shocked out of their peaceful abode, while bats flapped their wings blindly, awakened from their slumber.

Ratna, oblivious to the commotion her presence caused, looked straight ahead, as if seeing not with her eyes but with her deep inner being, her third eye—the compass to her soul. She felt a quiet peace enveloping her, sensing a gentle presence guiding her through all the rooms of her childhood haven. She raised her hand, where the temple bells used to be. Then covering her head, she bowed, folded her hands and closed her eyes.

When she joined Anu, it was close to three o'clock, so her aunt suggested they start walking towards the orange grove. As soon as they neared it, Anu exclaimed, 'Oh my god! Look at those trees. They look orange! Wow! You can't see any leaves!'

Ratna laughed. 'Amar chacha did a good job in picking the right plants for your orchard, didn't he?'

'I wish he could see how abundantly his trees bear fruit. He tended them with so much love.'

When they reached the meeting place, they found Razia Begum dressed in a burqa, waiting. Ratna did not remember ever seeing Razia Begum by herself, without a maid. 'Stay close by,' whispered Anu, before they joined Anu's friend.

'Anu, I'm sorry for not inviting you over to our house,' said Razia Begum. 'Hamid, our son, is not easy to have around. He left home to go to Lahore, so I took the opportunity to come here to talk to you in private—' Razia Begum broke down.

Ratna felt sorry for her, even though the woman had not acknowledged her presence. She wondered if Razia Begum suspected betrayal and murder of her husband.

Razia Begum asked Anu an abrupt question. 'Do you remember Kabir Sethi and his family?'

'Yee-es,' answered Anu hesitantly.

Ratna wondered where this strange conversation would take them. Why were they talking about the Sethis, in secret, in the orange orchard?

'I think you knew his wife. Didn't you?'

'Yes,' replied Anu. 'She used to visit us often at the haveli. If I remember correctly, she and the children left for India almost two months before Partition. Are they okay?' asked Anu.

'I'm sure she is fine. I wanted to talk to you about Kabir. During Partition, he was unlucky enough not to leave his home until it was too late. Then, in order to survive here in Pakistan, he had to give up his Hindu faith and become a Muslim. By and by, he became a very staunch Muslim and married my sister Azra. Do you remember her?'

Anu nodded. Ratna still wondered what this strange revelation had to do with Anu chachi.

'You must find my ramblings puzzling, but I don't know of an easier way to ask you this,' said Razia Begum. 'Did my husband have to convert to Hinduism in order to survive in India . . . like Kabir had to here? Did he remarry? Hai Allah! If only I knew the truth, then maybe I could carry on with my life.'

Ratna shuddered. On some level, Razia Begum seemed to have sensed Anu knew more about her husband than Anu had revealed earlier. Razia Begum came up with another more difficult question. 'Nadia, our daughter-in-law, mentioned she remembers seeing him with Gaurav at your brother's place, on their way to the Amritsar station. She says she met them when she and her family were in hiding at your brother's place in Garha. Is that true?'

Ratna hoped her aunt would tell only as much as would give closure to her grieving friend.

'Apa, let's sit here on the grass. I'll tell you what I know.' Putting her hand on Razia Begum's arm, Anu replied, 'Nadia did see him at my brother's house. Since my husband was down with typhoid at that time, we couldn't help Iqbal bhaiya return to Pakistan safely. We never heard from Gaurav after that day, but heard from another source that Iqbal bhaiya was . . . was killed at the Amritsar station. Apa, I'm sorry for not having the courage to tell you this the other day.' Anu moved to take her sobbing friend in her arms.

'Thank you Anu, for lifting a big weight off my heart,' mumbled Razia Begum. 'I know it's hard for you, but it gives me peace to know my beloved husband did not betray Islam. He did not convert and marry a kafir just to stay alive. Thank you, and Anu, I'm very sorry you have no news of Gaurav.'

Anu stared at her hands as Ratna sat thinking how innocent and trusting her aunt's friend was. Razia Begum seemed to have no idea that across the border, the option for a Muslim to convert to Hinduism did not exist. A Muslim woman, maybe, if willing and lucky, could adopt her husband's caste after marrying a Hindu. But for a Muslim man, such a luxury did not exist. There were no Hindu rituals, no prayers to facilitate his conversion. Only by taking birth in the home of a Hindu could make a person a true Hindu. What caste would a 'converted' Muslim fall into?

The next morning, Dev woke up early to visit the mango grove one more time. He sat one last time on the rock where his Uma ma had given him the mantra of the juice mango.

Salma got food and a sack full of oranges loaded in the car.

As soon as Dev brought out the luggage, Saleem motioned to him. 'Beta, your khalajaan and I have something for you.'

Dev joined his hands, palms touching as if in prayer. When Saleem gifted him Umesh's pocket watch, Dev cupped it reverently in his hands, and touching it to his lips, put it in his shirt pocket next to his heart. He looked up to find there was more to follow. Saleem also gave him Baoji's silver walking stick and his mother's wedding phulkari along with the photographs and his silver baby utensils. Thanking Saleem and Salma, Dev leaned against the wall to support his shaky legs weakened by human kindness.

It was time for good-byes. The family got into the car, and with warm invitations to visit again, Dev, Ratna and Anu took one last hard look at the haveli and left.

Raghu sat in the front, Dev directly behind him. Dev touched Raghu's shoulder and said, 'Raghu, I'm sorry, I've been so involved with my thoughts I forgot to ask how your visit went.'

'I'm glad I came,' replied the friend. 'It was good to see Naaz. She has grown into a lovely young woman. When we first met after so many years, she was rather bashful, but it didn't take long before we started talking and laughing like old friends.'

'Even her sister, Nadia, seems shy,' said Dev.

'She is. Naaz said Nadia lives a miserable life with her drunken husband, Hamid. Their parents are heart-broken at how unhappy Nadia is, and have vowed to educate and make Naaz self-sufficient before arranging her marriage. And Naaz plans to study medicine in England—' he stopped in mid-sentence as they reached the housing development where the Khan's resided. Turning to his father, Raghu asked, 'Can we stop here to say goodbye, one last time? Please?'

No one objected. As soon as Sanjay stopped the car, Raghu ran in, the rest followed him. The Khans welcomed them with much warmth and laughter, insisting they have chai with the family before their journey back. Ratna and the boys went to the inner courts with Naaz.

When they retuned to the car, Dev found Raghu, not just happy but glowing, which could only mean he had fallen in love. His friend talked incessantly about the visit, and about Naaz. Ratna and Anu sat without saying a word.

'I'm glad we took the time for this visit,' said Dev. He turned sideways to face his sister, and added, 'Ratna, I hope you too found closure by coming.' Ratna reached for his hands.

Crossing the border in the early afternoon, Sanjay dropped Dev and Raghu at their hostel, before dropping Ratna at Simranjeet's house.

Four days later, Dev returned to his uncle's house to receive his parents, and mamaji and mamiji. He was surprised to find his mother and his uncle looking more troubled than they did before they left for

Pakistan. After spending only an hour or two with the family, Raminder and Sukhdev left for Garha, having said nothing about their trip.

'I suspect they were unsuccessful in locating the missing family,' guessed Ratna.

'They certainly look troubled. I'm worried, Ratna.'

'I'll talk to mamaji. Maybe he'll give us some details.'

When she did, Simranjeet looked at her with an abrupt, 'Huh?' Then, straightening up, he replied, 'The neighbours saw our papaji leave the haveli, but he was alone in the car. We have no idea what happened to our bebeji and Preet.' He put a hand to his throat and coughed.

19
The Child is the Parent

Summer, 1956

Ratna and Dev came home for summer holidays to find their loving, chatty mother in a frenzy of decorating, seeming desperate to finish the house to its originally planned grandeur. Ratna had never seen her so agitated. What happened? Could it be the trip to Pakistan?

One day, while Raminder stood precariously on her tiptoes to stock a bookcase in their library, Ratna asked, 'Ma, is there something we can do to find the whereabouts of nanima and Preet masi?' She wondered what happened to their grandma and aunt Preet.

Raminder's hands froze in mid-air and she, along with a pile of books, tumbled to the floor. Tears clouding her eyes, she screeched, 'How does one find the dead?'

'I'm sorry . . . I'm so sorry Ma. Mamaji said you didn't know what happened to them.'

Raminder reached inside the neck of her kameez for the handkerchief tucked in her brassiere, and blew her nose. 'It's okay,' she said, 'you didn't know.'

'What happened, Ma?'

'Let me tell you both at the same time,' replied Raminder. 'Go and get Dev.'

When Dev joined them, they pulled chairs and sat in a circle.

Raminder started, 'We spent the first night in Lahore, where Simranjeet's house and practice used to be. Their servant Rashid now lives in Simranjeet's old dispensary. Rashid and his family made us feel very welcome.' She paused, and dabbed at her eyes. Ratna reached over to squeeze her hand and comfort her.

Raminder took a deep breath and sighed while exhaling. 'The next morning we travelled to Ugoke. Our house was still intact and Nasibaan and her husband, an old, loyal servant-family, lived in it. They invited us in and did what they could to make our visit less traumatic. We did not know what to expect, since during Partition we had fled our home, too stupefied with the loss of our Aman—'

'What happened to Aman?' interrupted Dev.

Raminder shifted in her chair, put her hand to her heart, and then folded both her hands on her lap to tell the story. 'On 11 August 1947, Nasibaan, our maid, had gone to pick up Aman from her school, but discovered that all non-Muslim children at the school had been massacred, and their bodies dumped in the school well—'

Eyes watering, Dev put his hands over hers, reminding Raminder to take a breath before continuing. 'Rioting and killing of non-Muslims spread so quickly that for safety's sake, Nasibaan packed a few things for the journey and helped us leave immediately. Our Sikh chauffeur had already left Ugoke three days earlier with his family, as had all the other Hindu and Sikh servants. Since your papaji was too paralyzed with grief to be able to drive the car, Nasibaan's husband, Mohammed, led us in the bullock cart to join a caravan to India.'

Ratna shuddered.

Raminder whispered, 'We didn't even have time to mourn our baby.' Weeping, she tried to wipe her face with the soggy handkerchief. Ratna fetched a dry cloth and gave it to her mother. Taking a deep breath, Raminder continued, 'Anyway . . . Nasibaan and her husband, who now live in our house, not only welcomed us, but surprised us with their loyalty. While dusting our old prayer room—that they kept locked out of respect for our beliefs—Nasibaan had accidentally found some loose bricks and found my gold jewellery in a hollow there. She returned every piece to me.

'She also pulled open boxes we had left behind. All were untouched. I hugged her and gave her permission to use whatever she could from those boxes. I gave her twelve of my heavy gold bangles as thanks.

'Besides the jewellery, I also wanted to bring back with me the *Guru Granth Sahib* and my daughter's things. As I touched my Aman's blanket, her clothes, her toys, I felt her presence and smelled her fragrance. My baby's essence was in the things she wore, the things she had touched, and with such vibes, a great peace replaced the horror of her death. I understood my Aman was in a safe place. No one could ever hurt her again.'

Raminder took in a calm, deep breath and got up. 'I'll be right back,' she said. Ratna and Dev looked at her and then at each other in surprise. She turned around to add, 'I need to introduce you to your sister, Aman.' When she returned, she carried a handful of photographs. 'Look Ratna! Aman had thick, long hair and almond-shaped eyes like you.'

Ratna rose and put her arms around her mother. 'She's beautiful, Ma. She looks like you.'

Raminder smiled and put the photographs against her heart. She kissed the bundle, before continuing her tale of the rest of the journey. 'After spending two nights in Ugoke, we left for Rawalpindi. We reached there late in the evening and checked into a hotel. The place where our parents used to live was not recognisable. New construction had taken place all around, and the names of the streets were unfamiliar. The first day there, we struggled to find a familiar face or a contact. The next day or two, still without a lead, we decided to go over each of the new streets one more time. Late on the third evening, while sitting in a restaurant I . . . I . . .' she stopped her narrative abruptly.

Dev squeezed her hand and Ratna hugged her as she shook uncontrollably.

'Biji, if it hurts, we don't have to talk anymore,' said Dev, and got up to get her a glass of water.

A small sip calmed Raminder enough to continue, 'I need to tell you everything. That evening, while sitting in the restaurant, I choked on my food thinking I'd seen a ghost. Before I could find my voice, a young boy of about seven or eight walked over. His right hand touching his forehead in respect, he said, "Abbajaan wants to see you all. Can you please come with me?" Looking around and not seeing the apparition again, I got up with the rest, and followed the boy into a private room at the back of the restaurant, to meet his father. There we saw. . . .' and she faltered again.

'Who was it, Ma?' prompted Ratna.

'Our father,' Raminder whispered, swallowing hard.

'Your father?' exclaimed Ratna. 'And . . . and . . . you didn't bring him back?'

'I'm not sure I knew who he was anymore. We were definitely his children but he was not our father! I . . . I don't know how to put it. He was our father alright, but he had a new family and he was dressed like a Muslim in a crocheted skullcap over shorn hair, and the little boy who fetched us was our half-brother.' Raminder sobbed.

Too dazed to help, Ratna and Dev gawked at each other. But Raminder wiped her eyes and took another sip of water. 'We met his Muslim wife, who seemed much younger than me. He introduced her to us by saying, "This is your ammijaan". Oh! It sounded so cruel. How could someone younger than us be our mother?'

'But where were your own mother and sister?' asked Dev.

'They both killed themselves. Oh! That didn't come out right. Vaheguru! Vaheguru!' She repeated the invocation to calm herself.

Raminder looked devastated by the weight of what she knew. 'During the riots of August 1947, he told us he was away on business when a Muslim mob attacked our haveli with fire torches, hatchets and steel rods. Bebeji and our sister Preet were home alone with a young, fifteen-year-old Muslim maid. All the Sikh and Hindu servants had deserted them. Times being such, he said, bebeji feared the mob would rape and kill them. So, saying a quick prayer, she wrapped her arms around Preet and jumped into the well with her. Maybe it felt more honourable to her to die willingly than to die tainted.'

Ratna gasped.

'I'm so sorry,' said Dev.

Raminder blew her nose and continued. 'The Muslim servant girl, an orphan, whom our parents had given a home and a shelter, survived the mob attack because of her religion. She, I believe, sat near the ruins for two days. By the time father returned, the mob looted and burnt the haveli. The young maid narrated the fate of his family, and offered to take him into her humble living quarters. Papaji learnt to recite *kalma*—a prayer for acceptance into Islam—while in hiding in her house. When he was ready to convert, he married the maid and started a new life.'

'But he was an old man . . . and, she only fifteen! How could he?' shrieked Ratna.

Raminder did not answer. 'Papaji said he was scared. By becoming a Muslim, he could still live on the land that gave him birth. Aside from the burnt down haveli, he still owned the rest of his properties and lands. After he found out what happened to bebeji and Preet, he had to deal with not only the pain of losing them, but also with paralysing fear. He knew of no way to travel safely to India, in search of us, his older children.'

Raminder sat in thought for a moment, then spoke out loud. 'You know, I am sooo . . . angry. How could he do this to us?'

'I'm sure he still loves you,' muttered Dev.

'I don't know. Simranjeet and I left abruptly.'

'He didn't try to stop you?'

Raminder thought for a second before answering, 'He might have wanted to. But we didn't give him a chance.'

'Why not?' asked Ratna.

'I don't know. We were angry and hurt. He seemed a lot calmer than we were. He said, "Please don't worry about me. Insha Allah"—by God's grace—"I'm happy and at peace. And I still love you." We left him standing there with his son and child-wife.'

Trying to help, Dev asked, 'Remember how a long time ago, I once asked you, "Biji, why did Anu chachi not find me?" Do you remember what your reply was?'

Raminder, startled by this unusual question, blurted, 'Nooo.'

'You said, "Beta, where was she to look?"'

'So?' Raminder asked, blowing hard into a cloth.

'Biji, don't you see? You are angry with your father because you feel, if he had loved you enough, he would have searched for you. But in your own words, "Where was he to look?" Should he have looked in Pakistan or in India? Should he have killed himself like your mother, or allowed the angry rioters to kill him, to prove his love for his first family? If so, prove that to whom. How was he to know that you and mamaji were still alive?'

Ratna marvelled at Dev's uncomplicated logic. She watched as her mother visibly straightened, as if unburdened by Dev's insight.

Raminder did feel some dissolving of the fierce anger. But, for her, the real issue was finding her father immersed in a new religion. She hated him for that. In her saner moments, she wondered why his conversion upset her so much. Could it be because he had shown them one path but picked a different one for himself?

The incongruity of her father's beliefs made her question her own convictions. Did not her children convert from the religion of their ancestors? Did she have a double standard—one standard to judge her father by and a different standard for her children and herself? She realised that it was tough to argue with feelings. Was it possible her feelings were neither right nor wrong? They were just . . . feelings.

She suddenly needed to know after all these years, if her children were still comfortable with their decision to follow her faith.

'Absolutely,' they replied in unison. 'Why do you ask?' asked Ratna.

'No reason. I just wanted to make sure.'

Somehow, her children's unhesitating response made it easier to live with her father's decision, granting him the right to a free will. She realised that her father had chosen to live his life the best way he knew, just as her children had chosen, and, just as she had chosen.

Once, when she was a little girl, her father had advised her. 'You are a Sikh. Always remember Vaheguru and thank Him for all the good that happens in your life.'

'I thought I should remember God regardless of whether I'm a Sikh, a Hindu or even a Muslim,' she had answered cheekily.

'You are right, my little one. Religion should bring peace to one's private world. But you happen to be a Sikh child, and the only way to reach God is the way we've taught you . . . and that is the Sikh way.' She could still hear his booming laugh.

It made sense to her now. Her prayers to Vaheguru brought her peace and if her father's new religion did the same for him, she would have to accept it. But how does one reason with the heart, she wondered. She was grateful that her own children had not forced her to go against her heart. Would she have been able to accept them as her children, if they had continued on a different path? Luckily, she did not have to explore and find out. The children believed with her. The only way they knew how to reach the One God, the Omnipresent One, was the way she had taught them.

A week after her talk with Ratna and Dev, she sat down to write a letter of thanks to her Muslim father in Pakistan. She wrote about being happy at seeing him alive and at peace with his world. She wanted him to know he would always be in her prayers.

But, she did not send him her return address.

PART FOUR
1958-78

*'There is a place where words are born of silence
A place where the whispers of the heart arise.'*

—JALALUDIN RUMI, 13th Century Sufi Poet
In the Arms of the Beloved
Translated by Jonathan Star

20
The Engagement

December 1958

Ratna and Dev returned to Garha for their winter vacation as usual. In the final year of college, Ratna wanted to continue her graduate studies in Indian instrumental music. Long ago, music, especially sitar, first whispered innocent, tranquil songs to her soul. Now, it oftentimes carried her on wings to peaceful places where dreams and reality merged.

Dev had joined The Medical College of Amritsar and started his medical studies. Ratna always knew he would follow in his mentor Simranjeet mamaji's footsteps by becoming a general practitioner and maybe, one day even join the uncle's practice. Dev had spent too much time at their uncle's dispensary to think of some other speciality. He had the temperament of a natural healer and, Ratna knew, he would make an excellent family doctor.

One morning, she and Dev sat at their favourite spot in Garha—on a bench under the juice mango tree. 'Dev, we need to talk to ma about your interest in Guddi,' said Ratna.

Taken by surprise, Dev stared at her. 'I still don't know how to approach it.'

'Do you want me to talk to her?'

'Do we have to? Can't we wait until I'm a full-fledged doctor?'

'We could, but you know how the parents of girls are—they want the girls married or engaged as soon as possible. You both are nineteen, a marriageable age for girls. If the engagement takes place now, you can get married whenever you are ready.'

They sat working out the details of Dev's love interest, when Raminder came upon them. 'There you are,' she exclaimed. 'I've been looking all over for you.'

'Is everything okay?' asked Ratna.

'Yes. Come to the drawing room. We have something special to share.'

Sukhdev, already seated in the drawing room, beamed at Dev and Ratna as they walked in. 'Wait here for just a minute. I'll be right back,' said Raminder, disappearing into her bedroom.

'What's up?' asked Dev, as he sat down.

'You'll find out,' replied a smiling Sukhdev.

Raminder returned with a small attaché case. 'We have a surprise for you. We couldn't disclose it earlier for fear of distracting you during your exams.'

Ratna saw Raminder nod at Sukhdev, who rose, and putting a gentle hand on Ratna's head said, 'We've promised our Ratna's hand in marriage to a doctor in the Indian army. An only son, he comes from a good family. The family owns a house in Delhi, and a big grain farm in Karnal.'

Ratna, her mouth open, stared at her mother.

Raminder smiled at her daughter. 'Ratna, you don't seem too happy with the news. Are you okay?'

'Ma, this is all so sudden,' stammered Ratna. The suddenness of the announcement tripped her, even though she had expected this to happen sooner or later. After all, she was raised to believe that marriage was the ultimate goal for a girl. Getting an education, she knew, was usually not a preparation for a career, but a 'waiting game' for an appropriate marriage prospect.

'The right boy showed up and besides, you've seen the boy and we suspect you like him,' answered Raminder.

'Wait a minute. Wait . . . who is he?' demanded Dev. 'How come I haven't met him?' A mischievous smile playing on his face, he winked at Ratna.

'You've probably met him too. He is Ravi, Manu mamiji's nephew and Waddeh Buaji's grandnephew. I believe he visited Amritsar last month, at Waddeh Buaji's invitation to check out Ratna,' said Raminder, lightly touching her daughter's cheek. 'Ravi liked her a lot and according to Waddeh Buaji, even Ratna seemed to like him.'

'Nobody asked my opinion,' muttered Ratna smiling, feeling a warm blush spreading on her face. She had to admit she did like Ravi. He looked so kind and handsome.

'That's because we didn't want to make you self-conscious.'

Ratna smiled and Raminder turned to her beaming son, saying, 'Dev Beta, do the ardaas prayer to bless your sister and her future family.'

Everyone stood up. Raminder reached for a shimmering red and gold dupatta veil from the luggage. Covering her daughter's head with it, she explained how it was a part of a gift set of clothes and jewellery that Ratna's future in-laws had sent to bless the promised bride. After the ardaas, she passed around laddoos to mark the auspicious occasion.

'Ratna, this engagement dupatta is a symbol meant to remind you that from this day forward, you will honour your new family's traditions and their faith in you,' explained Sukhdev. 'With the acceptance of this dupatta, you promise to honour and love your newly forged bond, your new family and your new life.'

One by one, each came to bless and hug Ratna.

'Papaji, I didn't get to meet him. So let's see if we approve of my future brother-in-law! A photograph please,' said Dev, laughing.

Sukhdev went to fetch his future son-in-law's picture and returned smiling, shaking his head. 'You know in our time we were not even told of our engagement. Our elders just informed us about our marriage maybe a day or two before the event. Look at you children now. You get to see what the future spouse looks like. You are so lucky.'

Dev plucked the black and white photograph from his father's hand and nodded his approval. 'He's handsome. How tall is he?'

'We are told he's six feet two inches.'

'Papaji, he's as handsome as you are and he even rolls up his beard like you,' said Dev.

'Well, our Ratna is so pretty and tall. Finding a tall boy from a good Sikh family was our biggest challenge,' said Raminder. 'Were it not for the height, our Ratna would have been married a long time ago. I'm glad we waited. With *Vaheguru di meher*'—with God's grace—'we've found the perfect match for our precious child.'

'Here,' said Dev, laughing and pushing the photograph in front of Ratna's face, 'our mother's precious child, does he meet with your approval? Is he a "perfect match" or what?'

Ratna's friends had often giggled at their own reactions when they were told of their engagements. But Ratna had never dreamt she too would get flustered at such a momentous occasion. Surprised at herself, she found she could not even be brazen enough to glance at the photograph. She smiled, but her huge eyes looked demurely at the ground.

'Biji, does mamaji know about this?' asked Dev.

'Of course! I just told you he is Manu mamiji's nephew. And it was mamaji and mamiji who carried the engagement gifts to the prospective groom's family in Delhi. Your uncle and family are coming in the evening. Tomorrow morning we have arranged to have prayers followed by an engagement party. Anu and everyone else we know in the village has been invited,' said Raminder.

'Great. Is my future brother-in-law and his family invited too?'

'Dev, stop being a comedian. You know they can't come before the wedding,' replied his mother. 'There are so many things to take care of . . . and so little time.'

Raminder showed Ratna the beautiful gold and ruby set—matching necklace, earrings and a ring—her future-in-laws had sent for her. 'The necklace and earrings are too heavy for everyday wear. Though, after the party, you may still wear the ring. We'll put the rest in a safe-deposit box for you.' Raminder rattled on in the same vein, while Ratna sat dreaming of a loving husband, a happy home and three little ones prancing about.

Thinking about her future husband seemed surreal. It gave her a tingling sensation, even though she still wondered about her feelings towards him. Could she learn to love him? Her parents did not say how soon she would be married.

Dev seemed to read her thoughts and asked, 'When is the wedding?'

'In May probably, as soon as Ratna completes her examinations for her Bachelor's degree. Actually, her future in-laws wanted the wedding during this winter vacation but we insisted she complete her Bachelor's degree before the wedding.'

Ratna understood she had no say in the matter but she did not mind.

Her mother continued, 'We wanted Ratna to complete her graduate studies before the wedding, but her future mother-in-law suggested otherwise. Being an army doctor, Ratna's fiancé Ravi, short for Ravinder, is often posted to non-family stations when Ratna will have to stay with either her in-laws or us. She could always complete her graduate studies then. So we decided not to wait. What do you think, Ratna?'

Ratna nodded knowing it was not really a question, but an affirmation for her parents that their decision was the right thing to do. It made sense to her. If she wanted to pursue her studies further, it could be done, as her mother suggested, whenever her husband's posting took him to a non-family station.

'Have you decided upon a tentative date for the wedding?' asked Dev again.

'Her in-laws haven't picked a date as yet, but as I mentioned, it'll probably be end of April or early May, after Ratna finishes her exams.'

'Does Ravi bhaji have any siblings?' inquired Dev, slipping easily into referring to his future brother-in-law as big brother.

'No. He's an only child—'

The phone on the side table rang, interrupting their conversation.

Dev answered, 'Hello. Yes. Thank you. Thank you. I'll get her on the phone,' and turning towards his sister said, 'It's for you—Simi on the line.'

Ratna had never received a long distance call from her uncle's family in Amritsar. All the things happening to her overwhelmed her. 'Hello,' she spoke softly.

'Speak up! Speak up!' her whole family prompted.

'Congratulations, Ratna,' said Simi. 'This is so exciting. We'll be leaving shortly after lunch and be at your place around five o'clock. Tell buaji all of us will spend the night with you. Papaji needs to be back at work, so he, mummy and Waddeh Buaji will leave after tomorrow's celebrations but I'd like to stay until the end of the vacation. Will that be okay with you?'

'Of course! I'd love that.'

'And Ratna, we'll be bringing another surprise with us.'

'What other surprise?'

'Not "what" other surprise, but "who".'

'Waddeh Buaji? She'll now be related to me through "his side" of the family. Wouldn't she?' As per custom, Ratna did not speak her fiancé's name.

'Oh, she's definitely coming. You know how much she loves you. She wouldn't miss your engagement for anything. But she is not the surprise. I'm not telling you who else will accompany us. Do make sure there is another bed for this person. You'll love the surprise,' and Simi hung up.

After lunch, the family set about making arrangements for the party. While the two maids prepared the food, the male servant went to borrow larger cooking utensils from friends and relatives. Sukhdev arranged for a colourful cloth canopy to be set up in their garden for next day's festivities and Dev took charge of seating arrangements. Raminder needed to compose herself. The mere thought of such a major event made her nervous, so she walked over to admire their picture perfect garden and complimented the gardener who had lovingly coaxed the roses, dahlias and chrysanthemums into bloom.

Ratna washed her long hair for the big event and Raminder insisted she take time to put wattna on her face—a mask made out of gram flour, turmeric and mustard oil. Ratna sat patiently with her mask while her mother painted her nails for her. She felt pampered, enjoying the attention, remembering her childhood in Shahadra and her bapu who had maintained she was special.

In the evening, the overnight guests began to arrive. Her uncle and aunt from Amritsar were the first ones to show up and with them came her surprise—Guddi. Simi had made a right assessment; Ratna loved the surprise. It made the occasion all the more special.

Waddeh Buaji, the one who had brokered her marriage, stepped out of the car and walked onto the patio beaming, her arms spread like a mother hen's wings, to greet Ratna. 'I am so happy Beti! I'm glad you are marrying into our family. I told Ravi he couldn't have wished for a better girl. You are gentle and smart and beautiful . . . and he even knows you have a dark complexion but he doesn't seem to mind.'

Ratna smiled, knowing the poor woman's views on God giving a lovely girl such dark skin. Everyone she had ever known, except her immediate family, laid great store by the colour of her complexion.

Guddi's arrival definitely made Ratna's task easier, the task of alerting her mother to Dev's keen interest in Guddi. Ratna was certain her parents would approve of her friend. The thought of having Guddi for a sister-in-law made her smile.

The family and friends hugged each other. Guddi looked radiant and Simi whispered in Ratna's ear, 'There's another surprise for you.'

'What?'

'We'll talk later.'

Simi's parents brought baskets of nuts, fresh fruit, laddoos and burfi sweets for the happy occasion.

Even Guddi brought a box of burfi and offered it to Ratna. 'My mother sent this for both the happy occasions, yours and mine,' she said.

Ratna's eyes and nose scrunched up into a question.

Simi looked at her. 'Oh! Guddi got engaged last week,' she said.

'My fiancé is a Captain in the army and is posted in Bareilly,' said Guddi. 'I'm getting married in the second week of January . . . in three weeks' time.'

Feeling the colour drain from her face, Ratna glanced at her brother. Dev looked stricken. Ratna knew the others heard nothing, but she heard the shattering of a tender dream.

Simi, surprised at Ratna's silent response to such momentous news, said, 'This is what I meant to tell you later. Isn't that great news?'

'Yes, yes. Congratulations, Guddi. The news just took a little long to sink in,' replied Ratna in her confusion. 'It just seems so sudden. Why are you getting married so soon before final exams?'

"My future father-in-law insisted, saying it didn't matter to them if I didn't complete my studies. They have no intention of allowing me to work outside the house anyway. Their son, they said, earned enough and didn't need a working woman for a wife.'

'And you don't mind?' asked Ratna, forcing a tepid smile. Why had she taken so long to talk to her mother? Her heart smarted at the thought of Guddi belonging to someone else. Ratna wanted to be happy for her friend, but her heart grieved for her brother's ache.

'Ratna, I do want to finish my studies,' replied Guddi. 'But my biji doesn't keep well. She wants to see me settled in case something happens to her. I cannot add to her worries by being stubborn about my needs. And then, the marriage broker assured us, my fiancé and his parents are decent people and there would be no problem if I wanted to appear for my exams after the wedding. My biji didn't want to lose this chance of getting such a handsome and educated son-in-law. I agreed mainly because they didn't ask for any dowry.'

'So, he's very good-looking? Huh?'

Guddi giggled. 'I believe so. I haven't seen his photograph but my biji has and she says he's very handsome.'

Ratna walked with Guddi and Simi to sit on the verandah with the family, but her heart remained uneasy. Anu arrived with Taara, Sanjeev and her nephew Raghu, planning to spend the night with them. The twins left to play while everyone else sat in the verandah sipping tea, talking and laughing.

Turning to Raminder, Waddeh Buaji said, 'Let me tell you something. Ravi is a good man and so is his father. But I want to warn you. Ravi's mother is something else.'

At the mention of Ravi's name, Ratna's ears, like antennas, picked up the conversation over the girls' giggling.

'What do you mean, Buaji?' asked Raminder.

'Well, I don't know how to tell you this . . . simply put, she is a bad tempered woman, a rotten shrew! I hope she doesn't give our Ratna too much trouble.'

'Buaji, I'm sorry to hear that. But my Ratna knows how to *thanda tattaa samona*.' Ratna knew how to temper the hot with the cold. 'Ratna can calm anyone's temper with her patience and compassion,' replied Raminder with pride.

'I know that. Ratna is a lovely person. It's her future mother-in-law I worry about. That woman can wear anyone down. After I lost my son, I could have lived with them easily, but I couldn't bear her crude, aggressive nature. Anyway, I'm glad I live with my niece instead. My Manu is sweet, kind and loving. Ratna reminds me of my Manu,' said the old woman.

Ratna heard the conversation but what she really heard was the pride in her mother's voice about her strength of character—patience and compassion. Deep in her heart, she knew she would do everything in her power to honour her mother's faith in her. Had her mother not taught her to believe that 'good begets good'? Ratna knew she could bring her prospective mother-in-law around with love and understanding. How difficult could she be?

The three friends slept in Ratna's room, talking long into the night. Guddi invited Ratna and her family to her wedding and Ratna felt relieved that neither her mother nor Simi were aware of Dev's crush on Guddi. With the way things had turned out, it was for the best.

The next morning the haveli bustled with activity. Everyone got dressed for the occasion. Raminder caught Ratna looking at herself in a full-length mirror, dressed in shimmering silks and gold jewellery her in-laws had sent.

'You look like a princess,' whispered Raminder, and walked over to wrap an arm around her daughter's waist.

Sukhdev's brother Harpal and his wife, Gursharan, arrived for the engagement, beaming from ear to ear. Raminder did a double take: what caused her difficult-to-please relatives to honour this occasion with their presence? Over the years, she and Sukhdev had dutifully invited the brother's family for every celebration, but Harpal and Gursharan had never bothered to acknowledge those invitations. Their arrival now caused a stir. Sukhdev walked up to Raminder and winked. "What happened?" he asked.

She smiled and shrugged her shoulders.

Harpal and Gursharan's intentions soon became apparent. They were on a mission to check out the rich doctor's daughter, Simi, as a prospective bride for their good-for-nothing son.

The prayers began and the two friends, Simi and Guddi, sat down together to do the kirtan, singing the hymns in blissful harmony. Once the prayers ended, the socialising began. Raminder watched as Harpal's wife, Gursharan, wasted no time in doing what she had come to do. She happened to be sitting next to Waddeh Buaji but not knowing the old woman, asked, 'Do you know which one is the doctor's daughter?'

Raminder had warned Waddeh Buaji about Gursharan. 'Why? What is she to you?' retorted the old woman. Gursharan arose abruptly, probably wanting to find a more civil audience.

Before Raminder could warn her niece, Gursharan found out about the prospective girl and walking up to her, hugged Simi while introducing herself as Ratna's aunt. Taking Simi's slim arm, Gursharan moved her hand over it, asking, 'Beti, how come you are so thin?'

'*Hain ji?*'—Excuse me?—mumbled the startled girl, withdrawing her arm. Then composing herself, Simi smiled her sweetest smile and asked, 'How come you are so fat, Auntie?'

Raminder smothered her laughter, as Gursharan's face registered the shock of being answered rudely. The woman, as most prospective mothers-in-law of her times, had probably expected the girl to smile coyly and accept the ungracious comment, but Simi answered her back. The child turned out to be a real *pataka*—a firecracker!

Raminder loved it, but Gursharan obviously decided she would have none of it. 'Rich or not, this girl is not fit to be my daughter-in-law. She has a mouth too big for her innocent-looking pretty face.' Raminder overheard Gursharan report the ill-fated encounter to her husband.

Gursharan's smile vanished and walking over, she said, 'Raminder, there is another engagement we have to attend. We are already late.'

Harpal joined her and together the couple wished her goodbye. They left as abruptly as they had arrived. Raminder sensed she would never see them again.

21
Marriages Made in Heaven

1959

In January of that year, Ratna, Simi and their respective families received invitations to Guddi's wedding. Ratna, however, had misgivings about Dev attending it. She knew it would make the situation more painful for him, but nothing she suggested dissuaded him.

Ratna's family reached Amritsar a day before the wedding. Anu chachi's eleven-year-old daughter Taara accompanied Raminder and Sukhdev from Garha. Taara had never seen a Sikh wedding and Guddi had extended her a personal invitation at Ratna's engagement party.

The night before the wedding, friends drew intricate designs on each other's hands with henna, while Ratna and Simi spent hours designing delicate filigree patterns with it on the bride's hands and feet. Ratna hated the smell of henna paste, but loved the motifs of glorious colour—the colour of deep terra cotta tiles—that the paste left behind. So, she took pains to mix the henna powder just right, with a touch of oil and lemon juice, hoping to ensure colours as deep as red poppies, to draw designs as delicate as butterflies. Her heart gave a leap when she noticed Guddi's mother checking her daughter's deep-coloured hands, smiling a secret smile. Everyone knew the oldwives tale—the more vibrant the colour of henna, the deeper the groom's love for his bride.

The morning of the wedding, Ratna, Simi, Taara and all the other friends took great care to dress the bride amidst laughter and singing of traditional wedding songs. Guddi's *churra*, her gold jewellery and the *kaliras*—the bridal trinkets—made all the joyous bridal sounds when she moved. Her gold and red salwaar kameez shimmered and her face glowed. Guddi's mother, Satwant, kissed the smooth forehead of her beautiful daughter bride, saying a quick prayer to bless her child.

When Dev saw Guddi in her bridal splendour, he asked Ratna for a favour. 'Can you talk Guddi's mother into letting me stand with her cousin brothers during the marriage ceremony? I'd like to help with the *widah* ceremony too.' He pleaded to participate in the bride's send-off ceremony too.

Ratna loved her brother dearly, but did not want to help him in this strange request. She did not want him to be the one to guide a veiled Guddi to follow her groom around the *Guru Granth Sahib*. She did not feel comfortable in helping him participate in the Sikh tradition of brothers and male cousins guiding their heavily veiled sister brides around the spiritual guide four times, to sanctify the union.

'You don't want to do that. It will be too unsettling,' Ratna said.

'I want to. I'm aware of what I'm asking. See what you can do.'

'But—'

'Behen, please?' he begged.

Ratna just melted whenever he called her 'behen'. So, she asked Guddi's mother, who gladly obliged. 'I am an only child like Guddi,' she said. 'My husband had four nephews but only one has come. I would love it if Dev helps out as a brother.'

As the ceremony started, Taara whispered, 'Didi, why is Dev bhaiya helping guide Guddi didi around the *Guru Granth Sahib*?'

'Because her face is covered with a veil and she can't see,' replied Ratna softly.

'Why is her face covered?'

'It's a tradition.'

'Taara,' whispered Raminder, 'by guiding a veiled sister around the *Guru Granth Sahib*, the brothers of the bride alert the groom and his family that if they ill-treat her, the brothers would stand up for her rights.'

'Auntie, you are so funny!' Taara giggled. 'First of all, Dev bhaiya is not her brother and secondly, Guddi didi is a good girl. Why would her new family not treat her right?'

Raminder and Ratna smiled and told her to hush.

Ratna completed her finals for her bachelor's degree by April, and her parents wasted no time in fixing her wedding date on the first Sunday in May. As soon as Ratna reached Garha after her university exams, she found herself in the midst of hectic preparations for her wedding. Raminder had hired a tailor who came to their home to stitch clothes for her trousseau. Every morning, she and her mother left to shop, returning late in the evening, exhausted.

Now that Raminder and Sukhdev were financially secure, they spent generously on their daughter's dowry. Dev assumed the responsibilities of a brother with pleasure, contacting chefs for the reception, buying the necessary rations for the wedding feast, making seating arrangements for the guests and arranging colourful cloth canopies for the ceremony. Sukhdev acquired accommodations for the *baraat*—the groom's party— and contacted the bhaiji at the local gurdwara for the ceremony. He also obtained the services of a florist for garlands and flower decorations, and made arrangements to rent a good music system for the prayers and the evening reception.

As soon as Ratna knew the date of the wedding, she invited Guddi and Inder, ensuring enough advance notice to allow time for travel plans. Simi and her mother came two weeks before the wedding to help with the preparations. Every afternoon, the girls sat under a ceiling fan in the shade of the verandah, laughing, talking and applying traditional gold and silver gotta-ribbons, on the edges of Ratna's dowry dupattas. They applied the gotta-ribbons by hand, so when the bride no longer wanted to advertise her newly wedded state, she could remove them easily.

Starting a week before the wedding, the haveli came alive every evening with twinkling lights, festive music and cheerful guests. The women from the village came to participate in the singing and dancing on a nightly basis. All the merriment and laughter made it a happy time for Ratna.

However, as the wedding day came closer, Ratna worried about not hearing from Guddi. Luckily, a couple of days before the wedding, she received a congratulatory card along with a note of apology from her friend. A difficult pregnancy, Guddi wrote, caused her doctor to instruct her to avoid travel during the first critical months. Guddi and Inder wished Ratna and her future husband much happiness. Ratna sat with the note from her best friend, disappointed, but wishing her better health.

Even though the pace of days prior to the wedding was hectic, they still were happy times for Ratna. She cherished her parents' loving hearts and her brother's indulgences. One of the few things Dev possessed that had belonged to his Uma ma was a necklace she had sent through Anu chachi before Partition. He gave that necklace to Ratna as a wedding gift, saying that he wanted her to have something precious, something meaningful from him. 'Ratna, whenever you wear it, let it remind you of juice mangoes and help you live your life with love and joy. Let it bring you peace and security.' Her eyes brimming with tears, Ratna could not find words to tell him how much the gift meant to her. She simply reached over and hugged him.

When the special day arrived, the twinkling lights on the trees and walls of the haveli, the arches of fragrant flowers and the loud gramophone music broadcast the celebrations to the entire village. Ratna's baraat arrived in the evening, a day before the ceremony. Her future mother-in-law and Waddeh Buaji accompanied the groom's wedding party.

Raminder insisted it was unlucky for the groom to see his bride prior to the wedding, so Ratna and her friends observed the proceedings through a second floor window. The bridegroom sat on a white horse, while his family and friends did bhangra dancing in front of the slow moving horse. Ravi's best friend, Gurdev, walked alongside his horse, carrying magenta and gold coloured shimmering umbrella over Ravi's head. Once the music stopped, the bridegroom alighted from the horse and Ratna's friends and cousins gaped in awe at her attractive groom. Even little Taara commented on how handsome the groom looked in his traditional garb of silk kurta pyjama under a long gold embroidered silk tunic called an achkan, wearing a turban trimmed with golden gotta ribbons. Ravi carried himself erect and tall like a prince.

Ratna tried to calm the flutter in her heart in vain. She watched both the families performing the *milni*—the meeting of two families—and saw them reciting the welcoming hymn, sung by the bride's family. But she heard nothing except her own singing heart; nothing registered except her own dreams.

Later that evening, everyone spent a pleasant time partying, listening to gifted musicians and watching hired professional bhangra dancers perform.

Early the next morning, the Sikh wedding ceremony called the Anand Karaj took place with melodious kirtan hymns sung from the *Guru Granth Sahib*. Ratna's face was covered by her gold and red embroidered dupatta, and her matching long skirted ghagara rustled as she walked tall and elegant, behind her groom, around the spiritual guide of Sikhs. Dev, Raghu and little Sanjeev guided a veiled Ratna around the sacred book. Simi and Taara sat behind the bride (a place of honour), helping her stand and sit without stepping on her flowing ghagara.

After the prayers and the ceremony, the congregation showered rose petals on the happy couple. Both sets of parents garlanded their children with fragrant flowers and fed them laddoos. They removed Ratna's veil from her face and she sat in her bridal splendour with her groom, flashing a coy smile, her dimples lighting up her face. Ratna's rustling kalira trinkets, the jingling gold bangles, the hanging tiara on the forehead, and all her gold jewellery gave her the look of a princess bride, while her prince, Ravi, stole loving glances at her.

The bride left with the groom's family immediately after the ceremony, as the wedding party had to catch the afternoon train to Delhi. Everyone wept joyously as they saw the newly-weds off.

The wedding party reached Delhi late in the evening.

Ratna's new home stood dark and lonely, with the moon peeping through rustling trees, bathing the quiet house with whispering shadows. Ratna's disappointment at her reception caused her to shudder. Ravi noticed and lovingly put a protective arm around her. Ratna's eyes filled with unexpected tears. She missed the twinkling lights to welcome her; she missed the gathering of friends and family awaiting the arrival of the newlyweds; she missed the welcoming prayers. She arrived as a bride in a 'house with a wedding', but found no friends and relatives with whom to celebrate the occasion. Her parents-in-law, tired from the journey, unlocked the house and went straight to bed. Ratna prayed silently, grateful for Ravi's protective arm around her.

The first morning in her new home, Ratna woke up to a quiet house. Her in-laws and her husband slept late, so she took a bath, said her morning prayers and prepared for the beautiful day. When Ravi woke up, he pulled her to the bed, kissing her sleepily, telling her how lovely she looked. Ratna blushed, sensing her husband's intentions.

When her mother-in-law woke up, she walked right into their room making loud warning noises with her throat, but without knocking. She greeted the couple, ignoring the startled bride's discomfort, telling her to make the morning tea for the family. The mother-in-law then casually turned around, dusting the curios in the room with the end of her dupatta, to allow Ratna time to collect herself. Ratna got up quietly and straightening her clothes, walked towards the kitchen.

On her way out, she overheard Ravi say, 'You could at least have given Ratna one day to feel special. Why couldn't you make the bed-tea one more day?'

'That's a sure way to spoil daughters-in-law. You don't want them to think they are princesses or something.'

'Biji! Biji!' Ravi shook his head.

Ratna came into the room with a tray full of teacups for the family. 'Child, you never serve morning tea without tea-time biscuits. Didn't your mother teach you that? Go and get some. They are in a tin sitting on the shelf next to the cooking stove.'

Ratna put the tea tray on the side table and returned to the kitchen to get the biscuits from the biscuit tin her mother-in-law had mentioned. When she returned, she stopped in her tracks. Her father-in-law busily rummaged through one of her boxes, inspecting her personal belongings—picking and shaking her intimate apparel and sanitary towels!

Seeing Ratna, he grinned, 'Heh! Heh! I was just checking to see if you had everything you'd need before you depart for your honeymoon. I wanted to ensure you had all the necessities a woman needs. Heh!

Heh! After I have my morning tea I will repack the boxes for both of you.'

'I can take care of myself,' replied Ratna, too angry and shocked to notice until much later, that neither her husband nor her mother-in-law found it bizarre to have the father-in-law peeking into her personal things. 'You forget,' she said, in a calm voice, 'I've been a woman all my life, and know what I need. And, I've always packed my boxes myself.'

'Well, our son can't pack. I've always packed for him.'

'I can pack too,' replied Ravi laughing. 'It's just easier to let you do it to avoid constant nagging.'

Ignoring the bantering between the father and the son, Ratna spoke quietly. 'That box has my jewellery you might want to see. This one here has clothes and jewellery for biji and you.' She guessed instinctively that aside from being uncouth, her father-in-law was like an impudent child—insisting on opening his gifts long before the birthday party was over. She knew her father-in-law was looking for the box with gifts for him and his family. Her mother-in-law showed disappointment at receiving a gift of a set of gold *karas*—heavy gold bangles—and a gold necklace with earrings, along with two silk salwar-kameez suits.

'Your parents should have saved on the jewellery and given us more *wadaigi*, which means cold cash, in case you didn't know,' mumbled her father-in-law. Ratna refused to dignify his comment with a reply. Her parents had given five thousand rupees in wadaigi and that was more than they deserved.

Ravi raised his voice. 'Papaji, how can you talk like that? It's disgusting. It sounds like you are begging!'

'Well, you are a doctor. You merited more than this. Your mother was expecting a much bigger dowry,' replied the father evenly.

'Whose marriage is it anyway? . . . Do leave us alone. I am delighted with my lovely bride, and I don't want to hear any more about what biji or you expected. It's my life and I am thrilled with what I got.'

That settled it and Ratna heard no more about it as long as Ravi was within hearing range. But behind Ravi's back, it seemed like a different story. Her father-in-law, with a tooth missing, smiled the lecherous smile of a hormonal teenager in heat. 'Ratna, how come your parents gave you only "single" sized quilts? Don't they know certain facts of life, like the necessity of a "double" sized quilt for newlyweds? Heh! Heh!'

Ratna, her face flushed, turned away without answering. The father-in-law joked about a topic that was taboo in her world. She remembered Waddeh Buaji telling them how difficult her mother-in-law was, but the old woman forgot to mention the crude and vulgar father-in-law.

In the evening, while Ravi stood tying his turban in the attached dressing room, Ratna ironed her clothes for the reception. Ravi's mother, not seeing Ravi, ambled into their room smiling. 'You know Ratna, I've been wondering why you are not as light skinned as your parents or your brother?'

Ravi stopped his turban tying in his tracks, stunned by his mother's rudeness. 'Biji, why are you bringing it up now?' he called from the next room. 'I told you about it. I love her complexion. You yourself are even darker than Ratna.'

Ratna felt in all fairness she had to tell them the truth, just in case they were not aware of it. 'I hope you know I was adopted during Partition.'

'What? We didn't know that! What if you were a Muslim by birth or worse still, the result of somebody's sin?' Ravi's biji huffed in agitation.

'Biji, how does it matter who her birth parents were? Will you please stop this nonsense? You are annoying!' said Ravi and walked into the bedroom with his partially untied turban trailing on the carpet behind him.

'It's just that no one told us about the adoption before the wedding.'

'No one asked. Anyway it goes to her parents' credit that they showered so much love on her that you couldn't guess.' Ravi glared at his mother and walked back to the dressing room.

'Waddeh Buaji probably knew and she too kept it secret from us,' grumbled the mother.

'Biji please stop! She did tell me. So please drop the topic right now!' he yelled back.

Ratna had never seen or heard so much bickering in a family, especially not between a mother and child. She stayed out of the discussion. As long as her husband loved her, it was easier to deal with his mother. She shuddered to realise that in spite of her good intentions, she would never be able to respect this woman, like she did her own loving mother.

At the evening reception, one of their family friends said to Ratna's mother-in-law, 'You must be so happy with such a lovely daughter-in-law.'

'Our son seems very happy with the *churail*—the witch. It doesn't matter how we feel.' She pressed her lips and smiled her sweetest smile.

Ratna overheard the conversation and something deflated in her chest. She had been judged and sentenced to being a witch, even before she had time to share the warmth in her heart. Later that week, Ratna was told in no uncertain terms, she was not smart enough or good looking enough for their *heere wargah puttar*—a son as precious as a diamond. Ratna bore the insults quietly, hoping her misery would end once she moved away from the family. To her relief, they soon left for their honeymoon, and from there went directly to their own home in Lucknow.

Ravi did not talk much about his parents. He once mentioned in passing, 'Ratna, my parents can be difficult at times. But their hearts are in the right place.'

That was easy for him to say, thought Ratna, but she did not tell him about her first traumatic week with his parents.

Spending a few days in her own home with her loving, considerate husband, helped Ratna get over the terror her mother-in-law caused and the indecency her father-in-law displayed.

Ravi's closest friend Gurdev met Ratna's cousin, Simi, at their wedding, and Raminder reported the meeting to her brother. 'Simranjeet,' she said, 'You better start wedding preparations for your daughter soon.'

'What are you talking about?' asked Simranjeet.

'I watched Ravi's friend Gurdev look at Simi and fall in love with her.'

Raminder's observation proved right. Gurdev's parents soon approached Simranjeet and Manu, who agreed that Gurdev would make a great match for their daughter—a handsome doctor with a private practice in orthopedic surgery.

Simi and Gurdev were betrothed within a week of Ratna and Ravi's wedding.

22
Making Do with Life's Lemons

Summer, 1959

A couple of months after her wedding, and to her utter delight, Ratna discovered she was pregnant, and her life turned sweeter. She received a letter from her ma looking for an invitation to visit Lucknow. Ratna replied promptly, 'Please come,' she wrote. 'I'm dying to see you. I get so lonely and homesick when Ravi is at work. Come. Please, please. I have a couple of surprises for you.'

Besides sharing the news of the arrival of a new baby, Ratna needed company to visit Guddi, who lived only four or five hours train journey away. From the few letters she had received, she gathered Guddi was in poor health. She wanted Ravi and her family to accompany her to Guddi's house in Bareilly, so her doctor husband and her wise mother could decide whether it was just a difficult pregnancy or something more serious.

Ratna had never been separated from her family for such a long period. The news of the visit threw her in a cycle of excitement and hectic preparations for their arrival. Two days before her family arrived, Ratna had excruciating pain in her lower back. Before she could reach her gynaecologist, she lost the baby. After the miscarriage, both she and Ravi experienced a strange sort of heartache. It was a pain that could not wrap itself around an object; a simple pain that floated around, tugging at their hearts in an awkward sort of way. Ratna and Ravi held each other but the embrace did not bring much comfort. Each had to deal with it alone.

'Why?' questioned Ratna.

'Only Vaheguru knows. Maybe the little soul was not ready to face the world,' replied Ravi.

By the time her family arrived, Ratna had come to terms with her misfortune. She knew she would still feel bad at times, but there would be a next time. And hope brought composure. Both she and her husband greeted the family at the railway station. They hugged and cried happy tears; much had happened in that short period and they talked and laughed more than they listened.

Ratna confided in her mother the recent heartache she and Ravi had suffered. When Raminder hugged her, it was enough to open the tap of her troubled emotions. Mother and daughter stood locked in a healing embrace. Hearing footsteps, Raminder kissed her forehead, and let go of her, saying, 'Anu sent some *pinnee* sweets for you.' Even though Raminder did not comment on the situation, Ratna sensed that her mother understood her pain. She wiped her tears and turned to face her brother.

'Dev made sure we arrived in Lucknow in time for rakhi,' said Raminder.

Ratna hugged her brother. 'Thank you for coming before the festival.'

At the breakfast table the next morning, Ratna suggested, 'Let's go sightseeing today. Tomorrow I have a big surprise planned for you.'

'What is it?'

'I would like us to take a train to Bareilly and visit Guddi.'

'That would be great,' said her mother, 'But—'

'But what?' asked Ratna.

'Tomorrow is the festival of rakhi.'

'So? This way even Guddi will be able to tie the rakhi on my wrist,' chimed in Dev. 'After all, they accepted me as her brother at the wedding.'

Ratna looked at her brother but decided not to comment. He was old enough to know what he suggested. He had already carried this 'brother thing' too far. If he really wanted to be Guddi's brother, then so be it. Ratna worried about him and his broken heart. If acting like Guddi's brother helped the healing, she would keep her mouth shut.

She planned to surprise Guddi. 'Who knows, Guddi could even decide to travel back with all of you to Amritsar, for her delivery.' Ratna knew that their customs dictated that a pregnant woman go to her parent's home for her first delivery.

The next morning, the train journey to Bareilly proved to be fun. On the way, Raminder gave Ratna the good news—Simi was getting married to Ravi's friend Gurdev in the beginning of September. And, Simranjeet had sent a personal wedding invitation for Ratna and Ravi. 'You'll receive the wedding card soon,' she said.

'You know how much Simi would love to have you come before her wedding and help with the trousseau,' said Sukhdev.

'Why don't you return with us?' Raminder added. 'Even Waddeh Buaji has sent you a personal invitation. She said, "There is no way Simi would get married unless Ratna joins the festivities".'

Ratna smiled and looked at her husband for approval. 'Of course you can go,' said Ravi with a wink. 'But do return soon after the wedding. I'll miss you.'

'What about you?' she asked.

'Well, it all depends on whether I can get leave around that time. But, even if I get the leave, I will not visit Amritsar with you. I'll come with the groom from Chandigarh. After all, Gurdev is my best friend and he was there for me at our wedding.' Ratna had not thought of that. She was happy either way, as long as he participated in the wedding. She agreed to return with her parents.

When the train stopped at the Bareilly station, Ravi asked, 'Should I call Guddi from the station and warn her we are coming?'

'No! No! A surprise is a surprise.' Ratna laughed. 'We don't have their telephone number anyway.'

'That's no problem. I can get it very easily from the army exchange.' She just shook her head and with twinkling eyes formed a quiet 'no' with her lips.

At the station, they rented a tonga to get to the army officers' colony. The whole family piled on the pony trap and set out to locate

Guddi's apartment. Once they reached the apartment building, both Sukhdev and Ravi walked over to ring the doorbell, while Dev assisted the women with the luggage. They had come prepared to spend one night with Guddi.

A young maid opened the door and looked inquiringly at the two well-dressed gentlemen. 'Is your sahib in?' asked Sukhdev.

'Kaptaan sahib is not home,' she said in a matter-of-fact way and slammed the door, acting as if being a maid in the captain's household gave her the right to be rude to guests.

Reacting with the finely tuned response of an army doctor, Ravi stepped inside, before the door shut. 'Is Guddi in?' he asked, standing at the door's entrance, keeping it ajar.

'Yes, she's in. But who are you?' asked the maid.

'Can we see her?' said Sukhdev, as Raminder and Ratna joined him.

'Who are you?' she repeated one more time.

'We are her relatives.'

The maid turned. 'Wait here. I'll go and check.'

But Ratna and Raminder decided not to wait. The maid shook her head as they followed her into Guddi's bedroom.

Ratna caught herself giggling like a schoolgirl at the thought of seeing the surprise on her friend's face. But she and her mother came to a sudden stop as they saw a form—curled up in foetal position—lying in a room darkened with heavy draperies drawn over the windows. As the maid switched on the light, they saw Guddi. Ratna screamed and froze. Raminder ran towards the girl, wailing, 'Vaheguru! Vaheguru! What happened to you, my baby?'

Guddi lay on a filthy bed, with ugly black and blue bruises all over her face and arms. For a couple of seconds she stared at the company with blank eyes, then, sat up mechanically and painfully. Little by little, recognition seemed to dawn and tears welled up in her eyes. The tears seemed to arrive uninvited from somewhere deep, from a place beyond pain, a place where the gushing water knew not where or how to flow.

Raminder had the girl in her arms and Guddi lowered her head on the woman's warm shoulders.

No one breathed.

Dev had followed his mother and sister into Guddi's room to check why their mother was so distraught and stood glued at the entrance to the room. By the time Ravi and Sukhdev joined them, Dev, his face twitching, bellowed, 'Where is that bastard? I'm going to kill him!' His eyes wild, he looked as if ready to punch the daylights out of Guddi's husband.

Ratna moved over to hug him, planting a calming kiss on his angry forehead. The veins on his temples pulsated, seeming ready to burst. 'Take it easy,' she whispered.

Guddi mumbled, 'I fell down the stairs.'

'What stairs, beti?' asked Sukhdev. 'You live in an apartment on the ground floor!' His tall body shrank with the shock.

'What took you so long?' asked the maid.

Raminder helped Guddi to her feet, as she was big, very big, with a child. Ratna helped to lead her to the drawing room, making her sit on the soft sofa with pillows, trying to make her as comfortable as possible. They all sat around Guddi.

Ratna shuddered, as she stared at her battered and bruised friend.

'Guddi, what do you want us to do?' asked Ravi, softly.

'We are taking her with us,' declared Raminder.

'What about Inder?' asked Ravi.

'He can go to hell!' Ratna screeched, surprising herself for harbouring so much venom.

'I'm going to kill him!' shrieked Dev. 'I'm going to kill him,' he repeated, kicking the wooden door.

'We should report him to his commanding officer,' said Sukhdev.

'We are getting her out of here right now!' screamed Ratna.

They argued, yelled and pronounced declarations as if the decision was theirs to make, until Ravi asked, 'Guddi, will you help testify against the bastard?'

Guddi nodded, and shut her eyes, as tears escaped through her long lashes.

Unbidden, the maid brought chai and placed the tray in front of Ratna who poured the tea for everyone. But Guddi declined her cup, as her lower lip, cut up and swollen, seemed on fire.

Ravi got up and asked Guddi's permission to examine her cuts and bruises. He straightened up to write a prescription and handing it to Dev asked him to get it filled at the nearest pharmacy. 'I think her arm is broken, maybe at more than one place. I'm not sure how she is handling the pain,' he said, talking like the rest of them—as if Guddi were not present.

'Can you fix it?' pleaded Ratna.

'I'll try my best to make her comfortable, until we can get the arm x-rayed and have a cast put on it.'

After Dev left, the family discussed options to get Guddi out of harm's way. Turning to her doctor son-in-law, Raminder said, 'I know you'll take care of Guddi's physical bruises, but is the baby in any kind of danger?'

'We can be sure only after she is examined by a gynaecologist—'

Ratna interrupted, 'Let's talk about doctors later. First, we have to get Guddi out of here. Now. Right now!'

Ravi turned to his wife. 'I believe the next train back to Lucknow is sometime in the evening. Anyway, this is a grave situation and we can't just take Guddi with us and walk out. We must feed her and I need to bandage her broken arm. We also need to ensure Inder never hurts her again. If we walk with her now, she'll be left without a penny, and without justice. In court, he would testify Guddi left of her own free will. The law will side with him, and in the end, she could even lose her baby.'

'Can't we call the police?'

'The police have no jurisdiction over an army officer's family matters.'

Just then the maid came in to say she needed to go to the market to buy vegetables for lunch. Sensing she was looking for money, Sukhdev took out a twenty-rupee bill and handed it to her. 'Buy whatever you need for lunch, and get some bananas and grapes also.' Ratna smiled at her compassionate father who had guessed that Guddi would be able to eat only soft fruit.

Before the maid left, Raminder asked, 'What time does your master, I mean your sahib, come home?'

'He is usually home by 2.00 pm, in time for lunch.'

The clock on the wall pointed to a little after ten o'clock. They now knew the time they had to plan their escape. Everyone sat in silence, thinking and sipping chai. As soon as Ratna finished her tea, she said, 'Guddi, tell us where your things are. We need to pack your stuff. You are leaving with us for good. Just tell us what you want to take.'

Guddi stared at Ratna as if her mind still could not wrap itself around reality. She sat uncomprehending. Raminder hugged her and taking a deep breath, started singing in a trembling voice, *'Deh Shiva Bur Mohae. . . .'* Ratna picked up the hymn in her melodious voice, and soon even Guddi joined them, mumbling—'God give me the strength to. . . .'

Sukhdev and Ravi joined them by singing the refrain. Soon a tranquil calm hung about the group, a calm brought by love and faith. Hands and hearts joined in prayer. The collective warmth of this loving act thawed the fear and immobility. Guddi did not or could not smile but her face acquired more colour. Her head once again sank onto Raminder's shoulder. Ratna hoped her mother's warm touch would help courage to flow from her to Guddi, like water to a wilted plant.

The men brought empty suitcases and metal boxes from the storage room. The women packed Guddi's things, stacking them against the wall in the drawing room. When Dev returned, Ravi splinted and bandaged Guddi's broken arm, applied salve to her bruises, and gave her glucose water to drink. Raminder mashed a banana and fed the starving girl. Ratna recollected another such scene that took place a long time ago. Then too the mother had nursed an ailing child through trauma, sickness and nightmares.

'Guddi, where is your wedding gold jewellery?' asked Ratna. 'We don't want to leave that behind.'

Guddi stared at her friend without blinking, as if trying to grasp her meaning.

'Do you know where your gold jewellery is, Guddi?' repeated Raminder.

'No, I don't. I never saw any after marriage,' she replied.

'But Satwant auntie bought such beautiful jewellery for you. She spent more than she could afford,' exclaimed Ratna. She remembered the day she had accompanied Guddi's mother to buy the gold jewellery for Guddi's trousseau and she remembered how most of it was bought on credit.

'You think it's with your mother-in-law, or you think Inder sold it?' asked Raminder.

'Sold it probably,' Guddi mumbled. 'He drinks heavily and spends his evenings with prostitutes.' She cringed as she sobbed, her face reflecting her inner struggle. Taking one long guttural breath, she added, 'Every evening when he goes out with those women, I feel my soul being dredged of any lingering illusions I still have about the future of our marriage.'

Ratna sensed that Guddi's fearful heart had already given up the fight. She was amazed at what had become of her cheerful and vivacious friend, who now responded vaguely or not at all. She found herself angry at Guddi's timorous acceptance of her situation, as it diminished not just the scared girl, but her too. It diminished every remembered life—past or present—which had mustered courage to nurse, nurture and lend its womb to the universe's dreams, its joys, sorrows and pain. She refused to concur with her friend's unspoken acceptance. Her soul screamed at Guddi to stand up and fight, if not for herself then at least for her unborn child.

With the cooking done and the table set, half an hour before Inder was expected, the maid requested Raminder and Ratna to talk to her in private. They both followed her into the kitchen.

'Bibiji,' the maid asked Raminder. 'Are you my memsahib's mother?'

'No, I'm the masi, her mother's sister,' Raminder lied.

'I hope God forgives me for saying this,' said the maid. 'That Kaptaan is an evil bastard. He gets drunk in the evenings and beats my memsahib, and then refuses to allow her any medical attention. We want to help her but can't, as he orders both of us—I mean his personal army attendant and me—to leave, threatening to fire us if we hesitate. Bibiji, we need our jobs. It's good money. Finding such a well-paid position is hard. But, watching the poor memsahib get beaten on a daily basis is unbearable. She needs to be in a safer place, especially during these last months of her pregnancy. Please help her or she will lose the baby.'

'We are planning to take her with us,' said Ratna.

'I hope he lets you take her.' The maid stood shaking her head. 'He is the devil himself.'

'How will he stop us? We are five of us against one of him,' said Raminder.

'Bibiji, please keep her safe. She might refuse to go with you because she is so scared of him.'

'We'll take care of that.'

'Bibiji, one more thing. He is a two-faced bastard, very civil and polite in front of company. Please don't let that fool you.'

'Don't you worry—' said Raminder hugging the maid. 'Will you be alright?'

'Yes, Bibiji. My husband is a chef in the army mess. He'll know what to do if the Kaptaan misbehaves with me.'

They heard a jeep stop in front of the apartment. The maid turned and started warming the food, while Raminder and Ratna scrambled to be with the rest of the family. Dev looked ready to kill. 'Don't do anything rash,' Ratna whispered, as she passed by him.

Ravi moved next to him, his arm around Dev's shoulder.

'Well! Well! Well!' blurted the Captain. 'Who do we have here?' He flashed the smile of a gracious host.

'Oh, I'm Guddi's mamaji and this is my family. This is Dev and that is our son-in-law Ravi, my wife and daughter Ratna,' said Sukhdev, acting the part of Guddi's uncle.

'Guddi, did you forget to tell me about their visit?' asked Inder, glowering at his trembling wife. When he turned sideways to face his guests, a pasted smile returned to his lips, while the air around him still quivered with tension.

Ratna realised she had made her first acquaintance with the 'Prince of Darkness'. With as much composure as she could muster, she said, 'Guddi didn't know'.

Sukhdev added, 'We came unannounced. It was Ratna's idea to surprise Guddi. And Dev wanted Guddi to tie a rakhi on him—'

'Why? He is Ratna's brother, not Guddi's,' Inder snapped.

'They always have been more of friends than cousins,' Ravi blurted a silly explanation.

Luckily for them, Inder seemed neither to hear Ravi's absurd clarification nor showed any further interest in their relationship.

'Did you see what happened to Guddi's poor face? Did she tell you how she fell down the stairs?' he asked, glaring at Guddi to see if she had divulged the truth.

'Yes, she did tell us about the fall. Her cousin here and I are both doctors, so we got her some medication,' replied Ravi.

'Oh! You really didn't have to do that. Guddi called me at work to tell me what happened. But she insisted she wasn't hurt too bad. Otherwise, I would have taken her straight to the military hospital. Thank you for helping her.'

'No problem. I'm an army doctor myself,' replied Ravi icily.

Soon, lunch was served, which they ate quietly. When done eating, Ratna felt uncomfortable, as the silence in the room grew heavy and palpable. When a child outside Guddi's apartment disrupted the quiet by bouncing a marble on the concrete floor, it heightened the quietude with every bounce. Ratna stared first at her husband then her mother, willing someone to speak. When no one uttered a word, she uncrossed her legs and re-crossed them, and clearing her throat gave a meaningful look to her mother.

Raminder turned to Inder and asked, 'What time does the next train leave for Lucknow?'

'There's an express train that leaves at 5.45 pm that should take you to Lucknow well in time.'

'In time for what?' Ratna demanded, as if she could no longer contain the itch to confront him.

'Oh! I just meant at a reasonable hour. It reaches Lucknow at 9.35 pm.'

'What time should we plan to leave, so that we make it to the station on time to buy the tickets and board the train?' asked Sukhdev.

'My commanding officer, Brigadier Mohan, lives in our subdivision and he says it takes about forty minutes in a tonga. But let me call the army driver to come around 5.00 pm to take you to the station. The jeep takes about ten minutes only. That will give you enough time to buy the tickets and catch the train.'

Inder dialled the number, giving orders for the jeep to be at his house at 5.00 pm sharp. That settled, Raminder requested for a cup of hot chai. When Ratna offered to get it, Inder objected. 'No! No! In our house, nobody needs to work. What are servants for? I never let my wife do any work. Then how can I let you do it?' Inder smiled. Acting the perfect host, he summoned the maid and ordered chai. He then led the guests to the drawing room.

With the tea served, Raminder took a sip and turned to Inder. In an even voice she announced, 'We are taking Guddi with us.'

Ratna walked over and sitting on Guddi's left, took her cold hands in her own. Guddi cringed, her swollen lip quivered.

Still oblivious to the vibes of a roomful of angry people, Inder forced a charming smile and replied, 'You don't need to do that. Guddi doesn't look too good after her fall down those stairs. She seems a little shaken even now. Give her a few days to recuperate and I will bring her over to Lucknow.'

'You don't understand. We are taking her with us. She is never coming back to this hell hole ever again,' Raminder's merciless voice howled colder than a Kashmiri winter.

Light dawning, Inder shrieked, 'Who do you think you are?' He jumped up, springing towards Guddi. Faster than lightning, Dev and Ravi pinned both his hands behind his back. When he settled, Ravi nodded to Dev and they let go of his hands, but stood there on guard.

'Guddi is going with us whether you like it or not,' hissed Dev.

'We don't ever want to see your blighted face again. If you ever trouble Guddi or her unborn child, I'll blast a bullet through your head. And that is a promise!' thundered Sukhdev, standing up to his full height of six-foot-two. Walking over, he sat next to Guddi on her right. Between him and Ratna, they flanked Guddi, almost daring Inder to misbehave.

Inder laughed a wicked laugh. 'This is ridiculous,' he said, shaking his head. 'I don't get it. Why would you or anyone want to help a spineless woman?' He asked with a smirk, as if expecting the audience to applaud or at least be amused. When no one responded, his face changed colour. 'Get out of my house! All of you.'

No one moved.

Ratna and Raminder sat staring defiantly at him, their faces showing mixed emotions of anger, revulsion and indignation. Their stare seemed to cause Inder to lose his bravado, and he lowered his eyes, probably for the first time in front of mere women.

Ravi spoke first. 'If you let go of Guddi of your own free will, we will accept it as an apology. Otherwise, I will make sure your commanding officer knows what a fiend you are. Then you stand to lose everything.'

Before Inder could respond, Sukhdev added, 'Inder, it's your responsibility to also tell your parents of this breakup. If you are man enough, own up to being an idiot and a bully. You've abused Guddi to the point of jeopardising not just her life but the life of her unborn child too. Your parents deserve to know what a fiend they raised.'

Inder laughed a sarcastic laugh. 'Old Man, how can you, in this modern age think a couple's breakup is a family affair? Guddi's my wife, and in my house, I'm the master. What do my parents have to do with it? Guddi lives the way I choose.'

'Master or not, Guddi deserves respect and justice.' Dev jumped, poised to kick Inder but Ravi restrained him.

'Ha! Go, knock on the court doors for justice,' Inder jeered. 'Ignorant boy, court justice is for the wealthy only . . . not for beggars like her and her mother.'

Guddi squirmed in her seat.

'Since you have no shame,' thundered Sukhdev, 'I will personally talk to your father. Maybe, he'll pound some sense into you.'

'Please do that!' Inder snickered. 'My father approves of how I treat this miserable slut. He always treated my mother the same way,' he boasted, wiping perspiration from his forehead with his shirtsleeve. 'I never had any use for this woman anyway. You can take her. Now get out of my house.'

'We shall leave when we are ready,' replied Raminder smoothly. 'How do we know for sure you will never cause her any more harm? And what about the baby?' she asked.

'What about the baby? The bitch can keep the child if she wants to,' he replied, starting to rise.

'Not so quick, my friend,' said Ravi pushing him down to his seat. 'Inder, you seem to have no remorse and no clue as to what you did. We can't leave until you give us a written apology for your brutish behaviour.'

'Ravi—that is your name, right? Now remind me again why I would do that?' Inder purred.

'Yes, my name is Ravi but I am Major to you, Captain. You have to do what your superior commands. And, one more thing—your commanding officer, Brigadier Mohan, is a school friend of my father's. One word to him and your career will be history,' promised Ravi.

Restless like a bird with clipped wings, Inder muttered, 'What do you want me to write?'

'What did you say?'

'What do you want me to write, Sir?'

'First, admit in writing that you beat your wife, Guddi, during her pregnancy. Promise to pay for any physical injury you may have caused her or the baby. If you ever abuse them again, you agree to pay alimony and child support for the rest of your life.'

Inder laughed an uneasy laugh. 'These sound like legal proceedings,' he muttered.

'Yes, in a way, they are,' said Sukhdev. 'I plan to do what your father should have done to teach you how to respect women. I know that *laton ke bhoot baton se nahin mante*—spare the rod and create a brat—we demand you pay Guddi five thousand rupees for delivery, and also for mental and physical anguish.'

Inder shrank in his seat. 'I don't have that kind of money. And besides, how do I know you will not use the letter against me with the military and the law?'

'You will never know. It's our word. Take it or leave it,' replied Ravi.

Inder called the maid to get him a pen and a writing pad. He scribbled a note apologising for his behaviour and promised to pay for any harm he might have done to the mother and her unborn child.

Sukhdev put the signed note in his inner coat pocket. 'What about the lumpsum money for Guddi and the baby? If everything else goes well and the unborn child is healthy, then five thousand rupees is all we ask.'

'I can only give her a check for two thousand rupees. The rest I'll pay in installments of five hundred rupees once a quarter, until the full amount is paid.' And he wrote a check for two thousand rupees.

'Write an "I owe you" note for Guddi, detailing how and when the rest of the money will be paid.'

After writing the note and giving it to Sukhdev, Inder sat in obvious disbelief, while the two young doctors stood at their posts close by.

Ratna and Raminder rose to pack Guddi's things.

Guddi sat like a zombie, looking lost. Her eyes revealed the turmoil in her heart. Her mind seemed to flutter from one thought to another, as if fearful to settle down in case it hurt.

'Inder, where is Guddi's jewellery?' asked Ratna.

'What jewellery?'

'The gold jewellery she got at the wedding.'

'The bandari, the she-monkey, didn't get any!' said Inder.

'Of course she did. I know because the jewellery she did not wear on her wedding day was packed with the rest of her trousseau. I packed it with my own two hands.'

'I thought it was for us.' Inder changed his tune.

'The gold jewellery is always for the bride. It is insurance for just such tragedies when the girl has nothing else to depend upon,' said Sukhdev.

Ravi laughed out loud. 'Since when have army Captains needed to wear bangles and gold trinkets?'

'Come with me,' mumbled Inder, leading Ravi and Dev to a room they had not noticed earlier. The jewellery lay in a trunk in the storeroom next to his bedroom.

'This is what her mother gave,' and Inder started sorting out Guddi's jewellery from a metal candy box he was holding.

Ravi took the metal box from his hands. 'All this belongs to Guddi,' he said.

'No! No! Some of it was given to her by my parents,' shrieked Inder, grabbing the box.

'If it was given to her, it belongs to her.'
'That's not fair!'
'What did you say?'
'That's not fair, Sir!'

Ravi smiled. 'This is not a reminder of my superior rank but rather a question about the "fairness" issue. Tell me, Captain, is it fair to treat another human being the way you treated your life partner?'

Inder stared. His eyes smouldered, but his half-open mouth stayed mute.

23
The Cool Breath of Security

Late July, 1959

The morning after their return from Bareilly, Raminder and others sat sipping their morning chai, gathered around the cane table in the verandah of Ratna's home. Dev, the last one to join the group, winked at the girls instead of calling out his usual morning greetings. 'I'm feeling neglected,' he said. 'See? No rakhis on my poor wrist.'

The previous day's chaotic drama had left no room for rakhi celebrations. Ratna scrambled to her feet and returned with two coloured strings as rakhis—one for herself and one for Guddi. The strings symbolised a sister's love and a brother's promise of protection. With a flourish, Dev offered his arm first to Ratna and then to Guddi, allowing them to tie rakhis on his wrist.

After hugging both the girls with brotherly affection, he turned to his mother and said, 'Shouldn't we get a lady doctor to check Guddi behen?'

Before Raminder could reply, Ravi spoke up. 'You know, she's technically still an army officer's wife. I can easily have her checked in the army medical hospital for free.'

'Nooo . . .' shrieked Guddi, suddenly coming to life. 'Please take me away from here.'

'We will Beti,' said Raminder, putting a calming hand on her shoulder.

'Can't we do this at Amritsar, please?' Guddi pleaded.

'We can't,' replied Raminder. 'The train journey to Amritsar is a long one. We need to have you checked before we start. We can take you to a civilian doctor if you prefer.'

'What if the doctor says not to travel? I'm scared.'

'Let me make a deal with you,' said Raminder smiling. 'If the doctor says you need more than a couple of days to recuperate, then Ratna and I will stay back with you. Your uncle and Dev will leave as planned and we'll leave whenever you are strong enough. Agreed?'

'Didn't you mention you had to be in Amritsar for Simi's wedding?' asked Guddi.

'I did. But her wedding is almost five weeks away. Delay of a week or two should not matter.'

Picking at her dupatta, Guddi whispered, 'I haven't been to see any doctor since I got married.'

'We know. Your maid told us. It's okay. You are safe with us,' replied Raminder.

Guddi still persisted in finding excuses. 'What if the doctor contacts him?'

'If we do not mention Inder's name, the doctor will have no way of contacting him. Don't you agree?' asked Raminder.

Guddi nodded, finally mumbling what seemed to be on her mind all along. 'Auntie, I have no money to pay the doctor.'

Raminder put a protective arm around Guddi's shoulders. 'Beti, if God forbid, our Ratna was in your shoes, you think we would abandon her? With Vaheguru di meher, we are in a position to help. In fact, we consider it an honour. Please don't worry about money. Vaheguru only knows, you'll have plenty of genuine worries in your life.'

Raminder took the frightened girl into an embrace and held her until she stopped shaking.

'Could I see a civilian lady doctor?' asked Guddi, twisting the corner of her dupatta between her fingers.

'Absolutely!' replied Ravi and went to the phone to arrange an appointment. After hearing the details of the injuries, the doctor asked that Guddi be brought in immediately.

Since Ravi had to leave for his office, Raminder and Ratna accompanied Guddi for her checkup. The doctor gave one quick look at her patient before reaching for her bandaged arm. 'What happened here?' she asked. When Guddi grimaced at her touch, the doctor turned to Raminder and asked, 'Are you the mother?'

'No, I am her masi,' she lied again.

'I'd like to speak to you in private.' The doctor led Raminder to her office, leaving Guddi in the examining room to change.

'Did her husband do this to her?' questioned the doctor. When Raminder nodded, she said, 'Let's hope there's not much harm done to her baby. Her arm is broken but you probably know that someone has already wrapped it securely.'

'Yes, my son-in-law is a doctor and he wrapped it until it could be x-rayed.'

'I can testify in court if you decide to go after her husband,' said the doctor, staring at Raminder.

'She is too scared of him and does not want to press charges.'

'I guessed as much. But be aware, you can put him behind bars with my help,' said the doctor.

'We know that. But she has been so traumatised that we had to promise not to mention his name before she agreed to see you.'

'He could come after her and the baby if you don't press charges now.'

'She is not thinking straight at the moment and is willing to take those chances.'

'In my profession, I've seen a lot of battered women, but never anyone so brutally beaten in such an advanced state of pregnancy. If it is any comfort, none of the victims has ever agreed to press charges. I wish there was something we could do to protect her. Anyway, if she refuses, there is nothing I can do other than check her, and maybe make her comfortable.'

The doctor moved to examine Guddi, while Raminder walked out to the waiting room to join Ratna. Soon Guddi came out, carrying a long list of necessary tests, x-rays and prescriptions for vitamins and medicines. To their relief, Guddi announced, 'As far as the doctor can tell, she thinks the baby is doing well. She says I might be able to travel by train soon.'

From the doctor's office, the women went to the free Government Hospital and waited in a long line for the prescribed tests and x-rays. During the early days after Partition, Raminder remembered having stood in similar lines at the refugee camps just to collect basic necessities.

While Raminder and Guddi waited for the tests at the hospital, Ratna walked over to the pharmacy to get the prescription filled. Waiting in line for the x-rays, Guddi stood ahead of Raminder, facing her sideways, asking hesitant questions, when she suddenly stopped talking and lowered her eyes.

'What is it, child?' asked Raminder.

Guddi made no reply.

Raminder reached for her. 'Are you okay?'

Barely audible, Guddi mouthed, 'Auntie, Inder is watching me—'

'Where?'

'On your right,' she mumbled.

Raminder turned to look in every direction but saw no trace of Inder. 'Where? I don't see him. Guddi, please stop worrying. He can't hurt you any more.'

'He was there,' Guddi whispered. 'Auntie, what will happen when you are not around? What if he goes to Amritsar and hurts my biji?'

'Beti, Dev and your uncle will ensure no harm comes to you or your mother.'

She nodded but did not look up.

They were out the whole morning, returning home exhausted in the afternoon. Raminder tried her best to make the traumatised girl feel safe again. The doctor had prescribed a high protein diet and Raminder and Sukhdev ensured she received it, caring for her as naturally as parents do for their newborn's needs.

On the second morning, Raminder noticed the swelling on Guddi's face had subsided some. At the breakfast table, Dev gave hundred rupee notes to each of the girls—a rakhi gift from the brother. Giving money like this, so casually, was Raminder's idea. She suggested and

Dev agreed, a little money of her own would probably make Guddi feel more secure.

After Ravi left for work, the rest of the family prepared for the day. Raminder said to Guddi, 'Ratna and I need to go shopping. Your uncle and Dev will take you to the hospital to get a cast put on your arm. Is that okay?'

'Auntie, I have no idea how to thank you for your kindness.'

'That is what friends are for.'

Since they had only one car, Ratna suggested her father and Dev drive Guddi to the hospital while she and her mother hire a rickshaw.

After Guddi and the men left, Ratna, a curious look in her eyes, turned to her mother. 'I didn't know you wanted to go shopping. What do you need?'

'A few things. Did you notice Guddi has nothing ready for the newborn? If the baby arrives early, she is ill prepared. She also needs comfortable clothes. What she's wearing seem like her maid's castoffs. I'd like to pick some cotton material and stitch one or two cool outfits for her to travel in.'

'Ma, you are amazing. I didn't even think about that!'

'Someone has to. Guddi is still so stressed she sees Inder everywhere. She is not thinking of the newborn.'

'What do you mean . . . "sees Inder everywhere"?'

'Yesterday while we stood in line, she insisted she saw Inder watching her.'

'Ma, she could be right. At the pharmacy, a man in civilian clothes and Inder's looks, winked at me, but before I realised what happened, he disappeared. I thought I was hallucinating.'

Raminder stared at Ratna. 'So . . . she was right. We have to talk to the men to ensure Inder does not terrorise her ever again.'

They summoned a rickshaw to go shopping and soon returned with bags full of baby wool and cotton fabric. That afternoon, both Raminder and Ratna started stitching, knitting baby things and sewing maternity outfits for the mother-to-be.

Guddi and the men returned before lunch. With her arm securely in a cast, the pain lines on her forehead looked all but gone.

That night after Guddi retired, Raminder talked to Ravi and Sukhdev to find a permanent solution and stop Inder from intimidating Guddi. Ravi promised to take a day off soon to go see Inder's commanding officer, Brigadier Mohan. Sukhdev insisted on accompanying Ravi when he talked to Inder in his commanding officer's presence, about staying away not only from Guddi but also from Guddi's mother in Amritsar.

By the third morning, Guddi looked well rested and she smiled for the first time while wishing everyone a good morning. 'If your appearance keeps improving at this rate, then, maybe we could all leave together,' said Raminder.

They were still at the breakfast table when Guddi excused herself to go for her bath. As soon as she left, they all started voicing their worries. They discussed the easiest way to break the news of Guddi's broken marriage and physical trauma, to her mother. Raminder and Ratna knew the mother had spent every penny she had saved over the years, on the wedding of her only child. How does one tell a mother that her greatest accomplishment in finding a suitable boy for her child is in reality her biggest blunder? That she had thrust her child into a fiery hell with her own loving hands.

'Maybe we should call Manu mamiji to personally go over to Satwant auntie's house and prepare her,' suggested Ratna.

'Prepare her how?' asked Raminder. 'How do you prepare a mother for this kind of tragedy?'

'We could enlist mamiji's help to prepare Satwant auntie for Guddi's maternity visit,' said Ratna. 'The real truth could then be disclosed gradually.'

Everyone agreed this might be the only way to give the troubling news to Guddi's mother in bite-sized blocks of heartache.

That afternoon, as they settled around the dining table, the phone rang and Simi asked to talk to Ratna. The only phone in the house sat on the sideboard in the dining room. Since Ratna could not talk in private, she just went ahead and blurted Guddi's ordeal and their decision to bring her with them.

'Do ask mamiji to prepare Satwant auntie for Guddi's visit and delivery, without mentioning Guddi's troubled marriage. Later when we arrive with her for your wedding, we will help break the news gradually.'

'Okay,' Simi mumbled.

'We are still not sure when we'll come. Just tell her mother that Guddi'll be returning with us for her delivery. Don't give her any specific dates. As soon as the doctor gives her the okay, we'll be on our way,' ended Ratna.

'Will you make it in time for the wedding?'

'We definitely intend to,' answered Ratna and hung up.

Nobody uttered a word. Ratna returned to her seat at the table without making eye contact with anyone. They stared at their plates, concentrating on their food as if it would escape if they did not keep vigil. Guddi, fighting tears, started eating with her good hand.

After lunch, Raminder suggested that Guddi should take a nap. While she rested, the mother and daughter sewed and knitted furiously. Within the next two days, Guddi's bruises and facial swelling faded. Even the torturous pain lines on her face seemed to have eased but she still grimaced when moving her right arm.

On the day of Guddi's second visit to the doctor, Ravi took a day off. He and Sukhdev went to Bareilly to take care of the sordid business concerning Inder.

After the men left for Inder's place, Ratna drove her mother and her friend to the clinic. When the doctor re-examined Guddi, she was amazed at the transformation in her patient's condition. 'If love and tender care can do this for you in five days, you can definitely travel with your family,' said the doctor.

When Guddi thanked her, the doctor replied, 'Don't thank me. Thank your relatives. I didn't think you'd be on the road to recovery so fast.'

Ravi and Sukhdev returned late that night, triumphant—Inder had begged forgiveness in his commanding officer's presence. Brigadier Mohan left no room for misunderstanding. 'This is the first and final warning,' he said. 'Inder, from now on, you so much as look at Guddi, her mother or the child, I'll personally ensure you are fired.'

Guddi sat playing with her food. Sukhdev turned to face her. 'Beti, believe us when we say Inder will never dare harm you or your loved ones. We'll ensure that.'

Guddi looked up to nod at him as her face turned wet with tears.

The family decided to travel by Howrah Amritsar Mail, and break their journey at Jullunder, while Dev planned to continue on the same train to Amritsar. Ratna felt this arrangement would give Guddi extra time to heal.

'There's another reason. Guddi needs more clothes,' said Raminder to Ratna. 'The two outfits I've stitched for her are not enough, especially since she has a wedding to attend. Once in Garha, I'll hire a tailor for her.'

When all the fuss of finding seats in the train and settling the luggage was over, Ratna sat listening to the rhythmic clack, clack of the train over its tracks. The sound soothed her. She took a deep breath, hoping, praying that Vaheguru would protect Guddi and her unborn child.

She marvelled at the way her family reacted to Guddi's tragedy. Her family's resources, physical, emotional, financial and even spiritual, all seemed channelled towards saving and supporting a life in crisis. Her dearest friend was in good hands, just as she and Dev were, when Sukhdev and Raminder found them so long ago.

Ratna looked over at Dev and wondered about his Uma ma's mantra of 'remembering the juice mango'. Was the advice too simplistic or could it help someone like Guddi reclaim her life? Ratna shuddered when she realised the advice made sense only if Guddi could believe in her right to breathe the same air, and live on the same earth that everyone else inhabited. In the face of ruthless brutality, her traumatised friend seemed embarrassed even to occupy the space her physical body took. She did not need any advice now. She just needed the *thandi waa*—the cool breath—of love and security, and Ratna knew her family would provide it.

During the journey, Ratna told Guddi for the first time, how both she and Dev were adopted. She also related the ordeal of their traumatic journey and humble beginnings after Partition, hoping this knowledge would ease Guddi into putting her own pain in perspective.

'Guddi, for your child's sake, you need to fight and survive,' urged Ratna. 'There are human farishte'—real live human angels—'like Dev and my parents, all around you, willing to give you a helping hand. Take the help and stand up tall like Vaheguru meant you to. Remember you are a "Kaur", a Sikh princess. Walk and talk like one.'

Guddi nodded, mumbling, 'Thank you for being my friend.' Then, turning to Raminder she said with quiet dignity, 'Auntie, accepting your kindness makes me feel humble—and yet stronger, much stronger. I can't understand or explain my feelings. Inder's ghost still haunts me day and night. And I know it will for a long time . . . but I get this powerful sense that hope turns more potent when passed from one human to another. If that is true, then, I can make one promise to you. Once I'm on my feet, I will do just what you did—pass "hope" along to keep its flame alive.'

'Oh Beti, you make it sound so noble. May Vaheguru bless you.' Raminder hugged her.

Guddi's face registered the struggle her vocal cords could not convey.

Once they reached Garha, Ratna was relieved that Guddi started sharing her emotions with her. She explained to her mother, how that in itself was a two-edged sword. 'On the one hand, I'm glad that Guddi is talking. On the other, it hurts to listen to her fears.'

'It does,' whispered Raminder. 'But it's still a good sign.'

She and Ratna joined Guddi on the verandah. They talked about the weather, local politics and other inconsequential things, before Raminder blurted what seemed to be on her mind. 'I wonder who recommended Inder to your mother? Was there a reason why you agreed to marry him?'

Guddi exhaled deeply. 'I've asked myself the same question hundreds of times,' she said, her eyes on distant horizons. Then, looking directly at Raminder, she continued, 'Auntie, biji never asked if I wanted to get married to him. She simply announced she'd promised my hand to Inder, and that was that. I was not raised to question the decisions she made.'

Raminder threw a quick glance at Ratna, who understood what her mother's furtive glance meant—none of the mothers ever thought to ask their daughters about their views on prospective grooms. 'Did anyone check his background?'

'My mother was ill. She depended on the recommendations of the marriage broker who showed her Inder's photograph, and assured her his family was not only respectable but also well educated. And, they didn't ask for any dowry. Also, my cousin, an army man, had met Inder at one of the army functions. Inder, as you know, can be very charming when he wants to, and my cousin was impressed. Biji liked what she heard. She didn't stop to think why Inder's family didn't want to wait, even for a couple of months, until I finished my studies. That would have meant more time to unearth their family's brutal secrets.'

Raminder and Guddi both took a loud breath at the same time, each immersed in her own thoughts. 'Talking of Inder's charm,' said Raminder, 'it seems he has two distinct personalities, almost like an elephant's two sets of teeth. *Haathi ke daant, khane ke aur, dikhane ke aur.* His one personality seems to be for day-to-day living, and the other, like the elephant's tusks, for appearances only.'

Guddi flashed a sad smile. 'You put it well. The thought of the "real" Inder still makes me shiver. It's distressing to talk about him. Auntie . . . did I mention my mother took early retirement last month because of ill-health?'

'No, you didn't,' replied Raminder.

'She wrote me a letter last month and I think she wanted me to offer to take her in. I didn't know what to do, so I never replied,' mumbled Guddi, breaking down. 'I was scared I would never see her again.'

Getting up and taking Guddi in her arms, Raminder said, 'There! There! Let's sleep over this for a day or two. One thing we know for sure is that you'll have to rejoin college to complete your studies. We'll figure out the other details after we have had time to think about it.'

'I'm sorry I put you through this.'

'Please don't apologise,' said Raminder. 'We look at it as an honour Vaheguru has bestowed upon us. It was He who led us to you when you needed us. Come. Let's drink our chai before it gets cold.' The servant had served chai while they were talking.

By the end of the first week of their return to Garha, Ratna asked Guddi if she was up to talking to her mother. 'I've been dying to talk to her, but she doesn't have a phone in the house. As I mentioned, she doesn't work at the school anymore, so we can't call her there. I know a neighbour who has a phone, but I wish I could remember her number.'

'Let's see what we can do. Maybe, we can call Simi's mother to invite your biji over and set up a time to call her. What do you say?'

With Guddi's okay, Ratna called her aunt to make the contact possible, making tentative plans to call her friend's mother the next afternoon.

'You know your biji the best. Guddi, what should we tell her about Inder?' asked Raminder.

'It'll kill her to know what Inder put me through. Auntie, can we just pretend I am returning for my delivery? Later, I'll tell her the truth that I might never go back.'

'I don't know how to stress this. There is no "might" in this situation. Child, your marriage is over. You don't want to go back to Inder, even if he apologises and begs you to return.'

'But Auntie, he's okay when he's not under pressure. In the first few months of my pregnancy, he hit me just once. It's only in the last three months that he went absolutely berserk. It was my fault really. I got him started by asking him where he spent his nights. I should have kept my mouth shut.' She sat wringing her hands.

Raminder reached over and put a calming hand over hers. 'Child, you do have a perfect right to ask questions. He's simply a rotten man, and it's not your fault.'

'But my kind mother-in-law said if I do as he says he wouldn't hurt me. She said he had a kinder heart than his father.'

'Beti, that makes no sense. It's simply the advice of one battered woman to another. Marriage is not a defensive sport. You are smart and educated and don't have to live your life by his warped rules or the desperate rules of your well meaning mother-in-law.'

'But I don't know what to do now. I have no money and my mother is too old to take care of me and my baby.'

'Exactly.'

'Huh?'

'Now it is your responsibility to stand on your feet and take care of your child and your sick mother. Of course, we are behind you all the way. Whenever you need to take a breather, remember we all are here for you to lean on.' Raminder wrapped her arms around her.

'You are so kind. Thank you for having faith that I can take care of my baby and my biji. I just get scared sometimes.'

'Oh! Oh!' piped in Ratna laughing.

'What?' said Guddi, puzzled.

Ratna laughed harder. 'I should have warned you.'

'Warned me about what?'

'About never using the word "scared" in front of ma. You got yourself into this one.'

'Yes, you did,' said Raminder, laughing too. 'You know what my bebeji used to say?'

'No,' said Guddi, shaking her head.

'You could never admit you were scared. Bebeji spoke her mind openly, as if what she thought was an obvious truth. She looked you straight in the eye and asked, "How can that be possible? Sikh girls do not get scared" and then she kissed you on your head like this,' and Raminder reached for Guddi, kissing her on her head.

Ratna laughed. 'I wish life were that simple and fearful-emotions that easy to banish.'

The next afternoon when Guddi called her mother, she handled the situation well. After putting the phone down, she turned to Ratna. 'Arthritis has made my biji almost an invalid. But she is thrilled about my visit in time for Simi's wedding.'

'Great. I'm so looking forward to the wedding myself,' said Ratna.

'Simi's wedding reminds me of my wedding. My biji was unwell even then, but I had many hopes and dreams, very few misgivings and no fear. Now, my life has turned upside down—'

'Guddi,' Ratna interrupted, 'take strength from friends and your loved ones. Stand up for your right to be happy.' Reaching for her friend's trembling hand, she squeezed it and continued more gently, 'Create a secure place for your baby and yourself—only you can make it happen.'

Guddi nodded, her upper teeth biting her curled lower lip.

'I mean it, Guddi,' said Ratna with more emphasis. 'Keep reminding yourself, you matter. You are special. Do you hear me? You are special.'

Guddi forced a smile and hugged her dearest friend. 'Thanks, Ratna. I'm trying. If only I could stop seeing Inder's evil face all the time.'

'Papaji and Dev will make sure you and your mother are safe. You know that, right?'

Guddi nodded and looking first at her swollen belly, then at Ratna, whispered, 'With your help, my dear friend, I think we'll make it.' She touched her stomach and smiled.

24
Bride and Mother

August-September 1959

Ratna, her parents, and Guddi were among the first guests to arrive for Simi's wedding. Simi, delighted that they made it on time, invited Guddi to stay with her family until after the wedding.

'Ratna,' said Simi, 'seeing Guddi's misfortune scares me. I've started doubting my fiancé and started wondering if he actually loves me as he professes. We hardly know each other. His attention pleases me but then who can predict the future?'

'Gurdev is an exceptionally decent man. That is what I hear from Ravi, and I believe him. They are the best of friends,' replied Ratna.

During the pre-wedding days, Guddi's mother, though ailing with arthritis, hobbled around back and forth, from her home to the house with the wedding, just to be with her daughter. She thanked Ratna and Simi again and again for showering so much attention on her only child.

The wedding, like all others before it, was loud and happy. Gurdev turned out to be the most romantic son-in-law this extended family of relatives and friends had ever known. For a fortnight before the wedding, every morning, Simi received a bouquet of red roses and every evening, the telephone rang with a long-distance call from Gurdev at seven o'clock sharp. Simi pretended embarrassment at this show of affection, but admitted to Ratna that she enjoyed this novel idea of him wooing her.

When Gurdev called in the evenings, every female in the house hovered around Simi, giggling and wanting to hear what the boy could possibly have to say to her before marriage. This kind of behaviour on the part of the prospective bridegroom was unheard of—unprecedented but interesting, thought Ratna. 'You know, its nice Gurdev sends you all these flowers but let's hope he doesn't turn totally unromantic after marriage,' she said.

'Are you saying there is a finite amount of romantic feelings in a human being? And if one uses up much of it so extravagantly, there will be precious little left after marriage?' Simi laughed.

'No, that is not what I meant.'

'Tell me. What did you really *mean*?' asked Simi, still laughing.

'Simi, Ratna is just concerned about you,' said Waddeh Buaji, changing the subject. 'Anyway, did I ever tell you my story?'

The girls grunted and made long faces as if tricked into suffering.

Waddeh Buaji started her story anyway—without waiting for an invitation. 'One day, a year after our marriage, my husband told me how daring he was in his younger days. In 1910, when his parents first told him about our engagement, he was seventeen and I only fourteen. He wanted to meet me before marriage, but there was no way his parents, or for that matter my parents, would allow such shameless behaviour.'

'So what did he do?' breathed Ratna smiling, sensing something juicy coming out of that old but impish mouth.

'Well, he decided to take things into his own hands. He talked to his older married sister, who helped him dress up like a pious man, a sadhu, in a reddish-orange robe. Thus attired, he arrived at my parents' house, hoping for a glimpse of me. I was a real stupid budhu in those days—very naive. Anyway, my mother sent me out with food for the sadhu who had come knocking on our door. He returned again and again for days. After several such visits, I remarked, "I don't think he is a real sadhu. He stares at me too hard." That upset my mother. "What's wrong with you young girls? Do show some respect for men of God," she admonished. After marriage, I found out the truth about my "man of God"!' Waddeh Buaji laughed a merry laugh.

'And the point is?' asked Simi, her eyes sparkling and lips struggling to hold laughter.

'The point is, my husband stayed the most loving and romantic man until the very end.'

'How? Did he ever bring you flowers or gifts?' she asked.

'No.'

'Then how do you say he stayed romantic?'

'Beti, have you ever looked into the eyes of a man in love?' Waddeh Buaji asked.

And that was enough. All young girls listening to Waddeh Buaji's story hushed, probably longing for just one such man in their lives.

Ratna, appreciating the good fortune of being blessed with just such a loving man, smiled at Waddeh Buaji. 'I know what you mean.' Then, thinking of Guddi, she shuddered.

Soon, the wedding day arrived and with it appeared the groom with a hundred red roses for the bride, leaving everyone speechless. The bridegroom's mother came with a special request from her son, who wanted his bride to be married without a heavy veil covering her pretty bridal face. Simranjeet and his family complied with the request with grace that belied their amusement.

'I'm glad Gurdev wants to part with the outdated custom of bridal purdah,' commented Raminder. 'Purdah is not a part of Sikh culture anyway. It came from Muslim culture.'

Simranjeet laughed. 'What else can one expect from a bridegroom who brings a hundred red roses for his bride?'

Watching the family laugh at the groom's request, Ratna noticed Simi smile at their amusement. Turning to Ravi who had arrived with the baraat, she whispered, 'It seems like Gurdev's request that Simi not cover her face with a veil during the ceremony scored big with her. Maybe she sees it as a good omen. After Guddi's tragedy, we all seem to worry about any new member who joins the family.'

'Am I still considered a new member or have I passed the family test?' Ravi winked at her.

Ratna blew him a silent kiss. 'With flying colors,' she murmured.

The guests talked with awe about it being the first 'love' marriage they had ever attended. In reality, Ratna guessed, this was probably the first time they had met a groom who acknowledged his pride at being in love.

Times were changing.

Simi made a radiant bride and Ratna prayed she be blessed with as good a man as her Ravi.

When Guddi returned to her mother's house after Simi's wedding, she invited Ratna for a visit.

'I'd be delighted,' replied Ratna. Before leaving for Guddi's place, she requested Dev to pick her up the following weekend to go to Garha. Ratna planned to visit her parents for a couple of weeks before returning once more to help Guddi during the delivery. Guddi's arm was still in a cast and Ratna knew she would need help when the baby arrived.

As soon as she reached her friend's house, Ratna got busy. First, she took Guddi to the bank to open an account and deposit the two-thousand-rupee cheque Inder had given her, and to rent a safe-deposit box for her gold jewellery. Then she got in touch with their old college teachers and friends to procure books, notes and syllabus for the final year of college. She did whatever she could to get Guddi started on the road to self-sufficiency.

Satwant's arthritic joints had disabled her, making it impossible for her to do housekeeping chores, but she could not afford household help. With Guddi's dominant arm in a cast, Ratna assumed the responsibility of their kitchen, realising that visiting Garha might not be an option anymore, as this was the time her friend needed her the most. She decided to talk it over with Dev when he came to take her home.

With Ratna's help, Guddi's life inched towards normalcy but the trauma of her past took its toll. She looked frail and tired. Ratna worried, requesting her doctor uncle to arrange a lady doctor for Guddi. She solicited Waddeh Buaji's help with the cooking, so she could concentrate on preparations for the baby's arrival. The elderly woman had always been a friend to the three girls. Ratna knew it would be okay to take her to Guddi's house without an invitation from the hostess, and she proved right. Both Guddi and Satwant welcomed the old aunt with warmth and love.

With Waddeh Buaji's help, Ratna was free to go shopping. Her papaji had given her the money to help Guddi with things she would need for her newborn. Ratna and Guddi decided to make use of the elderly aunt's services, requesting her to break the news of the broken marriage to Guddi's mother, which she promised to do at the appropriate time. It took a couple of days for Waddeh Buaji and Satwant to get to know each other, to laugh and talk like friends.

'Looks like Guddi's ready to deliver,' said Satwant one day. 'The delivery date is still a month away but her baby seems to have settled lower down her belly. I think it's time.'

'Yes, it is,' replied the old aunt.

'Waddeh Buaji, I'm worried. Inder has neither called nor written to Guddi since her return. I would have thought he'd be excited at the prospect of becoming a new father,' said Satwant.

'I don't know how to say it nicely, so I'll come right out,' blurted Waddeh Buaji. 'Guddi wants you to know something. Inder is not coming nor is he writing to her . . . ever.'

'Vaheguru. Vaheguru. Is he okay? Why do you say that?'

'Because he is a bloody bastard! He abused Guddi both physically and emotionally. Ratna's family had to remove Guddi from Bareilly and bring her to safety.'

'They did what? Who gave them the authority to do that? All young couples have squabbles. That doesn't mean every time a couple quarrels, the girl takes off to go to her parents. And, what a home to come to! I can't even look after myself, let alone look after her and the baby.'

'Satwant, please calm down,' said Waddeh Buaji. 'Guddi didn't take off after one quarrel. Inder abused her and denied her medical attention. If Ratna and her family hadn't gone over for a surprise visit, you'd have no child or grandchild now. He beat her even during this late stage in her pregnancy. He is the one who broke her arm. It was no accident. Raminder and Sukhdev got her out of that hell and brought her home. They have been nurturing her since then. We just hope and pray her baby is unharmed.'

Guddi's mother sat trembling, mumbling, 'Vaheguru. Vaheguru.'

Ratna and Guddi had been eavesdropping and now Ratna nudged Guddi to enter the room and speak up. 'What Waddeh Buaji is saying is true', said Guddi walking in. 'I couldn't bring myself to tell you all this for fear of worrying you . . . but biji, don't worry about the baby or me. I will stand on my feet and take care of both of you. Please trust me.' The mother and daughter fell into each other's arms weeping.

Suddenly, Ratna saw Guddi double-over. When she straightened up, she screamed, 'I think I'm bleeding.' Ratna realised Guddi seemed to have no idea how the delivery process started.

'No. Your water just broke,' said Waddeh Buaji taking charge. She commanded Ratna to run over to the neighbours and call her uncle to come over immediately. There was no time to find a "lady" doctor. Simranjeet would have to deliver the baby.

By the time Ratna returned, Waddeh Buaji had already got Guddi into a more comfortable outfit, and had her on a clean bed. Ratna started a fire in the clay coal-stove for boiling the water.

'How long will the pains last?' asked a scared Guddi.

'The first baby usually takes a long time—from a couple of hours to thirty hours or more,' replied Waddeh Buaji.

'What?' asked the disbelieving mother-to-be, 'How can one survive for so long with so much pain?'

No one answered.

Guddi's pains started coming every fifteen minutes and Waddeh Buaji instructed her to use her serviceable hand to latch on to the side of the cot, when riding her pains. Ratna came in to ask how she was doing and Guddi blurted, 'I feel I'm being thrust deeper and deeper into a chasm, as if I'm riding a roller coaster downhill with no way to get off this . . . this . . .' She let out a muffled scream. Ratna reached over with a wet towel, to wipe off the beads of perspiration from her friend's face, while Guddi clung to the side of the cot with her one good hand.

Guddi's pains started coming every ten minutes. Ratna rushed back to the kitchen to find the coal fire still sputtering and smoking. She panicked and dropped the pot of water.

Waddeh Buaji hurried into the kitchen and put a hand on Ratna's shoulder. 'Calm down. It will take at least another hour or two.'

Collecting herself, Ratna filled another pot and put it on the clay stove before she walked back to the birthing room. She watched Waddeh Buaji pull up an easy chair and order Guddi's mother to sit and recite "Sukhmani Sahib" out loud. The melodious recitation of the Sikh prayer served a dual purpose; it gave Satwant something to do for her daughter, and kept Guddi calm between her pains.

While Waddeh Buaji bustled around dispensing common sense and compassion, they heard Simranjeet's car arrive. Everyone breathed a sigh of relief. If things did not go right for the premature baby or his mother, the doctor would know what to do.

Ratna set about cooking supper for everyone, and her aunt Manu joined her in the kitchen to help. Within the next hour, they heard the first screams of a healthy baby, and hustled to see the newborn. They felt indescribable relief, knowing the tiny baby boy was healthy with strong lungs—as he raised hell with his screams.

Guddi looked at Ratna with moist eyes and whispered, 'It feels like I'm the first woman in the world to have accomplished such an amazing miracle.'

'You did accomplish a miracle,' said Ratna, hugging her.

Waddeh Buaji strutted around beaming as if she was the one who had done hard labour to bring forth the baby into the world. 'Guddi, this baby should forever remind you that Vaheguru is looking over you. May you and the little one grow in love, joy and good health.' She then walked into the prayer room to obtain the beginning letter with which to name the baby. She opened the *Guru Granth Sahib* at random and while searching the top left-hand corner of the page, realised the verse started on the previous page. Turning back the page to read the beginning of the sacred verse, the *waak*, she noted it began with the letter 'H'.

'Let us name the child Himmat—for courage,' said Waddeh Buaji.

So, Himmat he was from that day onwards. Guddi squeezed her newborn, and whispered, 'Himmat, my baby, I shall not fail you, ever.'

When Dev came to pick up Ratna, a tiny, sleepy baby greeted him, melting his heart. He remembered Guddi as a ravaged girl, but now she glowed with the beauty that accompanies motherhood; the glow of love, hope and courage; the glow of peace and acceptance Himmat brought with him. Dev knew before being told that there was no way Ratna could or would leave now.

In the baby's presence, he felt clumsy like an elephant in a room full of diyas, beautiful but breakable, crushable, earthen oil lamps, and he did not know how to tread softly. When Guddi handed him the baby, he held the tiny bundle, gingerly rocking it back and forth, back and forth. Baby Himmat felt more fragile than any expensive piece of crystal he had ever held, and, feeling awkward, he handed the baby back to his mother, all the while wondering how a demon like Inder could produce an angel like Himmat.

When Dev rose to take leave, Guddi had a request. 'Dev, on your way back, could you please bring auntie with you? I'd love to have your wise and loving mother visit us. And of course, this way Ratna will also get to spend time with her before she returns to Lucknow.'

Dev nodded. He noticed that Guddi's eyes had lit up, and a soft smile played on her lips when she mentioned his mother. Her eyes spoke of the respect she felt for Raminder more eloquently than any words could have conveyed. Dev loved Guddi all the better for being so warm and transparent.

25
And Life Goes On . . .

1961-70

During his final years of medical studies, Dev worked as his uncle Simranjeet's apprentice, leaving little time for other activities. But, as always, he made time for his extended family, which now included Guddi and Himmat.

In December of 1961, he received news that his sister Ratna had given birth to a baby girl named Simran. Dev and his parents were overjoyed and doted on the child, but Ravi's mother had a thing or two to say to him about her daughter-in-law being difficult and obstinate during her pregnancy. 'Ratna is very stubborn,' she said. 'She is not at all like you. Did you know, in spite of my repeated efforts, she refused to see a hakim to ensure a boy baby?'

'It doesn't matter.' Dev tried to pacify her. 'They sound very happy with their baby girl.'

'Do they have a choice now? When we could have done something, she clung to her misguided belief that the sex of the baby is determined at conception! You are a doctor yourself and must know it's not true. But then . . . who am I to complain? Even my doctor son, Ravi, does not listen to reason. He only dances to his wife's tunes.' Without giving Dev a chance to speak, she continued, 'Serves them right for not listening to wisdom. They deserved a girl baby,' and hung up.

Dev smiled, hoping she did not give too much trouble to Ratna. He knew how ecstatic Ravi and Ratna were with their daughter Simran, who had sweetened the love they already shared. He loved his sister and her family, visiting them at every opportunity.

After graduating from the medical school and successfully completing his residency requirements, he joined his uncle's practice in 1964. Under Simranjeet's guidance, Dev turned out to be an excellent doctor. Now that Simi was married and Waddeh Buaji had passed away, both Simranjeet and Manu offered to share their home with him, but Dev could not accept the offer. He wanted a place of his own, so he compromised by building a mansion adjoining his uncle's house.

In the years following Himmat's birth, he loaned Guddi the money to complete her doctorate in English Literature. By the time Himmat started his first year of school, Guddi found a lecturer's job in the university close to home. Her mother Satwant, by now an invalid, became one of his first patients. Dev often stopped to check on his patient on his way back from his morning walk. On one such "call of compassion", he found himself in an embarrassing situation.

'Beti . . . is there anything you want to tell me?' Satwant asked Guddi, as he stood unseen on their verandah, catching his breath.

'What?'

'Is something going on between you and Dev?' asked the arthritic mother from her bed.

'Not you too,' blurted Guddi.

'So you know people are talking?'

'Yes . . . and I don't care. People just have dirty minds. All I care is that you know the truth. Dev is your physician and comes to check on you. He also has a soft spot in his heart for Himmat. I'm sure you know that. As far as I am concerned, there is nothing going on between us.'

'Guddi, I was actually hoping there was some truth in the rumours.'

'Biii . . . ji!'

'Honestly . . . I would very much want Dev for a son-in-law. It would be such comfort to me to know you and Himmat are in good hands.'

'I love Dev but not in that way.'

'What way then?'

'Like a brother.'

'Are you sure? . . . I know you are fooling yourself. Aren't you?'

'No Biji, I'm not fooling myself. I am very sure. At this point in my life, I don't think I can bear the thought of marriage ever again. And then, technically, I'm still married to that devil. We never filed any papers for divorce. Remember?'

'Himmat is five now and needs a father figure. And Dev is so fond of him.'

'Biji, please, stop it. It's not going to happen. Do you forget, every year I tie a rakhi on Dev's wrist. He's like a brother to me and I love him, but I can never marry him.'

A discreet cough emerged from the verandah. Both Guddi and her mother looked mortified to find Dev standing in front of the screened door.

'I didn't mean to barge in like this . . . but I was out for my morning walk and came in to see how auntie was doing.' He stopped for a second to collect his thoughts. 'I also have a favour to ask. I'm planning to go to Garha for Diwali holidays and was wondering if Himmat could come with me?' he asked.

Guddi threw a quick glance at her mother. 'I'm sure Himmat would love that.'

He checked his patient, and straightening up, took his leave, declining an offer of a cup of tea. He could not trust himself after what he had overheard. 'I'll pick Himmat up on Friday evening around five,' he said, keeping his voice as smooth as possible, and left.

On his way home, he forced himself to take stock of his life, and came to the conclusion that Guddi's decision was for the best. She, at least, had not cut him off completely. She did care for him, even if only as a brother.

From then on, he devoted most of his waking hours to his medical practice and social service at Pingalwara, a one-man nonprofit agency at Amritsar, for 'God's rejects'—abandoned, orphaned and/or mentally retarded. Dev especially enjoyed working with the orphans there.

Helping children towards peace and happiness gave meaning to his life. Besides being their doctor, he gave some of his time, often taking these underprivileged children on picnics, to see movies and cricket matches. As time went by, his biji organised drives to knit sweaters and woollen socks for them, and his papaji provided them with used and refurbished bicycles.

He kept treating Guddi with respect and love, never revealing his true feelings to her. However, sometimes he still tortured himself by remembering the conversation between Guddi and her mother. But from then on, he tried not to entertain the idea of marriage and lived the familiar role of a brother to Guddi and an uncle to her son.

After losing her mother around Himmat's sixth birthday, Guddi started leaning more and more on him and Ratna for moral support. Himmat grew up to be a precocious child, exceptionally bright and very fond of Dev. Every time Dev visited Garha, he took Himmat with him, ensuring the child loved Raminder and Sukhdev as if they were his own grandparents.

Ratna cherished her brother, who, in his quiet way, always supported her. She wanted to see him happily married and settled. 'Dev, have you ever thought of asking Guddi to marry you?' she asked him one day, taking him by surprise.

'No. I can't ask her.'

'Why not?'

'Because she thinks of me only as a brother.'

'What about you?'

'I am fine with the way things are between us. I am Himmat's mamaji and that is good enough for me,' he replied, evasively.

'Is that so?'

'Yes.'

'Come on Dev . . . I know better.' Ratna chuckled.

'No, you don't,' Dev murmured.

'Really?' she asked with a twinkle in her eyes.

'Remember, when I was six years old, I had a riding accident in Shahadra?'

'Of course. How can I forget?' That was how you acquired your bulbous but cute snout,' she replied, pinching his nose and laughed.

'I suffered another injury then . . . an injury that prevents me from being a real man to any woman.'

With a sudden lump in her throat, Ratna walked up to him and putting her arms around him, whispered, 'Dev, I'm so sorry. I didn't know.'

After her talk with her brother, Ratna still thought it a good idea to broach the topic with Guddi. She decided life had bruised both Dev and Guddi enough to make them appreciate a marriage of a different sort—that of a loving companionship.

While she visited Guddi the next time in Amritsar, she asked, 'Now that auntie is gone, don't you feel lonely sometimes?'

'Of course I do.'

'So, how come you never remarried?'

'What for? I felt lonelier when I was married than I do now,' Guddi replied.

'No, really. Be serious.'

'Ratna, I am serious. You know, all these years the only time I ever heard from Inder was in the early years after our separation, when he sent the five hundred rupees every quarter. And even then, the money, and all communications were channelled through your papaji. I haven't heard from him since. I don't think he knows or cares if Himmat and I still exist and . . . and . . . I want to keep it that way.'

'Guddi, that doesn't make sense. Think about it. What does he have to do with your life now? As far as I'm concerned, he gave away all his rights a long time ago. He's not in the picture any more.'

'Oh yes, he is. We never separated legally. If I try to legalise it now, which I will have to if I decide to remarry, he will know he has a son.'

'So? He knew you were pregnant at that time and if I remember correctly, he said you could keep the baby.'

'Knowing Inder, he will fight to get custody of Himmat, if only to hurt me. The law will side with him, branding me an unfit mother trying to avoid responsibility by remarrying. No, no, no. I'll never be able to live with that. I love my child and cannot dream of jeopardising his happiness for anything.'

So her brother's painful secret stayed with Ratna. At long last, she understood Dev's wish to be Guddi's brother.

In October 1969, Dev received a wedding invitation from his dearest friend Raghu. After finishing his medical studies in Amritsar, Raghu had gone to England to specialise in neurosurgery. Since Dev and Raghu had grown up together in the same village, with their aunt Anu as the common link between them, they still related to each other as quasi-brothers.

Dev's parents and Ratna's family also received the wedding invitations. Upon discussing travel plans with Ratna, he learned she could not go, but coaxed his parents into attending the wedding. So, he made travel arrangements not only for his parents and himself but also for Raghu's father Sanjay, Anu and her son Sanjeev. Taara had other commitments and could not go.

Dev and these first-time travellers abroad boarded the airplane, excited, apprehensive and awed by the new experience. They landed in London at Heathrow Airport, and Raghu met them to take them to his home in Birmingham. The wedding was in two weeks' time. To keep them occupied until then, Raghu set up an exciting itinerary of short trips to the English countryside. Every morning, either Raghu or one of his friends drove them to a bus stop or a train station, for a fun-filled day of sightseeing.

Whenever questioned about his prospective bride, Raghu simply flashed a mischievous smile. He dodged all questions about her with the finesse of a seasoned ball player, refusing to divulge even her name. The only thing he revealed to his curious family and friends was his assertion that they would love her.

The wedding day turned out to be a blue-skied, sunny day—a rare event for England in mid-October. The guests started arriving with a punditji amongst them. The priest's arrival seemed to puzzle both Sanjay and his sister, Anu. Dev tried to calm their fears. 'At least, we know two things for sure. Raghu is neither marrying an English girl nor converting to another faith,' he said.

'That sounds logical,' replied Anu. 'But a priest in the groom's house and not in the bride's still seems curious.'

Raghu smiled when asked for clarification. He explained his bride's family could not participate, so the ceremony had to be performed in his house. When the bride arrived, the family stared with their mouths open. She was none other than Khan's daughter, Naaz, from Pakistan.

Dev had started suspecting the true identity of his friend's bride before Raghu revealed it. When he thought about the purpose behind Raghu's decision to go to England for higher studies, he understood. During their trip to Pakistan in 1956, Naaz had told Raghu about her plans to finish her medical studies there. He remembered Raghu mentioning, 'Dev, the only place where our romance has a chance to blossom, is in England—away from our suffocating cultures. As soon as I can, I'm going there!'

Raghu's bride, Naaz, had opted to convert, to relinquish her religion for love, a step her parents found unforgivable. At the marriage ceremony, Naaz gave up her Muslim name and became Vanneta from that day forward. Vanneta's new family, overjoyed with her sacrifice, welcomed her with open arms.

'I feel blessed that Vanneta being a woman can take my religion. A Muslim man wouldn't have been allowed to convert to Hinduism,' Raghu said to Dev.

Soon after the ceremony, Vanneta and Raghu left for their honeymoon. By the time the newly married couple returned, the family had done enough sightseeing in Scotland and Ireland and were ready to return to India.

'Before leaving, is it possible to spend a few days in London?' asked Dev.

'Absolutely! Vanneta and I will drive you there this Wednesday. That'll give you four days to sightsee,' replied Raghu.

Raghu and Vanneta drove the relatives in their van. London turned out to be as beautiful as Dev had imagined. However, the overcast skies and constant drip-drip made him yearn for the sunny blue skies of India.

On their second day in London, while returning to the hotel in the evening, a drunk driver rear-ended the van. Dev heard a terrible crash and pitched forward. Dazed, he vaguely heard Raghu's strangled cry. 'Is everyone okay?'

No one answered. That, more than the crash, frightened Dev.

He tried to step out but the van door would not budge. He watched as Raghu jumped out, and struggled to unlock Dev's door from the outside. As the door opened, Dev heard Vanneta's screams, 'Nooo . . . Anu Bua, Anu Bua—' He spun around, but saw only a mangled mass of blood and bones. Blinking and shaking his head to get a better picture, Dev now saw his papaji holding his unresponsive biji in his arms. His Anu chachi seemed beyond help and Sanjeev too incoherent to be of any use to them.

Dev, in his rush to help the injured, tried to step out but his leg refused to move.

'Broken,' he whispered.

'Just turn in your seat,' said Raghu. 'Help Naaz . : . eh . . . Vanneta. Your biji might still make it.'

'Someone please call the ambulance,' shrieked Sukhdev.

Even as he spoke, they heard the sirens.

The paramedics helped Raghu and Vanneta untangle the bodies. Anu, they realised, had died instantly, while Raminder, bleeding profusely with multiple internal injuries, lay unconscious. Besides Dev, who broke a leg, Sanjay sustained multiple deep cuts, while the rest escaped with minor injuries.

The accident happened at such speed that even after reaching the hospital, they still sat in shock. Once the doctors worked on his leg, Dev had to shake himself out of stupor, to make the heart-wrenching calls to India. He informed Ratna and Simranjeet about the accident that took his Anu chachi's life and left his mother in a coma.

The difficult task of breaking the news of her mother's death to Taara fell upon Ratna, who went over personally to give her 'chhoti behen' the shocking news. Taara took it better than Ratna had feared, but she clung to Ratna for a long time, sobbing. 'Didi, it hurts so much . . . I can't do it. I . . . I can't accept this tragedy.'

'You don't have to,' murmured Ratna. 'You let the tragedy accept you.'

'H-huh?' stammered Taara, jolted out of her sorrow.

'Taara, my little sister, I'm so sorry. This is the hardest thing you'll ever have to do. My biji always says, "You need to go to the heart of the tragedy and grapple with it. Then sit with it, knead it . . . feel the pain, experience the excruciating torment and then allow yourself to rise above it, hopefully wiser and stronger."'

26

Another Baby, Another War

1971-77

In February 1971, Ratna and Ravi found out the joyful news that by the end of September they would become parents for the second time. Ratna, at peace with her world, hoped for a son this time to complete the family. Her in-laws had mellowed over the years, but Ratna knew that the credit went to her mature and confident husband who ensured that his parents respected her.

It both gratified and amused her to watch Ravi dote so shamelessly on their daughter Simran. She teased him. 'Simran has you wrapped so tight around her little finger, I wonder if our new baby will have a chance with you?'

'You forget, every baby has his own set of little fingers.' He laughed.

She spent a happy time with her small but growing family. By July that year, Ravi received posting orders to a non-family station. Ratna worried, knowing a transfer to an unspecified border meant governmental preparations for a major turmoil in the area. 'At times like this, I'm so glad you are a doctor and not a soldier or a fighter pilot.'

'During a major crisis, we doctors are as much at risk as soldiers and pilots.'

'I don't want to think about a major crisis. As it is, I can barely concentrate. The possibility of not having you around at the time of our baby's arrival worries me to distraction.'

'Let's hope for the best. If no emergency arises, I might be allowed a short leave to see you and our baby.'

Ratna remembered how her parents and in-laws had both discussed the eventuality of a posting to a non-family station, even before her wedding. At that time they discussed it as if it was inconsequential, telling her she could finish her studies whenever such a posting took place. Now that it stared her in the face, she wondered why the thought made her so restless. Ravi was her life. How does one perform the act of living when 'life' is missing?

During the few tense weeks before Ravi left, his parents called. 'Ratna,' said her mother-in-law, 'I presume you will spend the last few months of your pregnancy with us. I'm so glad. After all, we all know how after last time's fiasco, you need guidance to ensure a male child.'

Ratna felt so flustered after the conversation that Ravi hugged her and said, 'I think in this, your last trimester, Garha is the safest place for both you and Simran. Just knowing you are happy and in safe hands will give me one less thing to worry about.'

'Will you talk to your mother and tell her? Please?'

'Of course.' Ravi bent down to kiss Ratna's stomach, and with his ear against it, said, 'Baby, are you listening? Papa loves you. Come, my baby, give me a signal to show you heard.'

Ratna laughed. 'Is this some form of telepathy?'

'Yes. See? The baby kicked. He knows I love him.' Ravi kissed her stomach again and straightened up.

'I wish you didn't have to go,' whispered Ratna, gazing into his eyes.

'I know. But that's the price you pay for falling in love with an army officer.' He winked, making her smile.

As soon as Ravi answered his summons for active duty on the east coast, Ratna left for Garha. Upon reaching her parental haveli, she found herself in the midst of major hustle and bustle. She learned that between Sanjay and her parents, they had found a suitable Hindu boy and arranged Taara's wedding.

Since Raminder still tired easily after the accident, Ratna was asked to help Taara with her trousseau. Ratna enjoyed the activities and the preparations. When the wedding day arrived, Taara looked breathtaking, doing justice to her name, Taara—a star. Ratna smiled at her mother and whispered, 'Hope Anu chachi is watching over her daughter today. Taara looks more radiant than the brightest star in the sky.'

Once the excitement of the wedding passed, Ratna thought more and more about Ravi, worrying herself sick over trouble brewing on the eastern borders of India. It smelled like another one of those futile conflicts that took place between India and Pakistan at regular intervals. She missed her husband with the ferocity of an unbearable ache and prayed for his return.

To take her mind off worrying over Ravi, she concentrated on her new life and enrolled her daughter in her own alma mater—St. Jude's High School. After the first time she drove Simran to school, her papaji insisted, 'Ratna, in your present state, your mother and I don't want you to drive to Jullunder. We've hired a chauffeur for the job.'

Amused, Ratna watched as Simran travelled in a chauffeur driven car, to and from school, just like Dev used to in his younger days when he was still the prince of Shahadra. Her parents not only pampered Simran but also ensured that she spent her days in a cocoon of love and security.

As Ratna's due date approached, Simran pestered her. 'When is papa returning? He promised he'd be in Garha for my birthday.'

'Simran, your father always keeps his promises. He'll come. Your birthday is still months away.'

But Ratna worried. India and Pakistan, like two contentious siblings, still had little spats at regular intervals. And Ratna, like the rest of her family, expected the tense situation between the two countries to ease by Simran's birthday.

During this long wait, Ratna spent a quiet time with her parents, often marvelling at how gracefully both of them were aging. Raminder had started using henna on her graying hair years earlier, and now, she noticed her mother's hair looked auburn while her father's untouched beard and mustache were still a mixture of salt and pepper. She guessed her mother to be in her early fifties. Both her parents were very good looking, still walking tall and erect like royalty. The question of her parents' age had never come up and she had never asked.

On one of his visits to Garha, Dev mentioned, 'Papaji turned sixty-three this March.'

'I didn't know you knew his age. How come you never ever mentioned it earlier? And how come we don't celebrate his birthday?' asked Ratna.

Dev shrugged. 'I didn't think it mattered. Papaji always says birthdays are for little children. He says he prefers to have each day celebrated for the gift of life.'

'Do you know ma's age?'

'Papaji once mentioned she is four years younger. Do the math.'

'If papaji is sixty-three now, he must have been thirty-nine at the time of Partition and ma thirty-five. Wow! I thought they were in their late twenties then.'

Her parents' haveli was a warm place where friends and relatives flocked at every opportunity. Guddi often accompanied Dev and Himmat to Garha, on weekends. Ratna knew Simran looked forward to weekends, hoping to see Himmat, who had become her close friend. Even Simi and Gurdev visited often with their daughter, Nimmi, who being the same age as Simran loved these weekend outings.

At Garha, besides socialising with family and friends, Ratna had the time for leisure activities. She got immersed in her sitar again. A teacher came from Jullunder to give music lessons to Simran. And Ratna, secretly amused, noticed Raminder talk of nothing but her granddaughter's melodious voice and accomplishments to anyone who was willing to listen.

By the middle of September, a week before her due date, Ratna delivered a healthy baby boy. Ravi could not be with her as the political situation had become volatile, and all leave for the army officers had been cancelled.

Ratna's parents went out of their way at the little one's naamkaran ceremony—the religious ceremony for naming the infant. Her in-laws, family friends and relatives participated in the joyous occasion. Everyone came, except her Ravi. His absence gnawed at her guts, even as the gathering of friends and relatives eased her enough to enjoy her good fortune. At the prayers, she named her newborn Mannat, meaning a 'prayed-for' blessing. Ratna and Ravi had prayed for a son and had chosen the name together.

Ratna watched Sukhdev and Raminder dote on her baby, as did his uncle Dev. She found her brother a little less awed, but more delighted by the miracle this time around. A lot of time and living had taken place since Simran and Himmat's births. Dev could now handle the delicate, but precious bundle with more ease.

As the year after the birth of baby Mannat wore on, the political situation went from bad to worse. Ratna prayed for the crisis to pass so that Ravi could return. He still had not had a chance to hold their precious new child.

The news media made her nervous, as it talked of nothing but the current crisis. West Pakistan was engaged in a civil war with East Pakistan. Since the two parts of Pakistan flanked India's opposite borders in an awkward fashion, the Pakistani civil war could only be fought by flying through the Indian air space. Ratna read in the papers the cause of this civil war: The Muslim Bengalis in East Pakistan demanded more autonomy but the governing body in West Pakistan refused the demand and instead launched a campaign of terror to intimidate them into submission.

Ratna had never paid much attention to Pakistan's politics. Now, because of Ravi being stationed somewhere near the troubled land, this crisis was too close to ignore. As summer turned into the monsoon season and the monsoons into winter, thousands upon thousands of Pakistani-Bengali refugees crossed the border into various Indian cities in Bengal, Assam, and other areas in and around Calcutta, looking for safety and reprieve. India, in an effort to stem this tide of refugees, offered support to East Pakistan, to ensure containment of their refugee influx into Indian cities.

On 3 December 1971, as Ratna and her parents sat in front of the television watching the news, they saw the Pakistani Air Force strike a number of Indian airfields, to stop the Indian government from supporting East Pakistan. And India, prepared for this eventuality, retaliated, starting a full-fledged war. Once the war started, Ratna spent all her time glued to the television. She watched the movement of large forces of Indian soldiers deployed to the eastern borders, to help East Pakistan. Her Ravi, stationed somewhere in the midst of these hostilities, drove her to pray as she watched, while India and Pakistan rehashed old wounds.

Within twelve days, the war ended. During this brief but intense moment in history, a new nation called Bangladesh—the Land of Bengalis—took birth.

East Pakistan became Bangladesh.

Ratna breathed a sigh of relief. The war was over and she hoped Ravi would be home soon.

One crisp winter morning, she sat in the sun, rocking baby Mannat in his jhula—a swing bassinet—that she had rolled from the verandah onto the paved patio. She sat under blue skies, one hand rocking the jhula and the other holding a newspaper. Raminder sat close by, knitting.

'Ma, listen to these headlines: "Indians Out in the Streets, Celebrating Victory Over Pakistan." I wish I could ask them what we Indians gained from the war. There are again thousands of refugees on the streets of Bengal and Assam.' Ratna shook her head reliving painful memories.

'Beti, every generation has to learn its own lessons. No one learns from history,' replied her mother.

'Ma . . .' she looked up without finishing her thought. A khaki uniformed mail carrier rode his bicycle through the haveli gates, jingling his bicycle bell. He got off and parked his bicycle against the gate, and offered her a telegram.

Cold slithered in Ratna's body from the ground up. The earth halted its spinning, as her hand moved slowly, slowly to reach for the telegram, to read the words she knew would be there. Her mouth opened to release a piercing howl. Holding her stomach, she fell to the ground.

Raminder picked up the telegram and read the words aloud, making them forever real. 'The Defence Ministry of India is sorry to inform you Dr Colonel Ravinder Singh was killed in a hospital bombing near Calcutta. We are proud to say he died a martyr in the line of duty.'

'Raviii—' shrieked Ratna.

Raminder helped Ratna onto a chair, before bending over to pick up the screaming baby from the cradle.

'He never saw his baby . . . our baby!' Ratna wailed.

Hearing her mother's screams, Simran jumped off the swing and ran towards her, crying, 'Mama, Mama.'

But Ratna did not hear. She pushed away the glass of water Simran brought her. 'Why?' she wailed. 'Ma, he was a good man. My Ravi was a good man. He . . . he never saw our baby. He never smelled our baby's smell.' With tears rolling down her face, she looked skywards and cried, 'Vaheguru, are you listening? Do you hear me? My Ravi was a good man.'

Cradling the baby in her arms, Raminder kissed Ratna's forehead. The gentle touch hushed Ratna's cries. 'Ma!' Ratna whispered, trembling, 'Ravi never kissed our baby. He never held him. . . .'

She cried for days until the tears dried up, but her heart still hungered for Ravi. She clung to her parents, and wondered what lessons she still had to learn in life. When Dev came, she drew a measure of comfort from his strength.

Ratna discovered she could no longer nurse her baby. Her milk dried up as suddenly as her heart shattered. Overnight, she watched her brother turn into the father her baby was never destined to know. Dev rocked baby Mannat, fed him and sang lullabies that she never knew he could. He learned to change the baby's nappies and warm his milk on kerosene stoves at two in the morning.

'Dev,' Ratna mumbled one day, 'remember I was Simran's age when we lost our families?'

'Behen, we survived. Remember that. And, I promise you one thing, Simran and Mannat will never lack a father. I'll be there for them. Always remember that. I can't bring your beloved back, but I'll make sure the children don't lack anything.'

Ratna inched closer, and putting her arms around him, put her head on his shoulder. 'Dev,' she mumbled, wiping her tears, 'why did it happen to my Ravi?'

'I don't know,' he whispered. And, gathering his sister in his arms, asked, 'Behen, do you still have Uma ma's necklace I gave you? Wear it. Let it remind you of the mantra of the "juice mango". I know, at the moment, the hurt is too raw and nothing will help. But trust me, with time, the mantra will make sense and give you courage.'

Ratna realised that she had to get a grip on herself soon for the sake of her children. She needed courage to face the nation during the January Republic Day celebrations, to receive a medal of bravery bestowed upon her Ravi posthumously. Dev sat with her, many, many times on the bench under the juice mango tree, and little by little, she gathered inner strength.

'My Ravi was a good man,' she whispered one day, as she broke down again.

Putting his arm around her shoulders, Dev said, 'He wouldn't want you to cry for him. He died a martyr, serving his country.'

'Yes, I know. Ravi died in glory, but . . . who pays the price?'

The unwavering support of her family nurtured her not only during the days, but also through dark nights. She stayed within the warm embrace of her parents' haveli until she felt strong enough to face her future.

Seven months after Ravi's death, Ratna's mother-in-law died in a car accident that left her father-in-law in a coma. With Ravi gone, she now felt it her duty to take care of him. So, taking her children, she moved to her in-law's home in New Delhi to look after Ravi's father. But, within three months, he too succumbed to his injuries.

Ratna suddenly found herself with two young children in a new home, a new city, and all alone. Moving back to Garha did not feel right. By now, she could think clearly enough to realise that New Delhi was a good place to raise Simran and Mannat. It had the best schools and colleges in the country. Besides better opportunities for them, she too had a chance at one of her dreams. So she decided to stay in New Delhi and complete her Masters in Indian Instrumental music, specialising in sitar.

Raminder moved in with her for all intents and purposes. Sukhdev visited them whenever he could, as he still needed to take care of his business and the farm in Garha. He seemed quite satisfied with the arrangement. Their unwavering emotional support helped Ratna heal. She appreciated their sacrifice, especially since she needed help bringing up her children. Simran needed assistance to adjust to a new school, a new environment and a fatherless life. And baby Mannat needed full time care while she and Simran went to school.

Dev and Sukhdev helped by taking charge of supervising the grain farm in Karnal that Ratna inherited from her in-laws. The monthly military pension, Ravi's insurance money, the proceeds from the farm, and the house her in-laws left behind, helped her lead a financially comfortable life.

Whenever Raminder visited Garha during the school year, she took Mannat with her, to allow Ratna time to concentrate on her music. During Simran's school vacations, Raminder and both the children went back to the village, with Ratna joining them whenever she could.

Ratna knew her children loved Garha. Simran insisted some of her happiest memories were of the haveli. Mannat too talked of garnering his most cherished memories there. It was in Garha, he told Ratna, that Dev mamaji taught him to play cricket and Himmat bhaji taught him to ride a bicycle and fly his first kite. There, in the haveli, her father related to Mannat the tales of Maharajas and Mughals, tales of Sinbad the sailor and tales from their Gurus' lives. Ratna knew why the bedtime stories meant so much to her little son. The secret lay in the way her father wove those tales. The same stories had nurtured Simran, and the same yarns had enthralled her and Dev when they were young. She understood why her children found the haveli in Garha a magical place. There her parents read them the same dreams she remembered; dreams as bewitching as a peacock's dance; dreams that assured them a song in their hearts.

Under her parents' supervision, she watched Simran grow into a poised fifteen-year-old, and Mannat grow into a well-adjusted five-year-old boy.

Soon after Mannat's sixth birthday, Raminder, Simran and Mannat came to Garha in October, for Diwali holidays. Dev and Himmat joined them there. One morning, Raminder got up from a chair, remarking, 'Dev Beta, I have this pain in my left shoulder. Can you look at it?'

Dev checked her and frowned. 'Does it hurt in your chest too?' he asked.

'Yes. I've been hoping it would go away but it's getting more and more severe.'

Turning to his father, Dev whispered, 'Papaji, we need to take her to the hospital immediately. She's having a heart attack.'

Sukhdev hurried to get the car started while Dev watched Raminder stumble towards the bathroom. He heard a loud thud inside the bathroom and knew. Himmat and Simran ran to get their grandfather. Upon opening the door, Sukhdev and Dev found her lying on the floor. Dev bent over her, checking her pulse, but she was already gone. Dev looked up and shook his head.

Sukhdev leaned against the wall, his mouth half open, his breath coming in spurts, looking at the crumbled figure. Slumping to his knees, tears rolling down his cheeks, he murmured, 'That's just like her. Departing the same way she lived her life—without complaining, with total acceptance of her Vaheguru's will.'

The first weekend after cremation, friends and family gathered to pay their last respects. Raghu and Vanneta came from England and so did the children from the Pingalwara orphanage in Amritsar. At the prayers after the cremation, Ratna, Simi, Guddi and Simran did the kirtan from the *Guru Granth Sahib*. Simi and Guddi sang shabads; while Ratna accompanied them on the sitar, paying homage to a life well lived.

Once the prayers were over, Ratna still sat cross-legged with the other women, on white sheets covering the ground. She did not say much, just pressed Simran or Taara's hand every now and then, as if gathering strength from her loved ones. One by one, family and friends got up to share memories of how Raminder had brightened their lives.

Dev got up to give a short speech. 'I've been blessed twice by the love of a mother,' he started. 'One gave me birth, the other re-birthed me into the world of the living, once again. One bequeathed a mantra of love to live my life by, the other taught me by her example to live it. Today I've lost both, but their legacy sustains me. All of you who knew my biji know how much love and compassion she shared with those around her. She made the world a better place not only for Ratna and me, her children, but also for strangers, friends and family. Biji breathed love into every life she touched,' he said, and paused, trying to calm his quivering voice. As he took a sip of water, many people, young and old, relatives and friends, dabbed their eyes, nodding.

He continued his heart-felt tribute: 'I want to celebrate my mother's life and not mourn her death. In her loving memory, with my uncle, Dr Simranjeet's help, I plan to build a two-roomed dispensary at Pingalwara's orphanage in Amritsar. Mamaji and I will provide our services, and make provisions to pay for medicines at the dispensary. Papaji is funding a foundation called "Vaheguru Raakha", biji's favourite phrase, to pay the salaries of a full-time nurse and a pharmacist at the premises. May Vaheguru bless each and every one of you.' Dev folded his hands and bowing, sat down.

His eyes wandered over his loved ones. He watched Ratna reach over for Guddi's hand. Guddi, tears rolling down her face, shook visibly. Simran sat sobbing softly, head covered and bowed, eyes red, with hands folded in prayer. Himmat, tears escaping through his long lashes, sat cross-legged, holding Mannat in his lap. Every now and then, Mannat turned around to wipe the tears from Himmat's face with his tiny hands.

Dev looked at his father, who, too distraught to talk, wore dark glasses to shield his moist eyes. After Dev's speech, Sukhdev took a long while getting up; making Dev acutely aware of his father's advancing age. With folded hands, Sukhdev looked skywards and said, 'Thank you Vaheguru for the honour of allowing Raminder to share her life with me. Thank you for her memories that like a lingering whiff of incense nourish and strengthen me. I will cherish her until the day I die. Vaheguru raakha.' God is our guardian.

Part Five
1978-91

'The song that I came to sing remains unsung to this day.'

—Rabindranath Tagore
Nobel laureate for Literature (1913)
Excerpt from *Gitanjali*

27
Cycles of Life

Spring, 1978

In a flurry of excitement, Ratna bustled around, making arrangements for the evening party to celebrate her daughter's acceptance into Lady Harding Medical College. Simran's admission to the Medical school, on merit, at the tender age of sixteen, gave Ratna tremendous joy and pride. Simran started on a fast track just like her uncle Dev.

Raminder had made it possible for Ratna to complete her studies and teach instrumental music in the university, just as she had helped mould Simran into the person she had become. Now, Ratna wished her mother could have celebrated Simran's extraordinary success with them. She knew Raminder would have been very proud of her bright granddaughter, as she had always seemed partial to the profession Simran planned to pursue.

Ratna's mind wandered to thoughts of her husband, Ravi, and the dreams they had dreamt together. During her last pregnancy, he would say, 'If we have a son this time, we'll make him a doctor'. She smiled thinking how Ravi probably never thought that his daughter could follow his footsteps as well. Simran's admission to medical school would have been such a joy to him.

Seeing tears in her mother's eyes, Simran asked, 'What is it, Mama? Why the tears on such a happy day?'

'These are just tears of joy. I wish your father and your nanima could see you now. They'd be so proud of you.'

'I know. They are always with me in spirit . . . isn't that what you taught me?' said Simran, and giving her mother a hug, walked away to finish her chores.

Ratna took a deep breath. Her Ravi and her mother had so much to offer, so much love to give. They had sung the songs meant for them to sing. And then there was her papaji. Such a rich song he sang. What about her? What was the song she came to sing in her lifetime?

After her mother's death, she knew her papaji had no interest left in Garha. She had talked it over with Dev, who insisted he take their father to live with him in Amritsar. Sukhdev had locked up the farmhouse and moved to Amritsar but before leaving, he had sold his bicycle factory in Jullunder to Taara's husband. After Ratna and Dev assured him they were secure financially, Sukhdev put aside half the sale money for his grandchildren's education. The other half he put in the Vaheguru Raakha foundation he had started in memory of Raminder, at Pingalwara, in Amritsar.

'Mannat!' she hollered at her six-year-old, as he ran by with his kite. 'How many times do I need to tell you to stop playing and get dressed? Everyone will be here any minute and you are still in your pyjamas! Go, take a bath right now.'

In order to celebrate Simran's special day, Ratna had taken two week's vacation from the university and invited everyone she knew. When a taxi stopped outside the house, she and Simran ran eagerly to answer the doorbell. Amidst much merriment, Ratna hugged and welcomed her guests. Along with her father and brother came Guddi, Himmat, and Simi's daughter Nimmi.

Ratna noticed that her father, now seventy years old, still walked tall and straight. He carried a silver walking stick. When Simran commented upon it, he answered, 'The walking stick is a gift from Dev'. Ratna recognised it as the same cane that belonged to Dev's Baoji. Sukhdev, his gray beard rolled up, a magenta turban matching his tie and a dark suit, cast an imposing presence. His shoes, black Oxfords, were polished and shining as usual.

Ratna remembered fondly how even during their post-Partition struggling days, he always wore polished and sparkling Oxfords. She had once asked her mother how they could afford such expensive shoes for him when the family had barely enough to eat. Raminder laughed. 'Oh! He had twelve pairs of fancy English shoes when we lived in Ugoke. He was wearing one pair when we left and our maid Nasibaan packed three more pairs with our luggage before we left home. That is how his feet at least are always smartly fitted.' Ratna smiled at the memory of old, worn out clothes hanging over sparkling, expensive shoes. The thought amused her then, it amused her now.

Simran exclaimed, 'Nanaji, you still look like a maharaja. You are so handsome.'

Sukhdev smiled, catching her in a bear hug. 'You are not bad looking yourself, my precious.'

Simran wiggled out of his embrace to hug Dev, Guddi and her favourite cousin, Nimmi.

Ratna wrapped her arms around Guddi. 'I'm so glad you came. How exciting that Himmat came too. Mannat's been asking about him.' Then putting one arm around Guddi's waist, she led them indoors, where everyone sat over a cup of tea, reminiscing about old days in Garha.

Seeing Mannat hover around Himmat, Ratna said, 'Mannat misses you a lot. He often tells us how you taught him to fly a kite and to play cricket.'

'It was so much fun teaching him the ways of a boy's world. Lucky for us the haveli in Garha had land to play cricket and fly kites. And then, of course, Dev mamaji and nanaji were always there to play with us,' said Himmat smiling at Dev.

The haveli, Ratna knew from experience was a happy place, a place where dreams came alive. She sensed her children and Himmat all felt the same way she did.

Ratna had invited the out-of-town guests for at least a week, as she had planned the weekend after Simran's party, for dastar bandhi—the turban-tying ceremony—for Mannat. Anu's son Sanjeev, a civil engineer, lived in New Delhi. Ratna invited Sanjeev and Taara's families to both parties. Taara lived in Jullunder with her three children and husband, a wealthy businessman. At Ratna's invitation, Taara arrived at her brother's, accompanied by her twin daughters and an older son, for at least a week.

On the day of Simran's party, Dev helped Ratna with the necessary arrangements for Simran's special day. Even Himmat and Mannat, recruited by Dev, helped put up decorations and offered to serve drinks and refreshments in the evening.

That morning, Taara called Ratna and asked, 'Didi, may I invite a friend, her mother and younger brother to the party? She and I studied together at Delhi University. This weekend is the only time she has when she can visit me, before she returns to her home in England.'

'Of course, you may,' replied Ratna.

So, Taara arrived at the party accompanied by Meera, her mother and brother. Ratna greeted her guests, smiling broadly, realising she knew Meera. Some years earlier, she had given private sitar lessons to her. After being introduced to the mother, Ratna led them to her drawing room. Just then, Dev signalled her from the kitchen. Excusing herself, she walked over to Dev.

His face twitching, Dev mumbled, 'Who is Taara's friend and the elderly lady with her? They look so familiar.'

'Her name is Meera. She's my ex-student. I gave her private sitar lessons a couple of years ago. She is married now, and I believe she lives somewhere in England. Those two are her mother and brother. Why do you ask?'

'Do you know her mother?' asked Dev.

'No. I've met her for the first time. However, I do know Meera's brother Deepak, who used to drive her in the evenings for sitar lessons. While she practiced, Deepak spent time with Mannat, who became very fond of him. Taara introduced the mother as Mrs Bhardwaj.'

'I knew it! I knew it! That's who she is. Sita chachi!' Dev almost danced around the kitchen as he became more certain of his discovery. 'Remember how Sita chachi had a black beauty spot on the right side of her chin and a light complexion? This lady also has the same height and the same dimpled smile. Of course, the name is a dead give-away.'

Sudden longing for his childhood made Dev jumpy. He found it hard not to smile as he remembered his 'Shweet chachi' who helped him with his English homework in Shahadra.

'You may be right,' replied Ratna, after staring at the woman. 'What should we do?'

Conflicting emotions collided in his heart. On the one hand, he wanted to embrace the woman if she indeed was Sita chachi, and on the other hand he was still infuriated with her husband—his Gaurav chacha—for being a traitor and a murderer of his Iqbal chacha.

Ratna said, 'I have an idea. Give me a few minutes to make discreet inquiries. If it is Sita chachi, we'll tell Taara and Sanjeev about it, as she would be their aunt too. Then we could make a joint decision how to handle the situation.'

'No! Don't tell them. I don't think they have a clue about Gaurav chacha's act of betrayal—it's something they don't need to know anyway. They never knew him. If necessary, you come back to the kitchen and we'll talk.'

Ratna asked Mrs Bhardwaj where her family was from originally. 'I'm from Delhi,' she answered. 'My husband was from Shahadra village near Lahore, in Pakistan. But, we lost his whole family during Partition.'

They talked some more, and when Ratna could leave without seeming rude, she rose and went to the kitchen. 'Dev, she is who you suspected her to be. However, Gaurav chacha passed away two years ago. Meera is her older child. Deepak is the younger son. What do we do now?'

Glad his uncle was not in the picture any more, Dev broke into a mischievous smile, and joked, 'I shall reveal myself now.' So saying, he walked up to the lady and asked if her name was Sita and if she ever lived in the village of Shahadra, near Lahore.

Concentrating on his face and furrowing her brow, Sita muttered, 'Yes.'

'Sita chachi! It's me, Dev. Dev Anand Bhardwaj.'

Sita stared at him, jaws partially open, eyes confused. He, with a graying beard and a turban, had just announced he was the little Dev the whole Shahadra family doted on. He wondered if she could even picture his childhood face.

'Is that true?' she mumbled, rising from the sofa.

'Yes, it is,' said Dev, smiling. 'How could I ever forget you? Every evening for more than a year, I sat with you in the library of our Shahadra haveli, sometimes doing my homework and sometimes staring at that black beauty spot on your chin. Remember how I lisped and couldn't say "sweet", so I called you "Shweet chachi" instead. You are the one who taught me my English alphabet. And, remember our first ride together in the black Austin Baoji bought just before Partition?'

'Oh my God! Look at that nose. Of course, it's you,' Sita said, her voice quivering. 'Alive all these years, when we thought we had lost the entire family!' She shook her head. 'Your uncle would have been so happy to see you.'

Ignoring the reference to his uncle, Dev reached and caught her in a bear hug. When he released her, Sita stood leaning on a wall for support. Seeing her so incapacitated, Dev guided her to the sofa, and sitting next to her, told her how he lost both his parents and Baoji during Partition. He also explained how a Sikh couple adopted him along with the punditji's daughter, Ratna. 'Taara and Sanjeev are Amar chacha's children.'

'I don't understand,' Sita whispered. 'When your Gaurav chacha went to facilitate Iqbal bhaiya's crossover from Amritsar into Pakistan, he said he stopped at Garha. Anu bhabi's brother gave him our jewellery and told him the entire family had been massacred at the border. Your Gaurav chacha was totally devastated with the news.'

Dev watched Ratna's stunned expression. But he did not think his uncle's lie mattered anymore—Gaurav chacha had already met his Maker and faced the moment of ultimate truth.

Sita chachi called Meera and Deepak to her. 'Come meet your cousin,' she called with that same lilting voice he remembered.

He felt as though no time had passed, that all the pain and sorrow were erased by Sita chachi's voice. But a remnant of the past's dark side remained. His aunt and Ratna stared at each other, unable to make that first move across the gulf—of a servant and master—that once separated them. Giving them time to digest this new development, he went looking for his father, to introduce Sukhdev to his new relatives. By the time he returned, Ratna had relaxed and was in an animated discussion with a smiling Sita.

'My goodness! Your father is so handsome,' muttered Meera, after the introductions.

Ratna smiled. 'He really is, isn't he?'

'Where is Amar bhaiya?' asked Sita.

'He died of typhoid shortly after Partition. The twins, Taara and Sanjeev, were born a few months after their father passed away. Our parents and both Ratna and I met Anu chachi when these twins were about six or seven years old. Our mother Raminder and Anu chachi became best of friends. They were like sisters.'

'How did Anu bhabi recognise you?' asked Sita.

'She didn't . . . Ratna recognised her. Anu chachi died in a car-accident shortly before Taara's wedding.'

Sita shook her head saying, 'My husband and I were blessed with abundant good fortune. I wish we could have shared the blessings with our loved ones. If only we had known you still lived.'

Sita's eyes glazed over. She seemed to look at something or someone that was not in the room. 'Did Gaurav somehow know his family still lived?' she whispered, as though afraid to voice what she was thinking. 'Why did he never go back to Garha or the Jullunder refugee camps? No, no . . . we couldn't have lived a lie.'

Dev lowered his eyes, granting his aunt dignity as she spoke aloud what had to be private. Sita shuddered, bringing her awareness back to the room. Seeing Ratna staring at her, she blushed crimson.

After the guests left, Ratna confronted Dev, demanding to know why he did not disclose Gaurav chacha's betrayal to Sita chachi.

'I guess I remembered the juice mango,' he answered, his eyes soft and compassionate. 'I needed to forgive my uncle's transgressions, not for his sake but for my own. Years of built up anger and hatred are difficult to overcome, but I needed to try for my Uma ma's sake.'

'I don't understand you, Dev,' yelled Ratna. 'Anger is not a simple emotion that goes away by simply willing it so. How can you forgive someone who robbed you of your innocence? Someone who was a murderer? . . . I can't.' Tears and frustration distorted her face. 'I hate him!'

'Behen, I agree with you. Anger is not a simple emotion, and for me, even forgiveness is not a lightly thought out decision. I've waited thirty years for forgiveness to envelop me and release the pain. But that has not happened,' said Dev. 'When I saw Sita chachi today, I realised it hurt too much to be locked in my own emotional prison. I have to forgive in order to love again, to be whole again. Don't you see, love and forgiveness dance in circles? One depends on the other.'

Brushing aside her tears, Ratna stared at Dev as he continued, 'I have to remind myself constantly that one khota paisa'—bad penny—'in a family does not make the rest of the family bad. Ratna, remember your bapu taught you that? What good would it do to tell Sita chachi the truth about Gaurav chacha? She's already in turmoil, wondering if her life with her husband was a lie.'

'Dev,' replied Ratna, 'I've spent a lifetime avoiding khota paisas like your Gaurav chacha, simply because it hurt too much to deal with bullies like him. But you may be right. Avoiding pain is as hard on one's psyche as dealing with it. You speak of powerful emotions and I need time to mull them over.' Taking a deep breath, she touched his arm before sitting down to calm herself.

The next morning, as Ratna stood in her kitchen cracking eggs for breakfast, she felt someone's warm breath on her neck. 'Behen, can we talk in private?' Dev whispered in her ear.

'Dev, why do you have to scare me?' She laughed and pushed against his chest. Leading him towards her bedroom, she said, 'At least now I know. Mannat learned to be silly from you! What is it you want?'

'What do you think of Himmat?' he asked.

'What kind of a question is this? You know I hold him in high esteem.'

'Is he good enough for our Simran?'

'Yes . . . but she is still too young for marriage.' She stared at her brother, wondering why she had not thought of this match herself.

'I know Simran is only sixteen, but I suggest we broach the subject with Guddi while she is visiting. I know both of them are still very young but they don't have to get married until they finish their studies.'

'You do have a point there. I think it's an excellent idea.' She knew this time around Dev did not want to leave anything to chance. She also knew that Himmat and Simran were fond of each other.

'Ratna, just so you know, I'm planning to help finance Himmat's studies abroad. He wants to go to America to specialise in cardiology,' said Dev.

'That would be perfect because Simran also wants to go to America for her higher studies. We don't have to have an engagement right away. The children are still very young. But as soon as Himmat graduates and before he goes abroad, we could have a formal engagement. Yes. That should work. You are right, my foolish brother. Let us make our intentions known.'

With a lopsided smile, Dev walked out of his sister's bedroom.

Ratna's suggestion delighted Guddi. 'You know, I always hoped we could unite our families in this manner. Yours is the only real family Himmat and I have ever known. This will make it official. Let's talk to the children and find out what they think.' Guddi beamed.

Amid a lot of blushing and stammering, Himmat and Simran loved the idea. All through their childhoods, they had spent many a vacation together at Garha. Ratna sensed they did not even know when they had fallen in love. She felt, Himmat and Simran's companionship as children had always been placid and serene, their friendship deep and warm.

Guddi and Ratna blessed this loving alliance with an ardaas. The prayer and the promise given by the two mothers were as sacred and as binding as an engagement.

A couple of days before the dastar-bandhi—the turban-tying ceremony—for Mannat, Ratna asked her brother, 'Dev, what do I call your Sita chachi?'

'Call her Sita chachi, of course! Didn't you call my other aunt, Anu chachi?'

'But that was different. Anu chachi was family and she always treated me like your sister.'

He winked. 'Well, make up your mind. Are you or are you not my sister?'

Ratna smiled at her silly brother. Anu chachi had never questioned the relationship because she had watched Ratna and Dev being treated as equals by their parents. But would Dev's aunt Sita understand, she wondered. Would she object to Ratna being treated as Dev's sister? Or perhaps she'd object to being addressed as Sita chachi by her? The only way to find out was to invite Sita and her family for the prayers at Mannat's turban tying ceremony, and see.

At the ceremony, Ratna relaxed when after addressing her as chachi, Sita smiled and hugged her. Even Sita's son, Deepak, seemed delighted with his newly discovered cousins.

Laughing and patting Dev on his shoulder Deepak said, 'If I grew a beard and wore a turban, we'd look alike, big bro.' Ratna sensed Dev's pleasure when Deepak addressed him as big brother.

The activities of the day continued to please Ratna. She remembered her mother's favourite saying. 'Having more relatives and friends is like having more arms with which to hug the universe.' She found Sita's family perfect for sharing her universe.

Ratna saw Deepak, Sita's twenty-one year old son, as a kind and loving young man, who still needed time to mature. His family's wealth seemed to have predisposed him towards laziness. Luckily, for Ratna, Deepak had the time and the resources to bond with Mannat, whom he remembered from Meera's sitar-playing days. After that first introduction, he started arriving unannounced at Ratna's house to take Mannat to a movie or a game of hockey or cricket. Ratna liked that.

Even Sita seemed delighted with the newly discovered relatives. As the two women came to know each other better, Sita revealed how she had lived an easy, satisfying life with her husband. Only after his death, life had turned harsh. To add to her difficulties, two other life-changing events happened around the same time. First, she retired from a teaching job in the university. Then, her only daughter got married and moved to England, leaving Sita to crave the warmth of an extended family. 'Ratna, you've filled a hole in my life. You remind me of Uma bhabi.'

Ratna accepted the compliment with humility. Uma had been a wise and gracious woman, loved by everyone.

Over a period of a few months, Ratna and Sita came to know each other better. Ratna often talked of her love of music and sometimes both she and Sita reminisced about old days. They discussed the last days each had spent at the haveli in Shahadra, and about the last moments of Uma's life. Ratna disclosed how Iqbal chacha never made it across the border, but she never mentioned the betrayal.

When Ratna related the horrors of their escape, the compassion she saw in Sita's eyes gave her courage to relate something very private. 'All through my childhood,' she said, 'I woke up from a recurring nightmare where I saw fields and fields of dead bodies covered in white sheets. The nightmare became a part of my very existence. As I grew up, I had the nightmare every time I was under stress, be it physical or emotional. In the beginning, I didn't even question it. And when I did start questioning, it made no sense.'

'Do you still have the bad dreams?'

'No. But I know one thing. My healing started with that visit back to Shahadra in 1956.'

'Ratna, you and Dev experienced what no child should have to suffer. That kind of trauma could give nightmares to anyone,' mumbled Sita, as she reached for Ratna's hands.

28
Spring Branches on Old Trees

1981-83

In the spring of 1981, Ratna heard from Guddi that Himmat had graduated from the Amritsar Medical School, and accepted an internship at Einstein Medical Hospital in New York. 'When does he have to leave for the USA?' she asked.

'By the beginning of July,' replied Guddi. 'Since Himmat needs to get his paperwork done at the embassy, we will be in Delhi by the end of May. And, did papaji or Dev call you? They plan to accompany us.'

'Yes, I know. I'm looking forward to seeing you all. Guddi, what if we have the engagement ceremony for Simran and Himmat in the beginning of June?'

'Sounds good.'

Luckily, for Ratna, the university had closed for the summer.

As per the plan, Guddi, Himmat, Sukhdev and Dev all arrived in the last week of May. On the first day after their arrival, Ratna sat polishing the silver for the engagement party when Guddi joined her. While helping her shine the silverware, Guddi said, 'I've given this whole thing much thought.'

Ratna looked up sharply, 'What thing?'

'Himmat and Simran's engagement.'

Ratna stopped polishing and straightened up. Pushing the graying strands of hair away from her face with the back of her hand, she asked,

'What about the engagement? You are not having second thoughts about their marriage. Are you?'

'No! No! . . . It's just that Himmat could be gone a long time and I was thinking maybe we should skip the engagement and have the marriage ceremony instead. It'll give him a strong reason to return to us.'

Ratna stared at her friend. 'This is so sudden,' she said finally. 'Do you think he might not return from America?'

'Himmat has never given me a reason to believe otherwise, but you can't say with young people. With new opportunities, sometimes attitudes, circumstances and even priorities change.'

'Can I talk it over with my father and brother?'

'Of course!'

Within a week of a few family discussions, Himmat and Simran were married. Ratna sighed with relief when the wedding, though sudden, went off well. The bride and groom left for a short honeymoon and when they returned, she sensed Simran's happiness. She could not believe how all along a perfect match for her daughter had been there under her nose, and she never saw it. She still found it amazing that Dev had to point it out to her. What could she say? She had a good brother, a loving man.

Exactly four weeks after the wedding, Himmat left. He needed to be in the USA by the beginning of July. Simran could not leave with him but Himmat promised to send for her as soon as her visa arrived.

Guddi and Simran left for Amritsar shortly after Himmat's departure. Simran wanted to make a pilgrimage to the Golden Temple to get Vaheguru's blessings before starting her new life.

Simran's visa came through in October and by that time Ratna and Guddi both knew Simran was carrying a child, due at the end of March the following year. They discussed the options Simran had as to where to have the baby—in the USA or in India. Staying back to deliver her baby in Delhi would mean help with the newborn from two doting mothers. On the other hand, giving birth in America would mean more opportunities for the baby.

'What about a third option?' asked Guddi.

'And that would be?' prompted Ratna.

'I can take early retirement at the university and accompany Simran to America. This way we can take advantage of both options. I will be able to help her with her new responsibilities, and the baby will be a US citizen.'

It seemed the perfect solution. Guddi applied for early retirement and procured a visitor's visa allowing her to stay in the US for six months.

As per the rules of the Indian government, Simran and Guddi were allowed a pathetically small amount of dollars to take with them to America. Ratna made frantic preparations to fit Simran with maternity clothes and western outfits for later use, thus ensuring that once in America, Simran would not have to spend her precious dollars on clothes. But Guddi, set in her ways, could not bring herself to switch to western clothes, and just bought a few new salwaar kameezes.

Simran and Guddi left for America by the middle of October. In an effort to help Ratna fill the void left by Simran's departure, Sukhdev returned to Delhi for an extended visit. There he set up his daily morning routine, while Ratna and Mannat went to school or work. His days started with morning prayers and a long walk, followed by yoga, breakfast and a visit to the local gurdwara. He rested in the afternoons, keeping the evenings free for the family.

Ratna's son Mannat, now nine years old, studied in the fourth class. He had never been a very expressive child. Now with his sister's wedding and Himmat's departure, he moped around the house doing nothing. Sukhdev worried. 'Ratna,' he said one day. 'How does Mannat get along with Sita's son . . . what's his name?'

'Deepak. Why do you ask?'

'Mannat seems to be withdrawing into himself. Maybe, if we help him bond with Deepak he wouldn't miss Himmat and Simran that much.'

'His withdrawal and lack of interest in studies makes me think maybe I failed him as a mother.'

'Don't go there.'

Ratna shrugged. 'I sure feel like I did,' she said. 'Mannat's mid-term exams are upon us, but he will not study. I've tried punishing him, rewarding him, bribing him, but nothing seems to work. He just will not touch his books! Why doesn't he listen to me? Papaji, what am I doing wrong?'

Sukhdev played with his mustache. 'I myself don't remember him this withdrawn, ever.'

'He wasn't. He listened to Simran and even Himmat.'

'He misses them.'

'I know that, but what am I to do?'

Sukhdev reached over and hugged her. 'I'll see what I can do.'

A few days later, Ratna returned from work to find Mannat sitting with his books. 'How did you do that?' she asked her father.

'I promised to coach him and his friends in cricket if he studied for his exams.' Sukhdev chuckled.

Once the exams finished, Sukhdev fulfilled his part of the deal and started coaching Mannat and his friends. Ratna's yard was big enough for the neighbourhood children to join them for an evening practice. Mannat's three closest friends started calling him nanaji and soon Sukhdev became jagat nanaji—a grandfather to the world—to children and their parents alike.

Every night, Mannat walked over to Sukhdev's room and sat cross-legged, talking, listening to bedtime stories, discussing his problems and his triumphs. One night he said, 'Nanaji, Dinesh says you are the bestest grandfather in the whole wide world!'

'Tell Dinesh it's because I have the bestest grandson in the whole wide world.' Sukhdev laughed, tickling him.

Mannat beamed. 'Did you notice I'm the fastest runner amongst my friends?'

'I noticed.'

'I have a secret . . . but don't tell mama.'

'Really . . . why?' Sukhdev raised his eyebrows and stared at him.

'Because mama gets angry when I talk of my future plans. All she wants to talk about is studies, studies and more studies.'

'And why is that?'

'She says I should study hard in school to become a doctor like Simran behen. She also tells me my papa would like that.'

'So, where's the problem?'

'I never knew my papa. He had no idea I'm the fastest runner... Anyway, the real problem is I hate studying. It doesn't make me happy.'

'Tell me your plan. How is your being a fast runner going to make you happy in life?'

'Nanaji, that's the secret. I'm going to do two things when I grow up. First, I'm going to be the bestest runner in the Olympics and then, I'm going to become the best bowler ever, in cricket.'

'I see.'

'Nanaji, mama once mentioned she was around my age when you found her. I told her if she had been a fast runner like me, she would have found you first!'

'You have a point there. I think it's a great idea to be the best runner in the Olympics. But maybe . . .' Sukhdev sat thinking, twirling his mustache.

'What?'

'I'm thinking it might not be a bad idea to study hard in school, so when you go out of the country to compete in the Olympics, people would say what a smart athlete you are.'

'You mean smart like Simran behen and Dev mamaji?'

'Exactly.'

'That makes sense. Thank you, nanaji.' Mannat got up and looping his arms around Sukhdev, kissed him good night.

Once the schools reopened, Sukhdev and Ratna watched in amazement as Mannat's class rank shot up to the second position.

'We are so proud of you,' said Ratna. 'Let's call your sister in America and give her the good news.'

Mannat beamed. 'I think I can easily top my class in the finals,' he boasted over the phone. He started paying more attention to his schoolwork. Ratna wanted to know what her father said or did to bring about the change.

'We just had a little chat.'

'Well, you did a great job chatting,' replied Ratna.

'Not really. It's Mannat who did the talking. I just listened and made a few suggestions.'

'I know. You did that with us too. You let Dev and me think we made up our own minds but all the while we did exactly what you wanted!'

Sukhdev laughed. 'Did I really do that?'

Ratna shook her head, smiling.

To keep himself busy while Ratna and Mannat were away during the mornings and afternoons, Sukhdev added another item to his daily routine. He not only visited the local Sikh gurdwara, he got involved with its day-to-day working. After being voted its president, he started managing the place. This gave him a purpose in life. He felt needed again.

Surrounded by so much love, he grew to be at peace with his life. The trauma of Partition, though never fully forgotten, no longer chipped at his heart every waking, breathing moment. He still missed Aman, his nine-year old daughter from Ugoke in Pakistan, but she now occupied a warm, fuzzy place somewhere deep in the folds of his heart. Life turned gentler and even the memory of his beloved wife became a warm emotion.

Sukhdev cherished not only his days with Ratna and Mannat but also the company of Sita's son, Deepak, who came over often for an evening of quiet chitchat or for a game of cricket with Mannat and his friends. He enjoyed Deepak's company because it reminded him of Dev's younger days. Dev and Deepak had a strong family resemblance, and even the temperament of the two cousins seemed very similar. Deepak seemed to be as gentle and funny as Dev. The only difference being that Dev had to learn every harsh lesson early in life, unlike Deepak.

Just as Sukhdev's relationship with Dev had become stronger while fixing bicycles, now the bonding between him and Deepak took roots while tinkering with cars. Sukhdev worked on Ratna's car and Deepak on his mother's vehicle. Mannat joined the two often, not because he was interested in engines but because it provided him male companionship. Sukhdev sensed this also helped Mannat fill the void left by Himmat's departure.

In March 1982, they received happy tidings from America. Simran had given birth to a baby girl named Aman. Sukhdev received the news with tears of joy. He knew Simran had named the new baby, in honour of his own daughter from Ugoke. He melted with this gesture of pure love and prayed, hoping baby Aman—as the name implied—would bring peace and joy to the family.

Aman's birth seemed to make Mannat feel very grownup. 'Nanaji, do you think I'm a big boy now?'

When Sukhdev smiled and nodded, Mannat asked, 'Will Aman sit in my lap and call me mamaji?'

'Absolutely.'

'Good. Then I'll tell her bedtime stories and teach her to run fast. I'll also teach her cricket.'

'I'll miss my little Mannat,' said Sukhdev kissing him.

'Don't worry, Nanaji.' Mannat patted his arm and giggled. 'I'm not going anywhere. I'll be around.'

'Even so, I'll still miss my baby.'

'I'm not a baby anymore . . . I'm a mamaji now. But I'll allow Aman to sit in your lap sometimes and you may call her your baby if you want to.'

29

Choices Pave the Way to Destiny

1983-84

In the winter of 1983, Simran, baby Aman and Guddi came for their first visit home. One morning, as Ratna sat knitting a sweater, Simran called her cousin Nimmi, who lived with her parents in Chandigarh.

Towards the end of their long conversation, Simran asked, 'Have you started working?'

'Not as yet.'

'How come? Mama told me you completed your Master of Business Administration with honours almost six months ago. Didn't you?'

'Yes, but it's not that easy—'

'What do you mean? Is it still difficult for a woman to find a good job, even after she does so brilliantly in her MBA?'

'No, that's not the problem. I did get an excellent offer in Jullunder and one in Ludhiana. But mummy and papa don't want me to work away from home.'

'I don't understand. Why not? They let you go to school away from home, didn't they?'

'Simran, I thought you knew about the Hindu-Sikh communal tensions. The conflicts and violence between them have intensified, and it is not safe for young girls to step out alone.'

'Really? So, young girls just stay confined indoors and wait to get married?'

'You sound so ridiculous. It's really . . . never mind. I have some exciting news for you—I'm getting engaged to Harjit.'

'Nimmi!' squealed Simran. 'Don't tell me you two are still carrying on! Doesn't he live in Bombay? Did Simi masiji agree?'

'How could she not? She and papa had a love marriage too. Remember?'

'Yes, I remember. A one-sided "love" marriage, his side!' teased Simran. 'But this sounds so neat. Congratulations! When?'

'When what?'

'When is the engagement, silly?'

'I think sometime in February, in the coming year. You'll come won't you?'

'Of course. I'm here till the end of March.'

After putting the phone down, she told her mother and her mother-in-law the good news.

That evening the phone rang. 'Hello Simran,' said Dev. 'I'm so looking forward to seeing you, especially the little one.'

'When do we see you, Mamaji?' asked Simran.

'Very soon. Tell Ratna—'

'She and Guddi masi are sitting right here. Let me give the phone to mom.'

'Hello Ratna. I was about to tell Simran that Simranjeet mamaji is preparing to retire in May or June of the coming year, in 1984. This will probably be my last opportunity to enjoy a long vacation with all of you. I plan to come to Delhi by the end of January and stay in Delhi until the middle of March. I'd like to bring papaji back with me.'

'Are you coming just to steal papaji from us?' replied Ratna, laughing. 'I understand we have to share him, but it's Mannat you have to convince. He's the maharaja around here. You'll have to get his permission when you come.'

She and Simran tried to prepare Mannat for his grandfather's departure but Mannat insisted, 'Nanaji is my coach. How can he leave before I become the best bowler?'

When Dev came, he was no more successful with his persuasion than Ratna and Simran had been. 'Dev,' suggested Ratna, 'you will be here for another five or six weeks. Maybe we should wait until it's time for you to leave, and broach the subject then?'

Dev agreed.

What Ratna enjoyed the most about Dev's visit was to watch him holding Aman. 'Guddi, isn't that the sweetest picture, grandpa Dev holding Himmat and Simran's baby?'

Guddi agreed. 'It almost rivals the lovely times we had watching him with the children in the Garha haveli. I wish Himmat was here to enjoy this too.'

As expected, in the beginning of February, they received an invitation from Simi, for Nimmi's engagement on 15 February. By now, tensions between the Sikhs and Hindus in and around Punjab had intensified to terrifying proportions, so Ratna worried. The two communities were on a collision course of destruction and she did not feel safe to travel with Simran and Aman. She confessed her fears over the phone to Simi. 'With the way things are these days, I don't feel comfortable in allowing the baby and Simran to travel by car to Chandigarh.'

'No, no. Come by bus. Buses are pretty safe. Car travel is risky, especially after dark.'

'Simi, I just don't feel comfortable. If papaji, Dev and Mannat attend the engagement, representing all of us, will that be okay with you?'

'No, it won't. You know how disappointed Nimmi will be if Simran doesn't come.'

'I can talk to her and explain. Please, Simi, it scares me. I hope you understand?'

'No, I don't . . . but I will respect your feelings. Take care. I love you.'

Ratna put the phone down to find Simran's smouldering eyes staring at her. 'Mama, couldn't you discuss this with me before deciding? Remember, I am an adult and can think for myself?'

'Maybe you can. But you haven't had a chance to grasp the gravity of the political situation—'

'Then, tell me! Never mind. Mama, I hate it when you treat me like a child.' Simran, red in the face, walked away without waiting to hear her mother's reasoning or her mother-in-law's explanation.

Early on the morning of 15 February, Dev, Sukhdev and Mannat left for Chandigarh by bus. Ratna wished she and Simran could have gone too. If Himmat were also visiting with Simran, Ratna would not have been so cautious. He would be there to protect her.

The day slipped into night, and Ratna did not hear from the men. Rumours of the past few weeks, of mob attacks on turbaned Sikhs, raised her anxiety level. Throughout the evening, her thoughts tumbled over each other—could they be in a bus accident, massacre or riots? Mannat, she hoped, was too young to be harmed, but, what about her turbaned father. Was he not too old? But then, Dev also wore a turban. She shuddered.

When the phone finally did ring, it startled her. On the other end of the line, Sukhdev wailed, 'Beti, *anarth ho gaya*'. Something unspeakable has happened. 'Get Sita's son, Deepak, to come to Karnal bus stop. Tell him to come by car.'

He hung up after insisting Ratna stay home with Simran and the baby. Ratna had never heard her papaji sound so devastated. Even when their mother passed away, he was calmer than this. Her hands shaking and heart pounding, Ratna dialled Sita's number, explaining what little she knew. Within twenty minutes, Deepak dropped Sita at Ratna's and drove to Karnal.

The next few hours trickled by. With every passing moment, Ratna recalled the horrors of her past, when she first saw her butchered family in the Shahadra temple. She relived the same gruesome fear, the kind that tortured her soul to its darkest, unknown depths. The acid in her stomach roiled. The images flashed with such vividness and intensity that Ratna had to talk to Sita chachi and Guddi about her bapu, mataji and Sheila, simply to relieve the tension she felt.

In an effort to calm her, Sita said, 'Remember how you once told me your mother taught you to recite "Sukhmani Sahib" in times of stress? Well, now is the time to pray.'

Ratna tried to pray but her mind wandered, and vivid, unwholesome fears kept intruding. Nothing but the path of fear that started with her father's phone call seemed real.

Simran brought a *gutka*, a small prayer book, and sat next to her mother, reading the 'Sukhmani Sahib'. But Ratna's mind refused to allow the words or the peace to sink in, as her mind and body stayed locked in fear.

Guddi and Sita cooked an evening meal no one ate. Sometime during this very tense wait, Simi called to ask why no one showed up for Nimmi's engagement and Sita explained. Ratna, too numb to talk, could not get herself to talk on the phone. She found her world threatening to crumble at a dizzying pace and felt helpless to stop it.

Late that night, Sukhdev and Deepak returned. Ratna's father staggered in, wearing neither shoes nor a turban.

And, Ratna knew.

Her father's face, dark and pallid, like a washcloth wrung out of moisture, stared at her. Taking a guttural breath, he pointed to the truck outside. 'Beti, anarth ho gaya.'

Ratna felt the unspeakable tragedy like a knife aimed at the spot where she, like most mothers, held her most precious, tender emotions. She doubled over, holding her stomach. When she could straighten up, she leaned against the wall and watched through the open door the bloodied bodies of Dev and Mannat lifted from the truck, to the ground. Neither a sound nor a tear escaped as she saw before her, two shattered pieces of her own heart, mutilated and covered in blood, lying next to each other.

Sita directed the pallbearers to bring the bodies inside the house. Simran turned hysterical, but Ratna stood staring, unaware of her body, until Sita and Guddi helped her sit down. She sat without glancing at the bodies, alternating her gaze from Deepak to her distraught father, and then towards nothing in particular.

It was past midnight when Sukhdev's voice drew Ratna back to reality. She summoned all her energy to concentrate on his face. 'When our bus reached Karnal,' he sobbed, 'a mob dragged down all young turbaned Sikh boys and men, and killed them with clubs and knives. I tried to shield Mannat but the mob . . . the mob—' Sukhdev gasped for breath through his tears. Guddi brought him a tumbler of water.

Ratna slipped into depths of heartbreaking grief, oblivious to her surroundings. During a few brief moments of cognizance, she heard Sanjeev and Deepak making arrangements for the cremation. No one slept that night.

Ratna did not remember the journey to the cremation grounds the next day, but remembered the flames that engulfed the pyres of her loved ones. Every now and then, visions of her papaji sitting next to her on the cloth-covered floor, talking of Dev and Mannat's last moments, floated in her mind. But nothing stayed long enough to understand and nothing made sense.

That evening, Sukhdev said, 'Beti, Dev asked me to give you a dying message. I think he said, "Behen, remember the juice mango". Do you understand what he meant?'

Ratna shook her head. She heard her father talk, but her mind sat idle like a machine without current—dead.

Later that evening, her father's words seeped into her consciousness, melting the iceberg encasing her heart. And she cried. Her brother's last thought had been to protect her. But remembering her brother's mantra did not calm the dark emotions enveloping her. An unsolicited thought of Mother Teresa flashed in her mind—"God speaks in the silence of the heart". Ratna wished her heart would go quiet so she could hear God through the angels of her son and brother.

But, the churning in her soul would not stop—why her innocent baby, and why her loving brother?

Sita comforted her, 'Ratna, they were in the wrong place at the wrong time.'

Those words kept resonating in Ratna's ears—her son and brother's fault had been to be in the wrong place at the wrong time. Sita chachi's measured, calm words failed to satisfy her. Her Ravi had died for his country. What did Mannat and Dev die for? Did the choice of one's religious beliefs change the colour of one's blood? Is a Hindu's blood different from a Sikh's, a Muslim's, or a Christian's? With a change of his beliefs, did Dev's Hindu Brahmin blood get tainted?

For weeks, she went through the motions of being alive. Then one day, the excruciating churning in the pit of her stomach, in her heart, in the depths of her soul suddenly awakened her to the truth. She was neither a Sikh nor a Hindu or a Muslim. She was, above all, a mother—simply a mother with a heart that could bleed and splinter without apology. Could she ever become whole again?

Her Simran and baby Aman could not fill the void in her shattered soul, a void that stung deep like a raw, open wound. Guddi's quiet presence was comforting, but it gave her tortured heart no answers. Sita held her many times, but Ratna could not still the relentless questioning of her heart. 'Why? Why the innocent?' she screeched.

A month passed. Ratna absent-mindedly fingered Uma's gold chain and pendent around her neck. She needed help, begging, praying to Dev's Uma ma. She needed to remember the juice mango. She needed to 'stay and live with love'. Her many angry thoughts and chaotic emotions needed soothing. She struggled to focus on what her brother's last message meant to remind her. But every night, she woke up from the haunting nightmare of her youth—the nightmare where acres of dead bodies lay side by side. The dead lay covered in white, looking like washed bed-sheets spread to dry across the fields. She awoke drenched in perspiration, her bedclothes jumbled in knots.

Anger consumed her. There were times when she knew the world was falling apart. At least her world was, even though the sun still rose every morning and the stars showed up every night. The birds still chirped and the flowers bloomed. Lovers loved, little girls still giggled and both Guddi and Sita chachi gave her a warm shoulder to cry on.

But the anger still seethed in Ratna's troubled heart.

Simran, distraught with the tragedy, became oblivious to the needs of her toddler. Guddi picked up the slack, tending to the baby's needs. It took days before Simran showed signs of coping. To Simran, her mother-in-law, Guddi, was always 'Masiji'—mother's sister. Simran requested Guddi to break the news to Ratna, the news that she was again with a child. Simran did not have the courage to share this irony of fate with her mother. She hoped the news of her baby, due in late August, would ground her mother to life once more, but instead, it made her more anxious.

'Guddi, take Aman and Simran back to America; out of harm's way. Please, do it now,' Ratna pleaded.

'I'll call Himmat and make the arrangements,' Guddi promised.

But Simran insisted they stay, to pull through the tragedy together.

Guddi, Simran and Aman left for America at the end of March, as per their original plan. Ratna accompanied them to the airport. Simran carried the last haunting image of her mother for a long time. She remembered her mother's hug and her gentle voice, but the mother she had known was missing—missing in action, in the simple act of living a life.

Almost like her father: "Died in the line of duty".

30
Broken

1984

Weeks turned to months, but Ratna's broken heart could get no peace. She resigned from her teaching position at the university. She had no more use for her sitar either. As the music within her died, she spent her days in front of the TV, mindlessly watching the news. The media bombarded her senses with pictures of horrors as painful, and as raw as her own tragedy. In June that year, three months after her world shattered, the hatred and anger seething amongst the Sikhs and the Hindus came to a climax.

As Ratna watched the news, the Indian army desecrated Harmandir Sahib—the Golden Temple in Amritsar—to flush out presumed Sikh terrorists. Every newspaper, every news clip on TV showed heavy army tanks levelling parts of the centuries-old gurdwara, killing thousands of innocent Sikh pilgrims inside the Golden Temple. Prime Minister Indira Gandhi's executive order caused irreparable damage to the Sikh-Hindu relations.

Ratna and her father did not comment much on the happenings around them, but when they did, neither had any wisdom to impart, no observations to give and no hope to offer. Every once in a while, they would hug each other, or squeeze each other's hand, willing their tears to dry.

Sometimes Ratna mustered enough energy to wonder why, decades after Partition, politics and religion were still being mixed in hateful proportions. The television showed images of dead bodies of men, women and children littering the Golden Temple premises. Her mother's gentle admonition floated into her mind. 'Every generation needs to learn its own lessons. Humans are incapable of learning from history.'

Why had she been singled out to bear witness to the follies of two generations—the older one, who killed her parents and this, her contemporaries, who killed her child and her brother? Maybe history had no lesson to impart. Could the one lesson, if any, be deduced from Sita chachi's unintentional advice: to avoid being in the wrong place at the wrong time?

Two weeks after 'Operation Blue Star', as the sacrilege came to be known, the phone rang as Ratna and Sukhdev sat down to breakfast. Getting up, she reached for the phone. 'Who? What? . . . All of them? Nooo—'

'What happened?' Sukhdev asked.

Hands shaking, she muttered into the phone, 'I'll call you later,' and turning to her father, said, 'That was Taara on the phone.' She trembled as she sat down.

'And?' he prompted.

'Baldev—the war baby—his wife, daughter and the newborn son, all died during Operation Blue Star. They had gone to the Golden Temple for Vaheguru's blessings.'

'Vaheguru, Vaheguru,' mumbled Sukhdev.

Reaching over the table, he took her trembling hands in his. Kissing her cold hands, he said, 'Beti, if you are up to it, we should go visit them. Sometimes, just the knowledge that someone cares helps heal broken spirits.'

Ratna nodded through her moist eyes.

Once the shock eased a little, Ratna called not only Taara, but also her Baljeet auntie and Harjinder uncle. As expected, Baldev's parents, broken by the loss of their only child and his family, could barely talk. Ratna did not have much to offer in the way of consolation, but the very next day she and her father left for Garha.

After their return from Garha, Ratna started accompanying her father to the gurdwara more often. She realised that the sacred rituals at the gurdwara brought her a small measure of peace. Living from day to day became a bit easier. But the habit of constantly expecting another catastrophe became as much a part of her life as the knots in her stomach.

Five months after Operation Blue Star, Ratna's fears materialised again. On 31 October 1984, two Sikhs assassinated Indira Gandhi, the prime minister of India.

For the next three days, life became a nightmare not only for Ratna and her father, but also for every other Sikh. All turbaned Sikhs were shot, massacred or burned on sight by Hindu mobs. The mobs burned turbaned Sikh men and boys by dousing them with kerosene or by garlanding them with kerosene-filled tires. Sikh businesses, houses, taxis and cars burned, some with occupants still inside. Agonised screams filled the air.

Her Hindu relatives—Sita and her son, Deepak—smuggled Ratna and her turbaned father to their own house as soon as the rioting broke out in Delhi after Indira Gandhi's assassination.

In a room in Sita's house, the heavy burgundy drapes on the window stood parted and Ratna sat glued to the view in the window, eating nothing, saying nothing. She watched Bharat Ma burn, and sat inhaling the residue of burned flesh.

On the second morning, Ratna still sat in the same place as the night before. Sita walked into the room carrying a tray, but stopped in mid-step seeing Ratna in the same chair by the window. 'Beti, you need to lie down. Take care of yourself for your father and Simran's sake.'

'I can't!'

'Please close the drapes on the window,' pleaded Sita. 'Come and sit on the bed.' Offering Ratna a glass of milk, she said, 'Take a drink of hot milk . . . it'll help you relax.'

'Sita chachi, I can't!' moaned Ratna.

Putting the tray on a side table, Sita took Ratna in her arms.

Her voice laced with pain and fear, Ratna whispered, 'Sita chachi, when I close my eyes I feel myself burn in the same angry orange flames that are hissing and crackling out there. I see my Dev and Mannat entombed in kerosene-filled car tires. When faceless crowds light the fire to the tires, I hear my son's screams and my brother's pleas. Their bodies turn into balls of fire, quivering in that inferno.'

Sita rubbed her back as one would a baby's, and Ratna let go a deep wail, unleashing a flood of tears. Pausing to take a guttural breath, Ratna persisted in telling her story, 'I struggle to help Dev and Mannat . . . but I'm unable to move, unable to scream, unable to breathe. I am frantic. My eyes beseech while my throat makes motions of loud pleas—but no sound escapes. I look helplessly around me and find the universe shrouded under thick blinders with no eyes and no ears . . . I don't understand. Why is the universe asleep when Mother India is spewing bubbles of molten oozing blood and vomiting blazing red-hot human body parts? Why does the universe feel nothing, see nothing, smell nothing and hear nothing? Look out of the window. Sita chachi, am I going crazy or can you see what I can see?'

31
A Heart that is Tender

November 1984

For a week after the massacre, every time Simran called from America, Ratna assured her that she and papaji were safe with Sita chachi. But Ratna could not fool her own heart. An aching need to share her troubled thoughts with a kindred spirit prompted her to write to Guddi.

She confessed her turmoil, saying all she knew was that she and papaji still breathed, even though their insides were molten lead. She asked Guddi if that could possibly be a good thing. Every morning, she said, she looked at Sita chachi's kind face, and wanted to believe both she and papaji had been saved for a reason. But the purpose eluded her. She wrote:

> It took three days and three nights
> > To avenge Indira Gandhi's assassination
> Three days and three nights to diminish us all—
> > Every thinking, feeling, human being in Mother India
>
> It took three days and three nights
> > Of unrelenting terror
> Before I, the shattered woman, asked what I, the collective mother
> > Could do to stand tall again

It took three days and three nights
   To turn my soul barren
So, how do I shed this baggage and face the sun
   To emerge a sunflower that my Vaheguru beckons me to be?

She ended the letter with a few more questions: 'Guddi, papaji says Vaheguru put us on earth to do good. If what papaji says is true then should Vaheguru not also guide us as to how to do it? When I sit down to think about it, the one gift He gave me is the gift of music. Then again, I haven't played the sitar for a long time. How do I know I haven't lost the ability to play it? And even if I did not, what good can I do with the gift of music?'

Within days, Guddi replied with a short letter. 'Ratna, Vaheguru gave you a heart that is tender and loving. Listen to its music. When you hear your heart's song—and you will if you pay attention—rise to embrace it. Vaheguru raakha.'

32
Physician Heal Thyself

November 1984

Simran sat with her newborn son Jasbir, in her two-bedroom apartment in New York city. Other than a used baby's bassinet, an old rocking chair and four straight-backed metal folding chairs, the room stood bare, like any other immigrant student's apartment. While her body moved to rock the baby to sleep, she worried about the recent massacre of Sikhs in India and the safety of her mother and grandfather. She still could not shake off the recurring images of the massacre of her kid brother Mannat and beloved uncle Dev. The despair and anger over their deaths had not subsided before this new terror of the riots appeared.

Even though Ratna told her repeatedly that Sita chachi kept them safe, Simran did not know Sita chachi well enough to take much comfort from that information. Aunt Sita was a Hindu and in Simran's present state of mind, every Hindu was suspect. So wrapped was she in her despair that sometimes when she rocked baby Jasbir, she did not hear him cry until Guddi reached for him.

One morning little Aman woke up crying. She waddled towards Simran and clamoured to sit in her lap. But as the child neared her, Simran turned the child around to face the kitchen, snapping, 'Go to your grandma. Don't you see the baby is sleeping in my lap?'

'Aman don't like baby,' cried the toddler. 'Give him back to 'ospital!'

Guddi walked over and scooping up Aman, kissed her and returned to the kitchen to feed her breakfast. When Aman settled down, Guddi said, 'Simran, I can take the baby while you spend some time with Aman. She needs you. Feed her breakfast, or rock her. Anything.'

Simran shook her head. 'I can't handle her. All I can think about is mama's and nanaji's safety.'

'Then don't just sit and worry. Do something,' Guddi said, her voice raised. 'At least get up and talk to your mother. Call her.' She then lowered her voice and added, 'It may help you feel better.'

'I can't do that. I'll just cry and feel worse.' The rocking chair creaked on the brown linoleum, echoing her frustration.

Guddi put her spoon down. 'Someone in the family has to be strong. If not you, then who?'

'I need time.'

'It's time we don't have.'

'Masiji, ever since Sita chachi's last call, I hear mama sobbing in the background and feel her pain. I can neither relax nor rest. Last night I woke up from a terrifying dream. I remember seeing nanaji's clothes and beard on fire. He carried a screaming baby Mannat in his arms as he ran towards the haveli in Garha. Nanaji saw me. "Mannat is going to be fine," he said. "Take care of him while your mother attends to Dev." He handed over Mannat to me, smiled, and crumbled into a heap of ashes. I looked down at the baby in my arms and it was my newborn Jasbir I saw. I'm not sure what my dream meant . . . but Masiji, it feels like a premonition. I just can't lose anyone else.'

'Oh Beti! After what the family has gone through, your fears are understandable. But Ratna and papaji both need your strength. Don't fail them. Don't fail yourself.' Guddi walked over and putting a hand over Simran's head, said, 'Vaheguru raakha! Put your trust in Him.'

Because of the ten-and-a-half hours time difference, Simran waited until ten o'clock that night before dialling Sita chachi's number in India, hoping to catch her mother in the early morning before the day's worries took over. She begged her mother and grandfather to leave India and move to America with them.

'We can't leave India. Not now at least,' said Ratna, but offered no reason.

For the next several days, Simran called at Sita chachi's house daily, but Ratna refused to discuss the move.

One late evening, while Guddi sat rocking the baby, Simran walked to the kitchen counter. She dialed her aunt's number in India. 'Sita chachi, is mama around?'

'No Beti, she and your nanaji left. They left about half an hour ago. Deepak drove them home and will stay with them until he's sure they are safe.'

'Thank you for everything.'

'You're welcome Beti.'

'Sita chachi, does anybody know for a fact who actually assassinated the prime minister?'

'Of course. It's all over the TV and the newspapers. Two of her Sikh bodyguards shot her.'

'Why?'

'Don't you know why—probably to avenge the deaths and sacrilege at the Golden Temple?'

'But I read the so-called "assassins" were behind Indira Gandhi. Didn't she get shot from the front?' Simran asked. Sita did not respond. 'I'm sorry . . . I shouldn't speculate. Maybe, time will reveal the truth. Anyway, why did the presumed decision of two men bring the wrath of a nation on all Sikhs? Why the mass hysteria against a whole community?' Simran's pitch rose as she felt colour warming her face.

'Beti, I don't know.'

'Sita chachi, we all know a Hindu fanatic killed Mahatma Gandhi. As is fair, only the guilty received punishment as opposed to the entire Hindu community. So, my question is, was Indira Gandhi perceived to be a better human being than Mahatma Gandhi? Why did the entire Sikh community need to be punished for her assassination?'

'I don't understand that myself.'

Breathing hard, Simran demanded, 'If Mahatma Gandhi had been killed not by a Hindu but by a Muslim, a Sikh, a Christian or a Parsi, would the massacre of the killer's community have avenged Mahatma Gandhi's assassination with better justice?'

'I don't know. Please stop asking futile questions. I don't have answers—only pain and prayers for healing.'

Simran slid to the ground. 'How will the healing start if the guilty are not punished?' she screeched.

'Are you accusing me of some crime?' Sita responded.

Sitting on the floor, her back against the kitchen counter, Simran pushed her free hand against the floor to control the tremor that shook her.

Guddi rose to put the screaming baby in Simran's lap and grabbed the phone. 'I'm so sorry for Simran's outburst,' Guddi apologised. 'It was uncalled for. She has not been her usual self since the family tragedy. Please forgive her.' Then, thanking Sita for taking care of Ratna and papaji, Guddi wished her goodbye and put the phone down.

Still red in the face, her usual calm voice raised, Guddi turned to her daughter-in-law and asked, 'Simran, are you holding Sita chachi personally responsible for what happened to the Sikh community?'

'She's a Hindu.'

'So? She is also the one who saved your nanaji and your mother.'

'There would have been no need if the Hindus had not attacked innocent people.'

Staring at her, Guddi demanded, 'How is your prejudice different from the prejudice of the mobs that massacred the Sikhs?'

Simran broke down, her body heaving with tumultuous sobs. Guddi still looking flustered, plucked the screaming baby from Simran's arms and sat on the rocking chair to rock him to sleep.

Little Aman dropped her doll on the carpet and walked over to her distraught mother. Putting one hand on Simran's shoulder, she wiped the tears from her mother's face with the other. 'Mama, don't c'y,' she whispered.

Looking at her daughter with wet eyes, Simran pulled her onto her lap.

Aman quickly looped her arms around her mother's neck, sobbing and snuggling. 'I love you Mama,' she said, kissing her. 'Pease don't c'y.'

Simran felt a sudden peace descend upon her soul with her child's warm touch. How could she be so self-centred to ignore her baby girl for so many months? Hugging her child tighter, she wiped her face and carrying Aman, stood up.

On her way to the kitchen stove, she turned to her mother-in-law, 'I'm so sorry. I was rude to Sita chachi and indifferent to your concerns. Please forgive me.' She took a loud nasal breath and said, 'I'm making tea for myself. Would you care for a hot cup too?'

Guddi looked up and nodded.

Still holding Aman in one arm, Simran proceeded to the stove and put the kettle on. Little Aman put her thumb in her mouth and lay her head on her mother's shoulder. While the water boiled, Simran absentmindedly rubbed her child's back in slow motion, wondering how she had lost herself so completely. How did she get so messed up? Even Himmat did not seem to have recognised her depression. Or did he? All through this sickness, her husband and mother-in-law had stood by her, picking up the slack she left, neither complaining nor giving advice. Only when she started being rude to Sita chachi did her mother-in-law lose her composure. Simran realised that she needed to shake herself out of this deep hole before she hurt the people she loved the most.

Was she not being educated in the art of healing? Did she not owe it to herself to heal her own heart before trying to heal others?

Before the water boiled, little Aman dozed off. Simran tucked her in bed and returned to pour the tea into mugs. She carried one mug to her mother-in-law, set it next to her on the table and reaching for the sleeping newborn said, 'Thank you for being so patient with me. I still need time to work out my problems but I promise to be more considerate.'

'Welcome back,' said Guddi. Smiling and touching Simran's cheek, she reached for the tea. 'We missed you.'

33
Search for a Meaning

November 1984

When Sita's son Deepak pulled the car into a stop in the driveway of Ratna's house, Sukhdev stepped out from the front seat while Ratna stepped out from the back, both facing the part of the property where Mannat and his friends used to play cricket. With misty eyes, Ratna stood staring at the playground.

'Didi,' asked Deepak, addressing Ratna as an older sister, 'Are you alright?'

'I'm not sure,' Ratna replied. 'Did you see what I saw?'

As Deepak shook his head, Sukhdev whispered, 'I did.'

'Why Papaji? Why?' she asked.

Sukhdev stared at the vacant field without replying.

Puzzled, Deepak looked from one to the other. 'What are you talking about?'

'Mannat's little friends. They were playing in the cricket field but as soon as they saw us pull onto the driveway, they all ran away. They never used to do that,' whispered Ratna.

'They probably thought they'd get in trouble for trespassing,' said Deepak.

'No, they came to play here even after Mannat passed away. They know they are welcome here. Why would they think we'd punish them for trespassing now?'

'Didi, these days even we adults are confused over what happened and what triggered the Sikh massacre. It's only natural that the children feel bewildered. They learn what they see.'

'But we didn't do anything,' mumbled Ratna.

'You are right, Beti,' said Sukhdev. 'We did nothing. Now, we need to do something to let them know they are welcome even if Mannat is no more.'

'How?' she asked.

Sukhdev put his arm around his daughter's shoulder and guided her up the steps to the raised verandah. 'Let's pray about it. Vaheguru will help.' As the father and daughter walked up the two steps, Deepak raced towards their backyard.

'What happened?' Ratna shrieked, but Deepak disappeared without answering.

They both stopped and turned. She looked at her father, who shrugged his shoulders. Just then, Deepak returned with a filthy, smelly teenager in tow. 'Speak up. Who are you?' he asked.

The girl came to a stop, as if paralysed.

'What were you doing in our yard?' he demanded.

She looked down, her hands frozen in fists, her lower lip trembling.

Sukhdev walked back down the two steps towards the teenager, and in a calm voice, said, 'Child, come here'.

The girl looked up at the gray-bearded man and before anyone could blink, she threw herself at Sukhdev's feet. 'Help me, Bapu.'

Sukhdev bent slowly to lift the young girl. 'Child, who are you?'

'Paro,' she mumbled. 'They . . . they poured kerosene and burned my father and brother,' she cried, gasping for breath, as tears flowed unchecked.

Ratna walked down the steps saying, 'Child, calm down. Tell us what you—'

'Hiding,' she muttered. 'They set fire to our house . . . I have nowhere to go.'

Ratna stopped. Taking a sharp breath, she exhaled through her mouth to quiet her pounding heart and put her arm around the girl's shoulder. 'Come with us,' she said.

'Didi, are you sure?' asked Deepak. 'She could have accomplices. Let's check her out thoroughly before you take her in.'

'No, Deepak. She's harmless,' replied Ratna, unlocking the door. Before stepping in, she turned around to look at Deepak. He stood mute. 'Her anguish echoes in here,' she said, lightly tapping her hand over her heart. 'It's close to forty years since I witnessed the massacre of my family in Shahadra, but the piercing pain still stings without remorse.'

Deepak nodded and moved to bring in the luggage and groceries. The girl stood shivering until Sukhdev asked her to sit on a chair. Ratna walked to the stove to warm a glass of milk for the girl, and to make three cups of tea for the rest. Taking a packet of gluco biscuits, a banana and an apple from a grocery bag, she fed the girl. Ratna then turned and asked her father to open the kitchen window. The girl's strong body odour had created a need for fresh air.

After a quick cup of tea, Ratna promised them lunch in an hour's time. Then, taking Paro to Mannat's old room, she started the hot water heater in the attached bathroom. 'Here's a fresh towel, shampoo and soap. In the cabinet, you'll find a soap bar for washing your clothes. You may bathe and shampoo your hair. I'll bring some of my daughter's old clothes to you.'

The girl walked into the bathroom and locked the door. Ratna rummaged through Simran's old clothes, looking for something short for the petite girl. She found a couple of old salwaar kameezes that looked like they would fit. Knocking on the bathroom door, she passed a warm cardigan and some clothes to the girl. 'Wear what fits the best. We'll get clothes of your size later.'

As Ratna turned to go, the girl whispered from the bathroom, 'Thank you, Auntie.' Taken by surprise, Ratna stopped. The beggar girl knew English. Could life have played a trick on Paro similar to the one it had played on Dev at the time of Partition?

When the girl came out to the dining table all scrubbed and washed, Ratna stared at her revealed beauty. She looked barely fifteen or sixteen years old. During lunch, they learned that Paro's mother used to be a seamstress, and her father a taxi-driver. Paro talked of how her mother died when she was only fourteen. By that time, she had already learned to stitch and sew. After her mother's death, her mother's dearest friend helped her pick up not only her mother's clients, but helped her with the sewing too, so Paro could still go to school full-time.

'Where do you study and in which class?' asked Sukhdev.

'I'm at Tagore Public School, in the tenth class.' Paro broke down.

'Would you like to finish school?' asked Ratna.

Paro's jaw dropped. 'You mean you'd pay for my education? And . . . I could live here?' Both Ratna and Sukhdev nodded, smiling.

Tears rolling down her face, her trembling hands pressed between her knees, Paro whispered, 'Thank you.'

Sukhdev put his hand on Paro's head and said, 'Vaheguru raakha'.

'Paro, you may call me biji,' said Ratna.

'And feel free to call me nanaji. Everybody else does,' said Sukhdev, smiling.

Still shaking, Paro nodded, struggling in vain to return Sukhdev's smile.

After lunch, Ratna took her back to Mannat's room. 'This is your room now. Here are some fresh bed sheets. Change the old sheets and put them in the hamper. Then you may rest.' The girl went to bed and did not wake up until the next morning.

Within a day or two, Ratna's life picked up its normal rhythm, and she convinced Deepak that she and Sukhdev were safe, so he took his leave. Every morning after that, Ratna watched Paro come to the breakfast table with swollen eyes. She knew Paro could not join a school until she had had the time to grieve and reach some sort of closure. So, one morning she offered to drive Paro to her old neighbourhood and on the way, talked of her own trip back to Shahadra years ago. While driving with one hand, Ratna reached over with the other, and placed it over the girl's trembling hands.

Paro's three-room house had burned to the ground. The girl found nothing in the rubble except her mother's scissors, a charred shoe and her brother's burned jeans. She cried and sobbed for days after, but other than offer a kind ear, a drink or a warm hug, Ratna allowed her to deal with her grief in private.

One morning, Ratna woke up to find Paro in the kitchen. She had already made the dough and had started frying the unleavened parantha bread for breakfast.

'You are up early today,' Ratna commented.

'I should have been up every morning to help you. Biji, your kindness is overwhelming. It reminds me of my mother.'

'Bless you for coming into our lives,' said Ratna, taking the girl in her arms.

Wiping her wet eyes, Paro asked, 'Is your daughter in college? And where's your son? It seems I sleep in his room.'

'My daughter Simran is married and in America. My son, my son . . .' and Ratna broke down, reaching for a handkerchief. It took a long time and a few wet handkerchiefs before the anguish of the murders of her child and brother finally spilled out.

Paro had switched off the stove to listen to Ratna's story. Now she got up to hug Ratna and make her a fresh cup of tea. Over the next few weeks, they helped each other navigate through pain, while their hearts healed in spurts.

'Paro, what do you enjoy doing the most? Do you have a hobby or a passion?' asked Ratna, one day.

'I love stitching clothes. The rhythm of the sewing machine calms me. After my mother's death, I found stitching clothes made me feel whole again. When I sit at the machine, I can feel my mother's presence and can hear her voice, even her tinkling laughter.'

'Good. Come with me. I'll get you my sewing machine. It's yours now. I hardly stitch anymore,' said Ratna. 'Start by cutting and re-stitching some of Simran's old clothes to fit you. Then we'll buy you some material to stitch new clothes. By January, you have to start school again.'

'Before I stitch clothes for myself, I'd like to make something for you and nanaji.'

'Child, at the moment Papaji and I don't need any new clothes—'

'Biji,' Paro whispered, 'the only way I can repay you for your kindness is by stitching for you. I have no other gift to offer.'

Ratna reached over to get the girl's hand in hers. 'Your presence in our lives is gift enough. And I promise, soon we'll let you stitch for us.'

Paro nodded.

Taking her to Simran's room, Ratna pulled out her daughter's old clothes. 'Take what you like. Fit it to your size. Later, I'll take you shopping to get material for new clothes.'

After the girl made her choices, Ratna took her to the storeroom and gave her the sewing machine along with spools of thread. Beaming, Paro moved the sewing machine next to the only window in the room. As Ratna helped her move Simran's old outfits, the phone rang. Dumping the clothes on the bed, Ratna ran to pick up the phone in the sitting area.

When she returned, she found Paro sitting at the sewing machine, a content look on her face, humming softly. Pleased to see a smile on the girl's face, Ratna walked back, out the room. 'Papaji,' she said to her father in the sitting room, 'I think Paro is on the road to recovery. A simple sewing machine has made her happy, just as sitar music made me content.'

'I know. Now that you mention it—how come you don't play the sitar anymore?' he asked.

Ratna's eyes filled up. 'Maybe, I will some day.'

'Why play some day—why not now?'

'Yes, why not now? Seeing Paro blossom at the mere sight of a sewing machine, I've become aware of the misfortune of losing myself. The music in my heart has been silent too long. And you are right. It's time to make an effort and reconnect with my spirit. But I'm not sure there is anything left to connect to.'

Sukhdev reached over to take her hand in his. 'During Partition, when I lost my Aman, I wasn't sure I could survive without her. Your mother, Raminder, was a wise woman. She reasoned with me. "If Vaheguru spared us, He is sure to reveal His intent too," she said. Then, you and Dev came into our lives. Maybe, this time it's Paro who is supposed to teach us some of life's lessons.'

At dawn the next morning, Ratna pulled out her sitar. The music returned just as surely as spring returns every year, and the sun rises daily.

The sitar soon became a regular morning ritual for them. Sukhdev started reciting morning prayers to the sitar's rhythm. Sometimes Paro sang a shabad to accompany Ratna's music. And hearts healed.

One day Paro said, 'Biji, your music is very peaceful. It helps me feel whole again.'

Ratna's face broke into a smile. 'Perfect! Now there are two things that make you feel whole again—your machine and my sitar. Does it mean that soon we'll have a doubly strong Paro?'

Paro smiled; her face a deep crimson. Ratna turned serious and looking at the girl said, 'May I ask you something?'

Paro nodded.

'Does the rhythm of the sewing machine feel like meditation to you? The sitar feels that way to me. It lulls me into that peaceful, trance-like state, where I sense these unusual stirrings. I get a warm feeling, and realise that the ultimate truth for me is "love", which is the only lesson I need to learn while on this earth. Just "love" in its myriad manifestations.'

'Biji, I'm too ignorant to even understand what you are saying. To me, love is a simple emotion. I loved my parents and they loved me. I loved my brother and he loved me. What you are saying sounds bigger than that. It sounds beautiful, but I don't understand it.'

'Me neither.' Ratna smiled at Paro. 'Love is an elusive and yet pervasive concept that seems to transcend human emotions. When I play the sitar, somehow, somewhere deep within me, I sense an awakening that urges me to understand and connect with those around me. Maybe, that's love.'

'If that is so, then you've already made a good start . . . with me,' muttered Paro.

'Beti, this is our life now. We want to do something with our lives. As papaji says, "Man was put on earth to help his fellow man".'

'Very noble indeed. But tell me, who came forward to help our loved ones? Where were all the noble men when Mannat and Dev mamaji pleaded for mercy?'

'Simran, please . . . you still sound so angry and—'

'What about you Mama? Aren't you angry?'

'I am, but helping others helps me forget. Actually, papaji and I are both working hard to become whole again.'

'And how are you doing?' Simran bit her tongue as she tried not to sound sarcastic.

'Not good, but we've made a start. We are trying to help a young girl who lives with us.'

'What do you mean lives with you?'

'I mean exactly what I say. She lives with us.'

'Oh, Mama! I mean who is she and why is she living with you? And why do you care?'

'We care because she needs help. Her name is Paro and she lost both her father and elder brother during the recent riots. She has no other relatives.'

'There must be thousands of needy children in and around Delhi. Why only her?'

'Because she came looking to us for help. The poor child was hungry, scared and filthy. Both papaji and I melted when we saw her plight. It reminded me of the time when as a child, I discovered my whole family massacred at the temple. The utter disbelief, shock and helplessness—'

'Mama, please don't go there. I know how you must feel, but that was a different time and a different situation. This child surely has some other relatives. What about her mother?'

'Her mother died when she was fourteen. She is an orphan. As I said earlier, she has no other relatives. She needed a place to call home and a family to make her feel safe again.'

'Isn't that the truth? We all need to feel safe again. But Mama, you've done your job of raising kids. You don't need any more headaches.'

'Raising children is not a headache but an honour,' replied Ratna. 'Anyway, she doesn't need much raising now. She is around sixteen years

34
A Daughter's Struggle

1985

Sitting in America, Simran read every Punjabi newspaper she could lay her hands on. Months after the mass hysteria, those papers still carried nothing but news about a reign of terror in the villages of Punjab, Haryana and Himachal Pradesh—states to the north of Delhi. The papers showed pictures of young turbaned Sikh boys who were disappearing like coins from a magician's hands.

One day, Simran called Ratna. 'Mama, is it true that young Sikh boys are being killed in Punjab simply because they wear turbans? The Punjabi weeklies at the Indian stores carry no other news except that.'

'Beti, it's sad but true. The decapitated bodies of missing boys oftentimes show up outside the families' home, or resurface in a ditch or a nearby field,' replied her mother. 'But,' she said, 'that's only half the story. Now, several Hindus have started disappearing too.'

'This was bound to happen,' Simran muttered. 'They asked for it'

'Child, what kind of attitude is that? How's it going to help sol anything?'

'I'm sorry, Mama. So much has happened and all I think about some sort of assurance that both you and nanaji are safe. Delhi no lon; sounds like a safe place to live in. Come to America. Please. Jasbir a Aman will love having you around. And, nanaji with his flair for st telling will be an instant hit with them. Please think about it. After what's left there for you?'

old and it seems she was raised with sound values and beliefs. In fact, her presence seems to cast a calming effect on us. Both papaji and I feel more at peace since she arrived.'

'I don't want to argue with you Mama. All I want is for you to remember we love you very much and want both of you to come and live with us.'

'Please Beti, stop worrying, and take care of yourself. We need our old Simran back. Be strong, and do pray. Oftentimes, that helps.'

'Even Himmat and his mother keep telling me to do this or that but nothing seems to work. I'm still angry,' admitted Simran, her voice quivering. 'I have no idea how to help myself Mama.'

'Your nanima taught me how. She said, "Do not ignore the dual emotions of pain and anger. Acknowledge and deal with them—the sooner, the better. Then and only then can you be free to move on with your life".'

'What do you mean? Of course I acknowledge I'm angry and in pain. That doesn't help!'

'Beti, nanima said, "Sit with the emotions, knead them. Feel the pain. Experience the torment and slowly lift yourself, rising above it—hopefully wiser and stronger".'

'I have no idea what you are talking about, but as usual, the philosophy sounds good. Mama, everything is easier said than done. Have you followed that advice yourself?'

'I'm still trying, and I've learned one thing. Understanding someone else's pain seems to help me deal with mine. But on some days, nothing helps. Maybe you are right. It's easier said than done . . . here, talk to your nanaji,' and her grandfather came to the phone.

The long chat with her mother and grandfather did not help her. Simran still worried about them and wished they would agree to immigrate to the States.

One day, Simran discussed the weekly Indian paper with her mother-in-law. 'I don't understand . . . Mama told me this months ago, but I didn't believe her. Now the paper confirms what she said. It says here that Sikh terrorists are now making rich and prominent Hindus pay for the sins of the Hindu mobs.' She shook her head. 'Doesn't make sense.'

'Anger in victims takes many forms—the least subtle of which is taking an eye-for-an-eye,' replied Guddi. 'But Simran, I'm glad you've found your peace and genuine concern for human life.'

'I'm not sure about genuine concern,' replied Simran. 'I'm still angry about the murders of Mannat and Dev mamaji. And I am angry about the Sikh massacre. All I can say is, taking revenge from random victims instead of punishing the guilty is . . . is unjust.'

'Yes. We know that,' replied Guddi. 'There seems to be no viable solution to stop this. But worrying about it does not help either. The only thing that does help is prayer.'

'It doesn't help me. My mind wanders when I try to pray.'

'Whenever your mind wanders, don't get frustrated; just bring it back to your prayer. Try talking to Vaheguru in your own words. Ask Him to show you the way. With me, the prayers from the prayer book bring tranquility when I'm already calm. When under stress, I need to talk to Vaheguru in a more personal way, in my own words. Try and see what works for you.'

Simran reached for her mother-in-law's hand and squeezed it.

Late that evening, when Simran was out getting groceries, Ratna called. 'Guddi, tell Simran someone kidnapped Taara's ten-year-old son Rahul. Papaji and I are very worried. Do pray for the child's safe return.' Guddi took the message and relayed it to Simran. Taara's family—an affluent, well-known Hindu political family—had no idea who did it and why.

Simran heard the news with a sharp pang of guilt, collective guilt. Could the newspapers and her mother have been right in saying that Sikhs had started retaliating?

For days and weeks, there was no news of Rahul. One day, a month after his disappearance, Ratna called again. 'Simran, I'm very worried about Taara. It has been confirmed that Sikh terrorists did it. Her son is still missing and papaji and I have decided to visit her.'

'Mama, how is your visit going to help? Jullunder could be dangerous with nanaji's turban. Please don't go there.' Simran begged.

'Beti, we can't stop living because of fear. Taara is my little sister. How can I let her suffer by herself?'

'The animosity between Sikhs and Hindus scares me, Mama.'

'Both communities are keeping scores that will never be even. Only we mothers can put an end to this. *Nehle pe dehla*—tit for tat—will not bring our loved ones back. Terrorising and killing the innocent in the name of religion only adds to the suffering, as hate and anger flows on like a toxic river, poisoning more lives. In order to end this madness, we have to build bridges between people and communities.'

Still, Simran found her mother's decision to go to Punjab extremely disturbing. After putting the phone down, she picked up Aman and sat down to rock her in the rocking chair. Turning to Guddi, she said, 'I don't understand how mama can put herself and nanaji in harm's way. After all, she can't help Taara masi get her son back. What is she going to do, call the police?'

'She can help by just being there. Simran, your mother and nanaji have always helped people in need. And this is Taara we are talking about. Ratna thinks of Taara as her chhoti behen. I don't think she could stay back in Delhi even if she wanted to.'

'Taara masi is not really her younger sister.'

'You know very well Taara has always been her chhoti behen—maybe not by birth but definitely by the bonds of love.'

'But Taara masi is a Hindu,' mumbled Simran.

'So? Even a Hindu can have a heart that beats with the warmth of a mother. And Simran, remember Sita chachi is also a Hindu? There are millions of Hindus who are good people,' said Guddi.

Simran grimaced, embarrassed by her implied religious intolerance. Somehow, even after recognising her feelings of anger and prejudice, she still could not forgive and forget. She heard the frustration in both her mother and mother-in-law's voices but try as she might, she could not curb her anger.

One evening when Himmat returned from work, he asked for the thousandth time, 'Honey, have you heard from mama?'

'Yes and no,' answered Simran.

'What do you mean?'

'Mama wrote, but it's not the answer I'm looking for. I've pleaded with her many times to bring nanaji and come live with us. I don't understand why she refuses. I'm tired of her stubbornness.'

'What was the excuse this time?'

'Nothing. She just sent me a poem,' said Simran shaking her head.

'A poem?'

'Yes, a poem.'

Simran got up from the rocking chair, and carrying little Aman, returned with her mother's letter. Handing it to Himmat she said, 'Read it out loud, please. Maybe hearing it will make sense to me. I just don't understand why she's so stubborn.'

'She was never stubborn.' Himmat smiled and started reading the letter. After the greetings and the usual inquiries about his work, the children's health and Guddi's well-being, Himmat found the poem. It read:

I've seen the eyes of hunger and poverty
Eyes of inconsolable pain

I've seen the joyous miracle of birth and
The ecstasy of a mother's love

I've seen the wounds that
Humans inflict on their fellow beings

Justifying the madness in the name of religion
Without heeding the lessons of history

I've seen a moment of fierce beauty
Caught between the wings of a butterfly and colours of a rainbow

But I've yet to see the essential me
The person I'm meant to be

Vaheguru, give me the wisdom
To birth a tranquil melody that would soothe shattered souls.

Eyes glistening, Himmat murmured, 'This is beautiful,' and handed the letter back to Simran.

'Hello? What's wrong with you?' Simran let out a strangled cry. 'Have you not been listening? Don't you see both of them need to be with us?'

'I know that. But I'm amazed after what she's gone through, she still has the courage to search for her essence, to find a real meaning to her life.'

'Himmat, if you'd seen her after the tragedy, you wouldn't talk nonsense. We have to get both of them out of there. Poems don't help! Do you understand?'

Himmat walked away silently, loosening his tie.

Guddi witnessed the tantrum from the kitchen. She washed her hands that reeked of garlic, rubbed them on the sides of the stainless steel sink, and ran water over them again. Smelling them and satisfied, she wiped them dry, and walked over to take the sobbing Simran in her arms. 'Beti, give them time to heal.'

'So that's what you think? Am I the one preventing their healing?'

'Simran, you know Himmat and I would do anything to help ease the pain but if papaji and Ratna are not ready to come into the family's embrace, we have to honour that.'

'I can't!' she shouted, and stormed into the bathroom.

Guddi sat down to rock the screaming toddler.

In March 1985, two months after Taara's son's kidnapping, Simran received a call from her mother in Delhi. 'Mama, I've been so worried. How was your trip to Jullunder? How are you and nanaji doing? And what about Taara masi?'

'We are doing well and so is Taara.'

'Has her son been released?'

'Yes, and he is well. But he lost one finger.'

'A finger? How?'

'Long story. The afternoon we reached Taara's house in Jullunder, before we even stepped out of the taxi, local journalists flocked around our vehicle, asking us questions—'

'What questions?' Simran interrupted.

'Questions like: "Do you know what else came in the package? Is there a ransom note in there? Anymore demands?", etc.'

'What package—?'

'Simran, unless you let me finish, I can't tell my story.'

'Sorry.'

'As we entered the house, a hysterical Taara fell into my arms. Sobbing, she showed us a chilling package they'd received that day. The package was stuffed with cotton wool and inside lay Rahul's little finger—a bluish piece of putrid flesh wrapped with care in soft cotton.'

Simran shuddered. 'Oh, my God!'

Ratna continued, 'Taara wailed, "I don't know where my child is, but I have his little pinkie!" and before I could respond, she doubled over to throw up in a wastebasket.'

Unable to stop herself, Simran asked, 'Was there a ransom note?'

'Yes. The kidnappers had the same demand all along. They were willing to exchange Rahul for the release of five Sikh prisoners in the Jullunder jail. But the police refused to negotiate.'

'So, how did it happen? Why was Rahul released?'

'Vaheguru has mysterious ways. It was His will.'

'Mama, did your visit help? Does nanaji still know anyone in Jullunder? Were you able to do anything?' Simran asked.

'No, we could do nothing, other than lend Taara a shoulder to cry on. And, we prayed. It was our Baljeet auntie and Harjinder uncle who did something big. We don't know how they did it, but somehow, they secured Rahul's release.'

'You mean they did something other than pray?' Simran chuckled.

'No. I mean, they prayed a bigger prayer. They did it as a tribute to their only child, Baldev, and his family, who died at the Golden Temple during Operation Blue Star. And they did it for Taara, a Hindu, because they love her. And, because they understand that love can transcend religion.'

Simran got the message as she bit her tongue in embarrassment.

35
Ratna Stands Tall, Again

Summer 1985

One Sunday morning, Sukhdev and Ratna sat at the breakfast table talking. 'Papaji,' said Ratna, 'I've been thinking about your suggestion of helping the victims of the massacre. It seems like a great idea. Since I need to do something just to hold on to my sanity, show me how. Please, help me.'

'I wish I could, Beti. I too like the idea, but don't know how to go about it. I have a million questions: Do we dole out charity or work? What kind of work do we offer? How do we decide whom to help? Where do the resources come from? And, the questions go on and on.'

'Maybe we can figure it out together,' replied Ratna. 'You were right about Paro being sent our way to teach us some life lessons. She has made me realise one thing—that all self-respecting people find it easier to give than to take.'

'Isn't that the truth!' exclaimed Sukhdev. 'Even our traumatised sixteen-year-old wants to stitch and cook for us! She seems to have a strong need to live with dignity and self-respect.'

'It's her example that makes me want to find work that not only gives the victims a means to survive but allows them to live with dignity.'

'How about teaching them the art of stitching custom-made clothing?' said Sukhdev. 'Is that doable? Paro often talks of how her mother earned a decent living as a seamstress. I wonder if the skill to sew and embroider can be taught to other needy women. Is there a market for such endeavours?'

'Yes and yes, to both your questions. Papaji, that seems to be the answer we are looking for. The skill can be taught to educated and uneducated women alike. We could open a centre to teach them and provide a channel to sell their finished products.'

Ratna watched as her father's eyes sparkled. 'And I could oversee the finances of the enterprise. I could even take an impressive title—the Chief Financial Officer! What do you say?'

'I say, let's do it.'

They reached over the table for each other's hands. Paro walked in on them as they both smiled and trembled with excitement. Putting both her hands over theirs, Paro chuckled. 'Count me in too—whatever it is you two seem so excited about.'

Ratna untangled her hands and pulled Paro into a hug. 'You already are in it. You are the one who provided the seed. Now, papaji and I will provide the soil and the nurturing.'

'What are you talking about?'

'Paro, you taught us a valuable lesson by handling your terrible loss with so much grace. There are thousands of young girls and women like you, who too have lost the only breadwinners in their families. Papaji and I want to open a centre for all such women—a place for them to learn a trade and earn an honest living. What could be more pertinent than to teach stitching and embroidery to both educated and uneducated women alike?'

With a smile on her face and tears in her eyes, Paro whispered, 'Thank you for being so kind. Biji, would it be alright if I ask a favour?'

Ratna nodded.

'I have an aunt, who is not related to me by blood but she was my mother's dearest friend and teacher. I called her Roop masi. She taught my mother to stitch clothes. After mummy passed away, she guided me in everything, including sewing. Can you take me to my old neighbourhood to look for her? She was a widow who lived with her mother-in-law and a young college going son. She is the one person I'd like to help at this new centre, if she is in need.'

dedicated this centre to Mannat and my beloved, Ravi. Now, I want us to start one in Amritsar in Dev's name and one in Garha for biji.'

Sukhdev's eyes watered, and almost choking, he answered, 'Beti, I've been thinking similar thoughts, but I also know we do not have enough resources to start anything else at the moment.'

'As you often say, "Vaheguru will provide".'

Sukhdev nodded. 'One lucky thing is that at both the places, we already have available buildings. In Amritsar, we have Dev's huge mansion and in Garha we have the haveli.'

'And I feel we already know people who will make good managers at both the places. Simranjeet mamaji at Amritsar and Taara at Garha would probably agree to take charge at no cost.'

'Beti, we'll still need initial starter money. And we don't have that at the moment.'

'Vaheguru will provide. Let's at least talk to them and see if they can raise some monies.'

Thus, Ratna called, and Simranjeet, now in his late seventies, loved the idea. He offered to raise the capital for the Amritsar branch. Taara on the other hand had a few misgivings. 'Didi, we do not have many massacre victims in and around Jullunder.'

'Taara, these are centres for all women in crisis, not just for survivors of the Sikh massacre. Even though the centre in Delhi was initially started for the massacre victims, last year we opened it to all women needing help. Many women around us have been abused. They are looking for protection against life's injustices. Taara, even you have survived suffering caused by the clash of communities. You understand what all kinds of conflict and abuse does to innocent women and children. Please think about it and talk it over with Baljeet auntie. See how she feels about this.'

Taara called back. 'Baljeet auntie wants to participate, so I guess, we'll do it.'

'May Vaheguru bless both of you.'

'We've discussed and decided between our families that we'll be able to come up with the initial capital. So, the plan is to visit Delhi next week, to learn how to get started.'

Thus, within five years of starting the centre in Delhi, Ratna and Sukhdev opened two more centres in Amritsar and Garha. Soon, Simi in Chandigarh and Nimmi in Mumbai also started toying with the idea.

36
Dawn

1991

One early spring morning, Ratna hung up the phone to the New Delhi International Airport Information and turned to her father. 'Papaji, Simran's flight is one hour late.'

In her rush to leave for the airport to meet her daughter's 3.00 am flight, she had tried to quell her craving for a hot cup of tea. Now they had an extra hour. Ratna turned to the stove and fixed three mugs of chai, for herself, her father and Paro. Since Sukhdev had given up driving after Dev passed away, and Ratna did not drive in the dark because of night-vision problems, it was Paro who would drive them to the airport. As they sat sipping their tea, Sukhdev asked if Simran knew about the non-profit shelters that they had opened.

'Yes,' replied Ratna. 'She has an idea but she does not understand how we can be happy and fulfilled doing what we do. She must see it and decide for herself.'

On the way to the airport, in the darkness of pre-dawn, Ratna wondered if she would find Simran any different after seven years. She herself had changed a lot since the family tragedy but her changes were mostly internal, other than her hair that had turned completely gray. For the first time since Mannat and Dev's deaths, Ratna wondered how her loved ones in America perceived her. She knew Simran thought her to be stubborn for not agreeing to immigrate to the States. Maybe, this homecoming would help her daughter understand. She wondered why she could not share her pain or her triumphs with her daughter. Could it be because, for her, finding a personal path towards healing was neither the result of a stubborn streak nor a conscious decision, but a visceral need?

Driving through the still sleeping town, they arrived at the airport abuzz with the comings and goings of international flights. Paro dropped them at the arrival gate and left to park the car. Ratna and Sukhdev watched a plane descend as they walked towards the entrance to the terminal.

When Paro joined them, Sukhdev held her arm and with the cane in his other hand, pointed to a few passengers who had started trickling out of Baggage Claim and Customs. 'Look for Simran. She will be the best looking amongst those arriving passengers.'

'I know. You've told me a million times how good-looking she is!' Paro chuckled, patting his hand.

Simran happened to be amongst the first few to step out. Ratna ran and hugged her while her father hobbled slower on his walking stick, with Paro beside him. Amidst tears, hugs and smiles, Ratna introduced Paro to her daughter. 'Simran, meet Paro. She is our inspiration. She helped create the centres for "Women-in-Crisis" in Delhi, Amritsar and Garha.'

'I'm impressed,' said Simran, as she moved to hug Paro.

'Don't be. It's not true,' mumbled Paro. 'It's biji and nanaji who made it happen.'

'No, Simran, your mama speaks the truth. It was Paro who whispered the song we two were meant to sing on this earth,' said Sukhdev.

'Nanaji, since when did you displace mama as the family's resident poet?' teased Simran, as Paro helped her push her luggage to the waiting car.

'Since the time I realised I can borrow poetic language from others, to say what I mean. Tagore, Wordsworth or Byron, are all fair game when I want to impress my little princess,' chuckled Sukhdev, and reaching over, hugged her.

As soon as they settled in the backseat, Simran turned to Ratna and embracing her, said, 'Mama, you look good. And Nanaji, how are you doing?'

'I'm doing well, my precious,' replied Sukhdev from the front passenger seat.

'I'm so happy to hear that,' said Simran, turning to wrap her arms around her grandfather's shoulders and neck.

'You are coming home with us. Aren't you?' Sukhdev asked, laughing. 'Let's do this hugging thing there. Don't choke me now.'

'Very funny, Nanaji.' Simran unwrapped her arms, and sat back smiling.

'How are Aman and Jasbir? Was it hard to leave them behind?' asked Ratna.

'I had to come for my peace of mind. I'm sure I'll survive three weeks without them.'

'What about them? Didn't they fuss when you left?' insisted Ratna.

'Jasbir shed a couple of tears but Aman seems to prefer her grandma over me. Mama, I think sometimes I'm not easy to live with.'

'Only sometimes?' teased her mother. 'You are lucky Guddi never complains about your temper, and Himmat of course is a jewel.'

'Mama, whose side are you on?'

They laughed and talked all the way. As soon as there was a lull in the conversation, Sukhdev asked, 'Simran, after you've rested, would you like to see Delhi's centre for Women-in-Crisis?'

Simran looked from her nanaji to her mother. 'Of course, I want to see what is more important to you than your own family.'

'Hopefully, you'll understand it after you see it,' said Ratna. 'We started the first centre as a temporary shelter for widows and children of the Sikh massacre. But, over time, it has turned into a safe haven for several of Vaheguru's wounded, and a reason for us to live.' A soft smile played on Ratna's face. No longer a victim, she sat tall and proud by her daughter's side.

Ratna looked out the window as the car slowed down to turn into the driveway. Her house, bathed in the early blush of dawn, had never looked as majestic as it did at that moment. The trees by its side danced in a gentle breeze, swaying to the silent music of approaching spring. The house, an ordinary four-bedroom structure built on a slight elevation, surrounded by brick-walls and hedges rose like a castle against an ethereal background of crimson, gold and blue.

'Simran, look at the house,' said Ratna.

Simran's jaw dropped. 'Wow!'

'I know, even I've never seen it look so breathtaking,' said Ratna.

'Mama, it's not the house. It's what you've done with the yard.'

Ratna beamed.

Driving over the long, winding driveway, Simran looked about her. A part of the property next to the main road, where Mannat and his friends used to play cricket, now carried a huge sign: 'Mannat's Playground/ All young cricket players welcome'. The hedge around its outer parametres had grown tall and thick in seven years.

Ratna explained, 'After Mannat passed away, papaji and I missed the laughter of children, so we encouraged young cricket players in the neighbourhood, to continue using the grounds. However, after the Sikh massacre, the children stopped coming. We had to put up signs to lure them back. When necessary, papaji volunteers to coach them.'

'And, I love it,' said Sukhdev.

Ratna tapped on Simran's shoulder, and pointed to the front lawn that she had converted to a playground for little children. The sign read, 'God's Tiny Angels'.

Paro had stayed quiet throughout the drive, but now she spoke up. 'I want to share something. Though no one ever asked, I suspect biji and nanaji probably wondered why I hid in their backyard, as opposed to any other neighbouring yard.'

Everyone turned to look at Paro.

'Interesting,' muttered Ratna. 'So, why did you hide in our backyard?'

'Before the massacre, every time we went for a drive in my papaji's taxi, we'd go by this house, and I'd notice Sikh, Hindu and Muslim children playing cricket in the yard,' replied Paro, as she slowed the car to a stop in front of the house. 'Something told me, any family who could share their beautiful yard with all the neighbourhood children, would surely assist someone like me.'

Simran reached over to put her arms around Paro's shoulders. 'Thank you for bringing me home in more ways than one.'

The front yard, with its fountain, swings, slides and a merry-go-round, provided a sheltered space for toddlers and little ones. A tall brick lattice wall divided the two playgrounds, with an iron grill embedded in the gate.

Simran stepped out of the car, and instead of walking into the house, she dragged her mother with one hand, opening the gate to the garden of 'God's Tiny Angels', with the other. The gate closed behind them. Simran sat on a bench and pulled her mother down beside her.

'Thank you, Mama,' said Simran. 'Thank you for honouring Mannat's life.' She put her head on Ratna's shoulder. 'Mama, I came because I thought you needed help. But, I'm the one who is still broken and angry. Do you think Mannat's playground will help me heal?'

Late in the afternoon, Ratna came into her daughter's room to ask if she wanted to visit the centre. 'Yes.' Simran smiled. 'Mama, give me just a minute. You, nanaji and Paro get in the car and I'll join you.'

'Paro won't be back from the university until later, and nanaji needs to rest. It's just you and me, kiddo.'

Simran nodded and still smiling, walked out. Opening the yard gate, she walked briskly towards the cricket grounds. Ratna watched her sweep her hand over the sign—Mannat's Playground— with reverence. Placing her hand on her heart, Simran closed her eyes and breathed deep, before walking back to the car. Ratna watched her with moist eyes.

Acting as if what just happened was inconsequential, Simran said, 'Mama, explain to me how this centre for Women-in-Crisis works. How many women do you think you'll be able to help this way?'

'I'm not sure about the answer to your second question. Papaji and I often ask ourselves that,' replied Ratna. 'All we know is that these unfortunate women needed a place to earn an honest living. They needed a place to regroup while keeping their self-respect intact. So, at the centre, we provide them training in stitching and embroidery for our made-to-order clothing business. They start earning immediately. Whatever they produce and sell goes to them after we deduct a small amount for overhead and savings for their family emergencies. The charges for providing one free meal a day is our responsibility. This was our pilot project. Once this one succeeded, we started another centre in Amritsar at Dev's old mansion and one more in the Garha haveli. Hopefully, soon Simi and Nimmi will join the enterprise too.'

'Mama, I don't even have words to say how proud I am of you.'

'Thank you, Beti. In truth, all we do is offer employment to able-bodied, needy women. The rest is in the hands of Vaheguru.'

'Do you make enough to keep this project going?' Simran asked.

'Barely,' answered Ratna. 'But when you see the smiles on those faces on payday, the whole thing seems worth it. Watching women who have been scarred by life rise from the ashes, is very humbling. Seeing their pain and struggles puts your own heartache in perspective.'

'I do see now why there's no hope you'll ever join us in America.'

'You are right, Beti. We can't leave until this work is finished,' replied Ratna.

'How long will that take?'

'Don't know . . . probably as long as Vaheguru directs me.' Ratna smiled her dimpled smile.

Simran turned sideways from her front passenger seat to take a long, hard look at her mother. 'Mama, I'm so proud of you. You've honoured both Mannat and Dev mamaji with your centres. You've used Dev mamaji's mantra to weave an intricate web of love, one heart-warming stitch at a time—' Simran stopped, as she choked with emotion.

'I hadn't thought of it that way, Beti.'

Simran laid a hand on Ratna's arm. 'Mama, when did the healing start?'

'I'm not sure. All I know is, once we opened the first centre, it just showed up, without much ado, like the fruit of a juice mango tree.'

Appendix
Cultural Titbits

- Traditionally, brides in India wear vibrant colours—reds, burgundy, gold, etc. White is a colour of mourning.
- Each community has its own mother tongue. So they refer to God by different names. The Sikhs speak Punjabi and address God as Vaheguru. The Muslims speak Urdu and call Him Allah. The Hindus speak Hindi (the national language of India) and call Him by various names like Lord Ram, Lord Shiva, Lord Krishna, etc.
- The young in India do not say the names of older relatives. Every relationship has a special term of address. This means that a woman 'Uma' could be addressed simply as Uma by older relatives or as Uma bhabi by a younger sister-in-law, as bahu by a father-in-law, and so on. These terms of address can be used as is, or combined with the first name.
- Acquaintances and family friends have no term of address, so they are simply addressed as 'auntie' and 'uncle'. That means, the English words, auntie and uncle, are not necessarily relatives.
- 'Ji' is a term of respect used for someone older/wiser than you, e.g. papaji, nanaji, etc.
- When addressing others, oftentimes a simple change of a vowel from an 'a' to an 'i' connotes the sex of the person addressed, e.g. mamaji is mother's brother and mamiji is his wife, the aunt.

Terms of Address Used in the Story

Apa	sister (Muslim)
Baoji	father or grandfather (Hindu)
Bapu	father (Hindu)
Bahu	daughter-in-law (Hindu)
Bebeji	mother (Sikh)
Beta	son
Beti	daughter
Bhabi	sister-in-law
Bhaiji	A form of address for the caretaker of a Sikh gurdwara
Bhaiya	brother (Hindu)
Bhaji	brother (Sikh)
Behen/behenji	sister (Sikh)
Bua/buaji	father's sister
Bibiji/biji	mistress of the house/mother (Sikh)
Chacha	father's younger brother
Chachi	wife of a chacha
Chhoti behen	little sister
Didi	sister (Hindu)
Khalajaan	mother's sister (Muslim)
Mamaji	mother's brother
Mamiji	mamaji's wife
Masi/masiji	mother's sister
Mataji	mother (Hindu)
Memsahib	mistress of the house

Nanima	maternal grandmother
Nanaji	maternal grandfather
Papa/Papaji	father
Sahib	a master or a well-dressed gentleman
Punditji	a form of address and a reference to Hindu priesthood

Glossary

ayah	a caregiver or nanny
Vaisakhi	festival celebrating harvest. For Sikhs it's also the day when their tenth guru named them 'Singh'—the brave ones—and decreed for them to keep an outward symbol of uncut hair
banyan	a long lived tropical tree with beard like growth
baraat	wedding party
bhangra	traditional Punjabi folk dance
bholee	simple, guileless
burfi	diamond shaped fudge milk bars
burqa	Muslim woman's cloak to cover the entire body except the eyes
churra	ivory bangles dyed red for brides
chapatti	Indian unleavened bread
daal	lentil soup
dhoti	loincloth
diwali	Hindu festival of lights
diyas	earthen lamps with oil and wicks
doli	wedding party returning with the bride
dupatta	veil
ghagara	long skirted outfit with a short matching top
ghats	a community washing place near a water source
ghee	clarified butter
gidda	Punjabi women's folk dance
gurdwara	Sikh place of worship

Glossary | 341

hakim	native herbal doctor
haveli	a mansion with an enclosed yard; a manor house
hijraas	what some call the third sex or hermaphrodites having both male and female sexual organs. They used to be social outcastes in India, where they earned a living by dancing and singing at a child's birth or a wedding
hookah	a native device for smoking, consisting of a bowl mounted on a vessel of water where the smoke is drawn through the water via a long tube
kabaddi	traditional Indian game of breath control. It combines the characteristics of wrestling and rugby
kachnar	a tropical flowering tree, with edible buds
kafir	non-believer
kameez	long tunic worn by Punjabi women
kaptaan	Punjabi slang for Captain in the military
karma	destiny
kikar	tropical thorny tree, its branches are used for oral hygiene
kirtan	singing of hymns
kismet	fate
kurta	long tunic usually worn by men/boys
laddoo	Indian sweet made of chickpea flour—eaten on auspicious occasions
langar	a free meal offered at Sikh places of worship
lathis	bamboo clubs
mango boor	panicles of tiny mango buds
mohra	pawn
murtees	idols
musalmaan	Muslim
neem	tropical tree with medicinal value, its branches often used for oral hygiene
paath	Sikh recital of *Guru Granth Sahib*, the spiritual guide for Sikhs
palki	palanquin—a carriage carried by four men, by means of poles borne on their shoulders

pashmina	expensive wool from Kashmir, native word for 'Cashmere'
peerhi	a low stool with a woven-jute seat, used mainly in old-fashioned Indian kitchens.
phulkari	an ocher hand-woven and hand embroidered cotton shawl
pinee	sweet balls/rolls made of gram flour
pipal	a broad leafed, long-lived tropical shade tree
pisti	something or someone small and precious like a pistachio
parantha	Indian unleavened, fried bread
purdah	to hide one's face behind a screen, a veil or burqa
rakhi	festival when a piece of string is tied on a brother's wrist as a declaration of a sister's love and a brother's promise of protection
rupee	Indian currency
shabads	Sikh hymns from *Guru Granth Sahib*
sadhu	a religious recluse, who usually dresses in ocher robes
salwaar	loose-cuffed pants worn by men and women
sari	six yards of material, tied as a long skirt, by Indian women
sitar	Indian musical instrument
tonga	pony trap—usually for hire